Broken Path

Books By
RUBY STANDING DEER

SHINING LIGHT'S SAGA

Book 1 – Circles
Book 2 – Spirals
Book 3 – Stones
Book 4 – Broken Path

www.RubyStandingDeer.com

Broken Path

A Historical Novel by

RUBY STANDING DEER

FIRST EDITION SOFTCOVER
ISBN: 1622539605
ISBN-13: 978-1-62253-960-4

Editor: Lane Diamond
Interior Designer: D. Robert Pease

Printed in the U.S.A.

EVOLVED PUBLISHING™
www.EvolvedPub.com
Evolved Publishing LLC
Butler, Wisconsin, USA

Printed in Book Antiqua font.

For Aya Walksfar... Tsi scuceblu.

And for my husband, Chuck, who now could be a gourmet chef for all the cooking he's done so I could write.

INTRODUCTION

I am honored to be asked to write the introduction for Ruby Standing Deer's important work, *Broken Path*. Through this powerful story, we see the continuing consequences of the European invasion of Native American lands.

Europeans brought a disease far more devastating than smallpox to the shores of North America — alcoholism. Even to this day, this disease continues to ravage the Native Peoples. According to a lawsuit filed by the Oglala Sioux, one quarter of their children suffer from fetal disorders related to their parents' alcoholism. Indian Health Services says that the rate of alcoholism among Native Americans is six times the United States' average for other ethnic groups. One in ten Native American deaths are alcohol related, according to Indian Health Services.

In actuality, these numbers are conservative.

My grandmother left her people to save her children from alcoholism and all the abuse that comes from it. Unfortunately, though she got sober, my mother succumbed to the same disease by the age of fourteen. She died at the age of forty. I nearly died before I finally got sober at the age of thirty.

Even when we run from our People, the disease has already taken root in our blood and we suffer from its terrible effects.

I am one of the fortunate ones. I found my way back to the First People and remain sober, yet I have watched even powerful medicine people, Holy People, suffer and die from this disease. Our families continue to be ravaged by the sicknesses that come with alcoholism: child abuse, once unheard-of among The People; domestic violence, again nearly-unheard-of among our People; sexual abuse, murder, theft, weakened bodies and shattered Spirits.

1

RUBY STANDING DEER

Broken Path tells of one Band's struggle to fight free of the deadly talons of alcoholism. Through this fictional story, based on painful reality, Ms. Standing Deer has shown us not only the dark abyss of this horrible disease, but she gives us the hope that there is a Shining Path that can lead us from this cold and deadly place called Alcoholism.

Sincerely,

Tsi scuceblu (Aya Walksfar)

1

Golden Fox bolted upright and threw off her sleeping robe. She reached for her mother's robe only to find it empty.

Sky Bird stood beside the open flap of the lodge.

Golden Fox jumped up and squeezed past her mother. "What happens? Father Sun is barely awake."

"Daughter, stay back. It is my crazy aunt racing through camp half-falling from her mustang. She brings more fire water and even three pale ones with her. We need to send someone to bring back your grandfather from his Time of Mourning. Too many hunters are gone. Only he can make our people, who crave the drink, listen."

Golden Fox put on her long tunic and leggings. "Mother, I will go."

"The pale ones dare not see you!"

Before her mother could grasp her tunic, Golden Fox pulled the lodge's flap wider and raced past her toward the herd of mustangs, a nose rope in hand. A whistle brought the black-grey animal splashed in white to her side.

She jumped on the animal and urged him forward. He nickered and jerked his head back to stare behind them.

"I hear the shouting, Swift Arrow. We go to find Grandfather!" She urged him on with a strong squeeze to his sides, then bit her lower lip and gazed all around. "I can only guess where he is. The land rolls and folds into valleys and then stretches out into grasslands. Swift Arrow, you go with him everywhere." She patted the animal's neck. "I give you your lead."

The animal trotted toward two hills that rose sharply into the sky, and into the narrow valley between the hills. The farther they rode, the closer the hills grew to each other, until the valley became a ravine. Sheer walls grew tall and bowed their heads close together at the top, so only streaks of sun striped the ground below.

The trail continued along the shadowed foot of the cliffs. The mustang stopped when the opening between the walls of the ravine became too narrow for his body to fit. A rocky path led up the steep side of the rough wall until it climbed out of sight near the top.

Golden Fox slid off Swift Arrow. "Sweet Mother, did Grandfather climb this path?" She stared around, but Swift Arrow stood with one hind foot tipped up and resting, his head drooped low as if he might already be asleep. "Swift Arrow, did you bring me here so you could sleep, or is Grandfather up above?"

The mustang barely opened his large brown eyes, as if to ask how she could doubt his knowledge.

With a sigh, Golden Fox turned to face the rough trail. Stones and sharp shards littered the hard ground. Fearful of sliding on the loose stones, she tested each footstep before moving onto the next.

"Why did I not put on my footwear," she mumbled to herself. Even with the bottoms of her feet hardened, she felt much pain.

The animal trotted past the first and second paths, which led inside two spiraling routs of deep orange and light red walls. He reached the third path, which offered only a narrow way in, then stopped and pranced.

"Go in, boy, we must hurry."

The mustang could only go in partway, stopping when the path narrowed. Two rocky paths split off from there, neither wide enough for Swift Arrow to walk through without tripping over the fallen stones.

"Sweet Mother, neither have tracks I can follow." She slid off the mustang and walked a little ways in, and yelled for her grandfather.

Nothing.

The second path proved no better. Light streamed through the wide open top.

Part way up the trail, she called out, "Grandfather!" Panic set in and her heart drummed when he did not answer.

More steps.

Awakened by her presence, featherless black-winged ones burst from a winding yellow slit in the wall above her head, and raced past, barely missing her hair.

She ducked and slipped. Heart racing, she scrambled to stop her slide, fell to her knees, and bit hard into her lower lip as the slick stones cut her knees and legs. Shaky, she eased back to her feet and sucked in her bloody lip. When her heart stopped pounding, she continued the climb.

"Eagle Thunder, where *are* you? Grandfather!"

A deep voice called out. "When you reach the top, look toward where Father Sun rises and you will see where I am."

The path became less steep as it crested the top of the cliff, where it meandered into a flat, sandy area with a small pond. A jagged tooth of the cliff's wall stuck up above the tiny meadow. Saplings grew in the tooth's shadow, and cattails dominated the rest of the area.

With his sleeping robe rolled in his arms, Eagle Thunder looked at the blood seeping from her knees and upper legs, and shook his head. "Swollen feet. Girl, will you ever learn to use footwear?"

"I... the band needs you! Yellow Moon has brought hairy-faces and fire water to our band. Her mustang carried much of the poison drink. The hunters have not returned —"

Talk as we make our way through the stones." He slung his robe over his shoulder. "Too deep in my sorrow, I did not hear the Spirits who may have tried to warn me. Your grandmother was hard to find." He dropped his robe and picked up Golden Fox.

"You are too old to carry me. Put me down and I will follow."

"Do not ever say I am too old to do something, little one. I am an elder, yes, and my hair is white, yes, but I am not too old to carry my fourteen-winters-old granddaughter who is lighter than a carryall of feathers."

Swift Arrow whinnied as the pair came from the narrow trail.

Eagle Thunder tossed her on the mustang's back, and leapt in front of her as she scooted back. Once clear of the ravine, he squeezed Swift Arrow's sides hard. "Too much smoke rises ahead." He urged the animal to go faster.

Hooves ate up the ground and left Golden Fox squeezing her grandfather's waist.

* * *

Sweat-soaked, Swift Arrow thundered into camp and past the first lodge before Eagle Thunder could lean back, signaling him to stop. Eagle Thunder and his granddaughter flew off the terrified mustang in front of two partly burnt lodges. Only charred poles marked where a third lodge had once stood.

Swift Arrow raced away toward the herd, and the lead mare set the herd to running away from the fire. Surprised foals whinnied and did their best to catch up.

Sky Bird and other women threw handfuls of dirt onto the blazing lodges.

Men dashed in and yanked out belongings, tossing them aside before hurrying to retrieve more.

Women tore at the lodges, ripping them apart and dragging the pieces away from the greedy fingers of the flames.

Eagle Thunder and Golden Fox joined the others who fought to kill the fast-moving blaze.

Drunken laughter reached those who fought the fire. "We can have much if we live closer to the white ones. Maybe they will teach us to make wooden lodges as they have. We can live as they do." Yellow Moon raised a rabbit fur-covered leather flask. Her slurred voice grew in excitement, and she laughed louder.

Eagle Thunder, covered in fallen ash, spun around and took fast steps to reach her. "You did this, did you not, old woman? Your heart is as black as our burnt lodges, and your Spirit dies even as you stand before me. It fades to grey and will soon turn to dust!"

"We can make new wooden lodges and live near the hairy-faces! More come this way with each full moon." She pointed to iron pots. "We already find their big pots better to cook in. When last did our people use an animal's bladder to cook in? The time of Shining Light, it was. They offer much in trade for your half-blood daughter, and your pale granddaughter. They will be angry when they know of what Sun Rising has done." She pointed at the dead hairy-faces. "Sun Rising must pay for what he did—shooting arrows without allowing them to speak. He is old and weak—of no use to us, the Sun People."

Sun Rising pushed her and she staggered back. "Shining Light warned of these times, and now we see what we are becoming and have a chance to change. Woman, your laughter sounds as a wounded coyote. A scar on our people is what you are—a scar that runs deep into the bone."

His eyes blazed like the flames around them. "Those crazy pale ones raced into camp without asking if they were welcome. Children play everywhere! Had I not acted, early rising children would have been run over." He spit on the ground before her and walked away.

6

Yellow Moon tossed four carryall pouches to the ground, and used a small branch on the tree next to her to hold herself upright. She shouted and waved with one hand. Her dress, stained dark brown down the middle of it, had one grey braid half undone. She stood with only one boot on and raised her arms. "Come drink with me!" She glanced at her bare foot. "I will get another hard leather boot from the pale ones!"

Her feet tangled and she stumbled sideways, kicking the pouch open, and flasks fell out. She blinked as if her eyes refused to focus. "The whites have much to offer. What we call footwear, they call mockosins... moccosens...."

She shrugged and laughed again. "They have hard leather boots that some of you wear. They do not wear out as our 'mocca-sins' do. Where do you think the beads you use with the quills on our clothing come from? The sky? We trade much for them. If we move outside of the wooden fort, we will get much more! Great gifts await us!"

The flasks lay scattered on the ground. One spewed and mixed with the ashes.

Eagle Thunder yanked the swaying Yellow Moon forward. "And why do you call these flasks great gifts, woman? I can smell your stench. The poisoned water in them kills our people. Never before have we needed to worry that a mother or father would hit their child, but with deadly fire water in their stomachs, some go crazy and harm their children, or harm the elders." He raised his chin. "I will kill the next white man who dares to come into camp."

Yellow Moon jerked free of his hold and sneered. "Once you were a great warrior, but now your hand shakes. Drop your bow from your shoulder before you *kill* yourself! You are as Sun Rising, weak old man."

He grinded his teeth. "My anger makes me shake."

A smile drew deep wrinkles across her face. Blackened and broken stumps of teeth showed against her dirty face. "The pale ones offer fire water that helps us to see into the Spirit Land, speak to the Great Mystery. I know *more* than Shining Light! Send your grey-eyed daughter and your ugly pale granddaughter back to Sky Bird's man. My ears have heard he wishes them back. Maybe they will forget about the dead white men that lie face-down in our camp, and will still welcome us if we give them those ... those two useless women."

"Her man threw her away! My hand shakes from anger, not weakness." Eagle Thunder pulled his obsidian knife and raised it to her neck. "What worth do you have?" He breathed deep, stepped back, lowered the knife, dropped his head in shame. "We are taught even as babies in our cradleboard that we do not harm one of our own. Yellow Moon, you must leave the Sun People before you cause more harm. I will even pack a mustang for you. I am certain others will gladly pull down your old lodge—"

"I go nowhere. You take your belongings, old man, and leave, alone. Be happy that the whites will take your two burdens. You will be rid of them."

People stared in silence and no one moved.

Yellow Moon lowered herself and reached inside the carryall pouch. She tossed leather flasks at the people's feet.

The elders who grabbed the flasks and passed them around received much praise from some, but others turned away in silence. The eldest among the people left the flasks where they had hit the ground, hurried into their lodges, and tied the flaps shut.

"Gutless, worthless...." Yellow Moon glared after those who left with no drink. She raised a flask of fire water and drank. Some of it ran down her neck and disappeared inside her stained dress. When she lowered the flask, she peered at the ones who stood watching and listening.

Several raised flasks to their lips, ignoring everyone as their chins dripped with their prize.

Yellow Moon sat legs splayed, and somehow managed to stand. "Bring me your bone necklaces, the colorful stones you carved holes into and made round, and your shells of many colors we traded for to make our clothing. Our decorated clothes, our footwea... moccasins are worth much in the eyes of many hairy-faces. They wish to take them over the salty waters to... to show how smart we are. Bring out your quillwork so we can trade for thick boots, blankets with colors, more iron pots, more met-al knives, and much fire water. Much fire water!"

Eagle Thunder's voice boomed. "We do not need more iron pots. We have good knives made of obsidian, for which we trade." He grasped her arm and shook it hard. "My lodge is gone. My daughter's lodge is gone. Sun Rising and his woman's lodge! Gone! So are two other lodges." He yelled in her face. "You will pack up and leave us! You are now thrown away. Go!"

Yellow Moon tumbled backward and sneered at him as another woman held her up. She staggered away. "You cannot throw me away. The Holy Man must do it, and he is hunting with the rest of our strong people, unlike you who runs into the canyons to hide."

Golden Fox hurried to grab the sleeve of his tunic. "Do not allow her to tear at your heart, grandfather. The band knows you left to grieve for Grandmother. We... we have much to clean up. The hunters will bring us humpback hides to scrape and make more lodges. The warm season comes, and we can sleep outside until the lodges are done."

* * *

Sleep did not claim Golden Fox, though her body ached with weariness.

Sun Rising had given her grandfather and them the lodge that his daughter and her man had slept in before the pale one's found the couple gathering berries during the Time of Falling Leaves, and ran long knives through them.

Sun Rising's daughter had lived long enough to tell him who had attacked them. He and his woman moved five sunrises away from the wooden fort, until Eagle Thunder brought them back to the safety of the Sun People and their sister band, who combined for even more protection. Sadly, most of the sister band moved even closer to the wooden fort.

Golden Fox stepped over her mother and grandfather and sped across camp. She made her way up to the top of the large stones, seeking solace before Father Sun woke.

From somewhere in the darkness, a mustang nickered and snorted, prompting Golden Fox to creep to the edge of the cliff and look down. She spotted Yellow Moon riding out of camp.

Why does she take three mustangs that do not belong to her, and what is in the packs that look so full? Surely she does not go back to the whites! Not that many people would give her their shells and quill-worked tunics and dresses.

2

Sky Bird flipped off the gifted sleeping robe another woman had given her, and stepped from the borrowed lodge. Songs from people singing their thanks to the Great Mystery for a new sunrise, a new beginning, lifted her heart. About half the lodges remained closed as people slept off the firewater, or groaned from hurting heads.

As her people's healer, she made poultices for bruises and wrapped bloody wounds from fights over the drink. She turned no one away, even if their breath smelled of the poisoned water. Whenever wounds ran too deep to heal, she soothed the person and stayed at their side until they breathed no more. Too many people already had been sung the songs to prepare them for their final journey, so they would find the right path, hopefully to Eagle Woman, who would guide them to the campfires of their relations... if they would have them—if Eagle Woman even found them worthy to reach out to. Many might walk the in-between land, where no one would remember them or pray for their release into the Spirit Land.

It had been three sunrises since Yellow Moon threw the carry-alls of poisoned water to the ground. For those nights, many of the people had danced until they fell to the ground, spewing stinking puddles of poisoned water from their mouths. Some had staggered to their lodges, where loud arguments had broken the quiet of darkness. Perhaps, the poisoned water had all been drunk up now.

Sky Bird would pray it was so.

When she repeated what Golden Fox had said about Yellow Moon sneaking away, some packed up lodges and left, while others only stared, dazed.

Her father refused to leave until the hunters returned, so sure that the Holy Man would throw away Yellow Moon.

Whenever she was not healing or making medicine, she helped Golden Fox care for the children of the young women who had gone on the hunt with the men. As was the way of the people, the women had left their small children to be cared for by the elders, and some of the children had been struck by men with drink-angered fists. Golden Fox and the elders who had refused to drink the poisoned water had moved the children to a safe lodge, away from those who drank.

After Yellow Moon left camp, Eagle Thunder had sent Sun Rising to the hunters' camp to speak with the Holy Man.

The Holy Man had left with the hunters to bless the hunt. If the hunt went well, some of the hunters would return for fresh mustangs to carry more of the meat back to camp.

Eagle Thunder kept guard with his longtime friends, lead scout Stands His Ground, and warrior woman Blazing Fire, to watch for Yellow Moon. No one had seen her since she burnt the lodges and Golden Fox saw her leaving.

Weariness weighed on Sky Bird's shoulders. Hoping Sun Rising would return soon with the Holy Man, she climbed a stone rise next to the slow moving waters not far from camp to sing and search for the men. She strained her eyes against the bright azure sky and Father Sun, in order to see movement.

With no one in sight, not even faraway dust, she turned and slowly walked back to camp.

Golden Fox met her on the path. "Mother, you are needed in camp."

"I head there now."

As they neared a copse of trees at the edge of the camp, Sky Bird flung out a hand to stop her daughter. "Lower yourself!"

She peered at the trees and, upon seeing the person ahead, dropped a hand to the knife sheathed at her side. "Yellow Moon, what is this you do? Sneak back into camp?"

Yellow Moon jerked her hand behind her back.

Sky Bird's gaze narrowed as she demanded, "What are you hiding?"

With brows raised, Yellow Moon stammered, "Nothing... I... hide nothing."

"I see the lie in your eyes." Golden Fox stood ready to shake off her mother's protective stance. "You lie!"

Anger colored Yellow Moon's cheeks red. "I am hiding nothing. I... I came to return, uh, your father's knife. I... I found it in the bushes." She tentatively held the sheathed knife out, offering it to Sky Bird.

Sky Bird snatched the knife out of her aunt's hand. "You come to steal what little we have, what little that did not burn in the fire you set!" Her shout brought several people to where they stood. "You do not belong here! How did you pass my father and the others unseen?"

Chin lifted, Yellow Moon glared at Sky Bird. "I know many paths. I go where I please. That old man cannot stop me. And you, where are your manners? I am your elder and your relation. You have no right to speak to me in such a harsh voice. You are only a half-blood with ugly grey eyes and hair the color of mud." Head held high, she stepped around Sky Bird.

Sky Bird spun to keep Yellow Moon in sight. "My father told you to leave and to not return."

"Your father," Yellow Moon spit out as she pivoted to face Sky Bird. "Your father has no power to throw me away. Only the Holy Man can throw me away." Hatred shone in her narrow eyes. "Your father is nothing but a weak old man." She turned away from camp and took a few steps before she twisted her head around to look over her shoulder. "Your daughter is more shameful to look at then you! Hair the color of dead grass in red dirt, and her eyes! Green as your white man's eyes."

Sky Bird cocked her head to one side and glared toward Yellow Moon. "How do you know the color of my daughter's father's eyes?"

Golden Fox reached a gentle hand toward her. "Mother, it matters not how she knows. He is not part of our lives. Maybe another pale one has spoken of him. She speaks their words better than most. Come, Mother, there is much for us to do."

Yellow Moon half smiled, her lip curled in contempt. "It is not the fire water that brings harm to our people. Fire water opens our Spirits to the ancestors, to Creator. Listen to your worthless daughter. Return to camp, gather your belongings, and *you* leave. Go to your man. Leave before your presence brings more harm." She spat on the ground and walked away.

Sky Bird shook with rage and shouted, "You know why I do not go back to him. Go sing, aunt-born-of-my-second-mother. Sing to the Great Mystery. Speak of your dark heart before your Soul dies of the poison inside you."

Yellow Moon waved a hand over her shoulder, but did not turn back.

"Come, Mother, we must go." Golden Fox tugged at her arm.

Sky Bird allowed her daughter to lead the way toward the center of camp. As they walked, her voice became sharp with worry. "Why are you not with the children? What if a person filled with crazy water—"

Golden Fox squeezed her hand, silencing her. "Do not be so concerned, Mother. Three elders are with them. I sought you only because one of the little ones has a belly pain. I gave her some peppermint leaves in hot tea, so she will be fine. You check on her, and I will get Swift Arrow and one of his mares for us to ride. We need to leave for a while, check on the elder woman's sore throat from the band who travels through our land. We are only a little ways from them. I did see Grandfather returning, so the camp will be safe."

"You are right. I will go to see the child, and then we leave."

***

Father Sun still gave some light as Golden Fox and her mother returned. Campfires burned low as people sat by their fires speaking. Some places where people should have sat were empty, and flasks lay about. After letting the mustangs go, they hurried to where Eagle Thunder sat next to Sun Rising at the nearest campfire, their heads close together as they spoke in low voices.

Sun Rising stretched and rose. "I must go. My woman waits for me. She has started to pack our belongings. I hope you will do the same. Even if you do not, the lodge is yours, as we cannot carry so much. Our Holy Man drinks when he can, and you know of this. I should have not brought him back with me."

Eagle Thunder added sticks to wake the fire. "I see my daughter and granddaughter have returned from where they had gone. No one in camp knew where my family vanished to."

Sky Bird knelt beside him. "Father, your granddaughter and I had to... needed to go see the sick elder woman in the traveling band before they left."

"Ah, I now understand why you both hurried away as I came into camp."

"Father, my blood ran hot after finding Yellow Moon in our belongings. Your granddaughter thought maybe a ride would cool my blood, and we really did need to see the elder woman."

She cleared her throat, grabbed a small branch, and stirred the low fire. She stared into the small flames as they fought for life. "When did Sun Rising return?

13

Why would his woman be packing all their belongings? They are safe at the small camp just beyond us. The season is many moons from changing to the time that we must travel." She handed the knife and sheath to her father. "You knife—"

"Sun Rising returned after you left." Eagle Thunder added sticks to wake the fire. "Come, sit, Daughter and Granddaughter. Eat while I speak." He felt where his knife should be.

"Yellow Moon spoke of finding it in the shrubs."

"Never does it leave my side, even if I carry my longer skinning knife!" He glanced around. "We will force her to leave. The Holy Man rushed to return with his son. His eyes brightened when Sun Rising spoke of the fire water. The hunters' mustangs and dogs are heavy with meat and cannot be rushed. We are on our own for maybe four days."

Sky Bird gazed around as she dipped meat from the pot, and Golden Fox followed her gaze.

Few sat long at the other campfires. They ate hurriedly, and then went to their lodges. Within a breath, some of them began moving packed belongings out of their lodges.

"What happens, Father?" Shy Bird sat legs at her side on the ground next to him.

Eagle Thunder's jaw muscles flexed and he looked away. He waited until Golden Fox served herself and sat on the ground next to him. "Blazing Fire caught her trying to leave only a short span ago, with more belongings that were not hers. When Blazing Fire took the belongings to the right owners, not all were happy with Blazing Fire. Some had given their beads and hides to Yellow Moon to trade for poisoned water."

Sky Bird gave a quick nod as she chewed and swallowed. "We know there are many who become sick without the poisoned water. This will never stop."

Golden Fox leaned on his shoulder, allowing her long, loose golden-red hair to fall across his chest.

He reached out and ran his fingers through her hair. "After I ate, I went to Yellow Moon's lodge. She had tied the flap closed and yelled at me to leave... told me the Holy Man would ban me soon."

Chills crawled over Golden Fox's arms like tiny spiders. "No one glances our way. They must be filled with the drink Yellow Moon brought again. Do you not wonder why no one looks our way, Grandfather?"

"The Holy Man—"He pulled his shoulders back and met her eyes. "By the time the Holy Man returned, Yellow Moon quickly offered him the fire water. After drinking a flask, he shouted that Yellow Moon belonged with the Sun People, that it was Eagle Thunder and his family who did not belong. In front of the band, the Holy Man threw us away."

His breathing came out slow and even. "Do not worry, children. Sun Rising spoke of five hunters who are to return sooner, maybe two days. When they come, I will join a few of our hunters and warriors, and we will speak to him then. We will build a sweat lodge and chase the angry Spirits from him. Once he is healed, we can help the others to become well."

He turned his face towards Sky Bird. "While Golden Fox cares for the children, you are to gather the plants you use for those sick from the poisoned water. I fear we will need many of the helper plants to cure our people. We are not thrown away if we can do this."

A loud scuffling, followed by Yellow Moon's slurred voice, came from just beyond the lodges. Blazing Fire and Stands His Ground, the lead scout, dragged Yellow Moon toward her lodge, tossed her inside, and quickly tied the flap closed.

Blazing Fire guarded the lodge as Stands His Ground walked over to Golden Fox's family. He squatted by the fire and dipped meat from the pot into a bowl sitting on a rock. "Eagle Thunder, I do not believe we will be able to chase the sick Spirits from the Holy Man, if they hold as tight to him as they hold to Yellow Moon."

Eagle Thunder picked up a small branch and flipped an orange ember back into the circle of stones around the campfire. "We will pray to the Spirits to guide us and to give us strength."

Stands His Ground grunted and swallowed. "There are times the Great Mystery must let us follow a broken path, one that will bring us much sorrow, to find a better way. I will pack everything I need." He glanced sideways at Sky Bird. "Several of us will do this. Perhaps, it is time to move away from the sickness that comes from the poisoned water."

Golden Fox rubbed her arms. "What about the children?"

Eagle Thunder shook his head. "Do not worry about the storm that has not yet come."

"But what if it does, Grandfather?"

He heaved a deep breath and let it ease out. "We have no right to take a child from its mother, Golden Fox. It is not the way of our people."

Sky Bird leapt up and hurried toward the borrowed lodge. When she trotted back toward them, she carried her 'memory pouch' — a leather pouch that held precious things passed down to her.

"Father!" She held the memory pouch up and shook it, then threw herself down next to her father. "The necklace and the carved beads my first mother gave me are gone! Yellow Moon stole them!" She jumped to her feet. "I will go to her lodge and tear everything apart until I find the necklace and beads!"

Before she could leave, Eagle Thunder sprung to his feet and grabbed her arm. "Daughter, you are still filled with too much fire. You will stay here. I will ask Blazing Fire and Stands His Ground to search Yellow Moon's lodge."

She pulled loose. "I do not need them to do what I must do! Yellow Moon needs to know I am no longer a child that she can treat poorly."

Eagle Thunder crossed his arms over his chest and shook his head. "You wear your anger as you do your dress — on the outside. Anger causes our bodies to become sick. Yes, it can feel like Power, make you think you are strong and that no one can defeat you.

"Slow as a small creature, it makes a path to the inside of your body, and ever so slowly, it eats at all the parts inside you. You do not feel your insides come apart until it has already happened. By then, you are sick and nothing can make you well. Your head pains you, your belly pains you, and the air you breathe smells as rotten meat and offers nothing except more pain.

"The heat of anger is a silent killer. When you understand this, it is too late. Anger consumes you, Daughter. Sit, breathe slow with me and your daughter. Long ago, these words were passed down by the Great Holy Man, Shining Light, who now lives in the —"

Sky Bird whirled and rushed from the camp.

Golden Fox stood and brushed a tear away. "Mother has much sadness. I could feel it. I feel sadness all around camp, Grandfather, and... I feel people who spin in circles inside their lodges, as if their minds are dizzy. Why is this so? Sometimes, I wish I did not have the gift of knowing another's emotions."

Eagle Thunder gripped her shoulders. "Never wish a gift to go away. Some lose their gift, and feel so empty they walk away from the band and never return. One day, this gift might save your life... or the band's life."

He dropped his hand and stared in the direction Sky Bird had fled. "I must go to your mother. We will pick plants together and, perhaps, this will help her heal. Do not worry if we do not return until Father Sun rises again. Go be with the children."

***

Head lowered, Sky Bird sat next to the boulders her daughter liked to climb. Long, dark brown-red hair hung past her waist, almost to the ground. When her father sat next to her, she held her head high, shoved her hair out of her face, and chased away tears. "Why do young ones always climb as high as they can go, and spend long spans up here?"

"Do you not remember a little Sky Bird sitting up high in the trees not so long ago? They see better what they cannot see down here. Just as a person searches in their mind for answers, the young ones find answers when they climb as high as they can, away from others." He waved one hand. "Why has my daughter come here, away from others?"

She picked up a handful of small stones and let them trickle through her fingers. "What if Blazing Fire cannot find the necklace and the beads from my first mother? What if Yellow Moon has already traded them for the poisoned water? Father, she stole that which meant much to me. I can never find another necklace or other beads that will mean what those meant. That small piece of my first mother is gone. Nothing could hurt me more. I hold my anger in now, but I do not know what I will do when I see Yellow Moon."

Her father scooted closer and took both her hands into his. "Daughter, what if Golden Fox was stolen by the hairy-faces? Would you give them your necklace and your beads to have her back?"

She jerked her hands away. "Why would you think I would not?"

"You would give them up, then?"

When she nodded, he took her hands again and gave a gentle squeeze. "This loss has hurt, but has not hurt so badly that you will not laugh again. The necklace was something you could hold. You could feel the love your mother had for you in the beads. It was important, as all such things are important, yet we have these things only for a short span—maybe as long as our lives, maybe longer, maybe shorter. Perhaps, what we think of as losing them is but them traveling away from us. Perhaps they have done their work here. The necklace and the

17

beads are gone, but are the stories I told you about your mother gone as well? Has the love in your heart disappeared, too?"

He let her think about that for a short span. "What is in our hearts, no thief can ever steal."

Ashamed, she dropped her head. "I am a grown woman, yet my father still teaches me."

He laid his arm around her shoulders and pulled her close. "I will teach you until I breathe no more, and you will teach me until I take my journey to the Spirit Land. We will gather plants, and then sleep here. Your daughter always leaves a sleeping robe in this place."

Father Sun peeked above the distant hills, offering light to guide Golden Fox. She hurried up to where her mother and grandfather slept. "Grandfather, Mother, wake! Yellow Moon cut her way out after darkness—"

Eagle Thunder jerked up. "No more words need be spoken, girl. We come."

Outside, a young warrior holding a flask turned his gaze away from Eagle Thunder's glare.

The warrior's older brother swayed next to a cold campfire, offering a crooked smile; he did not look away. He held a woman's hand and she leaned on his body.

A third man, one of the elders, shouted slurred words. "Eagle Thunder, my friend... we have found a new way of seeing the Great Mystery without she... sheekin a vision and fashing." He tossed a flask his way. "You wish to join us? You may stay if so."

Eagle Thunder caught the flask, a mix of sadness and anger flashing on his face. He opened the flask and poured it on the ground, and stared as the fire water made a stream that flowed through what remained of the ash.

The elder squawked as the fire water soaked into the ground.

"You are killing yourselves!" Grandfather yelled. "What new way? The way of blackened, dead hearts inside your bodies?"

Yellow Moon lurched across the camp, one hand hanging loosely at her side and gripping her sheath knife, probably the one she used to cut the hide of her lodge to escape. She swayed, and flopped against one of the lodges near Eagle Thunder. As she lifted the leather flask to her lips, she glared at Golden Fox, and then at Sky Bird. With the back of her hand, she wiped dribbles of poisoned water from her chin and sneered.

"Know wh... why I bur... burned your lodges? The pale ones sent by Sky Bird's man gave me much drink to burn them." She spread her hands wide. "As many flasks as the fingers on my hands, and more! Ha! Now you have no home but with the white-skinned ones." She pointed toward the end of camp that led the way to the fort. Her red, squinting eyes barely focused. "It is sad your grandfather also has also lost his home because of this. Your pale-skinned father maybe take you, ugly girl with green eyes and hair the color of dead grass and red dirt. They keep... keep you."

Sky Bird lunged for Yellow Moon, but Eagle Thunder held tight to his daughter. "It is not my granddaughter who is ugly! Inside, her Spirit is pure, and outside her face and body are pleasing to look at. No, it is not her who the Spirits are pained to look at. It is you! The fire-water has eaten away at your face and body. Only loose skin hangs from your body, and your face is so shallow, it is hard to see if you are human or maybe rotting flesh in the heat."

Yellow Moon snarled and took a swallow. "You, Eagle Thunder, are older than me. Do not speak of beauty you have never seen. The Spirits are angry at you for being a coward, and for not being willing to drink, so you can see the new way."

Blazing Fire stomped up and gritted her teeth. "I waited for Eagle Thunder to return, to decide what to do with you, but I think you are now an enemy, and you must die!" She unsheathed her knife, but Eagle Thunder grabbed her shoulder and stopped her.

Yellow Moon cleared her throat and held her head high in defiance. She faced Sky Bird. "Everyone in this band knows your *father* found you abandoned along a deer path. You are not *of the Sun People*. Who among our band has grey eyes as you? No *one*! You think you are better, wiser than me? You are wrong!" Spittle flew from her mouth, and her unfocused eyes seemed to see nothing as they moved back and forth.

"The fire water gives my mind visions as a Holy Person, but what would you know about visions?" She raised the flask. "Here ish Power. Here ish how Sprits whishper words to me. If you had drunk the Holy Water, you would have sheen, as I did. You do not belong here. Go back, half-blood, where you and your light-skinned daughter belong—with the white skins."

Much fire water was passed around in flasks, most of it in the hands of elders who no longer wore the valuable necklaces they had worn only three sunrises ago. They wore old, plain clothing, and staggered when they walked. A few still wore their decorated clothes, holding onto their dignity as they squatted at campfires, eating.

Yellow Moon tried to focus her gaze on Eagle Thunder. "Leave, ol... ol' weak man. You take Blazing Fire as well. Maybe the white men teach her some things."

Blazing Fire readied her knife and stepped toward the woman.

Eagle Thunder pushed her back. "She is mine, Blazing Fire."

Eagle Thunder, full of his own fire, walked close enough to Yellow Moon that his face was only a breath away. "Sky Bird is my blood daughter. You know this. I think you carry envy that has helped to blacken your heart. Your belly could never hold a child, and you blamed your man and sent him away. I see how you stare at other women who grow babies in *their* bellies. Now, you are past the time of children and have no one to blame."

Eagle Thunder's stare never wavered from the swaying woman. He shook her shoulders and his voice deepened. "You are not of my blood, but of my woman's, who now sits with her relations at their campfire in the sky. Know this, Yellow Moon: she casts shame upon you even from the Spirit Land. She turns away from you. You are not wanted at her campfire, or anyone else's in the sky. Not one of your relations will offer you a place at their fire. The whispers you hear are not from the same land where my woman waits for me, but a dark place that light has never seen."

He nodded at her breast. "A good heart lives there no longer."

Yellow Moon hissed, "You, Eagle Thunder, are a weak old man. Useless!"

"You are sick, woman! Have you no faith without this?" He pointed a trembling finger at the firewater she held, and then turned to the Sun People who had gathered. "Do *any* of you people feel shame?"

Some people moved away, while others only stared with empty eyes. No one spoke.

Golden Fox shouted at Yellow Moon, "It is you who is useless and weak." She spat on the ground and moved toward her to spit again.

Yellow Moon's body stiffened and her eyes showed great anger.

Golden Fox stared at the flask before speaking. "Your anger means nothing to me. Your mind is broken, as was my father's. Before my *grandmother* went to the campfires in the sky, she warned me to be wary of you, that you carried hate in your heart, unlike others who let their hate go before it turns their hearts black."

Yellow Moon's brows lowered and she clenched her broken-tipped flint knife. She took the stance of one ready to fight, but tripped on a small tree root and fell. As she pushed up from the dirt, the hilt of the knife slipped and the broken-tipped blade slashed the palm of her hand.

"Aiieee!" She kicked the open flask that lay on the ground. "You! I will get you for thish!" She pounced at Golden Fox.

"No!" Sky Bird lunged And used her shoulder to shove Golden Fox away.

Yellow Moon slammed into Sky Bird and they both fell.

Sky Bird leapt to her feet as Yellow Moon rolled on the ground, trying to stand. Face red with anger, Sky Bird pointed a stiff finger at her second mother's daughter. "You! You are what the Whites call a savage! You destroy our people and care not what you do."

Golden Fox rushed over and gripped her mother's shoulder "Mother, she is not worth as much as the oldest humpback robe in camp!"

Yellow Moon's face deepened to a dark red-purple as she sat on the ground, her dress muddied and torn. "You musht... reshpect...me!" She slammed her open palm against her thin chest. "I... elder. You know noth... nothin'." She crawled to her knees, picked up her knife and, after three tries, stood up. She sliced the air with her knife and snarled, and with her eyes focused on her target, she ran at Golden Fox.

Sky Bird raced at Yellow Moon with her arms outstretched. "No! You will not hurt my daughter!" She shoved Yellow Moon at the shoulder, sending her crashing to the ground. Sky Bird stumbled a few feet, then regained her balance, and turned back toward her fallen aunt.

Yellow Moon lay on the ground, face down, unmoving.

Golden Fox knelt down and rolled her over, and they all saw that Yellow Moon's knife had lodged in her chest. "Sweet Mother." Golden Fox stood and backed away, covering her mouth with a trembling hand. "If not for me... she would still breathe!"

Sky Bird pulled her away. "I know you are young and have never seen our people fight among our band. We have lived in peace for many cycles of seasons. Now we are broken, but this is not a sorrow that is yours to carry. My aunt has brought this upon herself."

Yellow Moon's two brothers, as much as the fire water had control of them, came forward and carried Yellow Moon away.

The eldest brother glared deep into Sky Bird's eyes. "This is not finished. Leave or die."

Eagle Thunder stepped in front of Sky Bird. "Do not threaten my daughter. She protected her own child. It was your sister who drank the poisoned water and became crazy."

The eldest brother let go of his sister's feet, and they thumped to the ground. He then pulled his obsidian knife, which held an edge much sharper than any met-al one. It could easily cut a hand to the bone with one slice.

Eagle Thunder locked gazes with the younger man as he readied his own obsidian blade. "I will break it off in your heart!"

"No, Father!" Sky Bird screamed. "I refuse to see you harmed over people whose minds drown in poisoned water, when good water runs past the camp. Even the Holy Man does not stir from his lodge."

Eagle Thunder stared at the knife in his hand and sighed. "We are no longer Sun People. We will go to the other camp, and take the good people with us. We will move on, become new Peoples in *our* new land."

Golden Fox tugged at her grandfather's hand. "Running Girl and her mother are not yet here. They come with the rest of the hunters. We must wait—"

"Girl, I know your friend will soon be here." Eagle Thunder nodded and watched the band fight among themselves. "Let us hope it is before we leave."

People spoke in small groups. Some came out of lodges with belongings packed, ready for drags, which the dogs and extra mustangs would pull.

Others held tight to their flasks and only watched.

"People are sick. Even now, if we walked into their lodges, I am sure we would find the poison hidden there. My eyes were blind to this before. I could not accept what the Spirits showed me. Perhaps this is why the Spirits allowed my woman's sister to burn our lodges."

* * *

"Father...." Sky Bird held tight to his arm. "When we traveled to the camp of the pale ones, I thought we traded our furs for blankets of many colors, iron pots, and knives made of what they called met-al. I did not understand we traveled to their camps for poison that kills the mind."

23

She nodded toward the band. "I watched our people dance at night, and fall to the ground. You could not see. Your grief lay as a heavy robe over your eyes after Mother took her journey a moon ago. You carried much pain and left camp to call on Mother's Spirit. How could I speak of it then?"

Her voice trembled. "I failed you, Father. I refused to think this would last long." Tears gathered on her lashes, and she dashed them away with her hand.

"Our people started to take more of the poison for their furs, instead of blankets, knives and arrow points, as other bands. Instead of returning with our mustangs, we lost some in trading. I know the pale ones stole as many mustangs as they could all cold season. I heard one say a red... filthy redskin savage... should never be allowed a mustang." She stared at her arm. "Is my skin red? Am I filthy?"

She shook her head. "I had hoped our Holy Man would make them take the drink back, but he took a bladder for himself. He offered it to his young son. The boy drank and fell senseless to the ground."

Eagle Thunder turned weary eyes upon his daughter. "I will go ready our mustangs to pull drags and carry what is left of our belongings." He pulled himself tall and spoke to those who would listen. "All who wish to leave with us are welcome." His eyes misted and he blinked to clear them, then strode away.

Stands His Ground and Blazing Fire helped each other take down their lodges.

Eagle Thunder asked for one of them to remain behind, to speak of what happened when the hunters returned. Perhaps they could return then.

The warrior woman led her mustang over to Eagle Thunder. "I will ride to where the rest of our hunters camp, and tell them what has happened. I will lead the ones who wish to walk with us, and we will catch up to you."

Sun Rising and his woman walked up leading their packed mustangs. Here and there around the camp, empty spaces showed where lodges had been pulled down and packed. People waited.

Among the gathered people, many held tight to leather flasks, or weaved as they stood in front of lodges still standing. Some staggered with stomachs full of poisoned water, though Father Sun had been awake for only a short span. A brother and a sister argued over a leather flask. All of a sudden, the brother pulled his fist back and hit his sister, knocking her to the ground.

Eagle Thunder called out, "Our people—the once-great Sun People—are sick. Even now, if we walked into many lodges, we would find poisoned water hidden among sleeping robes. Where is our Holy Man? Why does he not come and stand with me? Why does he hide while his people tear themselves apart?"

The gathered people parted as the Holy Man wove his way to Eagle Thunder with a leather flask dangling from his hand. "Do not tell me what to do for the Sun People!" Red splotched his cheeks, and red veins ran through his eyes. "You are not the Holy Man. Fire water opens our inside eyes to the Spirit Land. There is no wrong in this firewater. The wrong lies within your heart. You fear these visions. Go! You are no longer welcome here. You are not of the Sun People!" He spat on the ground at Eagle Thunder's feet, then turned and stalked away.

* * *

Some of the hunters came in the early sunrise, and helped their families gather their belongings. Dogs would pull the smaller drags, mustangs the larger ones. Warriors would ride the strongest mustangs, constantly searching the land ahead and behind for enemies. A few elders, whose legs could not journey so far, would ride mustangs, and sometimes, small children would sit in front of them.

Sky Bird tied the last bundle of robes on their drag. "Where is Golden Fox?"

Eagle Thunder nodded toward Running Girl and her little brother. "She begs her friend to come. Running Girl's grandfather is mean when he drinks. When I am no longer here, he will drink much poisoned water and will not hold his temper tight. My heart hurts for those who stay behind, and it hurts even more for the children."

* * *

Running Girl cried hard tears and held onto Golden Fox. "I will come when my brother, Strong Knife, returns from hunting. Someone has to stay with my little brother, and Father will not let me take him. I fear, too, for Grandmother. She drinks so much, it comes back up in her mouth. She might choke if I am not here. My parents drink as much poisoned water as Grandmother, and cannot help her. I must stay, Golden Fox, until my brother comes."

"I worry for you, Running Girl." Golden Fox swallowed the painful lump in her throat. "What if your father refuses to let you leave even after Strong Knife returns?"

"Father has much fear of Strong Knife's anger. He will let my elder brother leave with my little brother and me."

Golden Fox grasped her friend's hands. "Please, come. You cannot stay! We have been friends since we shared a cradleboard. Please, please, come with your little brother. Grandfather can talk to your father and make him say yes."

"Father will not agree. Eagle Thunder makes him angry. He says your grand-father thinks he is too good to share firewater at our campfire."

"I feel as if my heart will shatter like a cold spear of ice in the winter!" Golden Fox sniffed back tears. "Your father becomes crazy when the poisoned water is in him. I fear that the next time he beats you, if Grandfather is not here to stop him, he may not stop beating you until it is too late." She reached over with her fingers and gently wiped her friend's tears. "If you stay, I fear I may never see you again."

Running Girl wrung her hands together. "When the hunters return, I must help Mother make meat, or she will have none for the cold season. While we work, Strong Knife will speak with our father. Maybe Mother will come with us. Do not worry, Golden Fox. The Spirit of Grandfather will watch over me until I see you again."

Mouth turned down, Golden Fox lifted her chin in stubborn defiance. "I will stay with you, Running Girl, until Strong Knife can talk to your father."

Sadness filled Running Girl's eyes. "Your presence will only anger Father, and he may harm you. You go. Now!" She scooped up her little brother and settled him on her hip, and his chubby legs partly wrapped around her thin waist. With her back straight and her head held high, she marched toward her family's lodge.

Tears ran down Golden Fox's cheeks as she helplessly watched her friend walk away.

Eagle Thunder hung his head as he shuffled through the grasses. His braid dangled down his back in scattered strands, and a few white ones that had escaped wisped about his face.

Many from the broken band followed behind him. Now and then, a sob escaped one of the children, but was quickly stifled. As Father Sun rose higher, others from the shattered band joined those who traveled.

How is it I now lead so many people? Another curve, another stumble in the broken path of all our lives. Perhaps there is something beyond the broken, jagged edges that I cannot see. Life gives us many chances to look beyond what our human eyes can see. We must open our minds and our hearts to what the Great Mystery wishes to show us.

Eagle called.

Eagle Thunder raised his head to watch Eagle soar and circle above the people who followed. *Guide us, my Brother. Warn us of dangers that hide. Father Sun takes away his light. Everyone walks the heavy walk of sorrow, except the children. Perhaps, it is better to be young and not know things.*

Sky Bird caught up to him. Her red eyes and downturned mouth spoke much, but she would never complain. Medicine plants she had picked the last three sunrises filled the pouch she carried strapped over her shoulder. She kept tossing the plants in the pouch to keep them from going bad, and laid them out whenever they stopped. The yellow-orange sun painted on the pouch had only suffered minor burns from the lodge fire.

An animal path followed the shallow river. Children waded in the cold waters as their elders spread out along the narrow path. Though several of the young people were Golden Fox's age, she refused their calls to join them.

His granddaughter's aloneness did not escape Eagle Thunder's watchful eyes. "Good thing our women carry their own bows," he said to Sky Bird. "Golden Fox wanders out of sight much. She must worry for Running Girl."

He bent and picked up a good piece of thick flint. He could knap such flint and make them into arrowheads. He would make another bow for Golden Fox, as the fire had eaten hers, and now she carried an old one. This was a good time for Golden Fox and some of the other young ones to learn to make their own arrowheads.

Sky Bird interrupted his thoughts. "Father, we all tire. The water will cool our feet. Allow us to rest. Come sit beside me, and I will rebraid your hair and mine. The sick must rest, and we must all eat and sleep. A good time to stop, you think? I do."

Surrendering to her wisdom, he nodded, raised his hand, and called for the others to stop. With motions of his hands, he signaled that they would make camp in the meadow that spread beside the river.

Eagle Thunder and Sky Bird set their footwear back from the edge of the water. Eagle Thunder let his tired, sore feet hang in the slow moving river while his daughter fixed his star-dusted hair.

With his hair done, she re-braided her own hair. After a short while, she glanced over to where Golden Fox stood some distance away. A worried frown tightened the skin around her eyes as she pushed to her feet. "Father, I will go help Golden Fox gather wood before the darkness takes the light. I must hurry. She has only picked up three pieces, and now stares without seeing."

Eagle Thunder's granddaughter stood in stillness, not natural for one so young. "Daughter, I have concern, too. I had hoped her mind and heart would heal as we walked."

"After what she saw in camp, her mind wanders. I will walk with her after we make camp and eat. We can speak and share this experience together. I, too, have spent much of the last three sunrises thinking about what happened, living through it again."

He rubbed his chin. "I cannot help but worry she may try to turn back and get Running Girl."

***

Golden Fox hurried to clean up after eating, and carried her robe away from the fire to prepare her bed.

Sky Bird stopped her. "Daughter, I need to walk to take care of my needs. Please, come with me."

She stood with her robe in hand. "Mother, there is little to fear with the warriors so close. Some may have star dust in their hair, but they have the power of many cycles of seasons." She dropped the robe to the ground. "You wish to speak of something."

Sky Bird extended her hand. "Please? Besides, it is always safer for two to wander than for one to do so in a strange land."

"We have been out on the grasses for three sunrises, and now you have fear?"

"Even more so, my little one. We walk in lands unknown to most of us, except the hunters." She heaved a deep breath and let it rush out. "It is time, Golden Fox, to speak of what we...."

"Mother, I do not wish to speak of what happened. It is best left deep in my mind." She started to turn away when her mother hooked her arm.

"You have avoided your grandfather and me since we have been out here. Why not sit close to us when we rest, instead of moving away? Even in sleep, you lay your robe away from others. I have seen how you stare out at nothing for long spans. You do not see where we walk, but walk as if asleep. If you will not speak to me, speak to Flying Turtle. He is two-spirit and can see both as a woman and as a man."

Her mother brushed a stray strand of hair from Golden Fox's cheek. "There is no shame in seeking Flying Turtle's counsel, for even your grandfather and I have sought his counsel in time of need and sorrow. He is wise in ways that others, who are not two-spirit, cannot be."

Golden Fox kept her eyes on the grass at her feet. "I have much anger, and wish to go back to camp and bring Running Girl to be with us."

Her mother gripped her arm. "You will not do such a thing! Do you wish to die before you see fifteen winters?"

"She is the sister of my heart. Without her, I no longer care."

Too soon they had to move on. Father Sun had not yet awakened when the people ate and packed to leave.

Weary, Eagle Thunder led them along the river, following the call of Eagle, who glided above them. The river wound through the valley until it spilled out on spreading grasslands. His father had once brought him this far to hunt.

Tall, green grasses grew mixed in with the faded yellow-brown of last season's stalks. The children raced toward dark green shrubs, some heavy with red berries that held the promise of wonderful sweet juices. Flowers — red, orange, yellow, blue — added beauty to the green, silver, and purple-red grasses that stretched farther than anyone could see.

Sky Bird laid her hand on his arm and lightly shook it. "Father, the slopes grow thick with Sacred Sage, and the tall, stiff-spiked plants whose white blooms now fade are everywhere, more here than we have seen in the last two sunrises. We should gather the spiked plant's tubers for later. Some of us need to bathe, and the crushed tubers will make us clean. Father?"

He raised his head and peered around as if awaking from a dream, as mustangs and riders topped the crest of a rolling slope. "Hunters come with Blazing Fire and Stands His Ground in the lead."

Deer and ground birds hung across the backs of extra mustangs. The two lead hunters headed toward Eagle Thunder.

Eagle Thunder tilted his head toward the cooking fires. "Daughter, some of our hunters have come to be with us, with their women and children. Go and help make meat. Make sure Golden Fox helps. She drifts too far away in her own mind. Working will call her back to us." He raised his hand to block Father Sun's glare and see others approaching. "Many children come, too many to belong to the women who follow."

As Sky Bird hurried to the ring of women around the cooking fire, Eagle Thunder made his way toward the lone hunter and Blazing Fire.

Stands His Ground's face held no smile. "I greet you, Eagle Thunder. Let us speak away from others."

Both Stands His Ground and Blazing Fire slid off their mustangs and pushed the animals to join the camp.

Silence followed them out away from the others. "Hunters returned to the old camp. No joy came with their return. Some of the young warriors and their women followed us. I am sad to say our Holy Man stayed. More of the band was sick on the poisoned water, and many spoke angry words of Sky Bird killing Yellow Moon. We did not take any of their meat with us. The smell of rot blew on Sister Wind. We could not leave the children to starve. Not one mother or father cared when we pulled their children away from them."

Eagle Thunder clenched his jaw. "You both did as you should. No child could have survived this... craziness. Yellow Moon was crazy on poisoned water and fell on her own knife after she tried to harm Golden Fox. All who were there saw this."

Blazing Fire nodded. "That was Sky Bird's right as Golden Fox's mother. Still, angry words are being spread." She looked toward the busy camp. "This place is too open if Yellow Moon's brothers bring others after Sky Bird."

"We will soon find another place." Eagle Thunder squinted toward the mustangs. "If you left the meat, where did you find the deer and birds that you brought to us?"

A troubled look filled Blazing Fire's eyes. "A sunrise ago, we came across a camp of eight pale ones. The men were full of poisoned water. Five of them knew nothing until our arrows flew into their chests. Three of the hairy-faces jumped on mustangs and ran away. We brought the meat from their camp."

When Blazing Fire fell silent, Stands His Ground lifted his bowed head. "Two of our hunters chased the pale men. We did not find their bodies. We found *our* warriors, but all we could do was sing to help their Spirits on their journey. None of the men had women to grieve over them, so we wrapped them in their sleeping robes and placed them in the trees."

Eagle Thunder's head slumped. He moved small stones with his footwear. "Let us gather the rest of our elders. Please, Stands His Ground and Blazing Fire, take rested warriors and keep the people circled."

***

As a small group sat around a campfire, Eagle Thunder cleared his throat. "Let us send scouts back to follow our enemy. We are far away from the wooden fort, so this must be a small band of white men. Perhaps they do not follow us. but just journey in the same direction."

He pivoted his head to study the people who sat behind them. Many hugged themselves as if caught in the midst of a winter snow. Shivers racked their bloated bodies.

"More people show the craving for the poisoned water. Eagle Thunder, I know you see it, too." Sun Rising, the eldest in the band, looked at his oldest friend. "I remember your woman's story, about helping your mind come back, and what she had to do to keep you from journeying to the campfires in the sky. Soon we will need to care for the sick, and not be able to travel at all. It is clear that some sneaked flasks of poisoned water with them. They take small sips when they think no one looks. It helps keep them from shaking so bad."

Eagle Thunder dipped his eyes in remembered shame. "Without my woman, I would have gone to the campfires in the sky. After my mind returned, my woman taught me ways to help those with the poisoned water sickness. We will find shelter where the pale ones and Yellow Moon's brothers will not find us. The elders and the children need rest while we care for the sick. These past sunrises have been hard on them. If we do not do this, we will send more than just one man and his woman to the campfires in the sky."

He swept his gaze across their people. "The weight of a great stone sits upon my heart. We have lost many of our people. Some remained behind with the Sun People band, some came with us only to be pulled away by the craving for the poisoned water, and they left in darkness. Many of those who left will never reach the old camp, but no one could stop them. It is their right to choose how they will die."

He brushed away moisture from the edges of his eyes. "We will rest here until we know of a safer place."

Eagle Thunder walked away from the gathered elders, but soon stopped. "Granddaughter, you may use Fox's gift of hiding, but not from me. Shadows form no matter how well you become one with them."

She appeared before him. "I will one day hide in front of you and you will see no shadow. Do not worry, I will tell no one what has happened. Do you think Strong Knife will come with Running Girl and their youngest brother?"

"Blazing Fire said there were those who packed to follow us. Maybe he brings his sister and brother." He looped an arm around her shoulders. "I pray this is so, but only Great Mystery knows the answers to some of our questions."

She slipped away once more.

"Sneaky Golden Fox." He chuckled

He made his way toward Sky Bird and the many hungry children. "You have worries that burden your mind other than these children. We are safe for now."

Sky Bird nodded and her eyes showed no fear. Her shaking hands showed it instead. She cleared her throat and nodded toward where she had last seen Golden Fox. "I worry for her, not me. Her golden-red hair attracts attention. We should go into the canyons."

"Your daughter is not so easy to see when she calls upon Fox. Perhaps it is another worry?"

"Let us go sit among our belongings." She turned away from the children and other women who cared for them, and lifted her plain leather pouch over her shoulder. She carried all her sewing, clothing, paints, quills, medicines — everything a woman and a healer needed.

He took one of the rolled robes to shake out and spread on the ground.

After they had settled, his daughter's body moved in tight, jerky movements. Even after she fished out all the stones that poked her, she gritted her teeth. A body spoke so much.

He spoke softly. "You remember my words to you of how they reacted when I brought you to our band? Your dark, red-brown hair and grey eyes made some wish to leave you among the trees, so the Spirits could decide your fate. Daughter, look at me."

The command drew her eyes up to lock with his. "All bands have the good and the bad in them, like a bush with berries — not all the berries are sweet and good for you. Know this, Sky Bird: no one who follows us now, in our new band, ever thought of you or Golden Fox in a bad way."

The air between them remained still. Wisdom came with the cycles of seasons that one lived. All an elder had to do was watch a person to know what they carried in their hearts.

"Daughter, speak to me."

"I do not fear for myself." She folded her arms across her chest. "As Father Sun creeps behind the end of the land, sometimes I see pale ones hiding in the shadows. My heart beats fast, until I realize it is that I see only shadows. Even when Father Sun smiles at us from the highest part of the sky, I sometimes look and see in the fold of a hill, the shape of men who do not belong to the People.

"Father, Golden Fox is worth more than my own life. Why do the white men come now? Her pale-skinned father has never before wanted to see his daughter. Why does he now want her?" Her fists tightened until the knuckles turned white.

Eagle Thunder nodded. "It is wise to look closely at shadows, but we have scouts who keep watch over our people. To find trouble where none lives is not wise. To hunt for trouble when it has not come to visit us, is to find pain that you might have avoided. Daughter, I understand your fears. They are my fears, too. If the pale ones come, everyone in our band will fight for Golden Fox. Until they come, we have much work to do to save our people."

He turned his gaze. "Some of the elders have not yet come into camp. They sit by the trail and refuse to move. I am needed there."

He stood to leave. "Do not worry so. Find our sneaky little one and sleep next to her."

* * *

As darkness swallowed the last golden sliver of Father Sun, the campfires in the sky burned brighter, Eagle Thunder sought out his friend.

Sun Rising sat with his head bent back, staring at the blackness where the fires of loved ones burned. "I wonder which campfire my daughter and her man sit beside?"

"Ah, old friend, that is what I think when I look up. Which campfire is tended by my woman?"

"A warrior should journey to the campfires in the sky before his child." Sun Rising brought his eyes down from the sky. "I tire of this journey, Eagle Thunder." He motioned toward the silent woman seated next to him. "My woman tires of it, too. Perhaps, it is time for us to walk alone."

"That is a question a man, or a woman, must speak about with the Great Mystery. I have no answers, though you would both be much missed, if you decided to wander off into the darkness, as those other three elders did. You give courage to our hunters and warriors. You give laughter to our children with your stories. We have great need of both courage and laughter."

With a grunt, Sun Rising pushed to his feet and held a hand down to his woman, who also groaned as she stood.

As they drew near the camp, murmurs from weary people drifted among the campfires, as they settling in for the dark time. After eating, women readied their bows and laid them next to their sleeping robes. They tied dogs, used to wandering loose, to stakes around a family's belongings. At first, the animals had been restless, but after nights on the trail they had come to accept this new way.

Eagle Thunder sighed. *If only people could accept new ways as easily as dogs and children.*

It helped that so many greeted Father Sun with songs, and stayed longer to open their hearts to the Spirits. This shattering of their band had maybe reminded people of the important things in life.

As he dipped meat from the cooking pot, his heart told him what he did not want to know — the people needed rest. They could journey no more without it.

*　*　*

The night had grown quiet. Warriors rode and watched over the small band. Those too sick to sit by the campfires lay wrapped in sleeping robes. An elder cried out, and someone comforted him. The rest gathered around the cooking fire simply for the comfort of being with their people.

Eagle Thunder stepped close to the fire and raised his hand. He waited patiently for those who whispered among themselves to notice and pay attention. When everyone had fallen silent, he cleared his throat and tried to calm his fast beating heart. Eyes lifted to the campfires in the sky, he sang a short song known only to him.

The people remained still, giving respect to Eagle Thunder's call on the Spirits.

After his song drifted to a haunting close, his eyes settled on his daughter and granddaughter on the far side of the fire. Golden Fox squirmed beneath his steady gaze, and he wondered what made her eyes dart away from him. There would be time to find this out later; now he turned his attention to the gathered people.

36

The story needed to be told, and perhaps in the telling, the burden on his Spirit would be lightened. "Listen well to me, my people. For many cycles of seasons, I have held these words silent inside of me, ashamed to speak them so my people would hear. It is time to speak.

"When we drink the poisoned water, it makes our ears deaf. It drowns out the drumbeat of life. With deaf ears, we can no longer hear the beat of the cricket's call at night, or the joy in the bird's song at sunrise. As the song of life dies within us, darkness comes like a fog off the river. That darkness swallows our minds. We become as empty water bladders with nothing to give."

His hands fisted against the pain that pierced his chest. "Once, long ago, darkness swallowed my mind. My ears fell deaf to the drumbeat of all life. Warning dreams came to me and told me that I was killing my Spirit with every swallow of the poisoned water. I drank more, to keep the dreams away. As happens when we turn from Spirit's guidance, Spirit stopped sending the dreams."

He bowed his head for a short span. "Shame washes over me." When he lifted his face, his eyes held determination. "Great Mystery never abandoned me. I abandoned the Great Mystery. Like a wise parent, Great Mystery knew that I must travel a rocky, broken path. I could not be stopped. Like a child who believes he is wiser than the elders, I tumbled and fell. I crawled along the cutting rocks, and now carry the scars deep within."

He swung his arm wide and pointed toward Sister Moon. "So many gifts are lost to the mind that is broken. Eyes blinded by poisoned water cannot see our Sister. We stumble as if her silver light does not touch the land. The brush of Sister Wind cannot be felt. The small winged ones, who seek the flowers right next to us, go unnoticed. The soft hands of loved ones hold no joy, but feel like ropes wrapped tightly around our chests, crushing the breath from us. Father Sun no longer calls to us to sing as he rises from his bed."

Sun Rising caught Eagle Thunder's gaze and gravely nodded his respect. "Ah-ho, words of great truth spill from my wise friend's mouth."

Jaw clenched as he fought the water that wished to fall from his eyes, Eagle Thunder bent his head back and let the tender light of Sister Moon bathe him for a short span. "Great Mystery gives each of us the freedom to choose what we will do with our lives. It is up to us to choose with a wise heart, to remember that what we choose affects not only our lives, but the lives of all those around us."

He stared across the fire. "In shame, I did not tell my daughter that I once drank poisoned water." He caught and held her gaze. "You, Sky Bird, had yet to be with us. Your first mother and I drank together for a cycle of seasons. When my mother warned us about the poisoned water, I refused to listen. I took my woman and went to the wooden fort, back to her people, the hairy-faces.

"For many moons, we drank the poisoned water among those of our people who had come to the fort, like us. Many times, Father Sun rose on me not singing a song of praise, but lying in my own vomit as the mustangs of the soldiers splashed through the mud around me."

With great breaths to give his body the wind his words needed, so that all would hear, Eagle Thunder continued. "One morning, when I lay face down in a puddle of dirty water, an elder Holy Man gently rolled me over so I would not drown. Your first mother sat next to me, too weak from the poisoned water to turn me onto my back. The Holy Man squatted next to me until I opened my eyes. Father Sun burned them, and I squinted, barely able to see the elder's face. He told me that I had become a slave to the poisoned water, and to the hairy-faces. If I wanted to sit at the campfires in the sky, I must leave the wooden fort and the poisoned water and return to my people.

"My first woman spit on the Holy Man. He wiped if from his face and spoke kindly to her. He told her to follow me back to my mother's lodge, and to have our child within the embrace of our people. He warned her to listen well, so that she might be taught the ways of the Great Mystery. When the Holy Man left us, my first woman helped me to my feet, and we staggered outside of the fort. where we sat against the wall, too sick to speak."

Eagle Thunder drew air deep into his chest and let it ease from him. "Never did we speak of the Holy Man's words. For many more moons, I kept drinking the poisoned water, but it no longer kept the dreams away. I no longer laughed when those we drank with laughed. The poisoned water made me sicker. The Holy Man's words rode my mind like a man on a wild mustang must ride to stay on the animal. My first woman refused to leave the wooden fort. I begged her to leave for the child she carried. She refused. I left and waited in the forest nearby to see if my first woman would follow me. After many sunrises, I knew she would not come, and I could not force her. I traveled alone toward my mother's camp. She worried our child would be no good because of the fire water. She had seen it many times."

Eagle Thunder remained silent for so long that people started to fidget. They returned to stillness as soon as he began to speak again.

"By the time I came to my mother's lodge, I shook so hard that I fell from my mustang as it stood without moving, in the middle of the camp. My mother and another, younger woman rushed over to me. They tied me to a drag and took me away from the camp, out into the forest. By the time we reached a clearing in the trees, I fought hard against the ropes that bound me. Craving for the poisoned water burned like a fire through my body."

He stared down and traced a finger along the lines on the palms of his hands. "All pathways, like the lines of our hands, lead to a different place. We can blame no one else for the path we choose to follow, for Great Mystery gives us the power to choose our own path.

"There are many sunrises forever lost to my memory. The younger woman who tended me, and became my second woman, refused to speak of those days. It was my mother who told me what I had done and said."

Once again, the pain he had caused his second woman felt like a spear to his heart. His hand clutched at his chest until he could breathe again.

"This is what my mother told me about those sunrises. I shook hard from the bad Spirits that had entered me with the poisoned water. I shouted terrible things at my mother and at the one to be my second woman. My teeth ground together so loudly that my second woman placed a twig in my mouth to keep them from breaking. Voices told me that the women were trying to steal my Power, and that I would never be a man again if I did not drink of the poisoned water soon. I did not recognize my own mother, and fought against the ropes as if an enemy held me. Much water poured from my body, stinking of the poisoned water, and then shivers shook me as if I lay in a hard freeze in winter. Twice, my second woman touched my body, and it felt as if a fire burned within. My second woman and my mother bathed me in cool water. For three sunrises, I was like this."

A shudder shook his whole body. "Father Sun's heat woke me. I looked around and did not recognize the place where I lay. Ropes bound me, and I could feel dried blood beneath my nose. Along my arms, cuts stung, and I felt dried blood there, also. I felt alone, as if all the people had left our Mother. Tears ran from my eyes and into my ears. The salt from them must have cleaned my ears, because I could hear the rustling of a deer as it stepped from the trees around me. I gazed up at the bit of blue sky, and my eyes did not burn. Far above the trees, Eagle soared and dipped And danced around in circles, his body white as the soft, scattered clouds. I do not know how long I lay there, staring up as Eagle danced for me. Tears still streamed from my eyes when my second woman laid a gentle hand on my shoulder and squatted to be next to me. She, too, watched Eagle dance. Then, Eagle was gone. Not flown away. We simply could no longer see Eagle."

A good shiver rode along his back bone as he reached for the necklace made of braided mustang hair. He took it from his neck and held it so the others might see. A carved Eagle made from a white stone shimmered in the firelight. "As I lay shaking and shouting evil things, as the poisoned water left my body, my second woman carved this stone. When Eagle left, she pulled this from her pocket and looped it around my neck. For the first time in many moons, my Spirit felt free—truly free." He glanced around. "The one thing I know is this: -poisoned water will, sooner or later, kill all that it touches. Love can heal the wounds that the poisoned water makes, but.... We must choose to walk a path without poisoned water, and to let love work within us.

"My words are finished." He walked away into the darkness.

***

As she had taken to doing, Golden Fox picked up her sleeping robe and walked toward the mustang herd. Mother and grandfather knew she had a special way with animals, so they did not worry that she chose to sleep close to the mustangs. On this night, as Sister Moon drifted behind a cloud, she listened carefully to the rustling in the camp. At last, everyone seemed to have settled into sleep, except for the warriors who guarded the camp.

Golden Fox unrolled her robe and sat looking at the hidden things. A pouch held enough jerked meat to last for ten sunrises. A flask held water. The new arrows Grandfather had helped her make lay next to her bow. Her obsidian knife was safe in its sheath at her waist. The only thing missing was Swift Arrow.

She caught her lower lip between her teeth. For many nights, she had argued with herself that families shared everything, but a person's mustang was special. Grandfather would be angry when he woke and found Swift Arrow missing. One by one, she thought carefully about each of the other mustangs her family owned. None of them were as fast or as smart as Swift Arrow. She *needed* Swift Arrow.

She looped two thongs over her neck—the pouch's and the flask's. The pouch hung on the opposite side of her knife, with the flask lying on top of the pouch.

Her quiver rode behind her shoulder where she could easily get the arrows. She rolled the sleeping robe tight and tied it with a piece of flat leather she had cut from one of her dresses, which had been badly scorched by the flames that ate their lodge.

A quiet whistle brought Swift Arrow to her. He nickered softly as he approached.

She hunched close to the shadows of the trees until convinced no one else had heard, then slung her bow over her arm and patted the mustang.

Swift Arrow followed as she crept through the herd. The lead female lifted her head from grazing and called to Swift Arrow.

A scout rode from the darkness and peered across the animals. Slowly, the warrior woman nudged her mustang into the herd. The animals parted without panic as she passed.

Blazing Fire! Golden Fox grasped Swift Arrow's neck hairs and pulled him toward the far side of the herd. She could not let Blazing Fire stop her!

A tense span later, the warrior woman disappeared into the shadows of the trees close to the river.

Golden Fox sucked in a breath and hurried Swift Arrow along. At the edge of the herd, she placed the soft leather ties that would hold her sleeping robe on the mustang, tied the robe in place, and then hopped onto the animal's back. With a tap of her heel, she urged the mustang into a trot. She needed to cross the rise of the small hill a short distance from the camp, so the scouts would not spot her.

As she topped the rise and started down the other side, Blazing Fire rode out of the deeper darkness of the hillside. Her animal stopped in front of Swift Arrow. The warrior woman remained silent.

Unable to stand the tension between them, Golden Fox blurted out, "I could not sleep, and thought a small ride might help me rest."

"Hmm!" Blazing Fire grunted.

"Swift Arrow is the fastest mustang in our herd. I can ride back to camp quickly if an enemy shows."

With an audible sigh, Blazing Fire sat up straighter. "A short ride that needs a sleeping robe, a knife, a bow, a flask of water, and a pouch that most likely holds jerked meat. Such a long short ride, with our enemies perhaps trailing us, is not wise, girl."

Anger heated Golden Fox's cheeks. "I am a woman, not a girl!" She pulled herself taller on the mustang.

The warrior woman huffed out an angry breath. "Then perhaps, Golden Fox, you should act as a woman acts, not as a child acts—in ways that could bring trouble to her people." Tiredness lined Blazing Fire's face. "Go, Golden Fox, go back to camp. Settle your sleeping robe among our people and sleep, so that I do not need to speak of this to your Mother."

Shoulders slumped, Golden Fox turned Swift Arrow.

Before she got far, Blazing Fire spoke. "Do not ride into the night alone, Golden Fox. It is not safe for you or for our people. Many are yet too sick to move swiftly, to get away from an enemy. You must promise this to me, or I will be forced to speak to your grandfather."

With a brisk downward motion of her head, Golden Fox agreed to the warrior woman's demand. The tap of her heel on Swift Arrow's side nudged the mustang into a fast walk. "She said not to ride alone in darkness. She said nothing about when Father Sun is awake."

***

Father Sun woke the camp with a brilliance of gold rays shooting across the clouds. Warriors traded places with others, so they could rest and eat. Women took care of the younger children, who played quiet games.

Golden Fox's mother sent her to collect the prickly, purple-pink flowering plant that would help protect the sick people's livers from dying. Stretched-out clouds drifted across soft blue sky. She would return with the medicine plants, and clean up the area where they slept.

Grandfather will be busy making new arrows and watching over Sun Rising. Mother will be caring for the sick. I will find a way to go to Running Girl!

A smile creased her lips.

A different type of medicine plant grew along a small stream that veered away from the main waters. Its yellow flowers caught her attention. The rich green leaves were an extra gift. They grew in abundance at the bottom of a steep slope, which made her side-step her way down.

She squatted next to the plants. "Plant people, my people have a great need of your help. Many have much pain." She pulled out an offering of tobacco from a medicine pouch tied to her waist.

BROKEN PATH

The last trader to come by the Sun People's camp had brought tobacco with him. Sky Bird had traded a fine painted shirt and footwear for some. All the tobacco had not been lost with their lodge. Most of the bundled, Sacred plants had lain near the flap.

Golden Fox now offered tobacco to each healing plant.

As she gathered the plants, she thanked each one for their sacrifice. When she stood, a cool wind pushed her hair from her shoulders and tickled her warm skin. She closed her eyes and raised her face to Father Sun.

A faint drumbeat startled her, and her eyes jerked open. Faded images of long ago People, dressed in animal skins, danced in a circle around her. Her knees weakened, and the plants fell from her loosened arms.

"What is—" She turned to run up the hill.

'Granddaughter.'

Golden Fox spun back around. "Grandmother? How is it that you are here? And with Spirit People I do not know?"

'Little one, they are our relations. Once they wandered this land. You are connected to the Spirit Land around you, always. This is why you see them. When Eagle Woman came for me, I chose to stay close, instead of going to the campfires in the sky. I wished to be near your grandfather. Do not fear. Your grandfather leads the people along a good path. Hairy-faces offer nothing except pain, and our people need to heal and grow strong.

'Granddaughter, do not act in a foolish way. Much will happen in the sunrises to come, and you must keep your mind clear. You must become a woman of your people. They will need you.

Her grandmother laughed, a joyful sound.

'Tell your grandfather that to cross over from age is not so bad. When your grandfather joins me, I will once more feel complete. But he is not to join me yet. Danger hides everywhere, Little One, and you need him.'

Lines fell from her grandmother's face. Long, shiny, raven's wing hair sparkled with tiny specks of blue. She turned from her granddaughter and joined the Ancient Ones, dancing around their fire to the beat of the drums.

"Grandmother, please do not go! Tell me—why did this vision come to me?"

'Chosen.'

Her grandmother and the Spirit people faded, but the drumbeat went on.

Golden Fox danced to the rhythm, to the beat of all living things. When the beat faded and she could once more hear the chirp of birds, she frowned and gathered up the plants she had dropped.

What did Grandmother mean — do not act in a foolish way? Did Grandmother mean I should not go after Running Girl?

She gave her head a firm shake.

No, Grandmother would not want me to turn my back on my best friend. She must have meant to be watchful and to plan with care, instead of just running off at the earliest moment.

As Golden Fox headed back to camp, she scanned the sloping hills where small flowers scattered bursts of white, orange, and yellow among the green grasses. Shrubs with dark and light green and silvery leaves shimmered in Father Sun's light. Sister Wind stirred the leaves of the trees and they whispered among themselves. Black and white birds with black, spear-like tail feathers zipped through the air as they rushed to feed the chirping young in nests on high branches. Small dirt mounds were dotted with brown ground dogs who chirped warnings whenever danger approached.

She would have to be careful when she went to find Running Girl. The land between her band and the Sun People's camp was split with many ravines, places where enemies might lay in wait. Tall grasses could hide a whole hunting party. Now, she understood Blazing Fire's concern and her grandmother's words. Though her belly pained her and her hands shook to think of waiting, she must not bring danger to her band because of her impatience.

When she walked into camp, children giggled as they chased green hopping creatures. The slippery animals threw themselves into puddles of water between tall cattails, which grew along the slow-moving stream that branched off the river.

She stopped by the lodge where Sky Bird tended the very sick, and dropped off the pouch stuffed with medicine plants. When her mother did not motion for her to help, she wandered down to the river.

Running Girl, where are you, my sweet friend? So many sunrises and no sign of you. Why did Strong Knife not bring you and your little brother and ride with the hunters who came? Did your brother, Strong Knife, want to stay with those who drank poisoned water? I am not so strong without you! Sweet Mother, our people are broken, and I fear much for my cradleboard sister.

7

Stands His Ground often rode out alone to bring meat to the people and to scout the land ahead, leaving behind more warriors and hunters to protect the camp. He had been out three sunrises on this occasion, and had decided to begin hunting as he headed back to camp.

Off to the place where Father Sun rose every morning, a tiny spiral of smoke drifted up from a narrow valley. As he rode closer, he spotted a lone figure atop the steep hill. He rode the long way around to reach the opposite hill, where perhaps he could look down on the camp.

He tied the second mustang to a tree at the bottom of the hill beside a large boulder, where a few trees shaded the ground-covering plants, which were full with ripening red berries.

Father Sun had journeyed to the top of the sky by the time Stands His Ground reached a small area of grass near the crest of the slope. He slid off his mustang. The animal had been his since birth and had been taught to remain near until he returned. If the scouts of these strangers noticed his animal, they would think him to be one of the lone Stallions looking for a herd.

At the crest of the hill, he peered down at the camp, far larger than the one led by Eagle Thunder. He lay watching until Father Sun reached the edge of the land.

After he returned to his mustang and retrieved the other animal. He headed toward the opening of the valley in case he had to make a run for it. If these people were not friendly, they would have a hard time catching him.

Large iron pots hung over small, nearly-smokeless cooking fires as Stands His Ground rode into the camp.

Young children raced to hide behind their mothers. Older children grabbed rocks in their hands, determined to prove themselves worthy as warriors.

A smile tugged at the corners of his mouth. The thuds of mustang feet on packed earth sounded behind him, but he did not turn around; if they had wanted to put an arrow in his back, they would have already done so.

A woman with obsidian hair hanging in long, thick braids that reached her thighs made her way toward him. A light brown, short-sleeved tunic decorated with elk teeth and long fringe along the bottom swayed with her movement. Fringe ran down the sides of her leggings from hips to knees. By her clothing, she held a high place among these people, and possessed some wealth. She waved one hand and held a feather-decorated lance in the other. Her muscled body, the way she stood, and the way she moved spoke of a seasoned warrior.

In response to the woman's motion, her band moved closer behind her. Warriors stood watching him, waiting for some sign from her.

"Come, brother, sit at my fire circle and speak of where you come from and why you are here." She stabbed the lance deep into the ground, so that it stood on its own. "I am called Dances In Storms, Holy Woman of our people."

He slid off his mustang and let the nose rope of the pack animal drop to the ground. "I am called Stands His Ground, warrior and hunter for my people." *Both warrior woman and Holy Woman?* Always before, he had heard of women who became warriors, like Blazing Fire, or who became Holy Women, but he had never heard of a woman who carried both burdens for her people.

She led him to the main campfire and motioned for him to sit close to her. After they had given him food and water, the Holy Woman waited until he finished his meal for him to tell his story.

When he set his bowl aside, he spoke of his band seeking a new land, and that he had ridden ahead to scout and bring back meat.

Dances In Storms cocked her head. "I see in your eyes, Stands His Ground, that there is more to say. Speak."

Something in her voice allowed him to speak all the tangled feelings in his heart. "My band is broken. Many of our people drank the white man's fire water. There was much fighting and stealing." His head dropped to his chest, with shame covering him as snow covered the ground in the cold season. "Now, our band is broken. Many followed Eagle Thunder, who is a good man and a good leader, to find a land where the hairy-faces and their poisoned water do not live."

The Holy Woman nodded, her deep-set eyes shining with Power. "The fighting you speak of... it used to be seldom heard of, but now that hairy-faces invade our land, our lives, there has been much more fighting among people of the same band. Mostly, the people fight over the drink, and one of them does not walk away. Among the Sister Wolf Band, we make the one who wins gather their belongings and we cast them out." Pain showed in her eyes. "One cast out was my younger brother. He took the life of my other brother."

Anger narrowed her eyes. "These enemies overstep their welcome. Our people have banned them from our camp and from the camps of our sister bands. Still, they lurk on the edges, hiding and taking our women who walk alone. We have lost girls as young as ten summers. When we go to their camps and show our weapons, they let us search for our missing women and girls, but they are never there. I fear they are being sold as slaves to other pale ones."

Stands His Ground frowned. "Is that why your people camp here—to leave behind those in your band who drink the poisoned water? Do you also have a broken band?"

"There are many reasons why a person might be in a certain place, but we did not come here to flee a broken band. Your people, Stands His Ground, have much courage to search for new lands. It is hard when bad things come between the people of a band. It is as if fire from the sky in a bad storm splits the body of a tree. There is much pain. The tree is weakened. It takes great strength for the tree to heal and to continue to grow."

She pushed up and stood. "Your people are welcome to join us. We will be stronger traveling together. When we return to our band, Sister Wolf Band, I will speak for your people. We have need of those who are brave of heart and strong of Spirit.

"You can sleep by our fire tonight. When Father Sun rises, we will give you dried meat for your people and a deer skin tunic for your leader, Eagle Thunder. Take these gifts and speak with your people. In four sunrises, I will travel to where your people camp to speak with your elders and your leader. If they agree, I will return and lead my people to your camp. We will come together as one people."

With enough dried meat to feed the camp for many sunrises, Stands His Ground rode hard on his return to camp. The excitement of having more warriors and hunters filled his chest. Perhaps, the Holy Woman could also heal some of the people.

Well after the second sunrise since leaving the Holy Woman, he neared camp. The smells of cooking meat floated in the air and made his mouth fill with water. His stomach growled. His mustang slid to a halt in the center of camp, and he leapt off, tossing the nose rope of the pack animal to a young girl who stood close. "Unload the gift of dried meat, and then rub both animals with dried grasses. They have run hard. Where is Eagle Thunder?"

The girl pointed toward the lodge of the sick ones. A second lodge had been erected next to it—Deer Woman's lodge. His sister had come.

Without looking back, he took the gift robe and hurried across camp.

Before he could step inside the first lodge, Eagle Thunder slapped the flap aside and grabbed his arm. "Good! You are here, Stands His Ground. An elder's mind wanders and his body jerks hard. I have tied him down, so he cannot hurt another or himself. Go inside and help the women while I go to Sky Bird. If this elder is to live, we need more of her medicine."

A short span later, Sky Bird ducked into the lodge, where Deer Woman already squatted across from the elder. Sky Bird shouldered Stands His Ground aside and pulled out a flask of poisoned water. Not long after, she dribbled a few drops into the elder's mouth.

The elder's shaking stopped, and he fell into an unnatural sleep.

Stands His Ground followed the women out of the lodge. "You gave that elder poisoned water!"

"Brother!" Deer Woman gasped in shock at his rudeness.

With a nod, Sky Bird agreed. "If an elder is very old and weak, the bad Spirits of the poisoned water will take his Spirit as they leave his body. When I feed the bad Spirits a few drops of poisoned water, they are fooled. This gives the other medicines time to heal the elder's body. When the elder is strong enough, we can use medicines to cast all of the Spirits from the poisoned water out of his body." She pushed the flask into the medicine carry-all that hung from her shoulder.

His cheeks flamed hot. "I... I am sorry, Sky Bird. I did not know this."

She patted his shoulder. "You are a great warrior and a fine hunter, Stands His Ground, but you are not a healer." She turned her attention to Deer Woman. "Go to where my medicines lay on my sleeping robe, and find the small, rounded spiked plants I showed you. The hairs on top have dried, so the whole plant will have full Power to help the sick. There are only twelve left. It is the plant that came from the trader moons ago. Bring only enough to give half a plant to each of those sick from the poisoned water. The plants will make the people vomit before they work. Give them only to those who can stay awake. Watch them and help if they choke."

As soon as Deer Woman hurried off, Sky Bird started toward the cooking fire in the center of the camp.

Stands His Ground walked next to her. "Can we find the spiked plants around here?"

Wearily, she shook her head. "I have never seen them. The trader said they only grow in very hot places."

Eagle Thunder waved Sky Bird over to where he sat near the cooking fire. "Eat, Daughter. You cannot help others if you let yourself become weak."

Stands His Ground quickly waved for her to sit. "I will dip food for you." After he handed her a bowl of meat and tubers, he prepared one for himself and sat next to her.

"Stands His Ground, I am glad you have returned." Eagle Thunder sipped broth from his bowl. "As you can see, more of our people have joined us. When you are done eating, I will be glad to hear of your travels."

When he set his bowl aside, Stands His Ground untied a plain pouch from his waist. "On my way to look at the land ahead of us, I gathered flowers for you to dye quills, Sky Bird. I am sorry I have no quills to offer." Even as children, he had offered her little gifts. It pleased him to see her smile and blush, as she did back then.

Eagle Thunder cleared his throat. "Stands His Ground, what news do you have?"

The warrior handed the robe he had been carrying to Eagle Thunder. When the elder raised his brows in question, Stands His Ground told the story of how he had found a band of people. He spread his hands at the end of his telling. "Dances In Storms leads this camp of Sister Wolf Band people. She will come here in less than three more sunrises. If the elders and you decide to join with the

Sister Wolf Band, we can travel with them back to their home. She will speak for our people with the elders of her band."

"We will tell our warriors and hunters that a Holy Woman is coming." He held his hand up when Stands His Ground started to protest. "This is to be prepared if Dances In Storms is not what she seems. I have great respect for your ability to see the heart of others, Stands His Ground, but many of our people are sick and unable to help defend our camp."

Grudgingly, Stands His Ground nodded his acceptance.

"The elders and I will meet with Dances In Storms. After that, we will see what path the Great Mystery tells us to take."

Stands His Ground glanced from Eagle Thunder to Sky Bird and then back to Eagle Thunder. "I see my sister has joined our camp."

Eagle Thunder stood. "Sky Bird will tell you news of our people. I go to help in the lodge of the sick ones."

"My sister... she seemed well." Stands His Ground's shoulders grew tight.

"Deer Woman is well. Do not worry so."

"Others came?" A heavy weight lay in his stomach as he waited for Sky Bird to answer.

"The second lodge is not for those who are sick from poisoned water. It is for those who heal from injuries of the body."

"I know Golden Fox worried for Running Girl. Was Running Girl among those who came?"

Sky Bird's eyes swam with tears. She dashed them away with the heels of her hands. "Strong Knife, with his younger brother riding in front of him, brought Running Girl and their mother on drags. Both were beaten, as was Strong Knife. Only the little boy escaped being beaten. Running Girl and her mother lay among others in the trees, wrapped in robes, waiting for Eagle Woman to come for their Spirits."

He looped an arm around her shoulder and hugged her to his side. "I am so sorry, Sky Bird. I know how Golden Fox must hurt, and you for her."

"She blames herself for not staying to protect Running Girl, for not going back to get her." A silent sob shook Sky Bird.

Stands His Ground pulled her tighter. "We will help her understand that no fault lies with her. She is young. She will heal, though she will carry a scar inside."

Sky Bird pulled away and sat up straighter. "I know this is true. For now, she works with the injured and the sick. Her sleep is broken by dreams of blood and her friend's voice."

"Could the people who came tell you more about what happened?"

"Strong Knife said he and the other hunters had returned to the band with much meat. Several of the hunters, after leaving the meat they carried, packed up and took their women, and left. As we know, they came here. He remained behind to help Running Girl prepare the meat for winter for their parents, while he tried to talk their father into letting him take Running Girl and his younger brother, Little Knife, with him and leave.

"His father had drunk much poisoned water, but after a while he agreed. The next morning, as Strong Knife and Running Girl packed their mustangs, five hairy-faces came to the Sun People with much poisoned water. The Holy Man and Running Girl's father met with them in the center of camp. The people brought many furs to trade and laid them in front of the pale ones."

She wrung her hands and stared into the fire. "The whites packed the furs on their pack animals, then got on their riding animals. Running Girl's father demanded that they pay for the furs with the promised poisoned water. The leader of the hairy-faces tossed a few flasks to the ground and told Running Girl's father that is all the trade he would give. When the whites turned their mustangs to leave, Running Girl's father and some of the other men and women ran at the mustangs and tried to pull the packs from the animals. The white men pulled fire sticks and the fire sticks made great noise. Several of the band fell with holes in their chests, and their faces nearly gone. The rest of the band attacked. Running Girl's mother ran into the fight. Strong Knife and Running Girl ran to help their mother, and it was then they were badly beaten."

For a short span of time, she fell silent. When she began again, her voice sounded rough. "Warriors and hunters grabbed their bows and finally killed all the white men. The Sun People—hurt—pulled the packs from the mustangs and fought for the flasks of poisoned water."

Her face grew pale, and Stands His Ground wanted to tell her to stop, but knew she would not heed his words.

"One woman grabbed two flasks of poisoned water. A man demanded the woman give the flasks to him. When the mother refused, he pulled his knife. The mother ran at him and as they fought, the arm of the woman's young daughter was slashed open.

"All over the camp, people fought. Nine of our hunters and their women gathered children, their own and as many of the others as they could. They hid away from the band for two sunrises. When they returned, they found many dead. The others were sick, too sick to care about or to help the young ones.

"The hunters and their wives packed what they could and rode from the camp. The child with the cut arm and her mother came with them. Other children came here with no mothers and no fathers. This is not our way—to take children from their parents—but what else could the hunters and their women do? They could not leave the children to starve."

Stands His Ground rubbed circles on her back. "It is not our way to take children from their parents, this is true. But it is our way that a child belongs to every person in the band. We are all their mothers and their fathers. The children belong with those mothers and fathers who will care for them. What happened to the child with the cut arm?"

"The little girl is but five summers. She cannot use her arm. The cut bled much and drained part of her Spirit. She will not make words, as if she sees only inside herself. There is little I can do for her, except keep the bad Spirits from her wound. I used salves and packed the wound with moss. There is nothing else I can do. Her mother cries well into darkness. She rocks the child, who seldom closes her eyes."

Her fists lay on her lap and tightened until the knuckles shone white. "I have anger in my heart that burns like the heat of a great fire. The pale ones are as the white worm on rotting animals. They ruin a People and break the bands apart. If ever I see another white man, I will kill him."

"Did Strong Knife have word about Yellow Moon's brothers?"

"One of Yellow Moon's brothers hurt the child that is with us, and one of the warriors took his life. Yellow Moon's other brother jumped on a mustang and raced away. When Strong Knife told me this, I felt a cold wind blow though, but Sister Wind did not stir the leaves of the trees. I know he hunts us."

Before he could reply, Golden Fox walked over to the fire, followed by a dog.

Stands His Ground's brows drew tight over his eyes. "I have never seen this dog before, not even at the Sun People's camp."

Golden Fox ran her hand through the thick fur. "She is a blessing from the Spirits. The sunrise before Strong Knife came, I woke to find this dog sleeping next to me. Since then, she has refused to leave my side."

Golden Fox took the carry-all from her mother. "I thought you and Grandfather and Blazing Fire did not want me to ride away from camp alone. You said you feared the whites would find me." A frown twisted her lips. "This is what you said when I wished to go get Running Girl."

Sky Bird sighed. "Yes, and I still do not want you to ride alone, but there is no one else to go. The dried meat Stands His Ground received as gifts from that strange Holy Woman will not last, and the hunters must gather more meat. The women who are not tending the sick and injured are gathering tubers and berries for our people. I would send a warrior with you, but the ones we could spare have gone with the hunters."

Her mother put her arms around Golden Fox and squeezed. "My heart hurts for your sister-friend and for you, but it would have done no good for you to go to the Sun People. You heard what Strong Knife said—even he, as the elder brother and a good hunter, had a hard time getting Running Girl's father to agree to let her leave the band. He would not have listened to a girl, and he might have harmed you."

"I love you mother. I will ride Swift Arrow and go gather the medicine plants you need. There are few plants close-by, so I will pack enough for this day and for another sunrise."

As she whirled to leave, her mother called to her. "Remember, you are no warrior, Golden Fox. If you see any whites, or even any of the Peoples, do not go to them. Not all of our Peoples wish for peace, and we do not know who would trade you for poisoned water. I will pray to the Great Mystery for your safe return."

"Yes, Mother." She quickly gathered a sleeping robe, plant pouches to carry the harvest, a pouch of jerked meat, and a water bladder made from the inside of a rabbit hide. At her whistle, Swift Arrow trotted to her. With the sleeping robe wrapped around most of her supplies, she tied it to the mustang. The sheath for her knife rode on a belt around her waist. She slung the water bladder over one shoulder, and the quiver of arrows and her bow over the other one. The mustang stood still as she leapt on his back.

With a light tap of her heel, Swift Arrow moved into a trot, but barking from behind caused her to swivel her head around. A grin stretched her mouth. "Hurry, Dog!"

* * *

By the time Golden Fox found the plants, Father Sun had lowered behind a hill. If not for the tall stems of the old cattails from last warm season towering over the new green shoots, she might have ridden past them as the light grew dimmer. The plants she sought grew in the damp ground near cattails.

Head cocked, she listened for any sounds that might belong to people. When she heard nothing, she slid from Swift Arrow and quickly pulled the pouches from within the rolled sleeping robe.

After singing to the medicine plants and making offerings for the sacrifice of their bodies, she filled the pouches.

Along the distant edge of the land, Father Sun painted the sky a red-orange with streaks of bright yellow. A high bank that ran beside the river led down to a strip of land many feet from the water. Golden Fox guided Swift Arrow down the steep slope, and then slid from his back.

"Grass grows even down here. This is good. The river's bank will hide a small fire." She patted the mustang's shoulder, mostly black with a splattering of white. "I will rub you down after I find wood."

Around a bend in the dirt bank lay a fire circle. Golden Fox gasped and spun around, looking for the one who had left the rocks in place and a stack of wood close-by. Her legs urged her to run, to leap on Swift Arrow and race away, but she crept closer to study the remains of the fire circle. Small plants grew between the stones, which meant it had been a long while since anyone had been here.

Why did they leave the fire circle and the stack of wood? Mother always cleans up and scatters the ashes of a fire, and tossed the unused sticks of wood here and there. The stones she always returns to the places where they had lived. Did this mean the one who left meant to return?

Her heart began to pound again, as if trying to escape her chest. She peered around and tried to see through the gathering darkness.

Why has this person not returned?

Many frightening stories were told around the campfires about huge cats, giant wolves, and bears that stood as tall as two men. Perhaps, one of these wild ones had eaten the person.

She licked dry lips, and her fingers trembled as she lit the fire. When flames leapt among the wood, she brought Swift Arrow close and rubbed him with the grasses she had pulled. Afterwards, she laid her sleeping robe near the fire and pulled out the jerked meat and the water bladder, then scooted closer to the flames. "Good thing I brought a thick robe. There is a cool wind — strange for this late into the season of young animals."

The howl of a wolf split the night.

She leapt to her feet, spilling her pouch of jerked meat. Her eyes probed the darkness around her. The wolf howled again, and a shaky laugh tripped from her lips. The wolf was far away, and Sister Wind carried his song on the clear night air. Joy welled up in her and she howled back, a wild sound full of contentment.

After she picked up the pieces of jerked meat, she sat back down. "Grandmother once told me that if I fear, it is because I let bad thoughts fill my mind. I must fill my mind with good thoughts, strong thoughts."

A song wound its way up her throat and out of her lips, one Grandmother had taught her when she was a small girl given to fear of strange sounds in the night. The song soothed her. She stretched out on the robe with Dog curled against her side.

As sleep drifted through her mind, a coyote yipped from somewhere near. The 'oonk oonk' of night birds sang to her as they flew over.

* * *

Golden Fox bolted to her feet. The fire had burned out, and chill bumps rose on her arms.

I am so cold. Even with the fire out, I should not be this cold.

She pushed the robe aside and stood.

I feel... I feel... someone close.

Her eyes darted all around and she wrapped her arms around Dog.

Dog does not growl, and her hair is not raised along her back. Hah! I am a woman, but I jump at every shadow as would a girl!

Dark fog rose from the ground on the other side of the dead fire. Slowly, a figure took shape within the cloud.

Golden Fox gasped and rubbed her eyes, unable to believe what she saw. Knife unsheathed, she stared harder. "Yellow Moon? How is this so? Do I dream?"

Blood seeped from Yellow Moon's wound. She stood in deep grass, which did not move with Sister Wind's breath, as the surrounding grass did. Sorrow had replaced the cruel smile she had worn in camp.

"Yellow Moon, is this you? Why have you come to me?" She clutched Dog's thick hair and scooted away, pulling the animal with her.

Yellow Moon reached out bloody hands. *"Eagle Thunder spoke true words. When my Spirit left my body and rose into the sky, Eagle Woman flew down to me. She did not smile nor offer a human hand to me, as I was told she would when my time was ended on our Mother."*

The round face of Sister Moon shed silver light on the wet tracks of tears running down Yellow Moon's cheeks. Head lowered, she continued.

"Eagle Woman forbade me to follow her to the campfires in the sky. She said I must do good things or I will walk alone forever. This dark fog is my shame. It surrounds me like a heavy cloak, and will never be lifted unless I do good."

Her head came up and hollow eyes stared at Golden Fox. *"Eagle Woman spoke your name."*

"My name? I wish nothing to do with you!" Golden Fox scrambled even farther away. "All my life you have been hateful to my mother and to me for having hairy-face blood. When I was a young child, you spit on me. During the past cold season, you treated us even worse. Mother said the poisoned water had taken your Spirit and ate at your mind."

Yellow Moon floated closer, hands beseeching Golden Fox. *"I am sorry for treating you and Sky Bird with hate. I... I could not see past my... my envy of all that Sky Bird possessed and I did not. The poisoned water made me forget. It gave me dreams that I thought were true visions. Forgive me, please."*

She glanced away, and then back toward Golden Fox. Shame dragged the corners of her mouth down as she bowed her head.

Anger burned hot in Golden Fox's chest. Arms crossed, she glared at her aunt. "You brought much pain to my mother and me. The Sun People's band was broken because of your hate. Our people have no home now. My closest friend spoke of you bringing the poisoned water to her mother and father every time you came back from the wooden fort. You drank it with them. Sometimes, after the poisoned water filled their bellies, they beat Running Girl until she ran from their lodge and hid. They *beat* her! The next sunrise, they would tell her they did not beat her. She is now wrapped in a humpback robe and placed high in a tree because of you!"

Lips trembling, eyes narrowed, Golden Fox dropped her arms. She leaned forward on her toes as if she meant to attack Yellow Moon. "From Grandmother's teachings, I know this is not the way of our Peoples. I am sure she taught you the same, but you ignored her teachings and shamed her and Grandfather. You ask forgiveness, but forgiveness will not wipe away the pain you brought to us. Forgiveness will not give Running Girl and her mother their lives back." She turned away from Yellow Moon, and stared at the brown of the dirt bank.

"*Listen to me, please. I was foolish. Dreams came to my sister, Sky Bird. I wanted Mother to look at me the way she looked at Sky Bird, so I sought dreams, too. I prayed, I sang, I cut pieces of my flesh and offered it to the Spirits, yet no dreams came. When the hairy-faces told me the firewater would bring dreams, I wanted dreams so badly I ignored the feeling in my stomach that told me they lied. Please, hear me! I wanted so much to be as good as Sky Bird, to have our mother look at me like I, too, was special – the way she looked at Sky Bird as they talked about dreams. I am sorry, so sorry, Golden Fox.*"

Her form began to waver and fade. "*A Holy Woman comes your way, Golden Fox. Stay here and wait for her. She will help those who suffer from the poisoned water. Our people walk a broken path. For my part on placing our people on that path, I come to you and say these words. Listen well to the Holy Woman. She will help our people walk the broken path until they are healed.*"

Golden Fox pivoted around. "I cannot trust the words of a woman who hated me when she walked our Mother – hated me so badly she tried to attack me with a knife!"

"*You can trust the words of this woman because I must earn your forgiveness to save my Spirit. Someday, I wish to sit at the campfires in the sky with my mother. I wish to see her smile upon me.*" Yellow Moon's Spirit faded in and out. "*The Holy Woman will not be able to save all. Plants can ease only some pain. There are those with too much poisoned water in their bodies. They shake hard and no longer see, though their eyes are open. I sorrow that I helped to lead them to this dark place, but there will be many the Holy Woman can help. Listen well to her, Golden Fox. She has much to teach not only about plants and sickness, but about matters of the heart."* Sorrow darkened her eyes as she gazed at Golden Fox. *"Someday, I pray you find it in your heart to forgive me. Until you do, I will find ways to earn that forgiveness."*

Golden Fox bit her lip, her head shaking slowly from side to side.

Yellow Moon's form thinned until Golden Fox could clearly see the river behind her.

Panic grabbed Golden Fox by the throat and she yelled, "I forgive you, Yellow Moon! Please, you do not have to stay. Go to Grandmother's campfire in the sky." Tears fell from her eyes as she dropped to her knees. "If we cannot find it in our hearts to forgive others, we will never be able to forgive ourselves. We will forever keep a piece of our Spirits bound to the earth, unable to travel to the campfires in the sky. This is what Grandmother taught me, and this is what I believe. Yellow Moon, wherever you are, hear me! I forgive you, Yellow Moon!"

The dark-grey fog fell apart, its wisps teased away by the soft night breeze.

After a span, she pushed up from the dirt and made her way over to the sleeping robe. Curled into ball, with her arm tightly holding onto Dog who lay next to her, she drifted into an exhausted sleep.

9

Golden Fox batted at Swift Arrow's soft muzzle. He moved his head until she lay still again, and nibbled her hair.

"Go 'way, Swift Arrow." She pulled the robe up higher until only the very top of her head stuck out.

Unwilling to go away, Swift Arrow grabbed a corner of her sleeping robe and tugged.

She tightened her grip and squeezed her eyes more tightly closed. "Mustang, why do you torture me?"

He shoved her back hard with his head.

Frustrated, she flung her robe aside and glared up at him. "Swift Arrow, why do you wake me? And you, Dog, why do you sit and grin at me with your tongue hanging from your mouth? Am I so funny?"

An unknown voice spoke. "Perhaps, they wake you so a herd of humpbacks will not trample you in your sleep."

Golden Fox grabbed her knife and sprang to her feet to face the stranger.

A woman with loose, dark hair squatted on the far side of the cold campfire. Dressed in a man's tunic and leggings, she rocked on her heels. Bright, round eyes studied Golden Fox, shining from an oval face with high cheekbones. The square jaw, which would look manly on any other woman, only added to her beauty. "Be at peace, Golden Fox. I have not come to harm you. Yellow Moon spoke of me."

From behind the strange woman, someone walked toward Golden Fox's camp leading four mustangs with neck ropes.

Golden Fox's eyes slanted at the woman by the cold fire, then quickly returned to the stranger with the animals. Surely, this woman who had so silently come upon her sleeping could hear the hooves of the animals behind her. Why did she not turn to see who came?

Golden Fox tightened the hold on her knife and crouched into a fighting stance. *They must be together.*

As the second stranger came closer, she judged him with her eyes—a boy of not more summers than her own, but at least half a head taller. Dressed only in a breechclout, Golden Fox could still see that his was not the well-muscled chest of a man. He possessed the thin chest and arms of a boy.

The woman's face looked as if she fought a smile.

Golden Fox's heart thundered and her breath came in short, hard pants. She wanted to scream at the woman that this was not the time to laugh. Could the woman be so cruel as to enjoy the fear and pain of her enemies? Golden Fox had heard about such among the Peoples, especially in the Likes To Fight band. Was this woman part of that band? It did not matter. Golden Fox had decided she would not have her people remember her as one who ran like a scared child and led the enemy to their camp.

With the smoothness of a warrior, the strange woman stood up.

The black mustang jerked away from the boy and trotted a few steps toward the woman, bobbing his head and snorting in a playful dance.

Golden Fox slanted a glance at Dog and Swift Arrow. The tip of Dog's tail swung back and forth slowly, as it did when children in camp came toward her. Swift Arrow's head was up and he stood tall, staring at the black mustang, but in no other way did he show that he smelled an enemy. The mustang had always been able to tell enemy from friend. His actions spoke of no fear, no anger.

The strange woman turned toward the mustang and lifted a hand, palm up to the black animal. "Moon... saaa.... saaa." With slow steps, she walked up to him. He nickered and shifted his weight from one front foot to the other, as if he could not decide what to do. She ran her hands under his muzzle and down his broad chest.

"All is well, Moon. You do not need to prance and show the other stallion that you are strong." He calmed and stepped closer, and she wrapped her arms around the animal's neck and removed the hanging rope. His slick, obsidian-colored hair shone in the rays of Father Sun.

With the mustang at her shoulder, she turned toward Golden Fox. "I am Dances In Storms, a Holy Woman. We must be on our way. My people are but a day behind."

"Behind?" Golden Fox barely noticed how elk and deer teeth decorated the stranger's deerskin tunic from the waist up to the collar. Small pieces of shells shimmered blue along the collar. Long fringe from the waist of her tunic fell to her knees. Her clothes spoke of one who was important; yet, none of that mattered to Golden Fox.

Mouth agape, she stared at the woman and the mustang. "How did you teach him so well?"

The boy shuffled his feet loudly, drawing the women's eyes briefly to him. He shot the mustang a disgruntled look. "You allow him too much freedom for an uncut male." The boy backed away when the mustang moved his rump around so it pointed toward the boy's face.

Golden Fox would have laughed if this mustang had acted this way toward to one of her people. Any boy with as many summers as this boy would have known how to act with such a spirited animal. She held her laughter and her tongue, waiting to see how the woman would answer such disrespect. Perhaps, she would not see it as disrespectful. Golden Fox had heard stories about Peoples whose men showed disrespect to their women. Always in the Sun People, before the poisoned water blackened so many Spirits, men had shown great respect to women, and the young had shown great respect toward the elders.

The pain of losing so much lanced through her chest like a spear. She gritted her teeth against it and focused her attention on the two strangers.

Dances In Storms laughed lightly and shook her head, as an elder would shake her head at an youngster with too few summers to know better. "Keep your mouth still, Long Sun, or I will maybe make *you* ride him. See if you or Moon becomes the leader."

The boy puffed out his chest and lifted his chin. "I could ride that mustang! I would show him who is leader!"

With eyebrows lifted, Dances In Storms chuckled. "You wish to try, boy?"

He shuffled back a couple steps and looked away. "Um, perhaps another...." His eyes landed on Golden Fox and he nodded toward her. "She is good to look at, Storms. Perhaps I will take her as my woman. I like her shining, gold-red hair. Father Sun makes it even brighter." He grinned and whipped long, dark hair from his face with a quick sideways nod, then spoke to Golden Fox. "Your knees are covered in small pieces of dirt and sand. Perhaps you wish for me to wipe them clean for you?"

The boy's sudden attention caused Golden Fox to blush, and her eyes to shift from Dances In Storms. She tugged the short fringe of her dress. "You are a boy. I do not need your help." With one hand, she brushed at her plain, brown dress and dusted the dirt from her knees. A confusion, a feeling she never had with the boys in her band, filled her.

Dances In Storms' voice snapped Golden Fox out of her confusion. "Girl, do not just stare. We must leave. Long Sun and I sang healing songs and danced much of the night, and then hurried to catch up to you. There are those of your people who no longer breathe, but many of the ones sick from poisoned water need much care. We must hurry if we are to help them greet Father Sun for another sunrise."

She turned toward Moon, preparing to jump on him as she spoke more. "The whites poisoned water does things to our minds. Gather the healing plants you picked. They will help. I, too, have medicines that your people need."

Dances In Storms swung up on her mustang and took one of the other mustang's lead ropes from Long Sun. "Boy, stop giving her big eyes and get on your animal. I am sure she has had enough of your silliness."

Long Sun whirled around and gracefully leapt onto his animal. With the lead rope for the fourth animal tight in his hand, he followed Dances In Storms.

Pointed in the direction of Golden Fox's people, they tapped their animals into a smooth trot.

For a short span, Golden Fox stared at the puffs of dust that hung in the air as the strangers moved farther away.

Swift Arrow shoved her hard in the back and she stumbled forward, snapping out of the stillness that had taken hold of her. She ran over, grabbed her robe, the water bladder, the pouch of jerked meat, and the pouches of plants. Quickly, she rolled them into her sleeping robe and tied it to Swift Arrow, then leapt onto his back.

Dog raced after Dances In Storms, tongue lolling out of the side of her mouth, leaving Golden Fox and Swift Arrow behind. She tapped Swift Arrow into a gallop.

When she caught up, Long Sun glanced at her bare feet. "Perhaps you have forgotten something?"

Golden Fox's eyes dipped down. She smacked the palm of her hand against the side of her head. "My footwear! I must go back." She swung Swift Arrow around, but before she could nudge him into motion, Long Sun let out a whoop and raced toward her deserted camp.

Dances in Storms laughed. "He went on his first Vision Quest and had his Making A Man ceremony five moons ago, yet he acts like a boy."

They ambled along, so Long Sun could easily catch up without tiring his animal.

Golden Fox shot a sideways look at Dances In Storms. "Yellow Moon came to me in a vision last night. How did she know you would come?"

All laughter faded from Dances In Storms' face. "Yellow Moon is a faraway relation."

Before Golden Fox could open her mouth to question her, Dances in Storms tapped her mustang and trotted off. Puzzled by the Holy Woman's actions, Golden Fox pulled Swift Arrow to a stop and gazed after her.

Long Sun rode up and handed the footwear to her. "Did your mustang run out of air?"

Golden Fox's lips twisted into a wry smile. "If we found a path, he could run all the way to Father Sun!"

She snugged her footwear on and nudged Swift Arrow into a fast walk. "Are you Dances In Storms' son?"

He threw his head back and laughed. The sound was surprisingly deep and soothing. "She is my aunt. My father gave me to her when I was five winters old. He saw I held Power and would become a Holy Man." He sat up straighter on his mustang.

"Do you and Dances In Storms travel with a band? Is your family with you?"

Long Sun's animal, grey with black-striped legs, whinnied and pranced. "No, they are many days ride from us. I see them every cycle of seasons at the gathering, when we hunt and trade. When I am a Holy Man, I will return to them. Our Holy Woman is aging, and soon I will take her place."

"It takes many long seasons to become a Holy Person." She urged Swift Arrow to move faster. He lengthened his stride, and her tangled hair bounced on her thighs.

Long Sun urged his mustang to match the speed of Swift Arrow. "Storms speaks of how fast I learn. She spoke to my father a cycle of seasons ago and told him I would return before my brother was a man."

Golden Fox caught her lower lip between her teeth as she watched him struggle to ride as tall and easy as she while his mustang's stride bounced him around. "How old is your brother?"

"He was born eight moons ago." Long strands of night-black hair whipped around his face. He tossed his head to throw the wayward strands over his shoulder as he glanced at her. "Storms has a comb carved from bone. She would maybe let you use it."

"I have my own comb, bony boy." Golden Fox tapped her mustang into a run.

They quickly left Long Sun behind in *her* dust. She caught up to Dances In Storms, whooped, and passed her.

* * *

Father Sun rested at the bottom of the sky as Swift Arrow trotted into the busy camp just ahead of Dances In Storms and Long Sun. The smell of cooked meat made Golden Fox's mouth moist as she led the way to the place her grandfather, her mother, and she called their own. Their camp would move soon, so no one had put up lodges, except for the sick and the injured.

Though the embers of the cooking fire glowed red, the cooking pot sat to one side of the stone fire circle. "Mother and Grandfather must be with someone who needs them." She slid from Swift Arrow's back and checked out the pot. "Mother has cooked meat and tubers. I will heat up the food after I take care of Swift Arrow."

As Long Sun helped unpack Dances In Storms' mustang, he nodded toward Swift Arrow. "If you will trust me, I will care for all of our animals."

Golden Fox hesitated until Dances In Storms handed Moon's lead rope to the boy. "Though I tease Long Sun, he is good with animals."

She hesitated for a short span longer while Long Sun and Dances In Storms watched her. She rubbed Swift Arrow's broad forehead between his eyes and the mustang snorted. She looped his lead rope around his neck and, with a jerk, he pulled loose and trotted over to Long Sun.

Golden Fox laughed. "Swift Arrow trusts you, so I will, too."

Long Sun smiled as he caught Swift Arrow's lead rope and bowed to the mustang. "Oh, mighty fast runner, I am honored that you will let me rub your body with dried grasses and scratch the places that itch."

After Long Sun walked away, Dances In Storms cleared her throat and spoke. "How is it that you ride your mustang without a nose rope?"

Golden Fox tilted her head and studied the older woman. "This is how you and Long Sun ride, as well." She turned around and moved to the cooking fire. After she set the pot on the hot embers, she set bowls next to the fire circle.

"We are the Sister Wolf Band." Dances In Storms acted as if that explained the differences between her and other Peoples.

Golden Fox pursed her lips. "Mother told me that many cycles of seasons ago, when my Grandfather's grandfather was young, our people met a band who called themselves Wolf People. The Wolf People saw my band had no mustangs. They gifted our Holy Man, and a few elders and warriors with mustangs.

"Since no one in the Sun People's band had ever ridden one, the Wolf People stayed at our camp until our people learned to speak the language of the mustangs. When a person learns how to speak to mustangs, it is easy to ride using our legs to guide the animals, without need for face or neck ropes."

Golden Fox flicked a glance toward the herd and noticed Long Sun walking toward them. As she told the rest of the story, she added food into the bowls. "We use lead ropes only when a mustang might wish to go to his herd before he is rubbed down, and sometimes to keep a young animal close until he learns to do so with no need of a rope."

Long Sun's strides grew longer when he saw the wooden bowls of food.

Golden Fox smiled as she handed the first one to Dances In Storms. "The stories say that wolves lived with the Wolf People and their dogs and mustangs showed no worry. I wish I could see such a thing!" Wistfulness filled her voice. She cleared her throat, embarrassed to show such childish emotion in front of strangers.

Dances In Storms appeared ready to speak as she accepted the bowl, but only grinned.

Golden Fox dipped food into her own bowl and sat across the fire from Dances In Storms and Long Sun. Between bites of food, she continued the story. "Some cold seasons ago, we stopped following our mustangs and traveling in the grasslands. Our Holy Man and some others in the Sun People's band decided we should camp only four sunrises from the white men's wooden lodge to trade with them."

She sighed. "Grandfather warned the elders such closeness would bring trouble to our people, but since many people were happy, the elders refused to listen to Grandfather. At first, it was good. Our people got met-al knives and beautiful blankets and strange things none of us had seen before, in trade for robes and furs we did not need. Iron pots make cooking food faster. I have a clear stone flattened into a round circle, and I can see myself in it."

A shadow fell over Golden Fox's heart. "The whites began visiting our camp. At first, they brought the things our people could use—things such as we traded for when we traveled to their wooden lodge. They came many times, and one time they brought leather flasks of poisoned water."

Golden Fox's hands clenched the bowl. "They offered free sips of the poisoned water as they traded with our people. The ones who drank this poisoned water made poor trades with the white men. Instead of things their families could use, like warm blankets, they accepted flasks of fire water.

"At first, not many of the People drank the poisoned water. After the pale men left our camp, those with poisoned water offered others who sat beside their campfire drinks of it. They said it brought good dreams. Several sunrises after the whites had left, some of the Sun People drank much fire water. They staggered and fell down, like wounded animals.

"My mother, Sky Bird, is a healer. She tried to help these people who had fallen into a sleep close to death. There was nothing she could do, except watch and roll them to their sides when the food and drink in their stomachs came up through their mouths."

The heat of anger rose in Golden Fox's chest. "When these people woke, they talked of strange dreams and great visions. Those in the camp who hungered to be looked up to, and to be called Dreamers, began trading all they had for the poisoned water."

A hard swallow pushed down the lump that had become a boulder in her throat. Golden Fox set aside her bowl. "A couple of moons ago, Grandmother journeyed to the Spirit Land. This was only a few sunrises after our best hunters and warriors left to get meat.

"Grandfather, as a strong elder, held some Power over the people. When Grandmother left, Grandfather mourned so deeply, his eyes became blind and his ears became deaf to what was happening with the Sun People. Knowing he had to go on the Walk of Mourning to release Grandmother's Spirit, he left the camp."

Golden Fox's hands, lying on her thighs, formed into fists. "Not many sunrises after he left, my mother's sister, Yellow Moon, began gathering furs, robes, tunics made with quills, clay pots, and bowls from our people to trade for poisoned water. The bad Spirits in the poisoned water had blackened Yellow Moon's Spirit. When she did not have enough to trade, she stole from others in our band.

"The more poisoned water the people drank, the more angry fists were thrown, and much shouting between them happened. Some men beat their women and children. When the whites came to our camp, some of the women would sneak into the woods with them. Sometimes, these women did not return. We never knew if they went willingly or not. We had heard of the pale men taking women even if they did not want to go. Some of those women, it was said, were thrown away by the white men and returned to their People with bruised faces and broken Spirits."

Overcome with terrible memories, Golden Fox fell silent.

Dances In Storms set aside her bowl and moved closer to Golden Fox. Her hand rubbed circles on Golden Fox's back. "I have never heard as much words from one as I do you. Most girls... women... as young as you only shy away and hide. You are a strong one, Golden Fox. Speak your words, and allow them to escape on Sister Wind—allow her to take them away."

Not lifting her bowed head, Golden Fox rushed through the rest of the story in a dead voice. "The last sunrise we were part of the Sun People, many of our people and Yellow Moon had drunk much poisoned water. Fights left people bleeding. Mother and I helped an elder, one who drank no poisoned water, to move young children from lodges where much anger grew. Afterwards, my mother sent me to find Grandfather. When Grandfather and I returned, Yellow Moon had burned our lodges. Only a few belongings had been saved. Grandfather tried to stop Yellow Moon from doing more bad things, but she found ways around him. He sent Sun Rising to bring our Holy Man back from the hunt.

"Yellow Moon must have ridden her mustang very hard to beat Sun Rising to the hunters' camp. By the time the elder arrived, the Holy Man had drunk much poisoned water. When he returned to our camp, the Holy Man did not throw Yellow Moon away for stealing and fighting. He threw Grandfather, mother, and me away.

"As we packed, Yellow Moon tried to harm me with a knife. Mother shoved her away. Yellow Moon fell onto her own knife and I believe she died." Golden Fox pulled in a shaky breath. "Our band broke, and people stayed behind while others followed Grandfather to find a new land far away from hairy-faces."

Dances In Storms dropped her hand from Golden Fox's back and shook her head. "Many whites have black in their hearts. I wish none of our Peoples would trade with them, but some wishes are not to be."

She scooted around to face Golden Fox and gently touched her arm. "You do not carry the bad Spirits that live in their bodies, even if you carry their blood." When Golden Fox opened her mouth to speak, the Holy Woman laid a finger across her lips. "Not now. We must go to the sick, but we *will* speak of this."

Golden Fox hurried after the Holy Woman, leaving Long Sun seated by the fire.

As they neared the lodge of the ones sick from poisoned water, Eagle Thunder pushed open the flap and stepped out. He rushed over and grasped Dances In Storms by the forearm, and she returned the shake of one warrior to another.

A broad smile stretched Eagle Thunder's lips. "I greet you, Dances In Storms. Stands His Ground spoke of you with much praise. You honor my people with your presence."

The smile fell away when he nodded toward the trees some distance from the camp. "Nine of our people did not greet Father Sun. We would be honored if you would help us sing their Spirits to their relations who sit by the campfires in the sky." He gave a sorrowful shake of his head. "Our small band grows heavy with children who no longer have the family they were born into."

10

Golden Fox walked around the fire that blazed in the center of camp. Since the day she had ridden into camp with Dances In Storms and Long Sun, many had come to her asking if the Holy Woman would join their band. Not able to answer such questions, she had sent the people to her grandfather and Dances In Storms.

After a few sunrises, Eagle Thunder called for a gathering of the people. Even those still sick from the poisoned water joined the circle around the fire, helped by others if needed.

On the other side of Sky Bird, the wounded girl leaned against her mother. For many sunrises, Golden Fox had applied salve made by her mother, and wrapped the child's deep cut in fresh moss. The arm showed much improvement, but it had not been until the Holy Woman worked on the girl that she once again spoke and her eyes came alive.

Across the fire from Golden Fox, Long Sun patted a drum held in one hand. On the face of the drum, painted mustangs raced across open grassland. Beside him sat Eagle Thunder and Stands His Ground. The elder, Sun Rising, rested on the other side of Stands His Ground, his woman leaning on his shoulder.

With head bent back, Golden Fox stared up at the campfires in the sky. They shone with added brilliance that blessed this gathering.

All murmuring drifted into silence as the Holy Woman danced from behind the lodges for the sick and the injured. Shaking a turtle rattle, she danced and sang. Her hair, tightly wrapped into a single braid, bounced as her feet pounded the ground to the beat of the drum. She danced in and out of the firelight as she circled the gathered people, touching each person with the rattle. Each time the turtle rattle touched one of the people, Dances In Storms stooped low and whispered a blessing into their ear before moving onto the next person.

She stopped when she reached the same point from which she had entered, completing the circle. All eyes rested on her. "Five sunrises have passed since I came. Many of you are better, yet even when the poisoned water weakened your body and blackened your Spirit, you remained a part of the Sacred Circle of Life."

As she gazed around the circle, she let her eyes linger on each person. "From birth to young one to adult to elder to death, and then onto new life—such is the Sacred Circle. All living beings follow this circle. We grow, we learn, and we pass on knowledge to those who will one day take our place." She nodded toward a woman with a swollen belly.

"Though the Great Mystery created the Sacred Circle, each one is given the choice of how they will walk this path." She spread her hands to include every- one. "Some will walk this path with crooked feet, and stumble this way and that way. Some will walk with eyes squeezed tight, tripping over even the smallest of stones. These people walk a broken path, made so by their own choices. They make the path of life more difficult for themselves and for the ones who care for them, yet even a broken path will teach us much, each time we fall and crawl back up on our feet. It is up to us how long we take to learn the lessons of the broken path."

Dances In Storms pointed toward the wrapped bundles tied high in the stronger trees, a short distance from camp. "Trees where once we rested have become the last home of the bodies of those stolen away by the poisoned water. They walked a broken path, one broken by the fire water."

Though darkness cloaked them from sight, Golden Fox could see those bundles in her mind and with her heart, especially the bundle that was once her cradleboard sister, Running Girl.

"Did Eagle Woman come for them? Do they now sit with their relations at the campfires in the sky?" Dances In Storms dropped her head for a short span. When she lifted her face, tracks of moisture glistened in the firelight. "I cannot say. Only Eagle Woman can judge the darkness that stains their Spirits. Unless they come to us in dreams or visions and tell us where their Spirits live, we can never know. We can only sing the songs for their Spirit's journey, and pray to Great Mystery that Eagle Woman sees past the black streaks on their Spirits."

The Holy Woman's eyes locked on Golden Fox's face. "Some may become trapped on this side, tied to our Mother, unwelcomed by Eagle Woman. They will remain until they find a way to guide others away from the very path they took. Listen well to them, not only for the sake of *their* Spirits, but for your own.

"A few may be given a chance to wash their Spirits clean, to complete their journey and sit next to their relations around the campfires in the sky. These restless ones will come to those they harmed, and ask forgiveness. It is up to each person to decide if they find forgiveness in their hearts or not. Forgiveness can help heal a broken path."

The wood in the fire snapped and sparks flew up above the Holy Woman's waist, then lazily swirled back down to the greedy flames. "Whether you have dreams of those who walked the broken path of the poisoned water, know those Spirits surround you. Open your ears and hear their cries to *you,* their relatives. *Do not follow my broken path! Do not let the poisoned water darken your Spirit!* This is what they would say to you."

Her voice rose and became as growling thunder. "Only false dreams, false visions, come from the deadly fire water. True Power is found within us. Your mind is strong. Your Spirit is brave! Turn a deaf ear to the evil whispers and the lies of the poisoned water.

"Fling off the dark robe the poisoned water tosses upon your spirit! You are the People of our Mother. You are the children of the Great Mystery!" Dances In Storms threw her fist high above her head. "We are one in this battle! We are not alone... not ever!"

The Holy Woman turned and made her way into the night.

Those who could not stand alone were helped by others, as all around the circle, the people locked arms and swayed to Long Sun's drum. An owl hooted from somewhere near, and coyotes yipped, their song blending with the quiet beat.

* * *

Tired, Golden Fox slipped away and headed to the spot her family called their own. Once she laid her sleeping robe a little ways from her mother's, she stretched out and closed her eyes. The sound of the drum and the singing of the people floated on the warm air, wrapped around her in the same way it did when she was a child. Slowly, her eyelids sank lower.

In that half-asleep land, a white man's camp formed. Men and women of the Peoples squatted in front of wooden lodges, and laughed with the high-pitched sound of those with much poisoned water in their bellies. A strange object passed from hand to hand. Each person put the small, round end against their mouths and drank. One of the men yelled at the woman holding it. "Pass that bottle over here!"

The warmth of Dog pressed hard against her side, pulling her from that half-asleep state. Her arm flopped onto the thick-furred body. Without opening her eyes, she murmured, "Dog with no name... must give you...." Sleep closed over her head and she sank beneath it.

* * *

A faint voice, much like Sister Wind's on a hot season day, whispered Golden Fox awake. She rose from her sleeping robe while Sister Moon stood at the top of the sky, shedding silver light on a faint path not far from Golden Fox.

I don't remember that path.

Head cocked, she listened.

Voices. Should I wake Mother or Grandfather? No, they need to rest. I will blend into the night like Fox, and see who comes so near our camp. I must see if an enemy creeps upon us. If I need to, I can always come back or yell to awaken the others.

A few steps from camp, fog made it hard to see the path. Only a little of Sister Moon's silver light leaked through the dense forest. Rich smells of pine rode heavy on the air, And she breathed deeply of the pleasant scent. Somewhere not far ahead, the steady rhythm of a drum called to her. A tree with heavy boughs dragging the ground spread across the path. Even if all the people of her camp linked arms, they could not encircle the tree's large body. The insistent beat of the drum pulled at her, and she eased around the tree.

The fog had disappeared, leaving the tall, slender man standing in the middle of the trail easy to see. Golden Fox's stomach knotted and her heart thundered loud in her ears. Her legs half-turned to race back the way she had come, but something kept her planted where she stood.

A gentle voice filled her head. *"Do not fear, Golden Fox. I am Shining Light of the Wolf People. I called you here."*

Golden Fox found her voice after clearing her throat three times. "Where is here?" She raised her arms wide, palms up. "There is no forest close to our camp." Shrubs crowded around the bases of the large trees scattered through the woods.

A tiny mouse sat on Shining Light's shoulder. The fringes on his white, deer-hide tunic, and the ones down the sides of his leggings, danced in a wind that Golden Fox could not feel. On each side of him, a wolf sat--much like the painting on the front of his tunic.

The snort of a mustang drew her eyes past the man. A golden yellow animal pawed the ground behind him and nickered. When her eyes dropped back to the man, a white bear and her cub lay at his feet. A blue glow surrounded the animals and the man, creating a circle in the dark forest.

Golden Fox jerked back a step. *The bears were not here a heartbeat ago!*

Her voice raised in pitch until she nearly screeched, as she finally remembered what he had called himself. "Wolf People? Are you the Great Holy Man my grandfather spoke of? But... but... you disappeared many cycles of seasons ago. Why do you stand before me now? How did you get here? Why did you come?" A shiver shook her and she clasped her arms around her small breast.

Shining Light chuckled, a warm comforting sound. *"Words spill from your mouth, but you will not wait for an answer. Ah, Little Cousin, you sound much like me when I was young."*

"Cousin?" Her voice rose even higher. "We are cousins?"

Shining Light's eyes twinkled. *"Yes, Young One, we are cousins. If you will let me answer your questions..."*

When Golden Fox quietly waited, a laugh spilled from Shining Light.

"Ah, my grandmother will like you. It took her many, many moons to get me to be quiet and to listen. Now, to answer you – I chose to come and to stand before you because you need me, Little Cousin. Just as you need me, others need you. One of those who needs you is Yellow Moon."

Yellow Moon hovered behind Shining Light, her bloody hands outstretched. Her eyes pleaded with Golden Fox.

Golden Fox's words tangled as they leapt from her mouth. "I... I forgave her! What other need does she have of me? I do not understand. And... and what need do I have of you, Great Holy Man? Help me understand, Cousin."

"In the coming sunrises, you will have much to learn, and much to do. You must be brave, and you must be strong, but do not fear. Fear will only pull you away from where

you must go. You are not alone. Your people will join with Dances in Storms' people. Listen to the Holy Woman, for her heart has a place in it for you.

"Keep your knife ready, and carry the bow your grandfather made for you. There are those who hunt you and your people.

"All things become clear as sunrises pass into sunsets. This can only happen if you walk with a clear mind. Though you do not understand yet, you have Power, much Power. True Power can only be used if your mind, your body, and your Spirit are clean."

The blue light that swirled around him and the animals spread toward her. Her eyes grew wide and her breaths became pants as the blue light surrounded her. It tightened around her, and a tingling ran across her skin as it sank into every place it touched. When the blue light had been drunk by her body, she raised her eyes.

The Great Holy Man began to fade.

"Shining Light, wait! You speak words I understand with my ears, yet do not understand in my mind. Wait, I have much to ask... Cousin."

* * *

Golden Fox lay on damp grass. The swish of Dog's tail in her face tickled her partly awake. She rolled to her side and plopped her arm over her companion, snuggling her face into the long, brown- and white-speckled fur.

A hand on her shoulder shook her and a soft voice called her name. Really wishing to remain asleep, Golden Fox pried her eyes open.

Dark eyes, lit with kindness, stared down at her. Behind the round face of the Holy Woman, campfires burned thick in the sky. A few sparkled more brightly than the others through her hair.

Golden Fox shoved herself to a crouch and gazed around. "Why am I lying here in the grass, away from camp?" She rubbed her forehead with one hand. "I remember putting my sleeping robe only a little ways from mother's robe and lying down. Now, I wake up out here." Suspicion clawed at her chest. "Why are you here? Did you bring me out here?" She clutched Dog tight against her.

Moving slowly, Dances In Storms held a water bladder out to her. "Drink, Little Sister. You have made a long journey to the Spirit Land to meet Shining Light and his wolves. You are blessed."

With narrowed eyes, Golden Fox studied her. "How did you know I spoke with Shining Light? Was that a real Dream or only a child's imagining?"

Dog squirmed and sat on the ground next to Golden Fox.

With the animal no longer in her arms, Golden Fox accepted the water blad-der, sat down, and crossed her legs. As she drank, she eyed the Holy Woman.

"I knew where you were because Shining Light told me."

"Told you?"

Dances In Storms tightened her lips, then pushed out her breath. "Will you repeat the words I say, or do you choose to listen?"

Nostrils flaring at the sharpness in the older woman's voice, Golden Fox glared for a moment before giving an abrupt nod. "I will listen."

"Shining Light, Great Holy Man of the Wolf People, once lived in the Land of Tall Trees. He spoke of that forest as a magical place, where people never know death as we know it."

"What is this you speak of? No one escapes death! And you talk as if you knew him. You are not so old as to have known Shining Light. Even Grandfather only heard stories of the Great Holy Man."

A crooked smile tugged at Dances in Storms' mouth.

With a stiff finger, Golden Fox pointed at her. "I see by your face that you tease me!"

"I do not tease. And, you are right. I am only nine cycles of seasons older than you." She shifted slightly and settled again. "A woman called Dove was the daughter of Shining Light. A child of Dove's was one of my long-ago relatives. I am a Holy Woman who carries the blood of Shining Light's people. There are times when Shining Light visits me in dreams or visions."

"Why did Shining Light call me cousin? Are you and I related?"

The Holy Woman moved around until she rested her legs to one side and leaned on her hand. "Listen well to my story, so you may pass it on to your children. This is a story of love and of sadness. If we never know sorrow, we cannot fully know love."

She waited while Golden Fox squirmed into a more comfortable position. "Shining Light's two wolves had been with him since he was a child. It is said that the wolves, after living far beyond the life spans of normal wolves, made it known they wished to pass over. They longed to be with their own kind and to share a campfire in the sky with Shining Light's ancestors.

"Though he would miss his wolves terribly, he honored their wish and moved away from the Land of Tall Trees with the wolves and his family. Once away from that magical land, the wolves and the people aged much, as anyone does. Before long, the wolves let it be known that their time had come to leave. Shining Light shed many tears as he gave them his blessing. His woman, Animal Speaks Woman, and he missed the wolves with a deep ache inside of them. If they wanted to be with the wolves again, they could not return to live in the Land of Tall Trees.

"After his wolves traveled to the campfires in the sky, many cycles of seasons passed. Only once did Shining Light return to visit his relations who still lived in the Land of Tall Trees. After that, he chose to stay in the canyons and the grasslands."

Chills raced over Golden Fox's arms and she rubbed them with her hands.

"Stardust filled Shining Light's hair as age bent the Great Holy Man's back. His voice grew softer with the passing seasons. Animal Speaks Woman chose to speak to no one, except Shining Light. When her hair became pure stardust, the people honored her wish. Their band knew Animal Speaks Woman felt the pain, the fear that hunted animals feel, so they no longer asked her to call the animals to be hunted for meat."

Dances In Storms looked beyond the grasslands and into some faraway place. "Their band fared well and, over time, Dove and her man, Singing Stone, took the place of Dove's parents as leaders of the Wolf People. The band revered Shining Light and Animal Speaks Woman as great elders, but they let the two live without worries.

"One sunrise, Dove noticed that the flap of her parents' lodge remained tied. Concerned that they might need something, she hurried over to untie the flap. When the flap opened, peace filled Dove's heart. In the dim light of the lodge, she crept close to the hides where Shining Light and Animal Speaks Woman lay in a tight embrace. In the night, they had quietly traveled from this land. At last, Shining Light would be reunited with his much-loved wolves."

Dances In Storms pulled on a leather strand around her neck. A wolf carved from grey stone dangled on the thong. "It is said that when the Wolf People sang Shining Light and Animal Speaks Woman to the campfires in the sky, the whole land—canyons and grasslands and forests—rang with the howling of wolves."

She held the thong so that the carved wolf hung freely in the space before her. "Shining Light carved this wolf for his daughter, Dove. Since that time, it has been handed from mother to daughter to granddaughter when they became a Holy Woman."

"Does your band have wolves living with you?" Golden Fox leaned toward the Holy Woman, trembling with excitement. "Are we related?"

"Of course, we are related. Everyone is related. As for wolves... we have no wolves living with us. Yet, I have had dreams of wolves sharing lodges with the Sister Wolf People."

"Why do you call yourselves the Sister Wolf People?"

"Shining Light's people were the Wolf People. We are related, yet apart from them, as a sister is related yet apart from her brother."

"Do you know where the Wolf People are now?"

Dances In Storms shrugged. "No one knows. Perhaps, after Dove journeyed to the campfires in the sky, her people returned to the Land of Tall Trees. Or perhaps, out on the grasslands they still follow and protect their mustangs and live among their wolves."

Golden Fox pushed to her hands and knees and leaned closer to Dances In Storms. "Your eyes... they are dark, yet they shine with a blue light. How can this be? Why have I not noticed this before?"

"Ah, Young One, you cannot see what a valley looks like until you have journeyed through it. Golden Fox, you begin your journey this night."

Awe filled her as she sat back and stared at the Holy Woman. "Who *are* you? Why have I come?"

"You are filled with questions, Golden Fox, but not all questions will be answered when you first ask them." She jumped to her feet and looked down, meeting Golden Fox's eyes. "It has been foretold that our journeys — your journey and mine — will become braided together like the strongest of rope. For now, know this — all things will become clear as sunrises pass into sunsets." She turned and walked away. She started to walk away, but turned. "My people come. I must make ready for our bands to meet.

***

Golden Fox stared after her until she could no longer see the Holy Woman. Dog followed behind her for a short distance, then returned to Golden Fox and sat in front of her.

"Have you Powers, too?" She rubbed Dog's fur. "Hmm, brown speckles are mixed with your long, white hairs. Maybe there is your name, Dog?" She placed her hand beneath the dog's chin and raised the animal's face. "You have such beautiful brown eyes...." She leaned closer. "Your eyes shine blue, like Shining Light's eyes."

The blue in Dog's eyes intensified.

"Where are you from, Dog? I do not remember ever seeing you until after we left the Sun People. Have the Spirits sent you to me for a reason, too?"

Dog whined low in her throat and wiggled all over. Her tongue lashed out and licked Golden Fox's face.

"You are more than just a dog, Dog." Golden Fox laughed. "That is it! Blue Spirit Dog. This is your name. Not many will understand, for they will not see the blue that shines from your eyes, but it does not matter what others see or do not see."

11

Barking dogs chased giggling children in endless circles around Golden Fox as the band waited for Dances In Storms' people. Earlier, the Holy Woman had led Eagle Thunder out to meet her people. Led by Stands His Ground, seven warriors — Blazing Fire among them — and five hunters rode with Grandfather to welcome the new people.

Eagle Thunder carried his Pipe of Truth wrapped in a well-crafted deer skin, which was then placed in a humpback hide pouch to better protect it.

Golden Fox had sat next to Grandfather three cold seasons ago, when he made his new humpback hide pouch. A person should always be the one to make their own sacred things, so the Spirits would know that the person honored the Spirit Land. If a person was too lazy to make their own sacred objects, the Spirits found no honor when that person called upon them.

The bowl of the clay pipe — representing the woman Spirit, also made by her grandfather — separated from the stem that represented the man Spirit. Together, they became whole.

When she first learned about the importance of the pipe, it puzzled Golden Fox. She had gone to her mother. "If we must have a woman Spirit and a man Spirit together to be a whole, how can Fire Starter and Deer Stalker become mates? They are both men."

Sky Bird had handed her a partially woven basket to work on while they talked. "Not a woman and a man, Daughter. A woman Spirit and a man Spirit. Fire Starter and Deer Stalker are Two-Spirit people. Inside each of them live both the woman Spirit and the man Spirit. They do not need to join with another to be whole. This can happen also with a woman. She can have both the woman Spirit and the man Spirit living inside her. This is why many Two-Spirit people become Holy People or healers."

Golden Fox shook away the thoughts and took a quick look up at the cerulean sky. Puffy clouds drifted across Father Sun's face and dappled the land below, as strangers topped the small rise close to camp and stopped.

Sister Wind carried Eagle Thunder's greeting to Golden Fox's sharp ears. "I, Eagle Thunder, an elder of my people, greet you, people of Dances in Storms."

A respected elder woman—easily identified by the ceremonial clothes she wore—rode forward on a white mustang splashed with black and brown splotches. In spite of the distance, her strong voice reached Golden Fox. "I, Floating Cloud, greet you, Eagle Thunder. I am the elder of this band of Sister Wolf People."

Eagle Thunder and Floating Cloud slid from their mustangs and met between their people. Dances In Storms stood next to Floating Cloud, and Sun Rising stood beside Eagle Thunder. Her grandfather offered the pipe to Floating Cloud.

The elder woman smoked, and then handed it to her people's Holy Woman, Dances In Storms.

After smoking, the Holy Woman handed the Pipe to Sun Rising.

When the Pipe returned to Eagle Thunder, with great ceremony he put it back into the pouch. After he had put the Pipe away, two young men walked forward and stood one on either side of Floating Cloud.

The elder tugged the men's tunics. "My grandsons have come to watch over me. They fear their old grandmother cannot take care of herself. Ha!" The elder threw her head back and laughed loudly.

"Your people have traveled a long ways. My people would be honored if you rested beside our fires and ate from our pots." Eagle Thunder swept his arm toward the camp.

Floating Cloud dipped her head. "My people thank you for your kindness. We would be honored to rest and to eat with your people."

Eagle Thunder waited politely until the elder woman had mounted her mustang, then hopped upon Swift Arrow. In grave procession, he and his people led the strangers into camp, and the gathered band parted to let them pass. At the center fire circle, Eagle Thunder halted his mustang and slid off. Floating Cloud joined him, and they handed their mustangs to the eager hands of young boys and girls.

Eagle Thunder turned toward those gathered behind them. "Please, let my people lead you to their fires."

As the throng of people broke apart, with small clumps drifting to the scattered fire circles, Eagle Thunder motioned toward two thick robes lying close to the fire circle. "Please, be seated and let my daughter and my granddaughter serve you."

Floating Cloud lowered herself from her animal to the robes, and Dances In Storms settled next to the elder woman.

Across the fire circle, Eagle Thunder sat cross-legged on robes with Sun Rising beside him.

Golden Fox hurried to dip bowls of warm meat and tubers for their guests.

As Floating Cloud accepted the bowl, she smiled at the girl. "Thank you, Child." The elder woman did not glance twice at her yellow hair.

Golden Fox blushed and dipped her head as she handed a bowl to Dances In Storms, and Sky Bird served Eagle Thunder and Sun Rising.

The elders talked long past when Father Sun ducked behind the edge of the land.

The two elk Stands His Ground had brought for this gathering, and the deer his sister had felled, would have been meager food for such a crowd if the strangers had not brought much meat, tubers, and greens. Everywhere Golden Fox looked, people stood or sat near the cooking fires, laughing and eating. The strangers mixed with her people as if they were relatives come together after a long season apart.

* * *

Golden Fox sank down next to her mother. It had been a long day. She closed her eyes and let her tired body sag.

Eighteen warriors, and fourteen women with twelve children....

If Dances In Storms people and their people joined together, no one hunting them would dare come near.

She opened her eyes and stared across the camp. People still gathered around the dying cooking fires, and a few children laughed and chased each other while the dogs ran after them. The youngest ones collapsed here and there, safe in the camp.

No one had said anything bad within her hearing, but she had seen the strange looks Dances In Storms' people shot her way. "Mother?"

"Hmm?" Sky Bird dropped her eyes from looking at Sister Moon. The lines around her mouth had smoothed out.

"What will the new people do?" She picked up a twig and made scratches on the ground as a knot in her belly grew hard with worry.

"Do?" Her mother laid an arm across Golden Fox's shoulder. "Tonight, our people will show them places to lay their sleeping robes, and tomorrow, the women will gather at the cooking fires and talk about food and babies and the sick ones. They will do what our people do, Golden Fox. They are not so different from us."

Golden Fox's face drew tight. She sucked her lower lip between her teeth, worrying at it until a drop of blood touched her tongue. "They see you and I are not full-bloods."

Sky Bird pulled her close and laid her cheek against Golden Fox's. "Do not worry, Daughter. What happened in the Sun People band will not happen with our new band."

She jerked away from her mother. "How can you know this? All of my life I lived with the Sun People, yet many of the boys that teased other girls would not look at me. Their mothers frowned when I sat at their cooking fires and spoke with their daughters. You say these people are not so different than us. If that is true, perhaps they will turn away when they see my ugly gold-red hair and strange green eyes."

"Dances In Storms and Long Sun have not given you bad looks. And, no woman I worked with at the cooking fires curled her lip at my grey eyes and my hair that is the color of our Mother when she is wet. Yellow Moon had long been jealous of me, and her hate poisoned others against me and against you. She is no longer among us. Even her one brother who is with us smiles as he passes by." Sky Bird's hands twisted together like a ball of snakes that had been disturbed in their nest. "I am sorry that her words made your life hard. You must not let the words of Yellow Moon, and the cruel ones among the Sun People, put you on a path that takes you away from others."

"I feel as if I belong only when I am with Dog and the mustangs, or I am away from camp and listening to the wild ones." The confession felt bitter in Golden Fox's mouth.

"Stop it!" Her mother twisted around, grabbed her shoulders, and shook her hard. "You belong *here!* You belong with Father and me, and we belong to a line of ancestors that began when the Great Mystery put our people on our Mother!" She sucked in a deep breath and let it whoosh out of her. "When a person is jealous, when they envy another, a poison as strong as the poisoned water flows in their bodies."

Her mother dropped her hands from Golden Fox's shoulders, and her fingers rested on Golden Fox's arms. "I did not ask to be the one who dreamed. From the first dream when I had just become a woman, Yellow Moon envied me. I do not know what Power the Great Mystery gave Yellow Moon — I do not think Yellow Moon ever knew what her Power was, because she was too busy wanting the Power that Great Mystery placed on me. Look at me, Daughter!"

When Golden Fox met her mother's grey eyes, they glittered with Power. She had never seen such a look on her mother's face.

"When I was as many summers as you are, I too wanted to hide, to be like the other girls in the band with their dark brown eyes and long, raven black hair. None of them dreamed. I felt strange, different, and like you, that I never fully belonged with the Sun People. But when you are born to a People and you grow up among them, you know nothing else. It is normal to want to belong."

She looked away as she confessed to Golden Fox. "Yellow Moon was born only five cycles of seasons before me. She ran with girls who laughed at me. One day, Yellow Moon's friends circled around me and hit me, pulled my hair, and pushed me to the ground and kicked me. I went home with tears streaking my face and bloodied arms and knees. I cried to my mother — your grandmother — and said I wanted to go away to some place where no people lived. I begged her to tell me why the Great Mystery made me different from all of our people."

Silence fell over Sky Bird for so long that Golden Fox picked up her mother's hand and cradled it between her own. When she spoke to her mother, the words whispered between them. "What did Grandmother tell you?"

"These are the words your grandmother spoke to me...." Sky Bird's voice fell into a near whisper.

For a short span, Golden Fox's heart rejoiced. It was her grandmother's voice she heard coming from Sky Bird's lips. In the bones of her mother's face, she could see her grandmother's face. Why had she never noticed this before? Sky Bird's words pulled Golden Fox back to the night and her mother.

"You cannot hide from what you are, from who you are. There will be those who see your worth, and there will be those whose eyes are blind. Forgive them their blindness, but do not let them shape your life. They are a sad people who shoot arrows of envy because they refuse to honor the gifts the Great Mystery gives to each of us. Instead, they hunger for gifts they do not have. Their lives are small. Do not let your life be small." A grin broke across Sky Bird's face. "And, she had Blazing Fire teach me to fight."

Her mother leaned forward and kissed Golden Fox's cheek. "Some moons back, before our band became broken, I dreamed." Her eyes seemed to drift inward. "I dreamed of new Peoples, a new land, and much love and laughter. I dreamed that I lived among a People who looked at my grey eyes and hair the color of wet dirt as beautiful, not so strange. I had this dream as a child, but no Peoples like this came to our band. After a time, I accepted that it was not a true dream, but a child's wish. Now, I believe I saw Dances In Storms' people."

When Golden Fox stood up, her mother said, "Do not turn away from those who would care for you because of a past wound."

12

Golden Fox awakened before anyone in the camp stirred, and silently prowled around the edge of the camp and out into the grasslands. A short walk took her to the top of a knoll, where she settled in the tall grasses and gazed out at the rolling land. Sister Moon's round face spilled so much light that she could easily see the black river of humpbacks that flowed slowly in the distance.

Thoughts floated about her, about what her mother said, until Father Sun peeked over the edge of the land and pushed the darkness back. The sky bled from black to dove gray to a sharp blue. As Golden Fox sang her prayers to the Great Mystery, a peace filled her heart. Whether these people accepted her or not, those who had followed Grandfather did not care about her gold-red hair or her green eyes.

By the time she returned to her mother's cooking fire, Grandfather sat cross-legged eating his first food after greeting Father Sun. The tunic he wore was one that Sun Rising had grabbed out of their burning lodge. Mother had painted dark grey clouds with yellow lightning that shot out and vanished off the fringed bottom. The clouds hid the few black spots from the hot embers.

As she sat across from Eagle Thunder and ate, she watched her mother mix medicines for those who were getting better from the poisoned water sickness, but still were not strong. Sky Bird took whatever she found and made something better from it — like Grandfather's partly burned tunic, and the plants she made into medicines. Golden Fox had never before considered her mother's work in that light.

She finished her first food and got to her feet.

Sky Bird carried a bowl of her healing broth toward the lodge where the sick ones slept. "Golden Fox, we need wood."

"I will gather it, Mother." She cleaned her bowl and stacked it inside of Eagle Thunder's cleaned bowl. She would have to go farther to find wood, as they had already used the lower, dry branches of the nearby trees.

She scanned the ground, considering what she had overheard her grandfather and her mother talking about as she neared the fire this sunrise.

"Dances In Storms and Floating Cloud want to leave in a few sunrises. Sun Rising and I agree this would be good. Stands His Ground says this place would be hard to defend from hairy-faces if they still hunt Golden Fox and you.

"If we can wait four more sunrises, I think even the weakest will be able to travel on drags. They have passed through the time when they must fight hard against bad Spirits in the poisoned water. It will be sad to leave this place. We have the empty lodges of fourteen of our relatives, who lie bundled in the trees. No one will be here to Sing for them when the seasons turn.

"No one Sings for those we left behind in the trees of the Sun People. Our relatives understand this is something we must do if we are to survive as a People."

They must have heard her feet shuffling over the ground then, because they ceased their talk.

Even with Father Sun warming her back, Golden Fox shivered. *How could Yellow Moon think she saw the Great Mystery with that poison in her stomach? I wonder if Mother drank the poisoned water when she lived with my father in the wooden lodge?*

She bent and picked up wood as her mind filled with sadness. *More than fifteen winters have passed since father threw mother away. When I asked if she missed him, she asked how she could miss a man who was hardly ever there. Even before he threw her away, he left for moons at a time, claiming that he hunted. Who hunts for so long when there are many deer and humpbacks everywhere in the warm season? Perhaps, he hunted so he would not have to look at mother's grey eyes, or my gold-red hair and green eyes, in a face that is brown. Even among the hairy-faces, I do not belong.*

She gazed blankly across the grasses. "Am I to be an outcast among all Peoples? I see the young men stare, but no one approaches me. Am I that ugly, even to these new people? I saw in Mother's eyes that she prays this is not so. For her sake, I, too, hope these people are different. Yet, I fear they may not be."

A mother fox and her four young ones peered out from an underground hole. The entrance would have been hard to see behind the large stones and the low growing shrub whose berries had started to turn red, if Golden Fox had not seen the bright, black eyes watching her.

"Why would you be an outcast?"

Her eyes widened. "Fox?"

A voice snorted from behind her. "I am White Elk, not Fox."

"I said that out loud?" Heat climbed up her face. "I thought Fox spoke to me." Slowly, she turned, not wanting to face whoever was behind her.

A young man sat tall on a prancing mustang with tan hair.

Her mouth dropped open with surprise, and the wood in her arms fell to the ground. "You... your skin is as white as snow! Your... .eyes...." She ran out of words and simply stared.

A grin spread across the young man's face. "Yes, I know. My skin is pale as snow on the mountains in the cold season, and my eyes look red, but sometimes they look blue as the sky. My mother told me they change with the light. And, my hair is the color of a drifting cloud that carries no rain."

"Are... are there...." All of a sudden, shame stole her words. She was treating this young man as others had treated her—like some strange animal, instead of just another one of the People.

I hate that! Her head dropped to her chest. *How can I face him?*

The stranger's next words fell onto Golden Fox as soft as a light rain. "Do not feel as if you have hurt me. Many people I have met since I left my people have asked these questions. It is only as it should be when we are faced with someone who, at first, appears so different from us."

His words soothed some of the heat from her face and she looked up. "Where do your people live?"

He slid from his mustang and approached her, but no closer than was proper for a young man with a young woman he did not know. "Our land is where sky beads are found. It gets very hot. Among my people, I am not so odd. Grandmother had skin as mine. Though not many look as Grandmother and I do, our ancestors looked much like us."

He cocked his head. "We are not feared. No one sees us as outcasts. Dances In Storms' people have never treated me as an outcast. Are your people so afraid of people who look different that they make you feel like an outcast?"

She backed away, feeling as if he already knew too much. "I did not see you with Dances In Storms' people when they came into camp."

"I came later with the hunters. We brought ground birds to add to the cooking fires."

"Why are you with Dances In Storms' people? Do you follow a special woman?"

A warm chuckle bubbled up from his chest. "It is hard to follow a woman." He shrugged. "I wished to travel, to see the lands of other Peoples." He looked away, and then back to her.

Seeing White Elk struggle with words that wanted to hide behind his teeth, Golden Fox stepped forward and placed a hand on his forearm. "What is it that you are trying to share?"

"You would laugh if I said."

There rose inside of Golden Fox a feeling that she needed to hear what this strange young man was trying to say. "I promise, I will not laugh. You are safe to speak your heart to me."

Red eyes stared into hers. "Promise you will not run away? No matter what you hear?"

When she hesitated to agree, he rushed to add, "I promise, it is not a bad thing that I need to share, and I would never hurt you, Golden Fox."

She jerked back and rested her hand on her knife. "I did not tell you my name."

Hands raised in surrender, White Elk backed away. "I am far enough away now that you can take your hand from the hilt of your knife. I mean you no harm." His chest rose and fell as he breathed deeply. "How I know your name is part of what I need to share with you. Will you hear me?"

For a long span, neither one moved. Eyes locked with his, Golden Fox carefully considered his words.

White Elk did not fidget, but kept still, letting her decide.

Slowly, she removed her hand from her knife. "I will listen, but do not come any closer."

He bobbed his head in understanding. "I am many things, but I am no dreamer. Yet, the night that I had my Manhood Ceremony, I dreamed." He licked his lips and swallowed. "I... I dreamed of a young girl. She danced barefoot in the light of Sister Moon. Though she sang a beautiful song, I could feel the loneliness in her heart. It hurt me so much that tears sprang to my eyes. At last, she stopped dancing and sat upon the ground. A voice called to her. She stood and walked out of the forest. I believed that I dreamed the dream of a boy becoming a man. What boy on the night of his manhood would not dream of a beautiful woman?" He slid from his mustang.

Face turned down, he shuffled his feet and spoke to the ground. "Two cycles of seasons went by before she came into my dream again. This time, an elder woman spoke to me. She told me that I was to leave my people and travel to find this woman. This young woman would become a part of my life for as long as I walked our Mother. My heart jumped in my chest in happiness. What man would turn away from such a foretelling? I would have a beautiful woman with gold-red hair that flowed over her shoulders, and eyes as green as the first grasses after the cold season. The elder told me that her name was Golden Fox."

He lifted his head and stepped toward her. "I travel with Dances In Storms so I might find you, Golden Fox."

When he halted, he stood so close that she felt the heat from his skin. Her eyes wandered over his body, though her mother had taught her better manners than to act that way. Her fingers ached to touch his skin, to comb through his long, snow-white hair. It shimmered in Father Sun's light, looking almost blue. Now that he stood so close, she could see that blue ringed the reddish color in the center of his eyes—not the blue she saw in her mother's eyes, but a blue like the sky. The muscles of his bare chest rippled when he moved. Strands of blue-green sky beads dangled from his neck, reaching all the way to the top of his breechclout.

"Sweet one...."

Golden Fox shoved away from the stranger. Her breath hitched in her throat and her hands shook from wanting to touch him. Her legs moved in jerky motions as she hurried to put distance between them. "You should not call me such. It is not acceptable until... until...."

"Until what? Until I speak with your grandfather?" White Elk had not moved from where she had left him.

Cheeks blazing with heat, Golden Fox grabbed at the wood she had dropped. "You cannot speak to my grandfather! We have not... we just.... *Eerrr!* I do not know you. Now, go away. I have work to do." She snatched a few more pieces from the ground, then rushed toward camp.

When she reached their cooking fire, Eagle Thunder, Sun Rising, Stands His Ground, Blazing Fire, and warriors from Dances In Storms' people sat around the fire circle talking. It would be impolite to hang around the warriors talking, so she stacked the wood quickly, then hurried to where their sleeping robes lay. With no one else there, she flopped back and stared up at the pale blue sky — the same pale blue as the rings around White Elk's eyes. A tingly feeling settled between her thighs and butterflies fluttered in her belly.

She sighed and sat up. No boys in the Sun People's band, even when they did notice her, had ever called her beautiful.

Why does White Elk think me beautiful? The people I grew up with did not think me so. Not even my own father thought me good enough to look at.

She did not remember much about him, but she remembered one day when he came home while she was playing. He yelled at Mother and told her to get out of his way, and to take that ugly child with her. When she asked Mother about this, Sky Bird said her father said crazy things when he had a belly full of poisoned water. They never spoke of it again, but she always wondered if he said that because of the poisoned water, or because he really saw her as an ugly child.

Sky Bird made her way to the robes carrying two bowls of food. She handed one to Golden Fox, then settled next to her and began to eat.

The first taste of the tender meat made Golden Fox's stomach growl in anticipation. "These are not our bowls." She scooped a bite of tubers into her mouth. The juicy plant mixed its sweetness with the saltiness of the meat. The carved zig-zag design on the bowl was nothing like she had ever seen.

Her mother smiled. "A woman from Dances In Storms' people walked up to me and handed me four bowls like these." Sky Bird lifted the bowl to admire the design before she continued eating. Between bites, she told Golden Fox about the woman's gift. "I told her I had nothing to trade. She laughed with a sweet laugh and said they were her gift to her new sister-friend."

Dog trotted up and loudly threw herself to the ground beside Golden Fox. With a giggle, she hand the animal a piece of meat. "You are such a silly one, Blue Spirit Dog."

Brows lifted high, Sky Bird dipped the last of the food from her bowl, chewed, and swallowed. "Blue Spirit Dog?"

"Yes, for the blue in her eyes — the blue of Spirit."

Sky Bird leaned closer to Blue Spirit Dog, gazed into his eyes, and after a short span, sat back and shook her head. "Her eyes are brown, the same as the eyes of most dogs."

Golden Fox stared into the dog's eyes before she turned to her mother. "You truly do not see the blue in her eyes? It is a circle around the brown color. Sometimes, her eyes turn all blue, but mostly there is only this circle."

"Daughter, I cannot see this blue you speak of, but I have heard about it. No, not with Blue Spirit Dog—from my mother. It is the blue of the Spirit Land. Not all people are gifted to see it. How long have you seen this blue?"

"Since... since my dream of Shining Light."

"Ah, the Great Holy Man. How I wish to dream of him." Her mother's eyes showed a faraway look of longing. She blinked and the look disappeared. "You are blessed, Daughter, to meet the Great Holy Man, and now to see the blue of the Spirit Land. I have always known you would have great Power someday."

"Power? I have no Power, Mother!" She waved her hand in front of her face when it seemed her mother would continue to speak of Power. Without thinking, she blurted, "I met a man as pale as snow."

"Ahh. Where did you meet this man?" Worry clung to Sky Bird's words.

"Do not be concerned, Mother. He travels with Dances In Storms' people. I met him when I went to gather wood."

"You say his skin is as pale as snow? Are you sure? Perhaps, it was the way Father Sun shone on his body that made him seem so pale."

"No, Mother, he was born with white skin and white hair, and eyes that are blue, and then sometimes red."

"It is not proper for a young woman to walk alone with a man who has not spoken to her grandfather. Your grandfather would tell me if this had happened." She firmed her mouth into a stern line and crossed her arms, in the way that clearly said *this is not acceptable.*

"He did not mean to be impolite, Mother. It... he was riding and just happened to ride where I gathered wood. He has no interest in me that would make it proper for him to speak to Grandfather."

Sky Bird opened her mouth to speak, but the harsh voice of a man sounded from the trees behind them, cutting her short.

"When we find this girl of the Sun People, the hairy-faces will give us long knives and much firewater."

A second man, with the voice of one who yelled too much, spoke. "*If* we find this girl. I begin to think she exists only in someone's crazy mind."

"I tell you, I saw such a girl with gold-red hair. I know I did," the first man argued.

"Well, where is she?" The second man barked a sharp laugh. "I do not see her. Perhaps, this girl you saw wore a fox skin around her hair. Who knows what these savages might do. Unlike us, they were born wild and know nothing, act as if animals speak to them, as if even the land is alive. Our fathers were smart hairy-faces. We are better than animals and the dirt we walk on."

The other man grumbled. "That was no fox fur. She has to be here somewhere. We just have to keep looking."

"I thought you said you were a good tracker. I am starting to think you could not track a brown rabbit through the snow, much less this girl." Rude laughter sputtered from the man. "I have seen no girl with gold-red hair. I have seen no woman with grey eyes and hair the color of mud. We waste our time among these savages. I tell you —"

The sounds of a scuffle reached Golden Fox.

"Whoa!" The man of the rude laughter yelled. "What is wrong with you?"

"Do not disrespect me again," the other man growled low and dangerous. "I will find this girl of the Sun People. Did I not say these Sister Wolf people would meet up with the last of the Sun People? And, here we are. This camp is for the last of the Sun People. No others survived the fighting in that camp near the fort, so she has to be here, somewhere."

"All right! I believe you. Now, will you get that knife outta my face?"

"Just do as I tell you. We do not want these people to know we hunt one of their own. We might not get outta here with...."

Golden Fox could hear no more, as the men moved farther away.

Sky Bird hurried over to Golden Fox and tossed a robe around her head and shoulders. "Come! Hurry!" She urged Golden Fox to her feet and then rushed her to the lodge that had been for the injured ones. No one lay on the robes any longer, and they had meant to take the lodge down to prepare it for traveling when Father Sun rose again, but with so much going on, she had let it wait for one more sunrise.

As they darted in and closed the flap, Sky Bird whispered, "I wonder if perhaps the Spirits kept me too busy to take the lodge down."

92

"Who are they, Mother?" Golden Fox's whisper held fear and worry. "Where did they come from?"

Her mother put her mouth close to Golden Fox's ear. "I do not know, but we will find out. Stay here in the lodge while I go and speak to your grandfather."

"No!" Golden Fox clutched tight to her mother's arm. "They will see your hair and know I am here."

"I will keep this robe over my hair. It will appear to others as if I am one of those who are still sick and shiver even on the warmest night." Sky Bird slipped out of the lodge flap.

Alone in the lodge, worry rose like the waters of a river in the wet season. Golden Fox hugged Blue Spirit Dog tight to her as she waited.

Father Sun had dipped far below the edge of the land by the time her mother returned. Dances In Storms and Eagle Thunder followed her through the flap.

Dances In Storms rushed over to Golden Fox. "Are you all right?"

Trying to stop the chatter of her teeth, she hugged Blue Spirit Dog tighter, but unlike with the cold, he could not warm away the shaking from fear. "Do... do you know who... who these men are?"

Sky Bird handed Golden Fox a bowl of hot broth. "Drink. I have put in herbs that will help calm you."

She cradled the bowl between both hands and sipped the broth. The heat glided down her throat and into her cramped stomach. After a few sips, her stomach began to unknot. Eagle Thunder sat so close that the knee of his crossed legs touched her knee, and the touch calmed her as much as her mother's broth.

"You know who these men are?" The sternness in Eagle Thunder's voice said how unhappy he was that Dances In Storms had not told him of these men.

"I'm sorry, Eagle Thunder. I meant to tell you, but...." She spread her hands, palms up. "These men joined my band a sunrise after Stands His Ground ate at my fire. I could feel the evil that wrapped them, in the way we wrap ourselves in a winter robe. After much discussion, Floating Cloud and I thought it best to let them travel with our people until we could find out what or who they hunted."

Anger made Sky Bird sit stiffly upright. "How long have you known they hunted my daughter?"

Dances in Storms stabbed a finger toward the ground and said, "This night is the first that I have known who they hunted. Just before you came to get me, White Elk sat at my fire and told me about the men."

"What does White Elk have to do with these men?" Golden Fox startled so hard she nearly spilled the rest of the broth on Blue Spirit Dog, still draped across her lap.

"When the men joined us, White Elk said he would get them to trust him and find out what harm these men meant to do. As we waited to meet up with Eagle Thunder's people, White Elk acted as a friend to these men. They bragged of much knowledge of the Sun People, and even told how the Sun People had fought among themselves, and how many had died at the hands of their relatives. The sunrise after the fight between the traders and the Sun People, hairy-faces rode from the camp the traders had come from. In revenge for the deaths of the traders, these hairy-faces killed any of the Sun People who had not died. It is a good thing no children were there."

Disgust twisted Dances In Storms face. "White Elk found out that these two men rode with those who killed the last of the Sun People. We did not chase them from us because we still needed to know who they hunted. As Father Sun dipped below the tops of the trees, White Elk came to me. The men had offered him some of the firewater they would get when they took the girl with gold-red hair back to her hairy-face father, if he helped to find her. White Elk wanted to kill these men." She looked deep into Eagle Thunder's eyes. "It is not my people's decision to take or not to take the lives of these men. It is your decision. We will help you with whatever you decide to do."

Eagle Thunder lowered his head as a tear escaped down his face. "All those who remained."

* * *

Fretfully, Golden Fox shoved a strand of hair from her face. "Are those men *ever* going to leave?" She glanced around, the leather cover still hiding her hair. "Why does my hairy-face father want me?" Her anguished words burst out. "He threw us away when I was very young! He shamed you and called me ugly! Why does he hunt me now?"

Eagle Thunder stretched out in the warm sun beside their lodge, his hands under his head. "Girl, I hope we never find out, but know that *no one* will take you from us."

Sky Bird did not glance up from the deerskin tunic she sewed, with tiny stitches to make it more waterproof. She pointed her chin at the unfinished basket lying in Golden Fox's lap. "Work on the basket, and worry will not sit so heavy on your shoulders."

Too restless to follow her mother's advice, she set the basket aside and stood. As she drifted around the lodge, touching the bundles of plants hung for drying, thoughts of White Elk brought that tingly feeling to her body. "Mother, do you think White Elk is good to look at?"

Her mother glanced up. "Daughter, your thoughts are everywhere. You need to focus on making your basket for our new people." Sky Bird laid her work on her lap. "The inside of a man is more important than the outside. Do you care that White Elk's hair and eyes are so strange?"

"I... I found him strange when I turned and first saw him, but...." She flopped down onto the robe across from her mother. "He is easy to talk to, and... he sees me — *really sees* me."

"Like you see beyond the outside of White Elk, if he is the kind of man to spend your life with, then he will see beyond the outside of you." Sky Bird picked up her work. "Though he would be a blind fool to not see how good the outside of you is, also."

"Mother!"

With a tiny lift of her shoulders, her mother shrugged away Golden Fox's weak protest. "What? Is it not good for a mother to tell her daughter that she is beautiful?" Her hands sewed the tiny stitches Golden Fox had never had the patience to sew. "Just remember, he has not sat with your grandfather and he has not eaten at our fire."

Fire flashed in Golden Fox's eyes. "Grandfather said it is my choice who I take as my mate."

"Hmm! It may be your choice who you take as your mate, but no matter who it is, he will need to sit with your grandfather, and he will need to eat at our fire, if he hopes to be part of our family. There are some old ways that are good to keep."

Eagle Thunder chuckled.

***

By the time White Elk led the half-blood men who hunted her out of camp, Father Sun had lowered "White Elk has taken the men into the darkness," Blazing Fire said.

Carefully, Sky Bird folded the tunic she worked on, stood, and stretched. "Why did they wait until Father Sun's time to rest?"

Lip curled in contempt, Blazing Fire shook her head. "During the light, the men drank from hidden flasks of poisoned water. It was long after Father Sun peeked above the land before they woke. White Elk waited at their cooking fire while the men groaned and cursed and drank even more poison. The men became stupid, and more so as the light faded. Blazing Fire stood. "If no trouble comes to us, we will wait here."

* * *

For five sunrises, Golden Fox climbed to the top of the small hill and sang Father Sun up. Father Sun had risen for the sixth time before White Elk returned with three mustangs on lead ropes behind him.

Children ran to him and argued over who would rub down Runner.

White Elk hushed them and pointed toward a girl of no more than ten winters. "Girl Who Does Not Speak, will you look after my mustangs?" When the child nodded, he handed her the lead ropes. "If you find any of these others who know how to listen, you may have them help you—if you choose." He gave a hard stare at the gathered children. "Whoever you pick for this honor must listen to you, and do only as you say."

As the children clamored to be chosen, White Elk strode toward Sky Bird's cooking fire.

Golden Fox smiled at him. "I saw you ride in, and watched you with the children. It was kind of you to choose Girl Who Does Not Speak to care for your mustangs."

Light red touched his cheeks and he looked away. "I have watched her. She may not speak with her voice, but she speaks well with the animals."

Eagle Thunder waved toward a place on the robe across the fire circle from him. "White Elk, come, sit, and eat. Father Sun has almost reached the edge of the land. You must hunger."

Golden Fox handed a bowl of food to Eagle Thunder, and then another to Sky Bird. After serving the elders, she dipped up a bowl of food for White Elk. Before she could hand it to him, Dances In Storms walked over and lowered herself onto the robe next to him.

Why does Dances In Storms sit so close to White Elk? He has traveled with them.

Does she want him for her man? I did not think a Holy Woman took a man. Holy Men take a woman, so why is it a Holy Woman cannot take a man?

She pushed the uncomfortable thoughts aside and handed the bowl of food to Dances In Storms before again dipping food for White Elk, and then herself. Bowl in hand, she sat on the robe beside her mother.

No one spoke of the men until White Elk finished his food. By the time he set his bowl aside, Stands His Ground, Blazing Fire, and Floating Cloud also sat around Sky Bird's fire circle.

Eagle Thunder motioned with a dip of his head toward White Elk that the young man should speak.

"The time between the sunrise when we left," he said, "and when Father Sun drops behind the edge of the land, we did not make it far. The men—Luke and Adam—all during the time of light, cried and moaned as not even the youngest baby of our people would do. They drank more poisoned water after Father Sun left the sky, and I feared we would make no distance the next sunrise. Maybe they did not drink as much, because the next sunrise we rode over much grass-land and some hills. After the third sunrise of hard riding, I led them to where I did not think they could find their way back to this camp."

Humor danced in White Elk's eyes. "After we ate meat I had gotten for us, I told them we were very close to where the gold-red haired girl now lived, and that we should have a drink to show our happiness. We sat around the campfire until Sister Moon gave up and hid behind a hill. They drank one flask of poisoned water, and I encouraged them to bring out another flask. I do not know how many flasks they drank before they fell into the sleep of the poisoned water."

"Did they not demand that you drink with them?" Sky Bird's voice held many more questions than the words asked. She picked at her dress as she waited to hear the answer.

White teeth showing in the broad smile, White Elk made a puckered face like a person who had tasted something that is no longer good enough to eat. "It was good that they did not want to share the poisoned water, and only did so a few times. At those times, I held the flask to my lips and made throat motions as though I drank, but I never opened my lips. They thought my way of drinking very funny, and even more funny when I wiped my lips on my tunic after I drank." He flashed a look at Golden Fox. "I did not want poisoned water on my lips for even a short span."

She dropped her eyes when he caught her looking at him, but not before he winked at her. Heat ran up her neck and she hoped it did not stain her cheeks, or Blazing Fire would never let her forget.

White Elk returned his attention to Eagle Thunder. "They are half-blood brothers with two different mothers. They grew up at the wooden fort with their father. He drank much and beat them much. When they became men, they left the fort. Sometimes, they go back to get more poisoned water, but they live in a wooden lodge a short distance from the fort. They have much to drink. It will take many sunrises to find their way home."

"Did they say why my hairy-face father wanted me?" Golden Fox caught her lip between her teeth as she waited to hear.

"Your father has no relations. Not many moons ago, his white woman went back across the salty waters, and she took his only other child — a boy. They say he tires of living among his own kind and wishes to live a different way. He thinks if he had you, you would help him find this different way."

Scowling, Sky Bird huffed out a breath. "Perhaps, he tires of working and wishes to sell my daughter to the pale men every night. They do not care about their girl children, except to sell or trade them. When I lived among the whites, every sunrise I would see women of the People stumble to their lodges after sleeping the darkness with whoever their man had sold them to. Other whites sold women to clean men's lodges and cook." Anger poured from every part of Sky Bird's body. "While I lived among them, I saw women not only of the Peoples, but women with skin as dark as Raven's wing. Those women were treated even worse than women of the Peoples."

Pain flickered across Dances In Storms' face. "Yes, I know of what you speak. My... my older sister began drinking poisoned water and went to live at the wooden fort. Three moons passed when a pale man, who was a friend of my father's, came and told us that my sister's man sold her every sunset to men of the fort."

Tears filled her eyes, but she blinked them away. "My father, my mother, and I went to the fort to bring my sister home. We begged her to come with us, yet she refused. The poisoned water had blackened her Spirit. She attacked my mother. Still, my father and I tried to talk to her. It was no use. We had to abandon her at the wooden fort when her pale man brought many of his brothers. They threatened to hurt my father if we did not leave."

Sky Bird got up and walked over to Dances In Storms. She sat next to her and looped an arm around the other woman's shoulders. "What happened to your sister, Dances In Storms?"

"Five moons after that, a trader came to our camp. My father only traded with certain pale ones who did not trade their poisoned water to our people. The trader brought news of my sister's death. A hairy-face with too much poisoned water in his belly beat her to death. My sister's hairy-face man buried her in the ground, as is the way of his people. He did not even respect her enough to bring her home or, at least, to wrap her in her robe and lay her in a strong tree, so her Spirit could see when Eagle Woman came for her. All I can do is hope her body died only, and not her Spirit."

With nothing else to say about the men, everyone headed to their sleeping robes. Since even the sickest ones had healed enough to travel, they planned to move camp now that White Elk had returned.

***

Golden Fox woke to the chirping of birds. She stretched, got to her feet, and rolled up her sleeping robe. This would be her last time to greet Father Sun from her special hill. Quietly, she hurried out of camp and sat cross-legged among the tall grasses, gazing out toward the distant hills. They looked purple, and she wondered if they really were that color.

Did the Sister Wolf Band live close to those tall hills?

If they did, perhaps one day she would ride over and see if the hills were really purple.

Something rustled in the grasses behind her. She sat very still and listened hard—too heavy and too noisy to be an animal. Hand on her knife, she leapt to her feet, whirled, and pulled the knife from its sheath.

White Elk threw his hands in the air. "Aiiee! Do not use your knife on me, Golden Fox."

"Why do you come here where I greet Father Sun? Has your mother taught you no manners?" She sheathed her knife and sat.

Feet shuffling, White Elk walked closer. "May I sit beside you?"

His voice chased pleasant shivers down her back. Trying not to show how his presence warmed her, she grunted, "If you must."

He eased down and stared out at the distant hills. No sound crossed his lips.

At last, Golden Fox twisted her head to one side. "I am sorry that I spoke harshly."

A smile tugged the corners of White Elk's full lips as he faced her. "You are right to be angry. I know it is not polite to disturb another when they greet Father Sun. I...." His words fell silent and he looked away from her. "I worry when you are alone. White men could be close."

"Blazing Fire has taught me to take care of myself. It is not your place to worry about me." She turned away from him.

Long fingers wrapped around her hand. "It is my place to worry, Sweet One. Someday, you will be my mate."

She moved her hand away and stood. "I must be the one who chooses." She stormed back toward the camp.

Camp was nearly ready to move. The two lodges for the sick and the injured were tied to drags behind mustangs. Dogs waited patiently as the drags behind them were filled with the people's belongings. Even the smallest child worked.

Golden Fox hurried over to her mother and helped to pack the last robes on their drag.

It is perhaps good that the fire took much of what we had. We do not have so much for our animals to pull.

Before Father Sun peered over the tops of the trees, the Peoples moved out. As they crested the hill above the camp, Golden Fox stopped and stared back, noticing that White Elk stood close. Below her, not one stone from the fire circles remained; only the crushed grasses told of the encampment that had once been there.

Do they move so fast because of me? Have I become a burden on my people?

As Father Sun traveled across the pale blue sky, the people traveled, too.

White Elk walked beside Golden Fox, and she did not chase him away. His presence filled an empty place in her.

When Father Sun dropped lower toward the edge of the land, Eagle Thunder and Dances In Storms called a halt.

The weakest of the elders, and those still gaining strength from the poisoned water sickness, were placed near the first fire circle. A young girl prepared a pot of broth for the elders and the sick, while the rest of the people set up camp. Soon, other fire circles blazed with small fires, and women cooked. The men looked after the mustangs, and made the grasses flat so no snakes hid, and so that all the sleeping robes would lay in a way that was comfortable.

BROKEN PATH

By the time camp was set up, the mustangs rubbed down, and food cooked, Father Sun had dipped behind the edge of the land.

After eating and helping her mother with the elders and those still not quite healed, Golden Fox wandered a short distance away from the noise of the camp. Sister Moon hid part of her face, peering down on the Mother with a lop-sided grin.

Behind her, the soft voices of Eagle Thunder and White Elk rose and floated toward the campfires in the sky. Now and then, Sky Bird's higher-pitched voice would murmur a few words before falling back into silence.

It would be good to get Grandfather's blessing to have White Elk walk next to me.

A happiness grew in her chest and chased away some of the sharp ache from leaving Running Girl behind in the trees. Even the thought of her sister-friend brought tears to her eyes. Her heart ached for Strong Knife and his little brother, Little Knife. Perhaps on this journey, one of the women among Dances In Storms' people would smile at Strong Knife.

A wolf howled from some distance. The sound reached inside Golden Fox and called to her. Restless, she returned to camp.

White Elk had already left to sleep with the men who had no women.

* * *

As the bands traveled, after their morning meal, White Elk walked next to Golden Fox.

After Father Sun dropped behind the hills, White Elk came to sit beside their fire to speak to her grandfather.

Sky Bird pulled Golden Fox away to gather wood so the men could visit.

From the darkness forward, White Elk refused to be far from Golden Fox's side, and her grandfather smiled when he thought she did not see, but White Elk refused to say what words her grandfather had spoken to him.

Stands His Ground and her mother gave knowing looks to each other as White Elk sat near Golden Fox, as the campfires in the sky shone.

She tried to ignore the carrying-on of her elders, though her cheeks often heated beneath their gazes.

* * *

Blazing Fire, even as she took her turn watching the people, never went far from Golden Fox. Hope of Golden Fox becoming a warrior woman stayed with

Blazing Fire. The young woman had much courage, and often the two sparred away from camp. Golden Fox's ability to rapid fire her bow, and jump from a mustang and wrestle her to the ground, even if she allowed her to win, showed much promise.

This albino man might change everything.

* * *

As sunrises followed sunsets, the grasslands slowly folded into hills. These hills stood higher than any Golden Fox had ever seen. Eagle Thunder and Dances In Storms let the bands stop in a valley that wound beside one of the steepest hills. The shorter, thinner grasses of this land prickled against bare skin and exposed the light, orange-red flesh of the Mother. Stones jutted from beneath the thin skin of the land. Rough, grey boulders thrust up among dark-green trees with long needles that dotted the hillside. Here and there, rainbow robes of flowers—pink and snow white, brilliant red and deep yellow—blanketed the gentler slopes. Trees, with shrubs crowding beside them, grew along the river.

White Elk waved in the direction they traveled. "I am glad to be gone from the hunting camp where Stands His Ground first met us. We go to Dances In Storms' home with much dried humpback meat. The people will be glad to see us."

"What is Dances In Storms' home like?" Golden Fox scooped up pebbles and tossed them into the river.

Excitement shone in his now-pale-blue eyes as he pointed. "See those purple spikes that rise so high that some of their tips are hidden in the clouds?"

"Yes, I had wondered about them."

"They are mountains higher than anywhere else. In places, their sides are very steep. There are animals with small feet that leap along those rocky sides, going where even the best climber cannot go. Hidden by these walls and the jagged flesh of the land, canyons lie. Canyons are like valleys but with steeper sides, and more narrow. At the bottom of some canyons is nothing except red dirt, while in other canyons grow trees and plants you can find nowhere else.

"In the canyon where Dances In Storms' people live, a river of clear, cold water runs from the mountains above us. The water is so cold that, even in the hot season, a person cannot stay in it for more than a short span, or their lips become blue and their teeth chatter. Deer and elk and many small animals share the canyon with us."

Golden Fox felt her eyes grow wide as she stared at him. "These high walls, what do they look like?"

Eyes sparkling, White Elk's smile grew wider. "The flesh of the Mother that makes these walls has bands of many colors—grays and yellows, browns and reds. Sunsets can paint parts of that flesh, to make them as red as the muscle beneath an animal's skin. One time, I rode to the top of a high place and looked down. Spread out as far as my eyes could see, many canyons twisted and turned between the walls—like a nest of snakes racing between large and small rocks scattered on a flat land."

White Elk's voice became dreamy. "The sunsets have yellows so brilliant that to look at it hurts the eyes, and reds as shiny as new blood streak the sky. A light purple blends with a pale blue as Father Sun grows tired. When clouds hang above the canyons, blues and purples of many shades paint them. No sunset is like any other sunset." His eyes dropped to hers and his brows wrinkled. "Why do you look as if there is something frightening you, Golden Fox? Have my words painted a picture that scares you?"

She licked her lips and opened her mouth several times before she could push the words from behind her teeth. "I... I dreamed of such a place as this, White Elk. Ever since I was but a few summers old, I have had these dreams. They made my heart restless with wanting to travel. And now, I travel toward the lands in my dreams. What does this mean?"

He looped an arm around her shoulders and hugged her close. "I do not know, Golden Fox. In the sunrises ahead, I will walk beside you as you find what this means."

With her head lying on his muscled chest, Golden Fox's heart beat faster, but not from fear. She had never felt this way about any of the boys she grew up around, or any she had met when the Sun People would visit their relations in other bands.

Sky Bird cleared her throat as she approached from behind the pair.

Golden Fox's face burned as she moved away from White Elk.

Her mother came and stood next to her. "White Elk, when Father said we would go toward the great blue-purple mountains, I had some worry. I had heard that much snow fell there in the cold season, enough that a grown man could lose his way in it. Do the canyons where Dances In Storms' people live have such snows?"

With a frown, White Elk shook his head. "There is snow in the cold season, but it is not so bad."

Sky Bird nodded and humor danced in her eyes. "It is good that White Elk was only telling you, Golden Fox, about this new land where we will live." She headed toward camp, calling back over her shoulder. "It is time to eat before Father Sun hides behind the edge of the land."

Heat reddened White Elk's cheeks.

Golden Fox felt her own face burn hotter. "We had better hurry. Grandfather does not like to be kept waiting."

* * *

Two sunrises had passed since White Elk spoke of the canyons. Although he continued to walk beside Golden Fox as they traveled, her mother kept her busy with small tasks whenever they stopped for the dark time. There had been no more time to speak with him alone.

Father Sun had barely climbed from behind the land's edge as the people prepared to travel again. Golden Fox went to the herd to get her mustang. When Blue Spirit Dog walked with her, she stopped and stared at the animal. "You do not need to go with me, Blue Spirit Dog. I know my way to the herd."

Blue Spirit Dog nudged her hand and whined low in her throat, a sad sound.

With a shake of her head, Golden Fox shrugged and continued to the herd. Her old female that she never rode, but still cared for, had lain down in the midst of the mustangs. Stomach knotted all of a sudden, she made her way to the animal, knelt beside her, and stroked her muzzle. "It is time to walk again, my old friend."

The female grunted and tried to stand, but soon gave up and settled more comfortably on the short grass. Tears filled Golden Fox's eyes as she pulled a handful of grass and offered it, and the mustang turned her head away. She settled cross-legged beside the animal.

Blue Spirit Dog licked the mustang's muzzle and gave her a gentle nudge before lying next to the old animal.

As others came and called their mustangs away, several of the animals walked over and breathed into the old one's nostrils. Golden Fox kept singing as the mustangs said goodbye to one of their own. The shuffle of many feet on the dry grasses and the laughter of children told her when the people started away from the camp. She did not stop singing as she stroked the old female.

With a sigh, the mustang laid her head on Golden Fox's lap and stared up with one dark eye. Behind them, quiet voices blended with Golden Fox's song. At last, the old female closed her eye and breathed no more. Gently, she laid the mustang's head on the ground, kissed her face, and stood. "Rest well, my friend." Tears streamed from her eyes as she turned.

White Elk put an arm around her shoulder and led her away. Dances In Storms, Sky Bird, and Eagle Thunder followed silently behind the pair. Their mustangs followed along. When they had gone a short distance, Dances In Storms, Sky Bird, and Eagle Thunder jumped on their animals.

Golden Fox stepped toward her mother to ride behind her.

With a light hand on her shoulder, White Elk pulled her to a stop and handed her the nose rope of a tan and black female. "She has not told me her name, yet. She is young and untaught. I have had no time to teach her to listen without a nose rope. Though the nose rope does not harm her, she fights against it. I do not blame her, for there are many scars around her mouth where the iron piece tore her flesh."

"I cannot take this mustang." Golden Fox thrust the rope toward him.

Head tilted to one side, White Elk refused the rope. "There is no meanness in her, only a need for kindness and someone to talk to her. If you do not want to do this, I understand. It is hard to go from such a smart and kind animal as your old mustang to one who knows nothing. If this is how you feel, choose another of my mustangs. Only Runner cannot be chosen."

Head shaking strongly, Golden Fox tried to give him the rope, again. "A mustang is an important gift, not one that a man should lightly give to a woman without much talk between them."

Bright red spots appeared on his cheeks as he scuffed a toe against the grass. "What if we needed to get away in a hurry? A mustang carrying two women could not run fast."

Black stripes circled the animal's legs all the way up to her knees. Tan and black hairs flowed down the mustang's neck and tail. "She is beautiful and her eye is kind, but...." Golden Fox's voice drifted away.

Face set in stern lines, White Elk drew himself up tall. "I said I would not allow harm to come to you. I know this is a gift a man gives to his woman, and that we have not yet spoken of such things, but it does not matter. I said I would keep you safe, and a man keeps his word. I cannot do this if you ride a mustang that is too slow."

He reached out and laid his hand upon her arm. His eyes studied her face. "I have long dreamed of you, Sweet One. I am willing to wait until the time is right to talk of many things, but I tell you this: if you do not ever dream of me as I have dreamed of you, I will accept that. This gift does not tie you to me. It is only the gift of a man who would be a friend to you." He spun on his heel, walked over to his animal, and leapt up.

Sky Bird tapped her heels against her mustang's sides and the animal started away at a slow walk. "Daughter, you had best get on your mustang. The others wait for us."

***

Sister Wind blew a cooling breeze, causing the leaves on the trees by the river to shush together. Hunters from both bands readied nets to catch the black-speckled fish with the shiny purple and blue-green stripes running down their sides, which leapt out of the water and splashed back down.

After Father Sun slept for the night, White Elk sat beside Sky Bird's fire circle with Golden Fox. Eagle Thunder and Sky Bird had gone to visit some others in camp. Though alone at the fire, many eyes from the people flicked toward the young pair, reminding them to conduct themselves properly.

Blazing Fire swung by their fire circle and squatted for a short span, then headed out to guard the camp with the other warriors.

White Elk's eyes followed her as she faded into the darkness. "Among the People I come from, few women learn the ways of fighting, yet Blazing Fire trains several young girls, as well as the young boys, in the ways of war. Even you spar with her. It is the same with the Sister Wolf Band. If a young girl wishes to learn the ways of fighting, she is taught along with the boys."

Golden Fire stared up at the brightest campfires in the sky. "Traders have brought stories of people like yours, who are like this — treat women as if they own them. We find it strange that any Peoples would do this to their mothers, sisters, and aunts."

He broke a twig into small pieces, threw them into the fire, and shrugged. "We believe that women are more important than men. We do not wish to put them in such danger. They carry the children of the People. Without enough women, our people would be no more. Besides, women not only harvest foods from the land, and prepare the hides they use to make our clothes, they also build the places where we live. A woman should not have to be a warrior, too."

Lips pursed in thought, Golden Fox studied White Elk. "What if they choose to be a warrior or a hunter?"

White Elk only shrugged and remained silent.

"Among our Peoples, few choose such a hard life, but we have had women warriors who fight more fiercely than men. Some choose to never take a man, but live with honor in her parents' lodge, hunting for them and doing the work that her man would have done for his woman's parents. Some are even called to become medicine women, great healers. These women do not take a man, but live alone, honored above even a great warrior. All of the People take care of her parents. Such women are fewer even than those who choose a warrior's or a hunter's life."

Golden Fox grasped his arm and pointed upward. "Look! A campfire falls from the sky! Mother says when a campfire falls, it means someone's Spirit has chosen to return to our Mother, to be born as a helpless little one, so they can grow up to help their People. Perhaps, even more than one Spirit will return. No one knows how many share each campfire in the sky."

White Elk took her hand between his. "Sweet One, your eyes sparkle. I wish to always sit next to you at our fire circle."

The breath caught in her chest. She had to look away from him. Gently, she pulled her hand lose.

He asked in a brisk voice, "What have you named your mustang?"

She rubbed her hands up and down her arms to chase the bumps away, and smiled. "Splash. I call her Splash for the tan and black that comes together as fingers woven across her chest."

* * *

The quiet voices of her grandfather and her mother woke Golden Fox before Father Sun had drawn a golden line along the edge of the land.

"She is but a baby! I will not have my daughter--"

The rumble of Grandfather's voice interrupted Sky Bird. "You were only two cycles of seasons older than your daughter when you rode with your three-winters-old daughter in front of you and returned to the Sun People. You rode an old grey mustang, which had many scars from the hairy-faces and could hardly walk so far."

Golden Fox peeked toward Grandfather and Mother. She did not stare at them, but peered a bit to one side, so that the weight of her eyes would not tell them she watched. Never had her mother told her this story.

Arms crossed, Sky Bird grunted. "I could not leave the old female. She had become my friend — the only one I had in that terrible place."

A chuckle spilled from Eagle Thunder. "If our Holy Man had not dreamed of Golden Fox and you, Bear might have liked a taste of a baby girl and her mother."

"Father! I was a grown woman and had a good knife."

"Bear would have laughed at a knife whose blade was no longer than his claw." More chuckles rolled from Grandfather. "His laughter would have caught the attention of Mountain Lion. When Mountain Lion came, she and Bear would have fought over such tender meat. While they fought, Wolf would have come and carried you both to her den to feed her pups."

By this time, both Eagle Thunder and Sky Bird laughed hard.

"Enough, Father!" Sky Bird gasped and wiped at the happy tears in her eyes. "Father Sun will be awake soon and we have much to do. Dances In Storms wishes to give the people a rest this day. We will speak of this another time."

13

Sister Moon hid her face behind a bank of thick clouds, casting the night into such darkness that Dances In Storms would not have been able to see her own hand, if not for the fire she had built. The dancing red, orange, and blue flames threw a happy light on those closest to the fire circle. Her own people mixed with Eagle Thunder's band, blending the two Peoples together into one whole.

Children crowded close to the fire, and she smiled. "Sit back, so you do not wind up with burned noses."

Giggles poured from them, but they obeyed.

Children... for so long I have denied myself any hope to have them. A Holy Woman's life belongs to all of her people. She cannot be so selfish as to take a man. Yet, some Holy Men take women and are surrounded by young ones in their old age. Would a Holy Woman be able to carry a child and still take care of the People? If I had only one child, would I still think in ways that are best for the People and not just for my little one?

With a grim shake of her head, she shoved the thoughts aside.

I must wait for the Spirits to tell me what to do. One dream is not enough to be sure of my path.

With a cough, she cleared her throat. When quiet spread over the people, she began. "My people know some of the stories of Shining Light, one of my long-ago ancestors. The story I share this night is one that I have not yet told to my own people, for each story must be told in its own time."

An expectant hush filled the night. Dances In Storms let it build until the tension thrummed like the soft beat of a drum. "Long, long ago, a band of People lived who called themselves the Fish People. They lived as any other

Peoples did. The men fished, hunted, and sometimes went to war. The women cared for the camp and the family, and carried the stories given to them by their grandmothers.

"In such a time lived a boy called Feather Floating In Water. He had no desire to learn the ways of a hunter or the ways of a warrior. He was different. Even at nine-winters-old, dreams visited the boy during his sleeping time. Not knowing if he would sound crazy, he told no one of these dreams, not even his beloved grandmother. Often, after such a dream, he would go to a mesa—a flat-topped hill with steep sides—and open his Spirit to the Spirit Land. He thought no one knew his secret."

A peace wrapped around her, as it always did when she spoke of Shining Light. "One knew of Feather's dreams—his grandmother, Bright Sun Flower. When he went to his special place, without him knowing, she followed to keep him safe. Many sunrises passed before he spoke to his elder. He told of his visions and dreams, of his fears, and of things that no eight-winters-old boy could understand. He spoke to her of strange monsters with shiny heads, riding strange deer larger than any he had seen." Her eyes roamed over the people. "We now know that what Shining Light dreamed was the coming of the hairy-faces and their mustangs."

She gazed sharply at each person, and even the little ones who fidgeted on their mothers' laps settled. "All of my People have heard these words about Shining Light and his grandmother, Bright Sun Flower. The story I tell this night is one I have told no one. Last night, Shining Light told me that the time had come to tell this story."

Skipping over the faces in front of her, Dances In Storms pulled the memory of her vision close. "When the Fish People had to leave their beautiful land, they did not always walk a smooth path. The stories do not tell how, at first, the People walked a broken path. Disagreements and fear—that they followed a boy who did not know where he led—caused a crack in their path, and it grew. Their path became so broken that it was difficult to walk upon it. People can become sick in Spirit, in mind, and in body when this happens. Jealousy, greed, lust, wanting what another has—these things can cause a path to become broken, or they can create more cracks in a path that is weakened. So it happened with the Peoples who followed Shining Light."

Whispers from the men and the women who sat in the circle drowned out the sound of the crackling fire.

Golden Fox wrapped her arms around herself and leaned against her father.

At last, the whispers died away, and Dances In Storms continued. "Shining Light, as a young Holy Man and the leader of the Peoples, called upon Blue Night Sky, the greatest Holy Woman ever to walk upon our Mother. She sent Shining Light out alone to ask his Spirit Guides for help.

"With no food and only a few sips of water, Shining Light went out with only his wolves, White Paws and Moon Face, following him. On the fourth night, Mouse appeared on Shining Light's shoulder and nibbled the lobe of his ear.

"So, Human, you seek what you cannot see? I see plainly what your eyes do not. Close your eyes. They are useless. No one can truly see with their eyes. What good do they do in the darkness that covers the Spirit? Heed me, Brother. Your eyes will deceive you. See with your mind. Let the knowing inside of you be your guide. Build your nest well, so that all of your people feel safe and warm."

"After Mouse faded, Shining Light felt so alone. He raised his voice and sang to the Spirits, dancing until his legs wobbled and he fell to the ground. It was then that White Bear's rumbling voice vibrated in the darkness.

"Silence, Human. Go within the silence. Become the quiet and allow it to be your mind's guide. Remember the gifts I gave you — the gifts of healing and of patience. I am strength in the times of trouble, hardship, and suffering."

"White Bear stepped backwards into a land covered in snow, and became the snow. Shining Light thought he saw tall trees fade with him.

"Grandfather Wolf then appeared in front of Shining Light."

"Wolf is protector, young Holy Man. But, more important, Wolf makes all who are his a part of his pack, for he knows that one Wolf cannot kill an elk, not even when the snows are too deep for the elk to run fast. It takes the entire pack to bring food to them all, and to protect them all. Remember this, young Holy Man."

"Father Sun pried at Shining Light's eyelids, and he opened them slowly."

"I thirst. Where is my water bladder?"

"The bladder lay in front of him. He picked it up and lifted it to his lips. Sand poured out, instead of water. He dropped the bladder and stared hard at it."

"What is this? Why has the water turned to sand? I cannot drink sand."

"Blue Night Sky sat across a fire circle from Shining Light. All around them stretched a blackness darker than obsidian. He blinked hard.

"Where are we, Great Elder? Why has my water become sand?"

"Ah, young Holy Man, just as your body cannot drink sand, there are other things your body cannot drink and have your Spirit survive. This is the place of Nothing, Shining Light. Here our Spirits are free of all concerns. I have brought you here to re-mind you of a dream — a dream that haunted you as a child. In this dream, light-skinned Peoples crossed a great mass of water — water so big that no one can see across it. You have dreamed many times about these people. See this vision now."

"With those words, Blue Night Sky was gone. Shining Light opened his eyes to see lodges built of dead trees stacked upon each other. Around these lodges, many of the Peoples gathered — some sat upon the muddy ground, and some staggered into the paths of mustangs and were trampled. Still others laughed with a crazy laugh, and then attacked their sisters and brothers. They all carried strange containers. A man sat against the dead trees of the wooden lodge, and a woman in torn and filthy clothes of the People sat next to him. This strange container was pressed to her lips as she swallowed. The man grabbed at it, roaring with anger. 'Give me that bot-tle, Woman!'

"Blue Night Sky again wavered into being next to Shining Light."

"These hairy-faces from across the water will bring much death to our Peoples, as you have seen in your dreams. But of all the deaths they bring, this one will be the worst."

"She nodded toward the woman clinging to the bot-tle."

"The poisoned water the woman drinks will blacken her Spirit. It may become so black that Eagle Woman will not reach a hand to her, when she journeys to be with her relations at the campfires in the sky. Her relations at the campfires in the sky may not allow her a seat at their fire circle. This is the destiny you lead your Peoples away from, Shining Light — this killing of their Spirits. When you tire of the arguments and the petty squabbles of the Peoples, remember this.

"The poisoned water will destroy our People more than the long knives and bark-ing fire sticks that you have seen in your dreams. If the Peoples are to be saved, when this time comes — when the hairy-faces offer them the poisoned water — they must band together and fight this greatest of enemies. Remember this well, Shining Light, and pass this down to the Holy Men and the Holy Women who come after you. Do not let this story die, for the time will come when it must be told. Remember, if the people do not help each other turn away from the poisoned water, all of our Peoples will be destroyed."

Dances in Storms walked around the outside of the circle of people, letting the firelight and darkness flicker across her face. A short distance away, the mustangs nickered softly to each other. At the place where she had begun her walk, she halted. From the night, Moon, her mustang, ambled up and nuzzled her cheek. With one hand, she scratched his neck.

She nodded and continued. "Shining Light led his People to the Land Of Tall Trees—this is another story for another time—where Animal Speaks Woman and he had a daughter, Dove. As Dove grew, dreams came to her of a boy, Singing Stone, who protected mustangs.

"Her father remembered it had been foretold that his time among the Land of Tall Trees would only be for a while. Animal Speaks Woman and Shining Light followed Dove from the forest. They found Singing Stone's people and, after a certain time, Dove mated with him. The blood that flows in my body comes from that mating. Dove is an ancestor of mine. It is through our connection that Shining Light speaks to me. It is from them that my Power as a Holy Woman comes."

She pressed her cheek against Moon's cheek, patted the animal's neck, and then gently pushed it away. "But even Holy Women and Holy Men do not have all of the answers." Across the fire circle, she caught and held Golden Fox's eyes. "At times, what the Spirits tell us we must do is at odds with what our hearts demand. We cannot know where the Spirits lead us, only that they will never lead us on a broken path. No matter how difficult the path, we must walk tall, be strong, and heed the guidance of the Spirits. Never question them, for the Spirits see what our human eyes cannot see."

She pulled her gaze from Golden Fox and waved a hand in dismissal. "My story is finished, for now. I have spoken my words."

* * *

Before the others could climb to their feet, Golden Fox leapt up and dashed from the circle. White Elk followed, and from the corner of her eye, Golden Fox noticed her mother start to get up, but Eagle Thunder placed a firm hand on Sky Bird's arm and she could not rise.

Away from the sight of the others, White Elk grabbed her arm. "Wait, Golden Fox! Speak to me."

With a hard jerk, she pulled free. "It is my life she speaks of, Pale Man!" Heat burned through her words and lashed at him.

Hurt flashed across his face as he dropped his hand. "Your words hurt me, Golden Fox. I do not call you by the color of your hair or the color of your eyes."

113

Shame swamped her, but the hurt inside kept her from apologizing. She whirled away and stomped farther from the camp. Though the night was as dark as being beneath a heavy robe, she had studied the land around the camp before Father Sun ducked behind the horizon. That memory led her to the biggest tree near the camp.

Perhaps, I should be as Blazing Fire, and become the warrior woman she wishes to teach me to become.

"Sweet One, speak to me." White Elk stopped close enough that she could see his pale face.

The rough bark greeted her hands. She leaned against it, glad for something solid to help her shaky legs hold her up.

Why does it hurt so much? From when they first came to our camp, I have seen the looks Dances In Storms gives White Elk. Is he so blind to her beauty that he does not see? It does not matter. I will not share a man! Not even with a Holy Woman. It would be best if White Elk walked away.

She popped her knuckles. "Do not call me Sweet One! You know nothing of me. I... I have drunk the poisoned water and have come close to letting it blacken my Spirit. I walked away only because Shining Light came to me."

Chin squared and tilted up defiantly, she crossed her arms.

I have not known him for long. Why do I feel so strongly, as if my heart is shattering?

"I am to become a warrior woman. I have no time for a man. Dances In Storms has eyes for you, White Elk. Go to her."

Dances In Storms' voice carried from behind White Elk. "The Spirits do not show the whole future, not even to the greatest of the Holy People. They give us different possible paths, and it is up to us to choose which one we take, for each path holds a lesson."

Hands thrown up in frustration, Golden Fox snapped, "How then do we know which path is the right path for us to follow?"

Not answering her question, Dances In Storms walked closer and laid a hand upon Golden Fox's arm. "Young one, you have never been on a Vision Quest. It is time for you to seek the guidance of the Spirits."

"I am to go on a Vision Quest? When?" She stepped away from the tree and from them.

"Now, Golden Fox. You must go this night." Dances In Storms' body said there was no denying her demand.

White Elk removed four strands of sky beads from his neck, then stepped forward and carefully placed them around her neck. The carved beads of many shapes fell to her knees. "Visions are full of knowledge. Listen to Dances In Storms."

He lifted his hand as if he might caress her cheek, but Dances In Storms commanded, "Leave us, White Elk."

He left without another word.

"It is so dark." Golden Fox stared at the spot where the night had swallowed White Elk. "How will he find his way?"

A snort of laughter recalled her to Dances In Storms' presence. "Do you think that you are the only one who can remember the way to camp? White Elk is no boy, Golden Fox. One of his gifts is to see as a night bird in the darkness." With a stiff finger, she pointed to the ground at the base of the tree. "Sit, girl. We will wait here."

"I... I must go and tell my... my mother that I am to go on a Vision Quest."

"Sit! Your grandfather has already told her."

Golden Fox folded herself to the ground. "How does he know?"

"Still your tongue, child. It makes you deaf."

Bristling, Golden Fox propped her hands on her hips, though she felt a bit ridiculous doing it while seated. "I am not a child! I am a woman."

"If you are a woman, then act as one. Your grandfather comes. He brings your robe and a water bladder." Dances In Storms pushed to her feet and brushed the loose dirt and grass from the back of her dress. "Your grandfather will walk with you and explain things as best he can. When you return, we will have much to speak about." On quiet feet, she slipped away.

As her grandfather approached, Sister Moon slipped free of the clouds, but with only half her face showing, only a dim silvery light dripped to the ground. Yet, it would be enough to keep them from stumbling over tree roots and large rocks.

Eagle Thunder waved his hand. "Come, Granddaughter, we have a ways to walk." His feet crunched on last season's grass mixed with the new grass as he strode ahead of her.

She hurried to catch up. "Grandfather, where do we go?" She had to trot to keep up. "How can I go on a Vision Quest when I have not gone to a sweat lodge and have not smoked the Pipe?"

"When you find your place to speak with the Spirits, we will smoke the Pipe that Dances In Storms prayed over."

She planted her feet and her hands fisted on her hips. "How is this, Grandfather, that she has prayed over a Pipe for me? And how is it that you appeared to know what you must bring when you found us in the dark?"

Eagle Thunder swirled around and stomped back to where she stood. "Golden Fox, have you forgotten the manners your mother taught you?"

"No, Grandfather, I have not. I am too angry that others know more of my life than I do to pay heed to my manners."

Breath blew from between Eagle Thunder's lips. "Granddaughter, I am sorry that we must do this in a way that feels so rushed and confusing, but even a Holy Woman cannot question the Spirits."

Hands dropped from her hips, Golden Fox spread her arms wide, then let them slap down to her sides. "How long have you known about this, Grandfather? Who else knows?"

Face tilted toward the sky, Eagle Thunder did not speak for several breaths. "When Dances In Storms came to walk with me the first sunrise after her People arrived at camp, she told me that soon you would have to go on your Vision Quest, but she waited for the Spirits to tell her when. As the sunrises passed, I thought we would have time to arrive at her People's camp. I hoped this was so. She came to me this past sunrise and told me that the time had come. She instructed me on what to gather before she began the storytelling. As soon as the story was finished, I hurried to pick up the supplies I had lying in the dark outside of the campfire. It was not difficult to follow you and White Elk." A chuckle spilled from his mouth. "Your feet sounded as a great thundering of humpbacks."

He moved closer and laid a hand on her shoulder. "Dances In Storms cares about you. Though this Vision Quest seems hurried, she would not have you do this now without a good reason."

A gentle tug from her grandfather got her feet to move. Golden Fox's stomach growled. "It is good that I ate no food this day."

"The Spirits knew what they would ask of you."

Scuffing her feet along the grass, she chewed her lower lip. The rapid beat of her heart pounded in her ears. "Grandfather, I fear I will do something wrong. How will I know what I am to do? How will I know I have reached the special place where I am to wait for the Spirits?"

"Listen well." His long strides shortened, so she did not have to trot to keep up. "The Spirits will guide you to your place. When you get there, build a circle of stones large enough to sit inside. No matter what you see, no matter what you hear, do not leave the circle of stones. When fear rises up and chokes you, sing louder. When you tire and feel as if your eyelids are boulders crashing down a steep hillside, dance and stomp your feet harder."

Eyes wide, she felt moisture gather at the corners. "Where will you be, Grandfather?"

"Do not fear, Golden Fox. Though I will not interfere, I will watch over you."

She nodded, yet when a night bird called nearby, she jumped. He wrapped his arm around her shoulders, and she nestled against his side as they moved through the night. Not many steps later, she walked from beneath his arm and toward a group of four trees. An animal trail leading sharply up to the top of a mesa glowed silver in Sister Moon's light. When she got to the trees, she stopped. Fear gripped her and she shuddered.

"You have found the place that calls to you, Golden Fox." He walked over and handed her the light robe, and the water bladder made of rabbit skin.

With trembling hands, she gripped the robe and water bladder against her chest and stared up the faint path. Sister Wind prodded her back.

When she continued to hesitate, her grandfather spoke. "Your answers lie up there, Golden Fox. Power—to become who you are meant to be—is yours to find."

Reluctantly, she shuffled up the trail.

***

Rocks slipped beneath her feet as she neared the top. Behind her, Grandfather's breath came in short pants. Scrub brush dotted the flat top. A sharp spire of reddish rock thrust up through the hard dirt—a natural shelter from Wind's strong voice. Without being told, she began picking up stones that called to her, and laid them in a circle. Five of the stones bore shells within.

Circle completed, she laid her robe in the center, settled onto it, and stared out over the tree- and grass-covered land that rolled out toward the purple mountains hidden by the night.

"You were right, Grandfather. The stones did call to me—maybe not in words, but I felt each one in here." She tapped her chest. "The ones with the tiny shells whispered that once there was much water over this land." She ran her fingertips lightly across the ridges of the ancient shells.

"Stones are ancient beyond all memory. They carry many stories within." Eagle Thunder spoke his intentions to the stones before he stepped inside the circle. From the leather carry-all he carried slung across his shoulder, he removed a bowl and a bundle of Sacred Sage. "Face where Father Sun will wake."

The sweet smoke of the Sage wafted over Golden Fox as her grandfather lit the bundle, and she stood to receive the cleansing smoke.

With an Eagle tail feather, he brushed smoke over himself, and then over Golden Fox—over their heads, down the front and the back of their bodies, and even along the bottoms of their bare feet. Afterwards, they smoked the Pipe together.

When he took the Pipe apart, he carefully wrapped the two parts, and drew an obsidian knife no larger than her small finger. "The only thing we truly own is ourselves. To show the Spirits honor, it is our way to offer small pieces of our flesh. The pain opens us to the Spirits. I want you to start singing as I do some small pricks on your arms. The song will come to you as soon as you open your mind. It will guide you away from the cutting and lead you to the Spirit Land."

Holding her arms out, she stared up. The clouds had floated away and the campfires in the sky shone brightly. She began to hum, and the humming became a song. With this song, her body vibrated, and she raised her head and closed her eyes.

"Remember to stay in prayer when I leave," Grandfather said. "Ask the Spirits to come near, to speak of what you need to know. You will see many things—humans, animals, and things only you will understand, and some things you will not understand. Perhaps you will see when the waters flowed through here." As he spoke, he pricked her skin.

Her song reached a higher pitch, but she held still.

Soft words rumbled from Eagle Thunder. "This is the Circle of Life, of all there is and will ever be. We are born, and live our lives, as part of the never-ending Circle, just as every living being. We all share an equal place within the Circle. No one is better than anyone else. We are all in this life together—humans, trees, and even the smallest spiders. The seeds of the plants are as our unborn. We all have a right to live.

"When new life is born within the Circle, we have a chance to change what is out of balance, what was bad before, what was not for the good of all. We become teachers to those whose path is filled with broken, sharp stones, to help these people step over the sharpness and place their feet where the path is softer. Each Vision Quest is like that—a new beginning—not only for you, but for all living."

Her sight glazed over as she went inside herself, but some part of her continued to listen.

"Long ago, a wise person noticed that everything tried to be a Circle—trees, stones, plants, even our bodies. Our Mother is round, as is Father Sun and Sister Moon. The campfires in the sky are made in circles, just as we build campfires here. That way, no one person can say they alone lead. No one can sit at the head of a circle." He continued to cut small pieces from her skin as he talked. "This is your offering to the Great Mystery. Remember to sing for the animals and the plants, too. Thank them for everything they have given you."

She did not flinch as the knife pierced deeper into her skin than before. Small streams of blood ran down from her raised arms.

"I tell you only about a small part of the Circle. You will learn much more on your journey that is life. Breathe, my dear granddaughter, and take all there is into your body. Make it yours, as everything makes you theirs."

14

Golden Fox welcomed Father Sun with her arms raised, singing. As spears of golden light spread across the horizon, she thanked Great Mystery for this chance to become more. Her voice became hoarse as she sang songs of thanks to the animals and the plants that sacrificed their lives so that the Peoples could live. She sang praises to the stones who held ancient secrets, and to Sister Wind who nudged and whispered to guide a person. She danced with her head thrown back, as she begged the Spirits to pity her and show her the right path to follow.

As Father Sun climbed across the bright blue sky, she danced until her legs weakened, shook, and folded from beneath her. Fallen to the ground, she continued to sing, sweat running into her eyes as the day became heated.

At last, Father Sun lowered and orange-pink bands glowed, then faded until they blended into the soft grey of coming night. Soon, night swallowed even that meager bit of light. Sister Moon had hidden more of her face, but the campfires in the sky grew brighter.

Slumped on the ground, Golden Fox licked her dry lips. "I thirst."

A tiny mouse stood in front of her, squeaked, and jumped away as she reached for the water bladder. One swallow flowed down her parched throat as the rest of the water poured down her dress.

"Mouse! You chewed the bottom of my water bladder. Why would you do this?" She blinked and Mouse was no longer there.

Head swiveling from side to side, she searched the darkness. "Grandfather, are you there?" Heart pounding in panic, she shivered.

A gold-red fox with a huge belly popped up next to her. The animal barked once and waddled as she tried to run away. Between one heartbeat and another, Fox was gone.

She gathered her robe tightly around her, and looked up. Sister Moon played hide-and-seek, peeking out with one eye from behind the clouds scattered across the not-so-long-ago-clear sky. A mustang cloud galloped past Moon.

Wolf howled. Another answered, and then another. The howls sounded as if they rose from the throats of young wolves barely out of the den.

Head tossed back, she howled with them, pushed herself up from the ground, and danced on weak legs.

Sister Wind caressed her face as the campfires in the sky changed from white to blues and yellows. Her grandmother whispered to her; though she did not understand the words, courage grew stronger within her. She raised her arms high above her head and stomped the ground hard. No longer did her legs shake.

A young Eagle flew low and flapped wings in her face. She had yet to grow the pure white tail feathers like her parents. A white- and brown-spotted tail feather floated softly to the ground before Eagle faded into the night.

Sweat dampened the hair on her neck and ran down her cheeks. Her legs weakened once more, and she shuffled her feet through the dirt. "How can it be so warm when the nights are still cool? It is dark, is it not? I see campfires in the sky. But, I see Father Sun as well." Her voice sounded raspy. "How long have I been here?"

All she could do was whisper, her tongue so dry it could not moisten her cracked lips. Still she sang, and closed her eyes.

Did Father Sun go to sleep? She peeked. *No!* His brightness made her eyes squint. Exhausted, she sat down with her head lowered.

Why do I see both Father Sun and the campfires? Mouse chewed my bladder! Have to keep singing... am so thirsty and cold. Why does my face drip from the heat? I weaken! I am strong! I will do this.

She tried to stand, but her body would not respond.

"I can do this."

With weak arms, she pushed to her knees, then upward to stand. Her whole body shook. "I... will... do... this!"

Why do I hear mustangs?

She jerked her head as Eagle screamed and bore down on her.

"Eagle, do you wish your feather back?" A shaky hand held the feather high as it split into two tail feathers, each carrying the same color and splashes as the other.

A claw reached for her raised hand, but the claw turned into a human hand. It grasped hers, and then faded.

Fox barked again.

Blue fog surrounded her. The feathers glowed with an intense blue. On one tail feather, a large spider dropped from her sticky strand, ran across the ground, and crawled into a crack in a stone. Red oozed from the stone crack.

A bottle shattered, and red liquid splashed her face. It ran down her throat and burned all the way to her belly. She spat. The feathers in her hand faded, and her hands became bones. A scream ripped from her as the burning raced back up her throat, flew from her mouth, and set her hands on fire.

She jerked up and tried to stand, but her flesh burned away. She tried, but could not stand on her feet, which had also turned to bones.

Her skull dropped into her skeletal hands.

No flesh! She screamed in voiceless desperation.

"Fox Who Is Golden."

She tried to speak, but had no voice. No mouth to open. No eyes to see with. She had turned to a pile of grey dust.

"I am here, child who is a woman."

A warm hand picked up the grey dust. Her body grew a skeleton, and skin, and reformed.

She fell to the ground and curled inside her robe. Eyes squeezed shut, she gasped. "I see you with my eyes closed. Who are you? Why are you here? Do you know me? What—"

She opened her eyes. "How? I had turned into dust! I was no more."

"So many words.... Heh! Just as I once was."

"Who once was you? I... I mean... who once you?" She shook her head. "I mean to say—"

"Slow down your mouth. It cannot keep up with your mind." He grinned and shook his head. *"I am Shining Light. Do you not remember me?"*

A wolf appeared on either side of him, and a tiny mouse sat on his shoulder. His long black hair sparkled with blue specks. With shell beads braided into both sides of his loose hair, his hair and beads touched the ground as he sat cross-legged. His tunic and leggings shone so white that she had to shield her eyes for a brief span. Staring from a round, kind face, his dark eyes brightened with blue circling them. When he tipped his head higher, his square chin showed, the same one she had noticed on Dances In Storms.

An intense glittering blue moved in and surrounded him, the mouse, and the wolves.

The color drifted and enveloped her. It swirled around and through her. She reached for it, but when she did, it turned into blue sand and fell through her fingers.

"What is this... this blue?" Her words climbed from her throat on tiny, sharp feet.

When Shining Light smiled, the blue color became even brighter. *"Child, it is the color of our Spirits. You see the red mixed in next to the Wolves? It is the color of their Spirits. See the bit of yellow around Mouse? All of our Spirits make the colors of the rainbow — even more colors than Humans can see."*

Golden Fox gazed around. "Where are we?"

"I will let you explore that for yourself, but know you are in the Spirit Land. Fear nothing." He faded, and with him the wolves and the mouse.

Strength returned to her legs. She stood and walked around the circle, step by step. "So many colors...."

Hands of many browns, shades of white, blacks, and tans reached out, touched her, and faded into the rainbow. As she continued to walk her circle, human faces appeared and disappeared — so many faces with colors she had never seen!

People she did not know appeared, dressed in long furs. Hairy-faces and their wooden lodges appeared. People laughed as they raised bottles to their mouths. Once again, her throat burned and her hands flamed. Laughter vibrated, became loud, and hurt her ears. She covered them. The heat in her hands cooled. The laughter faded away, as did the people.

She stilled herself.

Spider crawled out of the crack in the stone, and wove a web before her. *"Fear nothing."*

She reached out and touched the web, pressed on it, but the web would not give.

"There is much strength when all is woven together. Everything living is a strand in the web of life. If even one strand is broken, the web becomes weaker."

She spun around as Elk bellowed. He walked up to her and bowed. A baby gold-red Fox sat on Elk's back. *"Stamina and strength is one strand. You strength lies within as well as without. Find it. When you would give up, reach deep inside and keep going. Use your strength to carry others."*

From above, birds called to one another as they faded into clouds of many colors. Elk turned white and became part of the rainbow cloud.

In front of Golden Fox sat a baby Fox. *"To hide in plain sight is your gift."*

Fox became a black Wolf, who sat and reached out a paw, which she accepted. *"Remember, young Human, a pack can overcome what one alone cannot. When you are pack, you are never alone, Human Sister."*

***

When Golden Fox returned to the mesa, Father Sun had just begun to climb above the horizon. She raised her face and sang a song of thanks. Throat parched, she glanced around her circle of stones. The water bladder lay close to her feet. She bent and picked it up, joy lighting her face. "It is full!"

Quickly untying the top, she drank until she could drink no more, and then laughed as she poured the rest of the water down her dress.

15

Golden Fox smiled up at Father Sun, spread her arms, and bathed in his warmth for a short span before heading down the steep path. Sister Wind brushed her hair away from her face. When she reached the bottom of the mesa, she realized that she carried her body straighter, and her steps grew more confident as she followed the trail. A wave of happiness washed over her.

It felt as if she had walked away from the life of a giggly, young girl, to take her place fully as a woman among her people. When she reached the foot of the mesa, Blue Spirit Dog wiggled her way. She knelt, ran her hands through Dog's thick fur, and hugged her around the neck. "You watched over me, eh?"

A deerskin lay on the ground. Grandfather had left her clothes for the sweat lodge. She shed her dress and her footwear, wrapped herself in the skin, and gathered her belongings. The sharp smell of burning wood filled the air. With a deep inhale, she pulled in the scent of pine.

"How did they know when I would come?" She grinned so wide her cheeks hurt. "Grandfather was always near, as he said he would be. I was never alone."

Arms spread, she twirled around. "I feel stronger. For the first time, I understand about Power. Even the flowers, and the trees, and the grass are brighter." Joy welled up in her and spilled from her mouth in a laugh.

Blue Spirit Dog trotted ahead of her, past a grove of trees and toward a small sweat lodge.

At the flap, White Elk waited. A wide grin stretched his lips as his eyes twinkled with happiness for her. When Golden Fox drew near, he lit a bundle of Sage and handed it to Dances In Storms, who waited across from him.

The Holy Woman waved the smoke over her body and even on the bottoms of her bare feet. She handed the Sage bundle back to him, then knelt and crawled through the open flap as she asked all her relations and all living to join her during this Sacred Time.

Golden Fox took the Sage from White Elk. In a soft murmur, she asked all her relations and all living to join her during this Sacred Time, while she wafted the smoke over herself. Done, she handed the bundle to White Elk, stopped, and entered the sweat lodge.

Blue Spirit Dog had taken up a position in front of and to one side of the flap. White Elk closed it from the outside.

The glowing stones in the fire circle in the center of the lodge gave off a muted red light. Golden Fox stopped just inside the flap and looked toward Dances In Storms.

The Holy Woman waved a hand toward the flap. "Always, we entered the sweat lodge from the place of beginning, where Father Sun wakes. The yellow sun painted on the flap honors Father Sun, who is the beginning of each day. I sit here in the direction of purity, and of the cold season of rest, because a Holy Person must purify herself before she can help those who seek her. Because in the sweat lodge, a person must give up her ties to the outside and let her Spirit rest, for she has come inside the womb of the Mother, and will leave a new person.

"In that direction...." She waved toward the place where Father Sun went to rest. "In that direction, we find the end of day as well as the end of life. Those who seek the sweat to bring an end to something — perhaps, to end the life they now lead — sit there, as do those who have traveled the path of their life and prepare to journey to the campfires in the sky."

Dances In Storms lit the Pipe of Truth. "You, Golden Fox, are young. You have gone on your Vision Quest and returned. You sit in the direction where Father Sun rises and blesses our Peoples with a new day, for you have come to the sweat lodge as a new person."

As Golden Fox settled with her back to the flap, Dances In Storms smoked the Pipe of Truth, and then passed it to her. This was only the second time she had smoked the pipe. Her hands trembled as she took it and lifted the stem to her lips. Once she pulled in the smoke and released it, every word she spoke inside the sweat lodge would find its way to the Great Mystery on the grey breath of the smoke.

Though being dishonest was not the way of her people, still she would have to judge each word to be certain it held not the slightest taint of dishonesty. Every word must come from her heart, without censor, or she must not speak it at all. Dishonesty after smoking the pipe was always punished by the Spirits. Such punishment came in many ways, and the person would never know when to expect it, only that it would come.

She sucked deep on the pipe and held the smoke inside her, so that it might twine with her Spirit and help her speak only the truth. Slowly, it eased out of her mouth. Only then did she realize that in the shadows at the back of the lodge, Long Sun stroked a soft beat on the drum. A song rose in her chest and burst from her. Dances In Storms' voice joined with hers.

When the pipe had been smoked and their songs had been sung, silence fell between the women.

Long Sun quietly made his way over to the fire and poured water on the hot embers. The lodge filled with steam, and he returned to his spot away from the fire.

Dances In Storms sprinkled Sage on the hot, moist stones, and waved the sweet-smelling smoke over herself. She nodded to Golden Fox to do the same.

"Tell me of your quest, Golden Fox." The Holy Woman folded her hands on her crossed legs.

For many heartbeats, Golden Fox talked of Shining Light, the colors she saw in the Spirit Land, the songs she heard, and of how she felt. Finally, she related the story of the water bladder.

Dances In Storms laughed. "I have yet to hear of a full water bladder until after a Vision Quest. Somehow, it is always either dry or has sand in it. As for the colors..." She poured more water on the hot embers. "The Spirit colors show you are never alone. All living is with you in this land and the Spirit Land."

Tossing another handful of Sage on the stones, she cocked her head. "Tell me what Spirit Guides came to you, and what you learned."

Golden Fox nodded. "Spider came and wove her web. She reminded me that all living things are part of the web of life. When a strand is broken, all of the web is weakened."

"What does that mean to *you*, Golden Fox?"

She considered her words carefully before answering. "We are stronger together, and no one is more important than any other. We all have an important place in the Circle of Life."

Lips pursed, Dances In Storms nodded. "What else did you learn?"

"Elk came, carrying a baby Fox on his back. He said that stamina and strength lie inside, and that I must use my strength to carry others. I am not sure how I am to do that." She scrunched her brows together.

"In time, that will be made clear, if you keep your mind open."

"Holy Woman, Fox said it is my gift to hide in plain sight. How am I to use such a gift?"

A chuckle spilled from the older woman. "Ahh, I am certain you have already used that gift, and will learn more about it as you journey on the Mother."

"Dances In Storms, Fox came to me and changed into Wolf." The heat of the embers brought sweat out on her forehead. She brushed it away with the back of her hand and squinted through the dim light. "Fox and Wolf are very different, and many times Wolf will chase Fox away, because they are both hunters and protective of the food they need for their young. How can it be, then, that one changed into the other?"

"All life is interwoven, Golden Fox. Fox and Wolf are not so very different. When you can find the sameness instead of the differentness, you will understand the most important lesson of all. Did Wolf have a message for you, too?"

With a nod, she gazed into the darkness at the back of the lodge, letting her mind return to the time Wolf came to her. "Wolf reminded me that when we belong to a pack, we are stronger, and we are never alone. But, what does it mean that I felt Wolf's paw on my hand? His paw was *real*, as real as my own skin."

Head tilted, Dances In Storms stared deep into Golden Fox's eyes. "Perhaps, you will have a wolf companion. That Shining Light comes to you makes me believe this might be so." A smile reached from her lips to her eyes. "We have waited a long, long time for Wolf to join our people once again. It may be that you will bring Wolf back to us."

Dances In Storms sat up tall, her body speaking of the importance of what she would say. "There is one more thing I must ask, since during your Vision Quest, Elk turned white."

"I believe I know what you wish to speak of with me, Holy Woman." Golden Fox flicked a look Long Sun's way.

Dances In Storms glanced between her helper and Golden Fox. "Do you wish Long Sun to leave?"

She dipped her head, but did not speak.

With a wave of her hand, Dances In Storms motioned toward the flap, and Long Sun silently left. Once the flap closed, she looked at Golden Fox. "What is this you wish to say that you could not say in front of my helper?"

Chewing on her lower lip, Golden Fox wrung her hands together. "When Elk turned white...." Her eyes darted away from the Holy Woman's.

I must speak the truth inside of me, for I have smoked the pipe, yet I am not sure I wish to speak of this with Dances In Storms.

After many long breaths of silence, Golden Fox gathered her courage.

The Holy Woman would not ask if it was not important. I must answer as truthfully as my heart will allow.

"When Elk turned white, I... I wondered if this meant I should look with favor on White Elk."

Hands clasped in her lap, the Holy Woman leaned forward. "How do you feel about White Elk?"

"He has been good to me."

"Is that all that you feel?"

Squirming, she refused to look at the Holy Woman. "I... it is like... like I can feel him—feel his honor and his respect. I could never do that before. Why can I feel this now?"

"Spider came to you. Think about how Spider must live her life—she must be constantly aware of everything around her, for many things see Spider as food. She must know whenever something touches her web, whether they come as food for her or as danger to her and to her web. She gave such a gift to you—to be much more aware of the lives around you."

"Does being so aware of... of White Elk mean we are to be together?" Shadows danced along the walls of the sweat lodge, dipping and swaying in harmony. How she longed for such harmony in her life.

"What do you think it means, Golden Fox?"

Hands spread, she cried out in frustration. "I do not know, Holy Woman. He... he makes me feel safe, and I do... could maybe... love him, but.... There is something I do not know. I feel it when I am around him." She raised her head and an ache settled in her chest. "Or, perhaps, I know, but am not willing to see what it is."

The Holy Woman sat very still, eyes locked with Golden Fox's for several long breaths. Finally, she dropped her eyes, reached out, and tossed more Sage on the embers. Smoke rose between them, obscuring Dances In Storms. "White Elk will be a part of your future, Golden Fox. Do you choose to let this happen?"

"Do I have a choice, Holy Woman?"

The Holy Woman's gaze met and held Golden Fox's as she softly answered. "There is always a choice. Even in those bands that do not allow a woman to choose her mate, there is still a choice for her to make."

Golden Fox tipped her head to one side and studied the older woman. "How is it with your people? Do they allow men to take more than one woman?"

Her eyes widened and, for a short span, she played with her fingernails. "I will tell you a story that I do not often share." Her shoulders pulled back and her chin lifted. "My mother came from a band where a young woman has no choice in who will be her mate, or in how many her man may choose. In my father's travels, he came through the camp where my mother lived with her father. At that time, my father had three extra mustangs with him.

"He only meant to sleep at their camp, and then move on, but my mother's father needed the mustangs, and offered to trade my mother and her sister for the animals. The next day, my father left the camp with my mother, her sister, one mustang, and the three dogs gifted to them by the people to carry my mother's and sister's belongings, and the gifts from their band. If my father had refused my mother *and* her sister, it would have shamed her sister. My mother's sister had already seen fifteen winters, and for a man to not look her way would have been bad. She would have been scorned. When they arrived to my father's band, he set the sister free to choose her own man. At first, she thought she had been thrown away, and she readied to leave, until my mother explained. She stayed in the same lodge, but three sunrises before, she had four suitors to choose from."

Dances In Storms stared into the fire pit of glowing stones, and laughed. "My mother had a choice, even when she was not allowed to choose. You see... my father set them both free. She refused to leave him. My mother and my father love each other as deep as I hear the salty waters are." She lifted her gaze. "Do you understand what I mean?"

Eyes darting away, Golden Fox replied in a voice that reflected the feelings battling within her. Head lowered, she pulled the purifying steam and smoke into her face, sat back, and flipped the hair away from her eyes. "I... I am not sure I could make such a choice as your mother made, not really knowing him as she should have."

"Love comes sometimes at first glance—"

"I... I know you hold a secret, Holy Woman, one you try to keep inside, but I can feel the edges of it like a sharp knife. I... I feel that perhaps White Elk is already spoken for. If he is, I am young, and Blazing Fire tells me I would make a good warrior woman. Maybe it is time for you to share your secret with me, Holy Woman." She locked her eyes on Dances In Storms and leaned forward, as if to dig until she found the secret hiding behind the other woman's eyes.

A sharp pain lanced through her head. With her fingertips, she rubbed her forehead.

Dances In Storms' voice lashed out at her. "Do not seek answers you are not meant to know! When your head hurts bad, as it does now, you will know you have invaded a person's mind without permission and without need. You are not to use your gift so that your life might be made smooth, like a stone from the river. Gifts are given to us to use for the good of all."

The older woman reached for the water bladder and sprinkled water over the hot stones, then crumbled three sprigs of Sage on the red embers. "There are things that must happen as they happen, and we are only given the choice of how we will act. Even as a Holy Woman, I must listen to the Spirits, the same as you, Golden Fox. There are futures that I cannot clearly see. I only know this: you will live in the canyons until the leaves are full again, and White Elk will be part of your life. What part, I cannot say."

"Cannot say, or will not say, Holy Woman?"

"Know this: you will live in the canyons until the leaves are full again. White Elk will be at your side when it is time for you to leave. I, too, will be there. More men will follow, if they are needed. What you are to do is save our people whose Souls barely live.

"Your father is not the bad man you think he is. He lives the life taught to him by his own father, and he knows no other way. This I have learned through a vision. He is part of your future. Remember, you are never alone.

"Know White Elk would give his life to save yours. He has a great love for you, unlike any I have seen. I, too, can feel emotions, woman.

"We must speak of the deep meaning of your vision, if you ask. This will be a hard time for you, girl. You must cleanse your body and mind from worry and fear. Many depend on the child within for much—to bring back joy, to not let the adult take complete hold, and to find answers only a child understands. I ask that you let your child go for now. She will always be part of you when you need her.

"Your grandfather, White Elk, Long Sun, and I will be close by. Stay as long as you need." She sprinkled more Sage on the stones, and spoke a silent prayer as she leaned over the stones, and left.

***

The darkness in the lodge left Golden Fox emptying her gut and sweating.

People lay wrapped in their death robes because they were unable to fight the pull.

She pulled up her legs, laid her head in shaky hands, then lay on her side clenching her belly.

Heat! So much heat.

She tried to speak to Dances In Storms, to tell her no more hot stones, no more steam.

Where is Dances In Storms?

She shook in someone's arms while they rocked her. Her body pained and she screamed.

"Too Hot!" Arms tightened around her. "I die!"

"No, woman, you do not die."

"I do! Please save me... me...."

Fox brushed soft, golden fur against tears on her face. *"Come with me. Follow me."*

Golden Fox uncurled from Fox, reached out, and fell silent.

Long, rich, bright yellow and white grasses swayed in the gentle breeze. The grasses rose so tall, they hid Golden Fox and the young foxes who slept curled next to her. Without a thought, she turned sideways, and brushed one of the baby's fur beside her. Twisting back, her eyes opened up to a deep, dark red sky, with a darker, dripping red sun fighting to turn yellow. She bolted upright.

Young foxes protested her movement and tried to pile closer around her. One called out, and the mother pushed the grasses aside. *"You have awakened. Good. Follow me. My young will follow us."*

"Mother Fox, where are we? Why is some of the grass white? And the sky —"

"I cannot tell you why. You chose the colors."

Faded images of humans wandered across the grasses, some in groups, some alone.

BROKEN PATH

"*Do not gawk at the Spirits. They might not like it.*"

"But, I know these people!"

"*I understand. Allow them to come to you, if it is their desire. Come, we will sit on this white sparkling sandstone at the base of the bright, yellow shrubs on the hillside. Beautiful, is it not? While we wait to see if any Spirits come, my young will play, and we will sit quiet and relax in each other's Energy.*"

"What do you mean, I chose the colors? Is this the Spirit Land? Yes, how silly of me.... Why else would Spirits be here? My pain... it is gone, but how? Why did I feel this pain? Why is not Father Sun—"

"'*You have yet to understand quiet, little one.*"

"I am a woman, not a little—"

"*Act as one. Be still and think about why the colors are the way they are. You must feel their pain to know it.*" Fox swished her thick tail and brought it forward to lick it clean.

"Running Girl!" Golden Fox jumped up to hug her, but her hands passed through her friend.

"*Gentle Golden Fox, I feel no pain, nor does my mother. It is my father who wanders. His own mustang kicked him off and stomped him. When he saw us in the Spirit Land, he ran from us into a dark shadow. We could hear many people cry. There must be a way to free them. My grandmother cries out from the shadows!*"

Fox spoke out. "Stay in the pure light, *Running Girl. Never venture into the shadow. Golden Fox will help your father, and more who seek the light.*"

16

The small campfire burned low as Sky Bird shifted on the scratchy grass. Restless, she picked up tiny stones and tossed them into the darker shadows away from the fire. A shiver raced over her.

The night is still cold for it being so warm after sunrise. She rubbed her arms and leaned closer to the fire, but it did little to chase the chill away. *Instead of letting the men take almost all the hides left behind when the others departed, I should have kept more than just the two needed for sleeping.*

She pulled the deerskin hide more tightly around her. Unable to sit still, she got up and paced the length of crushed grass where the people had made camp.

Four sunrises! Daughter, what do you do for such a long time? Dances In Storms should have allowed me to sit close to the sweat lodge. I would not have disturbed Golden Fox.

With a wry twist of her lips, she shook her head at such a thought. She was Golden Fox's mother and, as such, her Energy would have reached out to her daughter. Dances In Storms was right to make her stay at the camp, but it did not make the waiting easier.

Snores drifted from where Stands His Ground lay wrapped in his sleeping robes. With a sigh, she moved away from him.

Why can that not be me? He sleeps the sleep of a person with no worries, as he should. He is a good man.

A part of her wanted to go to him and wake him, so she could lie within his arms. She fought the feeling as she hurried farther from him.

Why do I run from Stands His Ground? He is nothing like Golden Fox's father. I have struggled to feel only as a friend toward him, yet... I cannot forget how he looked many cycles of seasons ago when he rode back into camp after traveling for a long span.

As always happened when she let herself think of Stands His Ground, warmth blossomed in her chest, driving out the chill of so many lonely nights.

He sat at my mother's cooking fire and I could not stop staring at him. I hoped he thought I stared at the sky beads braided into the sides of his hair. When he caught me, I mumbled that I did not know how these beads came to be. He cocked his head and a little smile played around his full lips, as if he knew it was not the sky beads at which I stared. Yet, he pretended to believe my words and told the story of how the sky beads were created.

His voice lives in my mind whenever I think of how he said the pale Sky envied the blue waters and wished to be as beautiful. The wish was granted. Before Sky could get used to the new heaviness of the blue, pieces of Sky fell to the Mother. The hills had not yet hardened when the pieces hit, and so those bits of Sky sank into the land. The dirt hardened around them. Sometimes, if the Mother believes you are worthy, she will push sky beads above the dirt, so they may be found.

Her feet shuffled across the brittle grass as she headed toward a spot beneath a tree whose head soared high above the Mother.

All the time Stands His Ground spoke, my heart pounded so hard I thought everyone would hear! My eyes would not leave his face. Instead of scolding me for having no manners, at the end of his story he held out his hand. In the palm lay sky beads.

Shaking her head at the foolishness of her younger self, she found a place that called to her and gazed toward the sky.

"I have brought these for you, Sky Bird," he said. Wanting to touch him, I stumbled over my father in my haste to reach Stands His Ground, as if I were still a child greedy for a gift. Oh, how the heat burned my cheeks when I fell into his lap! Without a word, he stood and helped me to my feet. His finger under my chin tilted my face up, so I had to look into his dark eyes. Instead of mockery, I saw desire in his eyes. A tingling feeling spread through my body, a feeling I had never felt with Golden Fox's father. Confused, I scrambled away from him, not even taking the beads he offered. With a knowing smile, Mother gave them to me as we prepared our robes for sleeping.

The soft clink of the sky beads around her neck pulled her hand to them. As she rolled the silky beads between her fingers, she wondered what it would feel like to have a man's arms wrapped around her at night. How would it feel to have Stands His Ground's sweet voice speak of love as they lay together?

She had never known any, except the touch of a drunk hairy-face — a man who felt only contempt for her and her daughter, a man who took what he wanted no matter the pain she felt. Her stomach clenched hard at the bitter memories, and she hastily chased them from her mind.

It is best to remain friends. I cannot risk the love we have between us by being so greedy that I demand more. Stands His Ground is young and will one day find a woman to warm his sleeping robes — a woman without bad memories to stand between them.

Gold light spread across the horizon as Father Sun began to rise, and grey-blue clouds turned bright pink. Crickets quieted, and bats called to each other as they flew to seek the cool dark of a cave or a crevice in which to sleep. In the distance, deer moved with their young fawns to the thickets near the water.

Sunrise creatures woke as night creatures sought their dens. A pair of Eagles took flight across the sky that lightened from black to grey to lighter and lighter blue. Two rabbits peered from beneath a shrub heavy with ripening, red berries. Tall grasses rustled with tiny animals as they hunted seeds dropped by the grasses. Birds sang from branches of trees hugging the edge of the nearby stream. Some of the winged ones dove through the air after the tiny, flying ones.

A song filled her heart and she lifted her hands to Father Sun. From somewhere near, the deeper sound of Stands His Ground's singing reached her, wrapped around her. Even as her song raised to the Great Mystery, a thought flitted through her mind.

Do I fill his thoughts as often as he fills mine?

As the last of her song wafted to the Great Mystery, Sky Bird's eyes focused on a shape riding toward her. "Golden Fox!"

When she started to run toward her daughter, a firm hand clasped her shoulder.

She twisted her head and looked into Stands His Ground's face. "She has been gone longer that I thought. I must go greet her."

With a stern look, he shook his head. "Allow your daughter to come to you. She has changed, can you not see? Look how straight she sits on her animal. She is a woman, and deserves to be greeted as one woman by another."

Blue Spirit Dog sped toward Sky Bird, puffs of dust flying up behind her.

The dog jumped into her arms, and Sky Bird fell backward, landing hard on the ground. She hid her face in the dog's thick fur. "I know better, but I am happy to see my daughter."

Though she tried to stand, Dog would not allow it. Her tongue soaked Sky Bird's face. "Dog, *pthh*... allow me to get up to greet my daughter." She shoved Dog to one side and rolled to her feet.

Dog leapt up and down in front of her, tongue darting and licking any part of her within reach.

Sky Bird turned her face as she laughed. "Dog, please! I am happy to see you, too."

Stands His Ground chuckled and pulled the dog away from her. "Never before have I seen a dog so happy to see someone! Heh... her belly is fat. Either you feed her too much or soon she will bring pups to us."

"Smart man," she teased. "I have known for a moon. Four pups, I think. Maybe five."

Splash, Golden Fox's mustang, headed toward Sky Bird. When Golden Fox leapt to the ground, arms wide, Sky Bird ran to greet her daughter.

After they embraced, she pulled back and stared at her daughter's eyes. "What blessings you have been given, Daughter. Some people go on many Vision Quests for such blessings, of which the brightness in your eyes speak. Can you say why you were gone so long?"

Golden Fox squeezed her mother's hand. "Because of the shame I felt, I have never told you that I have tasted the poisoned water, Mother." When Sky Bird's mouth dropped open, Golden Fox hurried on. "In the sweat lodge, I fought the bad Spirits of the poisoned water, and with the help of my Spirit Guides, I won the battle. I know that having tasted the poisoned water, I must be ever on guard against the whispers of the poisoned water Spirits. But, I know now they hold no power over me."

Tears leaked from Sky Bird's eyes as pride filled her chest. "Daughter, you have grown much."

"I have much yet to learn, Mother."

She looped an arm around her daughter's shoulders as they walked toward the cooking fire. "Your words make my heart glad, for if one believes they have learned all they need, they cannot grow." With the shrug of one shoulder, she dismissed the subject. "Many things seen during a Vision Quest may only be shared with a Holy Person, but share with me what you can. I hunger to know this new woman who is my daughter." Her arm tightened in a short hug.

"I have much to share, Mother, but only a little for now. My quest was not for me alone." She leaned her head on Sky Bird's shoulder as they shuffled through the grasses. "I can feel you, Mother. Not just the outside of you, but who *you* are." Head tipped so she could see her mother's face, she said, "You have never been on a Vision Quest."

A quick kiss to Golden Fox's forehead gave Sky Bird a moment to think. "No, I have never been on one. Some people never feel the call. But, tell me what you mean when you say you know who I am."

"I do not hear your words, but I feel your Energy. There are Spirits around me, around us, and I can feel them. They whisper in my mind the secrets in the hearts of others." She caught her lower lip between her teeth.

Sky Bird's heart stuttered as she waited to hear what her daughter said. What secrets might come from the mouth of her child? "Spirits are around all of us. It is the way of life. The Spirit Land is woven into the threads of our Mother, into all things living. They never leave us. There have been times I have felt them, but they have never whispered to me. Can you share the secrets they have told you?"

Golden Fox stopped and whirled to step in front of her, and grasped her hands. "I hear the song of your heart, Mother. It is a beautiful song, but there is much sadness and loneliness in it. In here—" She tapped her chest with one hand. "—the Spirits tell me that this need not be so. There is one who loves you, and whom you love. Do not let fear keep you from love."

Sky Bird pulled away from her daughter. When she turned back, she had hidden her feelings once more. "I see you wear the sky beads White Elk gave you. They look as if they were made for you. When we once more have deer and elk hides to make new clothes, I will search for plants that will make colors that bring out the colors in your beads." Brows lifted, she asked, "Perhaps, a joining dress?"

"Mother, I do not wish to speak of this."

"You have accepted sky beads from this man, and I see how he looks at you. Do you believe me blind? You have walked together on this journey of ours, and I have heard the whispers as you bend your heads close. Am I deaf as well?"

Shame flooded Golden Fox's face, reddening her cheeks and neck. "I... I am sorry I spoke in disrespect, Mother. It is... it is just that my heart runs faster than Swift Arrow when White Elk looks my way, yet my mind tells me not to be a fool. My belly twists in knots whenever I... I see a certain person sit close to White Elk. Perhaps, I should follow the way of Blazing Fire and become a warrior woman."

Sky Bird embraced Golden Fox, pulled her tight, and closed her eyes as she laid her cheek against her daughter's. "I am not one who knows much about love, Daughter, but this I do know—if you do not listen to your heart, you will regret it much as the cycles of seasons pass."

Do I speak to Golden Fox or to myself?

17

By the time Golden Fox reached the cooking fire with Sky Bird, Stands His Ground had already heated up the food left from the previous night. He handed a bowl to Sky Bird and another to her.

Before they finished eating, Dances In Storms, Long Sun, White Elk, and Eagle Thunder arrived. As they ate, Golden Fox helped Sky Bird and Stands His Ground prepare to leave.

Father Sun had nearly reached the highest point of the pale blue sky when Golden Fox mounted Splash and trotted away. White Elk drew up next to her and tried to talk, but she tapped Splash's sides and cantered off. Each time he tried to speak with her, she urged her mustang faster and left him behind with the words on his lips.

Though her heart thundered when he drew near, she did not know if she would ever be able to speak with him. It sounded foolish even in her own mind, yet she could not help the sharp ache that speared her chest each time she wondered if he really belonged with another. Several times, she caught Dances In Storms watching White Elk. The Holy Woman sacrificed much for the People, and if she desired White Elk, it would only be proper for Golden Fox to step away. Unlike some women of the People, she would not be able to share her man with another woman.

Why do I have to care about a man who has caught the eye of a Holy Woman?

She swiped at the moisture at the corner of her eyes.

I will ask Blazing Fire to work with me more. This will sharpen my skills, and maybe help me sleep without dreams.

Leg pressed hard to Splash's one side, she turned the young mustang and galloped to where Blazing Fire rode alone at the back. She swung Splash in beside the warrior woman and announced, "I wish to become as you are, a warrior woman."

If Blazing Fire was surprised, it did not show on her face or in the lines of her body. Almost lazily, she turned her attention to Golden Fox. "I have seen you walking with White Elk."

With a hard flip of her hand, she dismissed Blazing Fire's observation. "There will be time later for walking with men. My Vision Quest has made me aware that much is coming in the future, and I must prepare to meet it. I will need fighting skills to help keep the People safe." She sighed and breathed deeply. "I have not said this to anyone else, but I have had dreams. Bad dreams."

Blazing Fire waited for her to continue, and only the sounds of their mustang's feet upon the hard ground reached her ears. The others had pulled away to where she could not hear their words or the noises of their mustangs. The warrior woman gave her the respect of not prodding, of waiting for Golden Fox to speak as one warrior to another.

Her lips became dry. She reached for her water bladder and sipped. Determination hardened her resolve. Blazing Fire could help her understand her dreams. "I saw many of our Peoples' lying wrapped in their death robes. The skin stretched across their bones so tightly, I could count each bone. Their eyes had fallen into hollows, and their skin sagged from their faces. Bellies were swollen, but not with babies. Hands were puffed and red. The whites of their eyes looked as if they bled, yet these people lived. They fought to get free of the death robes, but each time they crawled away, a dark hand reached out and dragged them back.

"Farther away, near the dark wall of a wooden fort, many of our Peoples screamed and cried because they could not get in. Blood ran from open wounds on the chests of the men and women. When I looked closer, a dark hole appeared where their hearts should have been.

"Fox brushed against me as I stood in the shadows, watching. She turned into a black Wolf. Amber-yellow eyes stared up at me, as if Wolf expected me to help the people. A cold wind blew, and I shook so hard my teeth clashed together.

"Father Sun turned deep red, as the dark blood of a dying wound. The sky became crowded with black-grey clouds piling one on top of the other. Lightning flashed white and pink. Thunder rattled the trees, and lightning split them in half."

Words piled up in her throat and she had to swallow hard to push them down. "I wish to become a warrior woman, so I may free those who want to be freed."

Blazing Fire nodded toward White Elk. "There are many ways to free our Peoples, Golden Fox. Fighting such as I do is only one. If you wish to learn, I will teach you. Do not complain of blue-green bruises on your skin. I do not believe a warrior can be made without pain—pain of the body and heart." She took a deep breath. "Golden Fox, to be a warrior does not mean one cannot love."

* * *

Golden Fox rode with Blazing Fire during the days, and patrolled with her whenever Father Sun slept. They sparred while the others made camp. Her body throbbed and ached after each time, but she refused to complain. Even as tired as the work made her, she often found her eyes seeking out White Elk.

Now, he sometimes sat alone and stole glimpses at her, and at other times Dances In Storms sat next to him.

Whenever this happened, a hand squeezed Golden Fox's heart, and she forced herself to breathe through the pain.

Did I make the right choice?

White Elk would make a fine mate for Dances In Storms. He would understand the needs of a Holy Woman, and be there for her when the work became hard.

As she tried to convince herself of the rightness of her choice, her heart ached, and a hole opened up in her chest that no amount of work with Blazing Fire could fill. It did not help when she noticed how close Stands His Ground sat next to her mother. How could she not notice the way they leaned toward each other and whispered?

Loneliness wrapped around her, and her confused heart tightened.

18

Clouds exposed a yellow moon for a brief span, then swallowed it again. Wolves howled and their echo bounced off tall red-orange stones. The stones jutted from the ground, and disappeared into the expanding dark clouds that ate the campfires in the sky. A woman's laughing scream shattered the tall stones, and they crumbled into dust.

The settling dust choked Eagle Thunder. He rolled over onto his knees, coughed, and stood to brush himself off. He stared at the yellow moon, which glowed as if competing with Father Sun.

"Come, follow me." A woman's hand reached out with orange dust in her palm, grasped his, and pulled him toward the moon. "You must come this way."

He had no choice — her hand held much strength.

Strange sounds erupted from wooden lodges as people held onto bottles and staggered about. A woman yelled, and a hairy-face grabbed her by the arm and forced her inside his wooden lodge.

"Your destiny lies this way, as does the destiny of your pale-skinned granddaughter and half-blood daughter, Eagle Thunder. You will come, if you wish to save them."

* * *

Eagle Thunder yelled and startled himself from his sleep, his face dripping with sweat. "Yellow Moon?" Above his head, the campfires sparkled, and nowhere did a cloud drift past the beautiful white moon.

He stared at the quiet lodges behind him, rolled over, and stood. He used the bottom of his tunic to wipe sweat from his face, and whispered to himself, "I am so happy I slept outside. I wonder if anyone heard me. Need to walk...."

"Yes, you do, and I will walk beside you."

He spun around and faced Dances In Storms. "I woke you."

"No, I watched you dream, and followed you inside it. You were fighting your robe as if it was trying to take your life." She pointed to the crumpled sleeping robe he had tossed to the side. "I slept not far from you."

"How could you come into my dream?"

"Through the Spirit Land." She shook her head. "I am a Holy Woman. We need to speak of your dream and of Yellow Moon."

She motioned him forward with a nod. When he did not move, she walked forward and left him to stand alone.

"Wait." He caught up to her. "Moon is beautiful this night. She makes our shadows long."

"And sometimes she causes restless dreams when she is wide awake and so large." Dances In Storms joined her fingers together behind her back, and stepped lightly with her bare feet. "I have longed to speak with you. You are a good man. You care much for your people. They will follow you and always heed your advice. I believe you and my father will be great friends and depend on each other."

He glanced up at the campfires in the sky. "There is where I get my advice. Sometimes, I think I hear my woman reaching out to give me a push. She tells me to become still and listen to my inside voice. I have been without her too long. As for a man friend, my last was long ago, when my father was still with me."

"Always heed the voice of your woman, and other Spirits who watch over you. As you found out this night, Yellow Moon watches also, but she is trapped in the in-between lands. Perhaps, when she can cross over all the way, she will take her name with her, but for now we can speak her name, as you and I already have."

The bright moon showed lines starting to form on Dances In Storm's face. Her beauty sparkled though her dark eyes, and her high cheekbones rose as she smiled.

"Why do you stare so?"

He turned away. "I did not mean any disrespect, Holy Woman. I could not help but see a woman who is good to look at. You have a beauty, not just your face, but from deep within. You are one called an Old Soul."

Her soft laughter put him at ease, and he laughed also.

"Yes, I am an old Soul." She waved her hand. "We need to speak of other matters for now. I know much will take place after the next cold season. There will be many who must go on a hill, seek a vision, to find the answers they will need. We will build a new, larger sweat lodge so they can sweat first, as it should be. The Spirit of Shining Light purified your granddaughter in his own way, so we only did the sweat after. I am not yet sure why he needed her to seek a vision before we came to our camp in the canyons. Perhaps we will understand more when we need to. Sit, we will speak here."

She sat on one of the stones they came upon as they walked. "Soon, we will be home. I was not so sure Sky Bird and Golden Fox would go to the canyons with us. White Elk and I spoke of this, and now we know they must come." She stared down and rubbed the stone she sat on. "They feel rough, different from other stones. Often, I think I hear them sing."

She raised her head. "I had thought your granddaughter had another path, and made plans I should not have. Even a Holy Person can make a mistake."

He sat on a larger stone and ran his hand across the roughness. "Dances In Storms, tell me why we are here."

She took in air and blew it out slowly. "Yellow Moon... she will not be allowed to go to the campfires in the sky until she has done something worthy. Your daughter knows this. That is why I thought their path lie in another direction, not into the canyons." She raised her hand. "Allow me to speak, and then I will answer your question, if I can.

"Yellow Moon did very bad things, but so have others of your people. Many left to go to the hairy-faces to get the drink. Yellow Moon wishes us to help these people. I think you know how. It will take great courage. We must all decide on our own what we will do, if anything."

Eagle Thunder sat in silence and stared up at the campfire in the sky.

Woman of mine, where are you?

"My seeing Yellow Moon these past sunrises was not my mind's thoughts, but real?" He clasped his fingers together and leaned forward on his knees. "Why did you think my daughter and granddaughter would not go to the canyons and live in peace?"

"White men were to take Golden Fox to her father. I thought it would be much sooner. A vision showed them coming for her before we reached as far as we have. They did not come."

She nodded toward the lodges as a mustang approached them.

They both stood as hoof beats grew louder.

Sky Bird stumbled and nearly fell. Her breath came in short gasps. "Father, Golden Fox... rode... off on Swift Arrow.... Even White Elk could not catch her." She took a deep breath. "Both Stands His Ground and White Elk left to find her, and they, too, have not returned."

19

A growl filled the air. Golden Fox jerked around but the darkness of the night kept her from seeing what growled. A chilling hiss answered the growl, and her heart pounded.

"I have to find them before it is too late!" Urgency filled her chest. Her breath came in short, hard pants as fear draped over her. "Oh, Sweet Mother, help me!" Her bare feet skimmed the ground as she raced toward the sounds.

The sound of fighting ripped through the night. Yet, no matter how hard she ran, she could not get there. Tears streaked down her cheeks and dripped from her chin. A cold gripped her worse than any she had felt during the cold season.

The night went silent. Not even a cricket chirped.

Her heart jumped into her throat and a cry of despair tore from her lips. "Too late! I am too late!"

Tears poured down her face and her nose clogged with grief. She wrapped her arms around her stomach, bent over, and rocked back and forth. "Too late!"

"Not too late." Sister Wind whispered past her. "Not too late. Not yet."

Golden Fox leapt up and began running, but fell as her feet tangled in roots.

* * *

Golden Fox tore loose from her tangled sleeping robe and leapt to her feet. Not taking time to put on footwear, she raced for the mustangs grazing close by.

With a hard shove of her legs, she jumped on Swift Arrow's back, choosing her grandfather's mustang over her own Splash because of his speed, and nudged the animal in the direction her dream had shown her. With a light tap, Swift Arrow lunged into a gallop. As soon as they cleared the rest of the mustangs, she urged him into a hard run. She wrapped her fingers in the animal's mane, clamped her legs around his body, and leaned low over his back.

Sister Wind whipped her hair behind her, knotting the long strands. Her heart pounded from the fear the dream had stabbed into her chest. The mustang raced down a dry gulch, and loose rocks moved beneath the animal's feet, causing him to stumble. He caught himself before he fell, and never slowed his wild run.

The gulch widened out and spread into an area of flat ground. With a hard lean, Swift Arrow swerved around large rocks, nearly unseating Golden Fox. Grimly, she held on. Cold water splashed on her legs as the mustang galloped through a stream. It chilled her skin, but not nearly as chilled as her heart felt.

A hill rose ahead, with shrubs growing thick along its slopes. As they drew closer, she eased up straight and loosened her legs, and the mustang slowed.

"It is somewhere around here, boy. I hope we are not too late." Panic gripped her and beads of sweat started to run down her face. "Please, please, be safe!"

At the foot of the hill, she slipped off her animal and searched among the shrubs and along the base of the hill. Nothing.

Despair washed over her like a river in the wet days of the season of new growth. It nearly brought her to her knees. She stiffened her spine and, remembering how Blazing Fire taught her to push her emotions down, so she could better fight, she shoved the despair away.

She cupped her hands cupped behind her ears to better catch sounds, stopped, and held her breath. Sister Wind carried a faint whine to her on a light breeze. She walked on her toes, carefully, to make no sound.

There!

A little ways up, a rocky ledge jutted from the hill's side. Flat grey stone lay scattered in a wide area leading up to the ledge, and several large trees had fallen and slid, partly blocking her view of the ledge. It appeared the sound had come from behind the dead trees.

The loose, flat, slick rock slid beneath her feet. She fell, cutting her knees on its sharp edges. Jaws clenched, she clawed her way up the hill on her hands and feet. Several times, she stopped and held her breath, but not another sound drifted to her.

Too late! Oh, Sweet Mother, I am too late.

Tears blurred her eyes, and she angrily blinked them away.

No! I refuse to give up. I will not believe I am too late unless I see it with my own eyes.

Nearly crawling, she made her way to the downed trees, but there were too many stacked upon one another for her to see over. Mouth a tight slash, she gripped the rough bark and climbed to the top. A dark hole had been dug close to the downed trees and back into the hillside.

Sister Moon chose that moment to slip from behind a cloud. Her silver light bathed the bloody scene on the ledge that lay in front of the dug-out hole.

A sob choked her, as tears broke loose and trickled down her face. "The noise I heard must have been Sister Wind crying through these trees. I am too late. Poor Mother Wolf, poor babies... there is nothing I can do."

She gripped the bark and turned to leave, but a whisper of a whine caught her attention.

She whipped back around and continued her climb, slipping and sliding over the tree trunks on her way down. When her feet hit the narrow ledge, she skidded in the blood that had not yet hardened.

Why did Mountain Lion attack Wolf? That is not the way of life. Yet, this is what I saw in my dream. Perhaps, Wolf lived in Mountain Lion's territory, or perhaps Mountain Lion needed this den for herself.

She would never know unless the Spirits told her.

Intent on gaining entrance to the hole, she gently pushed the body of the mother Wolf aside and knelt in the blood. The stench of death filled her nostrils as she got halfway into the hole....

A hand grabbed her leg none too gently and yanked her out and through the blood. "Golden Fox!" White Elk snatched her up. "You do not know what animal is in there. My heart would die—"

"I know what animal lives here." Standing tall, she tipped her chin up, eyes narrowed. A wave of her hand took in the body of the wolf. "If you had looked, you would know, too. The one who claimed this ledge has traveled to her ancestors that sit by a campfire in the sky." Her loose hair clung to her sweaty face. Agitated, she tucked it behind her ears, smearing a streak of blood along her cheek.

"I do not care that Wolf lies here." He stubbornly crossed his arms and crunched his brows. "You do not know what else may live in this hole that Wolf dug."

Chin thrust forward, she pushed until she was so close that her breath mingled with his. "I know. I dreamed of the fight between Mountain Lion and Wolf, but I got here too late. I am sure that Wolf's babies wait in that hole for a mother who cannot come to them." She whirled around to return to the hole.

Stands His Ground reached out and grabbed both White Elk's and her arms. "Both of you stop. You act as children. Let us start a small fire, so we can use a burning branch to see. Do not glare at each other. Gather branches."

Not willing to wait for the fire, Golden Fox yanked loose and crawled into the den. By the time she reached the back of the hole, Stands His Ground had a small fire built. White Elk held a burning branch into the entrance, shedding enough light for her to see the three pups. They appeared less than a moon old.

Easing toward them, she crooned. "Poor babies. Poor, poor babies, your mother fought a hard battle and kept you safe from Mountain Lion, who would have killed you. I wonder if the sound of Swift Arrow's running feet scared her off before she could get inside here?"

She crouched close to them and reached out a hand, to let them each sniff her. "I do not know where your father is, but he cannot feed you—not yet. You are still too young and need the milk of a mother. You must come with me for a little while, until you are old enough to take care of yourselves." As she scooped the pups into the cradle she made from the bottom of her dress, they snuggled close. "Poor babies, I wish there was some way to tell your father that you are safe with me."

As she crawled to the entrance of Wolf's den, White Elk reached down for the pups. One by one, she handed them to him, and then made her way out. On her feet, she reached for the pups.

He handed them over with a grimace twisting his face. "You are covered in blood, and I see no knife on your belt. How were you going to defend yourself if Mountain Lion or Wolf had decided to make a meal of you?"

Heat flushed her face. She knew her feelings showed on her face, and wondered if Blazing Fire might know of a way to keep the telltale redness from blooming on her cheeks. "I dreamed, and in the dream neither Mountain Lion nor Wolf harmed me."

Nostrils flared, White Elk opened his mouth to speak, but before he could, Stands His Ground stepped between the two. With a finger, he stroked the heads of the pups. "This was a powerful dream, Golden Fox. I feel much good will come of it. How will we feed these pups?"

The sound of galloping mustangs yanked their attention to where their own animals waited at the base of the hill. With a sigh of relief, Golden Fox realized that it was Sky Bird, Eagle Thunder, and Dances In Storms.

They flew off their animals and glared up at her. Eagle Thunder rode Splash.

Swallowing her nervousness, she made her way down the hill. The pups made soft whines from the cradle of her dress as she walked up to her mother. "I am sorry, Mother, that I made you worry. I had a dream and felt great urgency to come here."

"What if the whites had found you?" Much anger flew from her mother's eyes.

"My dream—"

"Dreams do not always tell everything!" Her mother swirled around, leapt on her mustang, and raced away.

Dances In Storms stepped up beside her. "You and I need to speak of how to use your mind as well as your heart. Let me see the pups. Ha! One is white and a female. The little grey one is male. The one white paw and the white splatter down his face makes him very good to look at." She picked up the last one and held it before her eyes. "Pure black—not a speck of white—and another male."

Satisfied with the pups, she returned them to Golden Fox. "These pups are no more than a moon old, if that. How are you to feed them? If we were not days from the rest of the band, we might find a woman who has a baby and would share milk with these four-legged babies. But, the band is too far ahead of us to catch up before these little ones will die."

Eagle Thunder walked over, a scowl on his face. "Granddaughter, this is truly a Sacred Happening, but you brought great worry to certain ones among us." His eyes flicked over to White Elk, then he picked up a pup. "There will always be times when others will worry about what you are called to do. It is best if you saved those times for when you cannot heed their worry, for when you must act quickly in spite of their worry. *When there is no one around to call to.* Do you understand me?"

"Yes, Grandfather," she replied meekly.

When she would have continued speaking, he held up the hand that was not cuddling the pup against his chest. "Blazing Fire will have harsh words for you when she finds out you rode away without even your knife." He handed the pup back and laid a hand on her shoulder. "Your mother's worry about whites is not so wrong." He paused and stared into her eyes. "I rode *your* mustang. You will ride her back."

He placed his hand on Dances In Storms' arm, and they returned to their mustangs. He jumped onto Swift Arrow, and together they rode toward camp.

Only White Elk and Stands His Ground remained behind as she made her way to Splash. The mustang snorted at the smell of wolf pups and skittered sideways.

White Elk stepped close to her. "You can ride my male. He is well trained."

She lifted her chin. "I will ride Splash, but you are kind to offer."

Their eyes met and his hand reached for hers.

Stands His Ground walked over. "Hand the pups to me while you get on. It will help calm Splash."

In Sister Moon's light, red tinged White Elk's cheeks as he stared up at her. "Perhaps, you should hurry. The male may not be far away, and he may not like that his mate is dead and you take his pups." He eyed the top of the hill.

"You... you should get on your mustang and leave. Stands His Ground will ride with me."

"Then you have no need of me, and I will see you at camp." He leapt on his mustang, turned quickly, and rode away.

Stands His Ground helped her onto Splash. "Golden Fox, he only wishes to be your friend and, perhaps, someday to be your mate."

Long hair hid her face as she climbed on Splash and made a cradle for the pups. Once they snuggled safely in her dress, she glanced at Stands His Ground. "I have no need of a mate. I will become a warrior woman."

Without waiting for his words, she nudged Splash into a gentle trot.

She had not gone more than a few steps when a mournful howl raised the hairs on her arms. She twisted her head around and spotted a magnificent black wolf. Sister Moon shone on him, making his hair look frosted with white. Golden Fox answered with sorrow in her howl.

The male responded, and she again returned his call.

Stands His Ground stopped beside her. "What is this you do?"

Loss choked her, but she pushed the words past it. "I can feel his sorrow. I wish him to know that he is not alone in his pain."

Stands His Ground shifted around and, with one hand on the rump of his mustang, watched as the big male slinked away. "We must leave before he catches up. I have no desire to harm him."

Confidence oozed from her as she squeezed Splash into a trot. "He will follow us, but harm no one. He only wishes to know that his pups are cared for and safe. Perhaps, I should return to his hill and let him see his pups again—see that they are unharmed."

"No, woman, the time is not right for such a meeting. Come, let us get the pups where they will have warmth and we can find some way to feed them."

Reluctantly, she headed for camp.

When they reached the spot where the mustangs grazed, Golden Fox handed the pups to Stands His Ground and slid from her animal. With her feet planted on the grass, she took the pups back.

Sky Bird hurried to them, excitement dancing in her eyes. "Blue Spirit Dog has had her pups on Stands His Ground's sleeping robe. She must have given birth right after we left. The pups are already cleaned and fed, and they sleep with fat little bellies. Perhaps, we can get her to take these pups?" A concerned frown marred her forehead.

Before Golden Fox could reply, Blue Spirit Dog trotted toward her. She hurried over to meet her dog.

Sky Bird rushed toward her daughter. "Golden Fox, no! Do not place the wolf pups on the ground. She may harm them from fear for her own pups!"

Golden Fox disregarded her mother's warning, squatted on the ground, and lifted the pups from the cradle of her dress.

Blue Spirit Dog sat and waited until the last pup squirmed on the dirt. Head lowered, she sniffed the pups and used her muzzle to flip them onto their backs. With their little legs beating the air, the pups made pitiful mewling sounds. Blue Spirit Dog pushed them back onto their bellies, and closed her mouth around the back of the female's neck.

For a heart-stopping moment, everyone waited.

The dog trotted off with the pup dangling.

Golden Fox quickly gathered the other two pups and rushed after the dog, arriving in time to see the animal lay the pup among her own two sleeping babies. Golden Fox laid the other two in the pile of pups.

Blue Spirit Dog let go a long breath and flopped down with the pups nestled between her legs. She cleaned each one and nudged the wolf pups toward her full teats. After they began suckling, the dog again sighed and stretched out.

Sky Bird chuckled. "She has accepted them. Wolves and dogs are not friends, yet she has placed them among her own babies."

Sky Bird and Stands His Ground moved their sleeping robes away from the new mother.

Golden Fox lay on her side next to Blue Spirit Dog and watched the little ones breathe and snuffle against Blue Spirit Dog. She stroked the mother dog. "How did you know they needed you? Why did you accept them so easily? This is not the way of dogs with wolves."

The dog blinked sleepy eyes, the blue rimming them shining bright in the light of Sister Moon.

"Why did you choose to come with us, Blue Spirit Dog? *Where* did you come from, for I never saw you until we were sunrises away from the Sun People's camp?" Not expecting an answer, Golden Fox rested her head on her arm and let sleep claim her.

* * *

Blue Spirit Dog stretched out beneath a tree. Her pups wrestled with the wolf pups.

Golden Fox gasped and gazed around. "Where are we?"

Dog chuckled. "What silly questions you ask, Golden Fox. We are in the Spirit Land."

Panic raced through her and she dropped to her knees, and ran anxious hands over Dog. "Have you died, Dog?"

Her tongue lolled from the side of her mouth as Dog laughed at her. "Foolish girl, tell me, are you dead?"

"No, I do not believe I am."

She sat back on her heels. The black wolf pup ran into her and bounced off, gathered his fat legs beneath him, and raced off to join his brothers and sisters, very unlike a newly born pup.

"I bring you here —"

"You brought me here?" Her eyebrows shot high on her forehead.

"Of course, I brought you here. I brought you here to answer the questions you ask. After all, as Dog, I cannot speak unless we meet here in the Spirit Land."

Dog licked her foreleg, then sat up. "All of life has a purpose. None are without this — not the trees, or the birds, or the very small ones that crawl, or the four-legged. Not even the white people. It is when all living works together that the Circle of Life has harmony — when all respect the other. I walk with you for a purpose, just as you have a reason for walking on our Mother."

154

She licked one of the wolf pups. "We cannot know our whole purpose for being, for we would stop trying to become. Great Mystery lets us know what we need to choose the right path to walk. We may ignore the Great Mystery and choose to walk a different path. It is our choice.

"I choose to walk the path laid before me. Why this path brings these pups to me, I do not know. They will grow and I will teach them. We will know more as we need to know it."

Dog stretched out again, resting her head on her paws.

20

Golden Fox's mother slept.

Stands His Ground's sister faced the other side of the lodge, snoring enough to make a mother bear worry over her young.

The men slept outside and took turns guarding the small camp.

Golden Fox lowered the black pup, cuddled in her arms, next to Blue Spirit Dog, and slipped out under the bottom edge of the lodge. She cocked her head to the only sounds, those of crickets singing their mating song. The smell of rain clouds grew thicker and made it hard to see.

Blue Spirit Dog whined, and she turned back and whispered to her that all was well. Once again, she scooted out before anyone could realize the lump in her robe was not her.

She tiptoed backward to be as quiet as possible, and took eight steps before she slipped. "Ouch. What—"

"Me, Granddaughter. That ouch happens to be my legs. I heard you trying to be sneaky, but you are not so good at sneaky. Until eyes in the back of your head grow, you must learn to use the ones in front. You know which ones—the ones that are above your little short nose and below your thin brows."

"Grandfather, please say nothing. I did not mean to wake you. Wait. I *do not* have a little short nose. Ahh... you *were* awake. So all is well. I... I only need a walk. Am leaving now."

Eagle Thunder grabbed her leg and she fell squealing. "Ha! I bet that squeal will alert every night animal a meal is to be had right here if they swoop down fast enough."

She righted herself and squatted. "You tease, right?"

"Oh, no. Never. Why would a grandfather stop his granddaughter from wandering into the unknown darkness?"

"Please whisper before everyone hears us, Grandfather!"

"Those who did not hear your squeal have no ears, Golden Fox." Her mother stood over the pair, her brows lowered and her thin lips pressed tight enough to look as one. "Have you a place you need to go?"

"Um, yes, Mother. You understand. Sometimes when we sleep, our bodies wake us in need of release." She untangled herself from her grandfather and leaned forward on her knees to stand.

Sky Bird grinned. "Oh, I do. I have that same need. We can walk together, keep each other company." She took Golden Fox's hand and urged her toward the trees.

"Mother, I do know where to go! I am no longer your child."

"Little one, you will always be my child. Even when you have a child, I will call you little one. Never think I do not hear with the ears of a mother. Even when you and White Elk share a lodge, I will hear you."

"Mother!"

* * *

Dances In Storms chuckled. "I am happy I slept outside so close to the lodge. I would have been sad to know I missed this. Rain comes, and we have need to share the lodge. Gather your robe."

Eagle Thunder rolled over and sat up. "She had hoped to be sneaky and go find that male wolf. I know her mind."

"She is gifted, Eagle Thunder. She feels much, and I trust her to know about the wolf. Someday, people will depend on her to call the animals when none can be found."

* * *

Golden Fox had no choice but to lie next to her mother. She fumed until sunrise. "Animal Caller? Call them to die for us? Am I strong enough?"

Dances In Storms rolled over. "You will have no choice, if you wish the band to live through what comes our way. You must learn to think with your mouth closed."

157

Her mind kept busy with scattered thoughts. Sleep came for her mother, but not so much for her. Fully alert, she heard a distant herd of humpbacks.

Thunder came as a low rumble, building louder, and broke the calm of the darkness with a noise loud enough to make everyone in the lodge jump out of their sleeping robes. Yellow-orange fire lit up the land, and the lodge soon filled with the smell of wet leather.

White Elk, Long Sun, and Stands His Ground hurried to get wet clothes off and dash under sleeping robes.

"Good thing you did not sneak off into the darkness after that wolf, woman." White Elk shivered and scooted closer to the small fire.

The rain deafened Golden Fox's remark. Mostly. "I thought scouts, Holy People, and elders knew when a storm approached!"

"We did, Granddaughter. The mustangs raced away, and we smart ones stayed inside."

Deer Woman chuckled until a wet tunic hit her face.

Blazing Storm rushed in and over the top of everyone. "I must have not been one of the smart ones!"

Golden Fox grumbled and rolled over, pulling the sleeping robe with her.

Sky Bird pulled it back.

"Mother, the pups may chill!"

"How can they chill when your dog sleeps inside my part of the robe with them?"

Everyone else had already settled in... mostly.

Dances In Storms did not try to share a space inside. Everyone heard her outside, laughing and singing as the rain fell.

The lodge's bottom had been pulled tight enough that the rain made small rivers away from the people.

In time, Dances In Storms slopped her way inside, and met protests and yells.

"Hush! I am a Holy Woman to be respected. Give me a robe, or I will take one."

From somewhere a robe slapped her in the face.

***

Campfires in the sky faded and Deer Woman's cooking fire smelled wet and musty. She plodded through the mud in hopes of finding dry wood.

Too soaked to start a good fire, she woke Sky Bird. "We eat dried meat this sunrise, as we wait for the outside of the lodge to dry. The men are gone, maybe hunting the mustangs who ran away again."

Golden Fox jumped up and out of the lodge, forgetting her footwear. "Augh! Mud suck at my ankles."

"Daughter, I worry that you think too much with your emotions and not enough with your mind. There has to be a balance." Sky Bird tossed her a wet deerskin to clean her feet. "I have been overprotective and never allowed you to fully become a woman. You should have gone with the hunters before you became a woman, learned discipline, how to treat a man... and White Elk needs to learn as well how to treat a woman. And you must learn to put on footwear!"

Sky Bird chuckled. "I know your heart. I know you wish to go to Wolf, and you will, or he will come to you. Allow the Spirits to guide you, show you the right way." She hugged her daughter. "Let us make a drag for the pups."

Golden Fox cleaned her feet and put on the footwear she should have before. She then placed her hands to her mouth and made a sound like a mustang searching for the herd. "Soon they will be here, with *our* men running behind them."

Dances In Storms climbed out, her hair a tangled mess. When the women started to laugh at her, she reminded them of how she protected them by dancing in the rain to scare away more lightning. The other women's laughter grew.

***

Father Sun burst over the horizon as Golden Fox raised her arms high. Her song rang out over the land as gold spilled along the edge of the Mother. From the corner of her eye, a black shadow slipped along the trees.

Her mother had already made a drag with a nest of sleeping robes for Blue Spirit Dog and her mixed family. The drag was hooked behind her mother's mustang, an older mare that nothing startled. Sky Bird tied her sleeping robe to one of White Elk's stolen mustangs, the ones he brought back without the drunken half-bloods.

Eagle Thunder nodded toward White Elk and Dances In Storms, who played with the pups while Blue Spirit Dog watched. "He is a good man. A woman could do worse than to take him to her lodge, even if she would share that lodge and White Elk with another woman."

159

Golden Fox glared at her grandfather, filled her bowl, and walked over to where Blazing Fire ate. She sat cross-legged next to the warrior woman, feeling grateful that at least this one person did not prod her about White Elk.

Still, her eyes drifted the albino warrior's way.

"Long Sun was the one who heard you ride hard from camp," Blazing Fire said. "He came to me, and I sent your mother to find Eagle Thunder while the men rode to see if they could catch up to you." With her empty bowl set aside, she turned hard eyes on Golden Fox. "A warrior woman does not bring danger to her people by acting foolish, as a child would."

Head ducked low, she ate. There was no excuse for her actions, except that she had feared any delay would cause her to arrive too late. As it was, she had still been too late to save Mother Wolf.

"Have you no words to speak?"

"I... I had a dream. I knew I would be safe. I had to... to hurry. Even then I was... too late."

"Are you so unskilled that you cannot ride and tie the belt for your knife around your waist, or sling your bow and arrows over your shoulder?"

Mouth dry, she could not speak.

Blazing Fire pushed to her feet. "This day, you will ride alone and consider my words. If you wish to be a warrior woman, you must always put your people first. Always."

Golden Fox nodded. She could not help her yawn, and covered her mouth.

* * *

The howl of the wolf in her dream echoed in her mind. Restlessness poked her until she got to her feet and stared out into the darkness. If she left again, Blazing Fire might not teach her, yet how could she convince the others she had to go? The black wolf needed her. His sorrow reached inside her and clamped around her heart, making it hurt more than it did when she saw Dances In Storms laughing with White Elk.

She paced to the edge of their camp and, chewing her lower lip, fought against the call of the wolf.

"The wolf is close."

Long Sun startled her, and she jumped. "I did not hear you approach. Blazing Fire will be angry that I allowed another to walk up without me knowing it."

160

"Blazing Fire is hard on you because she wishes to keep you alive. Never see her actions as anger. She cares, as does Dances In Storms." The young man, who would one day be a Holy Man, crossed his arms over his thin chest. Have you not yet understood who you really are, woman?"

She shrugged. "*You* know?"

"I cannot speak of it. Dances In Storms told me never to speak of another's future, but... I can say you will have many children and guide them well. You are Mother Of The People."

She stared at her feet, and finally spoke in a whisper. "I love White Elk ." Her head snapped up. "I... I am very tired, as sleep did not find me."

Before she could say anything else, Long Sun walked forward, acting as if he did not hear anything, and jumped on his mustang. "Come, hunt with me before we must all leave."

* * *

They had not ridden far when Wolf's amber-gold eyes flashed from the edge of the trees. Golden Fox slipped from Splash and handed her nose rope to Long Sun. With slow steps, she eased toward Wolf, hand out, crooning as she had crooned to the pups, as the sky flashed its anger in the darkness.

"Wolf, I am your sister. We are one. Your pups do well."

Behind her, Splash snorted and pawed the ground.

Long Sun soothed her with a clicking sound and moved the animals away.

Golden Fox fell into the depths of Wolf's amber gaze. She blinked as Long Sun shook her shoulder.

When he saw her eyes open, he leaned back on his heels. "Where did you go, Golden Fox?"

She stared forward, then at Long Sun. "Where is Wolf?"

He tilted his head toward the thick shrubs. "He left only a few breaths ago. All of a sudden, he ran off." He got to his feet and held out a hand.

The offered hand brought on confusion, and weak-legged, standing was not going to happen. He helped her climb on Splash, and they tapped the mustangs into a slow walk.

Long Sun cleared his throat. "If you wish to share where you and Wolf went...."

"Where we went? Did Wolf also leave his body?"

161

"I have not ever seen an animal go on a Spirit journey like that. Did you travel together?"

"Yes, he took me running in a forest with tall trees, and we raced through the wet leaves on the path. Animals I have never seen flew, ran, and dashed up the trees. We ran and ran and ran. I felt so free. The wind rushed through my hair, and I had no trouble keeping up with Wolf." A sigh blew from her mouth. "That is all I remember. What did you see, Long Sun?"

"You knelt on the ground. When Wolf approached, the mustangs became restless and pranced sideways. With one eye on you, in case Wolf decided you looked like a meal, I soothed the mustangs. By the time their fear eased, you and Wolf gazed into each other's eyes. Neither of you blinked or moved, yet I could see you still breathed. That is when I realized a Sacred Happening had come to you."

He bent his neck backward and stared up at the cloudy sky. When he brought his eyes back down, he shook his head. "I do not know what happened, Golden Fox. Wolf was gone, as you were, traveling, and then he shook his head, cocked an ear as if he listened, and ran away. It was as if he heard something, perhaps some danger I could not hear." He paused and looked around them. "We must bring rabbit or ground birds so they know we hunted."

***

Golden Fox helped make the new drag and pull down the lodge. Father Sun had been awake for a good span. She yawned, closed her eyes, and leaned on Splash.

"We go, Daughter!" Sky Bird grinned at her before waving an arm for her to follow.

She stayed back with Splash to keep watch over Blue Spirit Dog and all the pups, making sure none of them bounced off—no riding for her today. Her mustang walked faster than normal, and twisted about as she adjusted to pulling the drag.

Golden Fox's eyes were half-lidded and her feet dragged. She forced her head up.

I am not a child! I can stay awake. Many of the people stay awake for days, if need be. I will learn to be sneaky. Sneaky Golden Fox, they will call me.

She stopped. "Fox is sneaky. Fox teaches how to hide while people look their way." She rushed to catch up with her animal. "I *do* have Fox medicine. I did see her in my vision. She gave me the gift of being able to hide in front of others when I was but a child."

A spider crawled up from the wood she had used to make part of the drag's frame. She slowed way down. "Perhaps, Spider, you can teach me how to be wary, as Wolf is."

Instead, visions of people drinking glazed over her mind. A young girl cried as her young brother called for her. Someone pushed him out of the large wooden entrance that hid the fort from outsiders. The boy begged to be let back in.

"Golden Fox, much goes on you need to prepare for beyond the pups, beyond your own safe world. Heed Wolf's words. Move away from the band and go with him. The pups will be safe. It is your kind that is not safe." Spider crawled back under the wooden frame.

Out of the corner of her eye, the black wolf frosted in white showed himself.

"Wolf, you have come back!" She put her hand over her mouth and stilled herself. His dark yellow eyes penetrated her mind. Everything vanished in a fog, until only she, Splash, the pups, and the wolf remained.

As Wolf neared Splash, she snorted and tried to run.

Golden Fox clicked her tongue and moved up by her head to whisper soothing words. The mustang held still, but her eyes went wide as the wolf neared. She snorted again.

"No, girl." Golden Fox closed her eyes and pressed her head against the mustang.

Feel me. I have no fear. There is no room for fear. Breath slow, easy. We are safe.

The mustang calmed some, but her ears pointed toward the wolf.

Golden Fox pulled away and walked backward to where the drag rested. The wolf sat close, but not near enough to make Blue Spirit Dog growl. She licked each pup rapidly, as she kept an eye on the wolf.

She patted the dog and moved toward the wolf. With each step, she spoke gentle words. She raised her arm halfway, offered the back of her hand, and approached him as she had before.

She spoke to the wolf, but with her mind. *You and I are brother and sister. Brother and sister....*

As her hand came close enough to touch him, he licked her. He raised his head and sat. The pull of his Energy held Power.

She would never fear him again.

Follow me, Brother, when you are ready. Do not worry. You are safe.

The wolf leaned forward, sniffed Blue Spirit Dog and his pups, but he did not run. As he walked beside Golden Fox, he raised his muzzle, and she rubbed his face and the top of his head.

She rested her arms on her mustang's rump and stared up into the clouding turquoise sky. "There is Energy in all of life, Power in all Energy. We are the same beings, connected by Spider's web, from tiny crawling ones, to trees, to us, to our Mother."

She turned to go back to Blue Spirit Dog, and glanced over her shoulder.

Eagle Thunder nodded her way.

Everyone watched her, but they listened also to her words.

21

The small group slowed to admire the land. Canyons showed off tall orange-red stones reaching for the turquoise sky. Some disappeared into dense clouds. The ground now carried a deeper cast of orange. Many pedaled white flowers with dark yellow centers, spread everywhere, and spikes with small yellow flowers grew along the sides of hills. Smaller reddish ones came up in groups alongside animal trails, and occasional blue and purple blossoms jutted up from the shorter grasses to compete for sun. Silver shrubs, and light green shrubs heavy with ripening purple berries, grew near the dark green pine trees that mingled on the rolling grassy hills as they entered the beginning of the canyons.

Familiar wild spinach grew everywhere. Wild lettuce, still blooming tiny yellow flowers, attracted the small winged ones, who were far too busy to pay attention to any distractions. The large sandstone boulders surrounded them in yellows, oranges, and deeper reds. White streaks ran through some of them like small rivers.

Soon they would be home. But whose home?

Golden Fox clutched the black wolf pup to her breast.

Will they want my people? Many had minds still not right from the drink, when the larger part of the band moved on. And the wolves! What will they say?

Deeper into the canyon, the waters became wider, and thick growths of cat-tails hid the river's edges. Berries on low-growing shrubs along the same waters had changed to deep red. As Father Sun lowered, soft pink and orange splashed across the few clouds that drifted by.

No one mentioned need for a lodge this night. With a mostly clear sky, everyone chose a place near the fire. They pressed the shorter grass down, to make walking around the camp easier, and to expose any hidden snakes. Two large water snakes slithered toward the waters.

The wolf vanished before anyone noticed, but I know where he went. Emptiness filled the Energy in Golden Fox's being. *Soon everyone will sleep....*

She pulled the grass around the fire circle to make the ground bare and safe from sparks. Like everyone else, she then used the pulled grass to rub down her mustang, and returned to her robe, which she shared with Blue Spirit dog and the pups.

Eagle Thunder lay on the extra robe Deer Woman had given him. The night air, warmer now, meant no need for robes to use as covers.

Golden Fox yawned and closed her eyes. She rolled over, faced the other way, and pretended to breathe an even rhythm.

Clouds drifted by, half-covering the now smaller moon. Nearby, mustangs moved about as they grazed. At sunrise, the group would eat cold food and ready to leave before sunrise. Within a short span, they would catch up to the main part of the band, which would be home by now.

What will they say about the wolf pups? My new adult wolf companion? No matter. They are part of my Soul.

She rolled off the robe, and reached to be sure her knife rested securely inside its sheath. Blue Spirit Dog stretched out and took up the room she left on the robe. With her footwear still on—she had never removed them—she crept away from the low burning fire.

She stiffened.

Dances In Storms does not sleep. I feel her watching me. She turned around and found the Holy Woman sitting up.

Dances In Storms waved her away and lay back down, but faced her.

She gave her permission to me. If anyone wakes, I will say this!

She slipped away and wandered out onto the new land. Sandstone boulders were large enough that she had to walk around them.

So many sandstones, and much less open grassland. We walk across the last of these tall grasses. We will never know if the mountains are blue and purple.

She ran her hands across the rough texture of the smaller stone next to her, as she used a stick to wave across the ground in front of her.

Could be a sleeping snake anywhere.

She waded through the clumps of strange new grasses.

Ha! Grandfather says I do not know sneaky. I do now. I am Sneaky Golden Fox. He did not stir, and.... I feel Wolf! I knew he followed close.

Her voice low, she called for him. "Wolf? Father Wolf, I know you are near me." She sat in the clumpy grass, leaned against a boulder, and pulled her legs to the side of her body. She half-whispered a song.

"Wolf of my being, I am here.

I am here. I have no fear.

Wolf who I feel in my heart,

I am here. I am here.

I wait for you, Wolf.

Wolf of my being, we connect."

She sang partly to let him hear her, partly to open herself up to him.

Before her, a blue mist appeared.

"What is this?" She scooted up and pressed against the boulder. "I have never seen this before." She stood the rest of the way and turned to run.

"Child, do not have fear. As you say, there is no fear."

"Shining Light? I have not fasted for a vision. Are... are you really there?" She reached for her skinning knife.

"You come with only your knife?"

"This night, I came seeking Father Wolf. I had no need for my bow."

"Ha! Mountain Lion would laugh at your small knife... right before she ate you."

"Mountain Lion is near?" A tremble ran through her body as her eyes darted here and there.

"If she is, what will you do, Golden Fox?"

"I... I do not know, Shining Light. Tell me, is Mountain Lion near?"

"Mountain Lion is not near, but you, Golden Fox, must let your mind grow to be like a warrior's mind. Always consider what you do before you do it. Only a child runs into the darkness with only a small knife."

Head bowed, she said, "Forgive me, Great Holy Man, for acting in such a foolish way again."

"You have brought no great harm to your people, but there are many ways in which a person might bring harm to their people without meaning to do this. Sometimes, it happens when the person ignores what a Holy Person sees in a vision. Not even Holy People

can always say why the Spirits show certain things. We must walk the path shown and make choices as the Spirits will it."

"Dances In Storms' vision? Is this what you speak of, Shining Light?"

"You are truly blessed, Golden Fox. It has been a long time since Wolf has chosen one to share his pack." His wolves appeared beside him. "This is White Paws." He scratched the wolf's head.

White Paws came out from behind Shining Light. Head cocked, ears up, he studied her, and then sauntered out and touched his nose to her outstretched hand. After a lick on the back of her hand, he ambled back to Shining Light's side.

"He... he touched me from the Spirit Land!"

"You think you are not in the Spirit Land?"

"I... I am not so sure."

"You are where you choose to be. One day you will understand." He reached down and scratched the wolf on his other side. "This is Moon Face. She has always been shy to touch another. Know she always backed up her mate. One day, you will do the same for your mate, as he will do for you." He raised a hand when she opened her mouth to speak.

"Let us speak of the frosted one. My companions are his ancestors. He will walk beside you until it is his time to join White Paws and Moon Face. Treat him and his pups as your blood relations. Remember, all strands in Spider's web are interwoven."

The blue surrounding him and the wolves glowed brighter. "All is connected. One being cannot exist without the other. When a strand of the web is broken, it affects every living being. If one becomes no more, waves will slowly rip apart the web, and all will die." He hugged White Paws and Moon Face close to his side.

"Every living being depends on the other. If one vanishes from our Mother, another will vanish, and another, until the Peoples themselves cannot survive and will vanish also. Far into the future, Humans dig deep into our Mother's body to search for treasures. The hunger for these treasures takes over, and the People's Spirits become blackened until they hunger only for such treasures, even if when it means great harm to the Mother and to the Web of Life. They forget who they are." He stopped speaking and stared at her.

She never wavered, and looked him in the eyes.

"A black thick substance deep in the ground will cause wars among Peoples, both here and far across the salty waters. Greed for it will bring much bloodshed. The waters needed to live will become poisoned, and many creatures will die. Many of the medicine plants, and plants needed to feed our four-legged relatives, will be torn up and thrown away. In their place, Humans will put plants that poison the animals, plants that belong in other places, and for as far as can be seen will be plants that easily sicken and die, leaving even the Humans with nothing to eat.

"The web weakens each time we destroy what is not ours to kill. The weaker the web becomes, the less it can hold. Humans will be given a chance to heal the Mother. If they do not work together to heal her, all will die. Listen to my words and pass them on. These things our Peoples have known since the first time Father Sun rose above our Mother. A long, long time ago, a Great Holy Woman, Blue Night Sky, made this my purpose — to pass this knowledge on to those who come after us.

"Listen well and remember... remember. Pass on my words, Young One. Many will not hear, as they cannot see beyond what is in front of their eyes. Their clouded minds will make all of their body blind and uncaring. You must find the Land Of Tall Trees to save those who will follow you." Shining Light and his wolves faded into the mist.

"Shining Light?" She spun and looked all around. "I will listen to your words and pass them on to others. Always, I will do this."

Where is the wolf? Did he not call to me in my mind to come out here? Or was it Shining Light?

Darkness still took the land.

Was I not here just as Father Sun woke? The Spirit Land... I was there, not here. Ahhh... everything stops.

The last of the night's crickets chirred to the beat of her heart. She danced in a circle and tapped her feet to the sound.

All are interconnected. I am the crickets' beat, they my heart.

She swirled until the blue became part of her, the bright blue she knew to be the Spirit Light — her Soul. Drums joined in from somewhere and rattles kept the rhythm. She danced until Father Sun spilled across land.

She laughed and sang her morning song and dropped to her knees.

How long did we speak? Was I in the Spirit Land, or Shining Light in this land? What do I hear?

"Wolf?" She bounced up onto her feet, knife in hand.

The wolf sat in the grasses.

"Wolf!" She sheathed her knife, took one slow step forward, another, and another, until she stood before him. She knelt and reached out her hand.

He leaned forward and smelled her, her hand close enough to scratch his nose. Then he scooted closer and lay across her lap.

"Wolf, you and I are one. Shining Light said so. We are going to be companions. Frost. I will call you by that name."

He sat still while she ran her hands over his head, ears, and down his neck. He allowed her to hug him. "Such fur I have never felt, so thick around your neck that I must dig my fingers in to touch your skin. Your amber-gold eyes peer deep into mine. You do not look away as a dog."

Frost growled and bared his teeth.

"What have I done?" She jumped and scooted away from the wolf.

She screamed when laughter beside her grew louder.

"So, here is the golden-red-haired girl. We have found you alone with a weak wolf. What wolf goes near a human? Your father wishes to see you." The man who spoke dressed as her people.

He is dark brown and has a beard?

"You will come." He pulled out a rope.

Another stood behind him, dressed the same way but with a lighter skin color. He pulled out a long knife and aimed it at Frost. "Gifts are promised to us for you." He reached for her.

The wolf gave no more warning. He lunged and grabbed the stranger's arm, and pulled him down.

The man screamed and dropped his knife. He tried to protect himself with his good arm, but to no avail. The struggle ended quickly, as Frost silenced him with one quick bite to his neck.

The other man held his knife in front of himself as he backed off. He then whirled away and ran.

Frost caught up to him and bit into his leg.

He fell, and swung the knife toward the wolf, but caught only air.

Before the man could scream twice, the wolf jumped on his back and shook him until he lay still.

"Wolf, Frost, you saved my life!" She ran and hugged him in spite of his blood-coated fur. "Who... What—"

Blue Spirit Dog came out of the long grass. Wolf and Dog faced each other.

Golden Fox scooted over to be in-between them, but Blue Spirit Dog moved around her and wriggled her body. Frost repeated the same motion, and inched his way toward the dog and sniffed her nose. Satisfied, Frost moved away.

"Golden Fox!" Dances In Storms jumped off her mustang and ran to Golden Fox's side, saw the wolf, and backed away as he growled. She scanned the bloody ground. "I knew Shining Light wished to speak to you, but I did not see the men!"

The Holy Woman nodded. "They had no chance to ready themselves. Your wolf knew what to do. This I why I did not see the men. Your wolf proved himself well. Never will I feel as if you are not safe."

Golden Fox hugged Frost tighter. "I wanted to see Frost so much. I did not pay heed to anything else. I have much to learn. Shining Light proved that."

"You call him Frost? Shining Light? What is this you say?" Dances In Storms turned.

Running mustangs stopped short of the scene.

Sky Bird had eased off her mustang and slowly walked closer to her daughter and the wolf. "Daughter, I wish to know who this new person in our family is."

Though Sky Bird stood tall, Golden Fox noted the quaver in her mother's voice. "Come closer, Mother, but do not look him in the eyes." When her mother was close enough to touch the wolf, Golden Fox gave more instructions. "Kneel on the ground and put you hand out, so he can sniff you."

Sky Bird twisted her head around and eyed the fallen men. "Daughter, tell your wolf that I need both hands to cook food." Though her words teased, her voice betrayed her fear.

A light laugh made its way from Golden Fox. "Mother, he has does not want to eat you. You are much too old and too tough."

Frost leaned forward and slurped Sky Bird's outstretched hand.

She made a squished face and laughed. "He slobbers more than Blue Spirit Dog."

Her laugh called the wolf closer, and he began licking her face all over.

Still laughing, she threw up her hands and fell to her rump on the ground.

The wolf turned his back and sat down on her legs, his tongue lolling from the side of his mouth.

"Aiiee! Wolf, you are too heavy to sit on my lap like a small child." She pushed at him until he finally moved.

Frost plopped down next to her, rolled onto his back, and kicked his feet up in the air.

Golden Fox moved closer and rubbed his belly.

Her mother's hand also glided through his hair. "His fur is so soft, almost as soft as the fur of his children." Sky Bird eyed the fallen men. "Sweet Mother! How did they know where to find you?"

Dances in Storms walked to where the men lay. She circled them and came back. "I do not know them. So foolish I have become. Wanting to hurry home, I asked no one to watch this night. They could have found us all sleeping." She smacked her head.

Golden Fox wrapped her arms around the wolf.

Eagle Thunder and White elk rode up. Both jumped off their mustangs and walked around to the two dead men.

Eagle Thunder spoke first. "What is this? Why has this happened?"

White Elk walked up behind Eagle Thunder. "This night, I too was foolish. I slept."

Dances In Storms nodded toward Eagle Thunder. "Leave them where they lie. Eagle Woman will fly down from the campfires and deal with them. She will decide where they are worth taking to, and I am sure it is not the Spirit Land."

Frost moved away, but did not try to hide.

White Elk gave Golden Fox a hand up on his mustang, and he urged the animal toward their camp.

Frost trotted behind.

22

Golden Fox held tight to White Elk, her head rested on his shoulder.

Deer Woman's mustang ran circles around the other animals, then raced toward Deer Woman.

"Her mustang is crazy. He always returns to Deer woman, but sometimes he takes off before she is ready to jump on him."

She turned to look for the wolf. He trotted next to them, and she motioned for him to follow. "I must walk with him... alone. Frost, companion, my brother... let us walk, alone." She slipped a leg over and slid off White Elk's mustang before the animal even slowed, and walked toward a stand of trees.

Before she moved too far away, White Elk took of his tunic and tossed it over her shoulder. "You need something without blood. You do not need to attract animals. Take my tunic. It may be a bit big, but it is clean. Maybe I will stay close."

He smiled and put his finger to his lips.

Golden Fox nodded and carried his tunic with her. Once out of his sight, she replaced her dress with it. She had to roll up the arms, and it fell to her knees. "Yes, a bit big." She rolled up the ruined dress and left it behind. She would return and retrieve it to see if she could use any parts for patches.

Those men, why... why were they trying to kill me?

She wrapped her arms around herself and stopped. Frost rubbed against her and she rubbed his ears. When he stared up at her, she knelt down and faced him. "You came to me, saved me from those men. I owe you much, and would give my life to protect you, as you protected me. Why did you do this? I took your pups and left you to grieve over your mate. Did you understand I wished to save your pups?"

***

As White Elk snuck up toward the pair, the wolf turned and stared up into his eyes. White Elk stopped.

"Not to worry. I am sure he knows you are with me."

"Sure?"

She smiled and shrugged. "Maybe."

"Golden Fox, please tell me he will not tear my leg off."

"He will not tear your leg off."

"You speak the truth to me. Right?"

"Has he torn your leg off yet?"

"No." He stepped beside them.

"Watch it! He licks his lips."

"Golden Fox! Do not scare me so." He moved back.

"I do not scare you. Do you see me lick my lips?"

"You are being mean. You wish to tease me? You are teasing... right?"

"I walk while looking for medicine plants. Mother says to never waste a walk, to always search for tubers to eat and useful plants. I have no tine to tease. Are your eyes always that wide? Do you do that to see better?"

"My eyes are not wide! I am not frightened as a little girl!"

He stepped closer to her and kept his eyes on the wolf. "I am grateful he took down those men. To have lost you to them.... I would have hunted them down."

She shook. "I try to put them out of my mind by wandering, but I cannot. I am a hunted woman and maybe put the band in danger. I feel safe with Frost, but he cannot outrun an arrow. I have watched him lower when he sees someone, or turn to watch another. He knows who he can trust and cannot. He has the knowing."

Frost, caution in every step, came closer to White Elk. He stretched his body toward the human's hand, sniffed it, and moved away.

"Frost must not be hungry." Golden Fox half smiled. "Why did you follow me?"

"I have something I wish to say. You have a mind of your own, unlike the women of my old people. I am used to women who do as they are asked. I will try to understand your stubborn ways. I do not want you to leave camp without my—" He raised a hand before she could speak. "If Dances In Storms did not see where you had gone.... Woman, please understand that I mean well. You cannot go off as you wish anymore."

"I cannot always see into another's mind—only if they feel happy, or guilt, sorrow. Anger shuts me out, and I have never felt anger from you, but I wish to know why you sorrow."

"Out of worry. To not know where you are is not right."

She scrunched up her brows, changing the mood along with the subject. "I also need to speak. If you still want me for a mate, I will be happy. If not, I will understand. I will never allow you to tell me where I can go, nor when. In my Vision Quest—" She lowered her head, turned, and walked away.

He hurried to keep up as her steps grew longer. Frost stayed between them, and White Elk pulled back some.

Her voice rose in pitch as she stopped and faced him. "I... I saw the fort, and people. Some of ours laughed and drank. One woman screamed as a hairy-face grabbed her and took her inside his wooden lodge." She cleared her throat and continued to walk. "I am to help these people, but I do not know how. I know you are willing to help anyone who needs it."

She sped up to jump a small stream, with Frost at her heels. "I may never have a life as the mate you wish of me. I am not one to sit by our fire and wait for you to return. The women of my people are strong and can fight if need be. If you go off to fight, I go also."

She turned toward him. "I must know why I feel such sorrow from you. Is it about a woman?"

He hopped over the waters and spoke with a sad voice. "You are not seeing deep enough, Golden Fox. I must tell you something about me, something no one knows. It is a guilt I will always carry, and I do carry anger. It is why I sleep away from everyone."

He sat on a wide sandstone and motioned to her. "I left my people because of a woman—not one I loved, but one who only wanted me for the color of my hair and skin. She wished to show me off to her family at the gathering when I reached fourteen winters. Her breath always smelled like fire water. She always wished to follow me and speak about our joining. I never said yes, or no. I heard her speak to her women friends about the gifts her parents would give her for having me, an odd one, who maybe held great Power. She told her friends she held no love for me, but for the things I might get her because of my color. This caused me to feel great anger."

He reached down, clenched a bunch of dried stems, and hurled them through the air. "When she walked away, alone, I followed her to the river's edge where she sat. I wished to tell her of how bad she always made me feel, and that I could not mate with a woman as her. Surprised to see me, she staggered and fell in where the river ran fast. I did not help her out. I wished for her to drown. Another jumped in before I could decide to help her or not. He saved her and saw me standing beside the river's edge."

White Elk clenched his fists until the veins on his hands stood out. "She told the band I threw her in. I did not even defend myself. My grandmother went to be alone and never came back, as was custom among the last sunrises of the elders, so I had no one, no family left. I gathered some things, an old mustang no one would miss, and left. I wandered for two cycles of seasons before Dances In Storms found my small camp and asked for food. It was not food she wanted, but to hear my story. By then, I had no mustang, only tattered clothes and a knife. She took me in."

White Elk reached for Golden Fox's hand, and started to pull her close, until he heard a soft growl. "I thought my mind made you up, but wherever our band traveled, I searched for you. When I saw you, I wanted to run away, but could not. I had fallen deep in my heart for you long ago. I had to see if you were real."

He let out a soft sigh. "The dreams I had of you are true. And now, you know the truth about me." He released her hand and turned to go.

She grabbed his hand before he was out of reach. "I cannot share you with another. Never will I do this." She turned, raised her arms, and let them flop back down. "I do not know what to do! Mate or not?"

She ran down the way they had come, Frost beside her.

* * *

Sky Bird stayed hidden, and waited until White Elk left. Then she showed herself and approached her daughter. Eyeing Frost first, she reached for Golden Fox's hand and pulled her close.

The wolf stepped back.

"Please," she said, "never leave camp alone again, until we understand why these men hunt you. Dances In Storms, your grandfather, and the three warriors

176

followed their tracks to see if they could learn where they came from. They vanished into the waters. You do not have enough fear in you to be wary! You *must* learn now, girl. One sunrise—"

Frost nudged Sky Bird's hand.

"So you accepted me, Frost? Do you understand this fearless woman is my daughter?"

The wolf gave her many licks and did not pulled back, but instead stayed in place.

Sky Bird knelt next to him.

He crouched and half crawled, ready to run if anything spooked him as he approached her.

She reached out and ran her hand across his head. "You will protect my daughter. I see this." He came closer, and she put a hand on either side of his head and scratched him. "Heh... I touch a wolf. His fur is coarse, yet also soft. I love his deep golden eyes. It is as if he sees beyond mine and feels my being." She raised her head. "And, he listens... unlike another I know."

Frost licked her face and pressed against her, then backed away and trotted into the brush. He turned his head and looked back, cocked his head at Sky Bird, and turned away again.

"He is as gentle as a newborn deer. It makes no sense. He is a wild wolf!" She stared after the wolf, who did not try to hide as he climbed the stones on the hill.

She shook herself. "Daughter, it is time we speak as a woman to a woman." She could no longer contain her small smile. A wider one replaced it. "Perhaps we should make sure our lodge is on the other side of the camp until my father speaks to White Elk, and the boy brings gifts—many, many gifts. We approach the Sister Wolf Band, and many men will look your way."

Golden Fox lowered her head. "Am I worth so much?"

"I value my daughter more than all the land we walk upon. I would die for you." Golden Fox bowed her head. *Please Spirits, do not let this be so—ever.*

* * *

Sky Bird took in the sights as they settled one last night before going into the canyon. Frost lay next to Golden Fox near the cooking fire to her left. Blue Spirit Dog lay on her other side, as the two sets of pups wrestled on a sleeping robe not far from them.

177

"They are yet so young," Sky Bird said. "I wonder if they will always be as this, playing and sleeping with one another?"

Stands His Ground sat cross-legged next to her. "They were half-bloods. We hurried so to catch up to our bands, because I did not have scouts watching behind us, as much as I should have." His head drooped as though he had failed his people.

Sky Bird patted his arm. "We all pushed to get to our people. I, too, should not have let us forget that the whites hunted Golden Fox and me."

Dances In Storms sat across the fire, tossed a twig into the fire, and spoke. "If there is blame, it belongs to me, as much as Stands His Ground or anyone else. These past few nights, I have not gone out alone to listen for what the Spirits might tell me."

Eagle Thunder, sitting next to Dances In Storms, cleared his throat, and all eyes turned to him. "No one person carries the burdens to feed our people, or to clothe our people, or to raise our young. No one person bears the burden of keeping our people safe. Even our women are often warriors and hunters. There is no need to feel shame. We have traveled a long ways, and our minds and Spirits are fogged with tiredness. These men are dead. The newest person in our band has proven himself a warrior."

Frost lifted his head, glanced around, and yawned before laying his chin on his forepaws and closing his eyes.

23

Golden Fox, at Blazing Fire's insistence, rode Splash at the rear, several mustang lengths away from the closest rider. Splash had gotten used to the wolf pups' scent, and ignored the presence of their father walking next to Blue Spirit Dog and the pups' drag.

Golden Fox shook her head. "Frost would never eat our mustangs!"

Blazing Fire shrugged her shoulders. "The other mustangs wish to be brave, but cannot forget that Father Wolf looks at mustangs as hot meals." The warrior woman chuckled, but all humor fell from her face as she nodded at Frost. "He has much to teach you about being a warrior, Golden Fox. Father Wolf sees life as it is, not as he wishes it to be. When we can look past what appears, and accept things for what they really are, then we can see the dangers that come toward our Peoples. Given a sunrise or two, the mustangs will see the wolf for what he has become, and not fear him. Until then, please ride back here with me. We do not want the mustangs ahead of us racing all the way to the rest of our new band."

All the time Father Sun crossed the sky, Golden Fox considered Blazing Fire's words. After camp was set up for the night, she drifted away from the cooking fires and the talk. Sister Moon shone less light than she had the night before, but the darkness helped her clear her mind.

Though she did not hear his footfalls, she knew Frost followed her. When his muzzle suddenly rooted beneath her hanging hand, she scratched behind his ears.

Easing to the ground, she crossed her legs and shut her eyes. The songs of crickets filled her ears, as did the swish of night bird wings above her. Frost lay tight against her leg, and his warmth made her feel less alone.

The *shh-shh* of feet across the brittle grass snatched her back from her half-aware state. Frost lunged to his feet and whirled, a growl rumbling in his chest as Golden Fox drew her knife and bounded to her feet. Together they faced the intruder.

White Elk halted, his empty hands held out to his sides. "I...." His eyes dipped to Frost. "I come in peace, Golden Fox. Please, tell Frost I am not a warm meal."

She sheathed her knife and crossed her arms. "Why should I tell him this when you disturb us?"

"Because I do not want my leg torn off."

"He will not tear your leg off."

He eased a step closer.

"Watch it! He licks his lips."

White Elk scrambled back. "Golden Fox, do not scare me so... again! We had these words before!"

"I do not scare you, White Elk who comes where he is not invited."

A huff of air blew from White Elk's lips. "You are being mean once more. Why does he still growl at me?

"Ask him. Maybe you smell good."

He took a step closer, though his eyes drifted often to where Frost now sat. "I... I wanted to say I am glad we have such a fine new warrior to travel with us and to help keep you safe."

He stopped when Frost rose and plopped himself in a sitting position between him and Golden Fox.

Her foolish heart sang at his words. "Is this why you searched for me? If it is, you have said your words, and I thank you for your worry, but you can leave us now."

He raised one hand as if he desired to reach out and stroke her cheek. It hung in the air for a short span before falling to his side. "Will you listen, Golden Fox?"

Eyes narrowed, she considered his request. After a short span, she gave a brusque nod. "I will listen."

"I dream only of you, Sweet One." When she opened her mouth to protest his special name for her, he held up a hand. "I am sorry. I will not use that name, the name I feel in my heart for you, Golden Fox."

She bobbed her chin once to let him know she accepted his apology.

"I see you looking when Dances In Storms sits close to me, and when we laugh together, I *feel* your frown even if I cannot see it. It is not as it appears. I do not desire the Holy Woman to be my mate. I desire only you. But the Spirits have given Dances In Storms the dream of a child of her own in her arms. In this dream, you and I are with her in a lodge. We are all gathered around the child, smiling. I laughed only because I thought how clumsy I would be holding such a small creature. I do not know what the Spirits would have of us. I only know that you, and only you, are a part of my Spirit and all of my heart."

Not waiting for an answer, he turned and shuffled away.

She let go a deep sigh. "We sleep here, Frost."

24

The grasslands had given way to rolling hills, and now those rolling hills climbed sharper and higher. The rivers foamed white as they roared through narrow valleys.

Golden Fox fidgeted on Splash as she stared around at the many places whites could hide. Thick patches of trees spotted the land.

Eagle Thunder rode back to Blazing Fire and Golden Fox. "We need you to scout ahead and find a place to camp." He peered around. "I have a bad feeling that we are not alone."

Blazing Fire nodded briskly. "Golden Fox, stay back here and watch behind you. If you see anything that does not look as if it belongs, tell Stands His Ground."

When she opened her mouth to say she could see what followed, Blazing Fire shook her head hard. "You ride a drag with fur children on it. They are as much our band as any two-legged, and we must protect them."

Understanding filled Golden Fox's mind as she slapped a palm against her forehead. "I am as a child! I should have thought of this."

Humor twinkled in the warrior woman's eyes. "You do not act as a child, but you have much to learn." With that, she tapped her mustang into a slow run.

As Father Sun crossed the sky, Golden Fox turned many times—nothing behind them, though a spot between her shoulders kept itching. At last, she told this to Stands His Ground, he nodded and rode off to check behind them.

When he returned, he spoke in a soft voice. "I saw signs of men and mustangs with those met-al spinning things on their feet. I will circle around to the trail behind." Each time, he returned with no news of who followed.

Father Sun dipped behind the taller, sharper hills by the time they rode into a narrow valley that Blazing Fire found. Blood red walls climbed so high that dark crept in and pulled a grey robe over everything. The narrow mouth widened all of a sudden. Trees grew next to the rough stone face on three sides of them, although the center of the closed canyon lay open.

Boulders grew as tall as three or four men stacked high on each other's shoulders. Four such boulders clustered together, mostly hidden by trees. At one end of the cluster of boulders, the valley wall rose. The rest of the boulders nearly created a circle out from the wall. Hidden by the boulders, a cave opened in the canyon wall, offering plenty of space for the small group to shelter.

Grass grew tall in the circle created by the high walls of the valley. The tight mouth into this space would provide a place to ambush and stop any attackers.

During the grey span between Father Sun going behind the horizon and true darkness, two sharp whistles from a night bird echoed. This was the signal.

Bows drawn, the people hid behind boulders and in the black beneath the trees.

Two mustangs staggered into the flat space surrounded by the high walls. The men hunched on the animals' backs lifted faces covered with black hair, and stared around at the mustangs grazing calmly in the thick grass. By the time understanding jerked them straight on their animals, seven arrows pointed at them.

After carefully pulling their hands away from their fire sticks, one man began jabbering in his own language. When no one replied, he drew a breath and tried again. His grimy hands waved as he poured a mix of words from his language and from the People's speech.

When the half-blood with black hair stopped speaking, the man with hair the color of dead grass in the middle of the cold season tried.

White Elk stepped from the shadows of the closest trees, and cocked his head.

The one with dead grass hair smiled, showing yellowed teeth as he turned and signed at White Elk. Before White Elk could translate for the others, the sweat-covered red mustang the man rode staggered.

Stands His Ground and Golden Fox dropped their bows and raced for the animal. They caught the animal as its legs began to fold from exhaustion. When Eagle Thunder ran over to help, Golden Fox reached up and yanked the man off the mustang's back. With hard kicks to his ribs, she yelled at him.

Dances In Storms grabbed her around the waist and pulled her away from the man, who had curled up on the ground.

With a wave of his readied bow, Long Sun motioned for the other man to get off his mustang.

The second man quickly glanced around, and climbed down, his hands held high above his head.

Golden Fox fought to get loose from Dances In Storms' embrace, but the older woman held tight.

Blazing Fire stomped over to Golden Fox. "Stop it! Act as a warrior. We have captives and need to know what they have to tell us."

As soon as Golden Fox stopped fighting against her, Dances In Storms released her. She followed the warrior over to where both men sat on the ground, surrounded by arrows pointed their way.

White Elk squatted in front of the one with dead grass hair. After much chattering that made Golden Fox's ears cringe, he stood up and moved away from the captives.

Eagle Thunder, Dances In Storms, Blazing Fire, and Golden Fox surrounded White Elk. Blazing Fire and Golden Fox stood so they could still watch the captives that Stands His Ground, Long Sun, and Sky Bird circled with drawn bows.

White Elk stepped back. "In traveling, I have learned some hairy-face words and some of their hand signs. When I put these with the words of our People, this is the story they told.

"Five other whites attacked these men, who are traders. These men fought and killed two of the ones who attacked, but their fire sticks quit making noise and they had to run. For a long ways, the other men chased them. Even after they let go of their pack animals, the men kept chasing them. These two rode in a river with fast waters and finally got away. They have been without food for three days. They thought they were riding toward the wooden fort."

Sky Bird crossed her arms. "I understand their words, but do not speak as well as you do. They speak with their hands waving all over. How do we know they do not lie? Perhaps, their mustangs are very tired from chasing us."

Blazing Fire raised a hand to be heard. "Without pack animals, how can we know these men tell the truth?" She looked at Dances In Storms. "Holy Woman, can you see into their hearts?"

Sharp arrows of anger shot from Golden Fox's eyes toward the men. "I do not care if they ran from other hairy-faces or if they chased us. They have treated their mustangs badly. Let us take their mustangs and tell them to walk to their wooden fort."

"Would you take one of Blue Spirit Dog's pups, Granddaughter, and put it in the middle of the woods with nothing to eat and no family to help him?" Eagle Thunder nodded toward the men. "These men are as one of the pups. They have no way to live if we do not help them."

"Father, what if they come to harm Golden Fox?" Sky Bird turned worried eyes on Eagle Thunder.

Lips set in a grim line, he said, "Then they will die." He looked toward the Holy Woman. "Can you tell what is in their hearts?"

Dances In Storms shook her head.

Blue Spirit Dog rubbed against Golden Fox's legs, and when she looked down, blue swirled in the dog's brown eyes.

***

She must have fallen, for when she opened her eyes again, her mother knelt next to her, her worried face hanging over Golden Fox's.

Sky Bird put her arm around Golden Fox's shoulders as she struggled to sit up.

Dances In Storms knelt on her other side. "What did you see, Golden Fox?"

"Blue Spirit Dog told me these men speak truth. Both Frost and her say this is so. They mean us no harm, and have much fear of what will happen to them. They are in great need of help."

All eyes turned to Eagle Thunder, who said, "This is not my decision to make alone. Golden Fox and Long Sun will care for their mustangs. We will build a cooking fire, and feed these strangers and ourselves. After this, we will make them sit where we can watch them, but far enough away so they cannot hear our words. In this way, we will decide if they will live or die."

***

After the mustangs had been rubbed down and allowed to rest, It appeared they had been well fed, and no sores had been made by the ugly met-al against their sides or mouths.

Golden Fox settled across from her mother at the cooking fire, where White Elk handed her a bowl of meat and greens. "Mother, the mustangs have not been badly treated. Perhaps, I let my anger run away without my heart."

"Maybe, my daughter, this would be a good time to ask White Elk to tell that hairy-face you are sorry you brought him harm without reason."

She did not want to apologize to a half-blood, but she felt Blazing Fire's attention on her.

The warrior woman nodded. "A warrior is never too proud to admit that she made a mistake. No one is perfect, and we cannot learn unless we are willing to make mistakes—and to set them right, when we can."

Golden Fox chewed and swallowed the meat in her mouth. "White Elk, would you speak with the man and tell him I am sorry I hit him without reason?"

A grin stretched White Elk's lips. "No, but I will show you how to say it."

"I... I...." A glance at Blazing Fire had her swallowing her protests. "Thank you, White Elk." Though her words were humble, the look she shot him would have set the grasses on fire.

White Elk smiled. "We will do this after we eat. The people sitting at our cooking fire have been without food for too long. It would not be right to disturb their meal." He nodded to the men, who stuffed food into their mouths and swallowed though they had not given themselves time to chew.

When the two men had finished, White Elk signaled for them to follow him a little ways away from the fire.

As Golden Fox started to follow them, her mother handed her clothes, footwear, and the special plant they used to bathe and wash their hair. "Tell them to go to the small creek that runs over there. They need to be clean before I give them sleeping robes. I do not wish to find white worms from their hair in any robe."

Golden Fox jerked her hands behind her back and vigorously shook her head. "I have no wish to speak with these men, except to right the wrong I did."

As Sky Bird pushed the bundle toward her again, Blazing Fire ambled past and said, "Think of this as learning more of the white's speech, Golden Fox. All warriors learn as much as they can about the enemies of their people."

Reluctantly, Golden Fox accepted the bundle and made her way to where White Elk had led the captives.

Father Sun rose high above the steep walls of the valley, and touched a finger to the place where Golden Fox lifted her arms in song. Blue sky with no clouds spread above the Mother.

At the mouth of the valley, where the land spread in all directions, the men sat surrounded by Stands His Ground, Blazing Fire, Sky Bird, and White Elk.

Blue Spirit Dog stood next to the drag behind Splash, where her pups slept.

Frost sat a little ways away from Splash's side.

Though no bows or knives had been drawn, the two men fidgeted next to their mustangs and gave fearful glances around.

In a grave voice, White Elk gave them the People's decision.

Clothed in clean tunics and leggings, and with soft footwear, the hairy-faces grinned big. They would join the People who had saved their lives.

25

Father Sun had not yet reached the highest place in the sky when Dances In Storms led them into a land of many canyons.

Golden Fox stared with big eyes and a mouth agape at the walls of red-orange that reached so far above the Mother. Sister Wind echoed off the rough walls, creating a hollow sound—like the whispers of long-forgotten people. Some canyons had walls so close together, she could almost touch both sides at once. Father Sun barely reached a finger of light to the bottoms of these places.

Dances In Storms led the way into a narrow canyon where only two could ride side-by-side.

The fast-moving river they rode beside roared so loudly that Blazing Fire had to shout for Golden Fox to hear.

Frost walked closer to Blue Spirit Dog and the pups, as he eyed the strange land around them. A sharp bend in the canyon caused Frost's hair to raise along his back, but Blue Spirit Dog did not appear upset.

Golden Fox poked Blazing Fire on the forearm and pointed at the wolf.

With a grin, Blazing Fire pointed up toward the top of the canyon wall, where four warriors stood staring down at them.

Blazing Fire leaned close. "Father Wolf was watching when you were not. Did you not see Dances In Storms raise her arm to them?"

Head ducked, Golden Fox picked at the fringe on her dress. "I feel as if I may never become a warrior."

Blazing Fire patted her back. "You have only been learning for a few moons. Do not worry. You are already as good as many warriors who have studied for a cycle of seasons."

The canyon finally widened. Trees and grasses rolled out for a long distance, until several openings in the high walls led into more canyons and kept Golden Fox from seeing any farther.

White Elk rode back to Golden Fox. "Dances In Storms asks that you stay back with Frost until the she waves for you to bring the wolf forward. She worries that others will let fear take them. These people would never hurt a wolf unless they felt afraid for the children."

With a wave of his hand, he motioned at a pile of large boulders that looked as if they had tumbled from the wall behind them. "She asks that you and the wolves remain next to those boulders until she comes for you. She hopes everyone will see how Frost does not slink as a hunter, but walks as a friend to you. Perhaps, it will be good that they will see Blue Spirit Dog and our mustangs are not afraid of the wolf."

White Elk nodded toward where lodges stood. "Let us hope that Frost does not see the People's mustangs as many meals for him."

* * *

Dances In Storms smiled even as a tightness wrapped around her. Her parents stood at the front of the gathered people. Without a word to anyone, she slid off her mustang and allowed Long Sun to lead the animal away. The people she brought with her remained mounted. She hoped that Golden Fox had heeded her words and now stood with Frost over by the boulders, where the people could see the wolf, and yet be far enough away to feel little fear of him.

Her eyes searched those gathered for Eagle Thunder's people who had come ahead of her small group. She had not been with them long, but she should easily see the sun they had painted on nearly all of their clothes. She saw only a few.

What happened? Were they attacked before reaching my People's camp? Have more died from the poisoned water sickness?

The only lodges with the sun sign sat on the edge of the camp, as if the people who lived there had not been welcomed.

Why would my people turn them away?

She pushed the questions aside.

Her mother and father stood in front of the people with their arms crossed over their chests. No smiles greeted her; rather, her father spun around, and her mother silently followed as he made his way to their lodge.

Dances In Storms' heart pounded against her ribs, and she swallowed the fear that threatened to gag her as she followed her parents.

Even the would not meet her eyes; they all glanced away.

What has happened to make the band so unhappy?

Once inside the lodge, Calls Elk motioned for his daughter to sit.

Her mother offered her a bowl of hot food that she gratefully took. Her ears rang in the silence. The fire had only enough glow for heating food. A gap at the bottom of the lodge, raised for cool air, carried whispers of people who stayed back just enough to not look nosey.

After she finished the food and set the bowl aside, she met her father's hooded eyes. "We had good hunting, Father. I see the hides rest between trees and have been scraped already."

"A good hunt is always welcome. When the cold season comes, the bellies of our people will not cry out with hunger."

"The lodges of the Sun People are set away from the lodges of our People." Dances In Storms waved behind her with one hand.

Her mother's light voice answered the true question. "They chose to set themselves apart."

Dances In Storms' eyes darted between her mother and father. "Only those who have shame set themselves apart from the band."

Her father sighed. "Those with relatives who are sick from the poisoned water have much shame."

Head cocked, her brows pinched together. "Father, many sunrises ago I helped Eagle Thunder's people fight the bad Spirits from the poisoned drink. What shame is it that a person has fought against such Spirits and won?"

Her mother cleared her throat. "When a child is taught that a fire is hot, but reaches out and is burned anyway, the child's mother will heal the hurt. Most children learn from such pain. Yet, the fire will call to some of those children, and no matter how many times they are burned, as soon as they are healed, they will return to the fire."

Dances In Storms' stomach cramped, and she closed her eyes against her failure.

Voice softer, her father commanded, "Open your eyes, for closed eyes will not make Father Sun rise when it is Sister Moon's time to shine."

"I failed Eagle Thunder's people — the ones I was sent to save." Grief tore at her chest, and she clutched her tunic as if to stop the pain.

"When they walked into our camp, no one drank the poisoned water. Their eyes were clear and they spoke with a clean mind." Calls Elk wiped his hand down his face. "I should have seen that something was not right when many insisted on putting up their lodges so far from the rest of the people. I thought only that it must feel strange to be among those you do not know. Sun Rising argued against setting themselves apart, but too many raised their voices and drowned out his counsel."

Her mother, Small Feet, got up and dragged a hide from the side of the lodge. "Inside, you will find five empty leather flasks. I do not know how many they had hidden in their sleeping robes. Your father spoke to the men, and I called a women's counsel. Many ears were closed so tight that boulders could have fallen on the camp, and they would not have heard them."

Her mother knelt and stared at the lodge behind Dances In Storms. With a soft *saa – saa*, she comforted whatever lingered in the lodge's shadows. "Come, Little One, it is safe to come."

A rustling sounded but, afraid of startling whatever her mother called, Dances In Storms did not turn.

Finally, a small girl crept over to Small Feet. Sucking her thumb, she crawled into her mother's lap and hid her face against the older woman's chest.

If Dances In Storms' heart could have shattered, it would have then. "The child?"

Her father answered in a gruff voice. "The girl's mother said we could keep the child if we gave her something to trade for the fire water. The child is only two winters old. I threw the mother's belongings to her and told her to never return, that the child belonged to the People, not to one who thought she was worth nothing more than a flask of poisoned water."

The little girl cringed at Calls Elk's harsh tone, and Small Feet frowned at him. If it had not been such a sad time, Dances In Storms might have laughed at the red spots on her father's cheeks.

Her mother resumed. "Those who left had fire water with them. Half-grown children cried and tried to pull their mothers and fathers away from the poison drink, begging them to stay. One young boy clung to his mother, and his father gently pulled him away and told him his mother no longer wanted him." Small Feet's eyes squeezed shut. When she opened them, they were wet.

Dances In Storms shook her head. "The ones who live in the lodges.... Why are they still living on the edge of camp?"

"They feel shame that their relatives brought poisoned water to our camp." Calls Elk shifted and rubbed the part of his thigh where a bear's claws had left four scars. "Sun Rising said his people will not move their lodges closer until they have been cleansed by our Holy Woman."

"What say you, Father? Do you wish for these people to become part of our band?"

"The people who stayed all worried about the children, the little ones the sick ones took with them. Sun Rising asked for a few warriors to ride with him and Eagle Thunder's people, to bring the young ones back. When darkness hid the land, our warriors followed Sun Rising and his people to where the ones who drank poisoned water slept the sleep of the dead." Her father paused and looked at Small Feet.

"The little one sleeps," she said.

He turned to Dances In Storms. "Some of those who drank the poisoned water had not fallen into the sleep of the dead. There was fighting, and four of those sick on the poisoned water went to the campfires in the sky. One girl of about six winters old was trampled by one of the sick one's mustangs, and she too went to the campfires in the sky."

"Will they come looking for the young ones, Father?"

With sorrow in his eyes, he shook his head. "Father Sun has risen six times since the children were returned to the lodges in our camp. No one came. Those who did not die have continued to travel toward the whites' lodges. They did not have much poisoned water left, so most will not make it. The shakes will come on them before they reach the wooden fort."

He glared at the empty flasks. "Daughter, I must tell you—this poisoned water carries a very powerful Spirit. After I had chased away those who drank it, I lay down and tried to sleep. The flasks called to me though I had never drunk of the poisoned water. I got up and searched through them until I found one almost full, and one half-full. I wished to understand these people, and why they would give up their band to chase such poison."

His head dipped, but he lifted it so he looked into her eyes. "I crept out of the lodge and went to where the boulders lean against each other. As Sister Moon watched me, I drank from the flask. With every swallow, I felt stronger, as if I became young once more. I felt wiser, as wise as the most powerful Holy Man. When I fell into this sleep that is not sleep, I dreamed. It has been many years since last I dreamed. I could have cried for happiness."

Dances In Storms stared at her father and felt as if she did not know him.

"When Father Sun woke me, my head hurt so bad that I groaned out loud. I felt lost, confused, sad, and very angry, as if someone had stolen my most loved mustang. I walked and fought the Spirit of the poisoned water all day. When Sister Moon rose again, I crept out to the boulders and unburied the last flask. I drank it. Again, I had wonderful dreams, powerful dreams. When Father Sun woke me, my stomach cramped in want of the poisoned water. I came to your mother and told her what I had done. She told me not to return to our lodge until I sat in the sweat lodge and forced the bad Spirits from my body."

"Father, do you still crave the poisoned water?" Dances In Storms asked quietly.

Lips tight, the muscles in his jaw bulged as he fought to speak. "Yes, Daughter, it shames me to say I hunger for the poisoned water sometimes — not for the strength I felt, for I know that was a lie. I crave it for the dreams that left me when I took your mother for my woman. I grieve for the Power that once lived inside me. For a short span, the poisoned water returned those dreams, though I know they were not real dreams, but false ones sent by the bad Spirits in the poisoned water." His gaze locked on hers. "When the people are settled, I ask that you come with me to the sweat lodge to heal me."

"It would be an honor, Father. Shame feels as a heavy robe on my shoulders. I am sorry that I caused you to step onto a broken path created by the ones I sent here."

With a firm shake of his head, he continued to speak. "I was the one who listened to the whispers of the poisoned water. You would have counseled me against it, as would your mother, had I talked with her. This broken path is one my feet needed to step upon to break the pride that blinded me. We all choose the path we walk, Daughter. All those who love us can do is to take our hand when we reach out to them for help."

Small Feet shifted the sleeping child in her arms. "What have your dreams told you, Daughter, that you can share with us?"

Worry shot through her as she studied the fine lines around her mother's eyes, and the deeper lines across her forehead. "This I can tell you — I will be staying here during the cold season. There is much work to be done, for when the season of new grasses comes again, Golden Fox, who you will soon meet, will leave our camp for a time, and I must go with her. And, Father, she has a wolf with her and his pups. We are as Shining Light's band. The wolf will cause no harm. It is good to be among wolves again."

She cleared her throat and looked away. "We have two whites with us. They wished not to go back among their own people. They work hard to learn our words, and have helped to watch over our small camp in darkness. They are fine hunters. They wish to find their new names here, among us."

He remained silent.

"Father, what say you?"

Calls Elk pushed to his feet. "Walk with me, Daughter, and help me greet those who have followed you here. Even the whites will be welcomed. I know you would bring no danger to us. We will speak to those who feel shamed, let them move closer. They no longer carry any shame. If they wish, I will go into the sweat lodge with them to sing and pray."

Dances In Storms reached out for the child on her mother's lap, but Small Feet shook her head. "She cries if anyone except me tries to touch her." She brushed the hair from the little girl's face. "I do not mind. Go with your father. I will come after I place her on a sleeping robe."

***

When Dances In Storms called the people together, Golden Fox stood up and brushed the pieces of grass from the back of her dress. Frost nudged her hand and she scratched behind his ears. "Soon, Frost, she will come and we will have to follow her. I do not like so many eyes on me."

A young man pranced across the grass toward her. His eyes darting often to Wolf, he stopped only a mustang length away. "A golden-red-haired white woman? Who do you belong to, so I may trade for you?"

"Trade for me?" Golden Fox drew herself stiff and tall.

"Ahh, this is good. You understand and speak as we do. I will have to offer at least three mustangs for you. I wish for the wolf to be part of the trade. Tell me, woman, who captured you?"

She pulled her knife. "Perhaps, boy, you should learn to keep silent unless you know of what you speak. Go away from me before I show you how a warrior woman of my people handles a boy with no manners."

Frost stepped between Golden Fox and the boy. A snarl lifted his lip and his long, white teeth gleamed in the bright light of Father Sun.

The cocky grin fell from his face as he shuffled back a few steps.

"My wolf has not eaten since Father Sun rose. Maybe you would make a good meal for him."

The boy's eyes widened. "It... it would not be polite to let your wolf eat one of Dances In Storms' band."

Her hand dropped to the wolf's neck.

White Elk ran over, stopped, and grinned. "Ahh, I see you have offended Golden Fox and Frost, a most Powerful wolf. You had better apologize before the wolf decides to teach you some manners, Sun Who Rises Early. I do not think you could hunt so well with only one hand."

All color drained from the boy's face. "You... you would not let...." He swallowed hard and licked his lips. "I... I did not mean to offend. I was... teasing. Tell her, White Elk! I tease girls who are very good to look at."

Golden Fox lifted her chin. "I find it offending to be called a *White Woman*. I am granddaughter of Eagle Thunder, leader of our band."

"I... I am sorry. Never have I seen such bright hair on any of our Peoples."

She flipped her head and the strands that had hugged her cheeks fell behind her shoulders. "I spoke with a sharp tongue. My mother says there is no shame in carrying some white blood, that it does not make me less of the Peoples."

"Dances In Storms wants you to come now, Golden Fox." White Elk turned toward the boy. "Sun Who Rises Early, perhaps it is time for you to greet your sister, Dances In Storms."

The boy ducked his head and hurried toward the main part of the camp.

White Elk chuckled. "He does not mean to anger you. He is Dances In Storms' youngest brother, and spends much time alone making bows, so he does not understand how to talk to young women.

"He is the best bow maker among several bands. Many warriors come to him, and he dreams of the bows they ask him to make. Each bow fits that person as no other bow ever has, and the arrows fly true from its string. Do not be surprised if you awake one morning and find a new bow outside of your lodge. Sometimes, it is his way of showing he is sorry to those he offends with his teasing."

As Golden Fox drew nearer to the gathered people, her heart throbbed in her throat. Her feet shuffled to a halt. She wanted to run away, to hide behind the boulders until everyone slept. Splash lowered her muzzle and shoved her hard between the shoulders. With reluctant steps, she began walking again, Frost at her side.

A man who could only be Dances In Storms' father, who she knew to be called Calls Elk, leader of the Sister Wolf Band, stood in front of the people with crossed arms. Beaded on the front of his tunic was a wolf's head, thrown back and howling. Fringe followed the side of his leggings from hip to ankle. Beads decorated each fringe and clinked whenever he moved.

With trembling hands, she dug deep into Frost's neck as sweat beaded on her forehead. She stood several long strides away when the pups raced past her and leapt up on Calls Elk's legs. The black wolf pup grasped the toe of Calls Elk's footwear and tugged, giving little puppy growls as he shook his head. Blue Spirit Dog's pups danced back and forth and barked with high-pitched puppy voices.

Frost sat down on one side of Golden Fox, his tongue lolling from the side of his mouth as if he laughed at the pups' energy. Blue Spirit Dog let out a sigh and lay down next to Frost.

Searching for her voice and the ability to move, Golden Fox dashed forward. "Night Wolf, no! Stop that!" She reached out and grabbed at the pup, but he bounced out of reach, only to race back and grab another piece of Calls Elk's footwear.

She grasped the white wolf pup by the scruff of her neck, but not before she yanked one of the fringes from Calls Elk's leggings.

At first, Golden Fox did not hear the laughter. Finally, Calls Elk's voice reached her panicked mind.

"Golden Fox, these must be your wolves. Leave the young ones to play. They have been too long on the drag I see behind your mustang."

She stopped and straightened up to meet the Sister Wolf Band's leader. "I... I am sorry."

He waved her apology away. "It has been generations since last we had wolf pups grabbing at our clothes. It fills my heart with happiness to see them among us again."

"Your dogs... your mustangs... you must tie them so they...."

He held up one hand and stopped her words. "No, let them be. Our dogs and our mustangs come from those that once traveled with Shining Light's Wolf Band People. I do not think they will fear these pups." He nodded toward Splash. "Besides, your mustangs will give them courage that the wolves do not see them as food. Only your Father Wolf might see the dogs as food, but your dog shows no fear."

"Frost has told me that he will honor your dogs and mustangs as he honors those who belong to my people."

Eyebrows shot high, Calls Elk looked at her. "Ahh, do you also have Shining Light's gift of talking to the wolves?"

Scuffing her toe in the grass, she lowered her head. "I do not know if I can talk to wolves. I only know that Frost will talk to me."

"You bring my people a Sacred blessing, young woman. Come and sit at our cooking fire, so we may share food and talk."

* * *

Golden Fox wandered around the busy camp. Calls Elk had insisted that they place Eagle Thunder's family lodge near his own. With the help of many hands, their few belongings were soon in a new lodge. Many people came with gifts, and soon their lodge filled with fine things, which they shared among the rest of the once Sun People.

Her mother gathered around cooking fires with the other women of their new band, sounding like the black- and white-colored birds that gather in the trees and chatter loudly. Sky Bird had shooed Golden Fox away, telling her to meet the other young women around camp, and to let the Sister Wolf Band people ask questions about Frost and the wolf pups.

A group of young men had taken White Elk somewhere. Golden Fox could only turn her head to follow him until he blended into the trees.

Dances In Storms had taken Long Sun to the lodges on the edge of the camp.

Blue Spirit Dog and the pups, after much excitement, had fallen asleep on robes inside Eagle Thunder's lodge.

Frost had left, as he sometimes did, to seek his own food. Perhaps, he needed time away from so many people and dogs. It must have been as difficult for him as for her in letting others become comfortable with their differences.

Will I ever feel as if I belong among any Peoples, or will my gold-red hair and green eyes always make me feel alone?

A man's voice shouted. Her head whipped around to locate the voice, and the man shouted again. "Golden Fox!"

Finally, her eyes found the man hurrying through clumps of people, his face creased in a wide grin. As he drew closer, she noticed the small of amount of hair that grew on his chin.

"Golden Fox, I welcome you to the Sister Wolf Band. I am called Fast Runner."

A woman hurried forward and stopped a half step behind him, her eyes cast shyly to the ground.

He reached back and pulled her forward. "This is my woman, Sings Loud."

Never good at knowing what to say to strangers, she dipped her head to the woman as she studied the man from the side of her eyes. "You carry white blood?"

"My two brothers and I, yes. Our father was of the Peoples. Our mother is sister to Small Feet, Calls Elk's woman."

"Do all of you live here?" She scuffed the toe of her footwear in the dirt, not used to being so nosy. Her mother had taught her that people would tell her what they wanted her to know, and it was impolite to be as Bear, pushing his nose into everyone's past. Yet, it seemed as if this man expected her to ask after his family.

"Only sometimes. Our mother follows our father when he goes to his wooden lodge in the canyons. He refuses to live near the fort where poisoned water is passed around." He peered around. "Where is the black wolf who travels with you?"

"Frost hunts for his food."

A small boy crashed into Fast Runner and clung to his leg. The man laughed as he picked the boy up. "Perhaps, he looks for a boy to eat?"

The boy squealed with laughter and wiggled until Fast Runner put him down. "Big dog no eat me." He held clawed hands up and growled. "Eeeerrrrr! I eat you, maybe."

Fast Runner pretended fright until another boy ran up growling. "I am Bear!"

After the children ran off, Golden Fox nodded their way. "He has hair the color of the yellow sandstone that we saw as we rode in the canyons."

Sings Loud shyly spoke up. "That one fears nothing. He is called Lightning Boy. As Dances In Storms, he runs out and twirls in circles when the Thunder Beings roar. The other young one is his cousin, Boy Who Laughs."

A smile twinkled in Fast Runner's eyes. "Our son has less than half the blood of the People, yet no one of Sister Wolf Band cares about this. Perhaps, with your gold-red hair and green eyes, you have wondered how the People will be toward you." When she did not answer right away, he continued. "Here in the Sister Wolf Band, we know that our People do not always come from the same blood, but always they come from the same Spirit."

The smile died away and sternness came over his face. "Young One, I have heard the stories from Eagle Thunder's people—how there were Sun People who did not accept your mother because she is half-blood like me, and those who did not accept you because your mother is half-blood and your father is white. Know that you are not alone. Among our Sister Wolf Band, you will find that people are judged by their hearts, not by the color of their hair and eyes."

Sings Loud tugged his arm and gazed up with loving eyes. "Enough said, my man." She turned her eyes to Golden Fox. "Know this, my sister: I have heard many good things about your mother and about you. You are both welcome in our lodge and at our cooking fire." She handed Golden Fox a clean tunic and leggings. "They have yet to have any quills or beads on them, but the stitches are tight and will fit you well. Your mother spoke of this as being your choice of wear. We dress as we please, men and women."

Before Golden Fox could respond, the woman ran after her children.

26

Golden Fox rested high on the rim of a canyon, gazing out over the winding rock walls below. She had ridden up here with Blazing Fire, joining the warriors who guarded the camp. She cushioned her chin on clasped hands as the warmth of Father Sun loosened tired muscles. They had been with the Sister Wolf Band for the hot season, and Blazing Fire continued to train her. She, in turn, had helped Blazing Fire with the younger girls and boys in the ways of fighting.

Leaves had begun to turn golden and orange-red, losing the greens of the warm season. The rock walls held the heat, and the breeze danced through the trees. Loose leaves twirled through the air and started to cover the ground.

The women and children of their new band carried woven cattail baskets in a 'V' shape as they gathered ripe berries. The shape kept the berries on the bottom from being crushed. The women would add the berries to meat mixed with fat, making pemmican for the cold season, when food would become scarce. Some of the berries would be dried and put into baskets. When the women moved from bush to bush, a good portion of the berries still clung to the spindly limbs — they left these for the birds and other animals, and to become seeds for more plants.

Behind her, Sky Bird painted a picture of the canyons on a soft deer hide. All warm season, she had painted beautiful red canyons with trees that jutted outward and struggled to grow toward the sun. With her gifted hand, she had detailed roots that entangled themselves around boulders and pushed their way into small crevices.

Golden Fox loved the paintings of the plants that struggled to grow most of all. She took courage from them.

The only paintings she had seen that were as good as her mother's paintings were a few from long ago, by a woman called Falling Rainbow. Small Feet had one such painting in her lodge. Dances In Storms — a distant relative of Falling Rainbow — had two small paintings by the gifted woman hanging in her lodge.

Dances In Storms... what is she going to do about White Elk?

When the people gathered, Golden Fox often saw Small Feet watching her daughter with pity in her eyes. Dances In Storms must have told her mother that both of them were to share a man.

Anger and confusion flashed through Golden Fox like a stream that raced over rocks, white foam and mist rising from it. She shoved the thoughts away. It was more important to learn the ways of fighting than to worry about having a man. That much she had learned from Blazing Fire.

As the warm season ended, she thought perhaps Blazing Fire spoke the truth. The dream of the Peoples dying at the fort had been returning nearly every night.

The only one she studied as closely as Blazing Fire was her mother. Every day, they gathered medicine plants, and Golden Fox learned medicines and new ways to protect her people. Her mother had begun painting the medicine plants on scraps of deer hide, so that any who wished to learn about them could do so. Other women of the Sister Wolf Band heard about this, and often came to show her mother yet another plant that grew only in the canyons.

She flopped to her back and stared up into the branches of a pine tree. Two brown squirrels chased each other around and around the trunk of the tree. Blue-grey birds, with feathers that rose on the top of their heads when angered, loudly scolded the squirrels. Farther away, snow dusted the high peaks. Soon it would fall on the canyons.

Frost shoved his muzzle beneath her hand and she scratched behind his ears.

Although Calls Elk only allowed certain traders to come into the camp, Eagle Thunder and Sky Bird felt it best if Golden Fox stayed away when they came. As the traders arrived, Blazing Fire would take her and other young people out into the canyons, with three of Sister Wolf Band's warriors, to teach them tracking and scouting. Once White Elk had asked to come, and she welcomed him, but only to watch.

Sky Bird, with her grey eyes and hair the color of mud, would leave with Dances In Storms to gather medicine plants when the traders came... until her painting became desirable.

She painted squirrels chasing one another around pine trees, never missing the detailed lines on the tree's bark. Small colorful birds of yellow and black, brown birds with orange breasts, and blue-grey ones with feathers that rose up on their heads, became of great interest to her. Some she quilled, others she painted and quilled together, and she used traded beads to add brilliant colors she never had before.

A small hawk sat and watched on a nearby branch. She caught his every color as sunlight glistened on his white, brown, and yellow feathers. The changing seasons brought even more beauty as snow dusted the high peaks.

Twice she painted herds of deer and elk as they grazed near streams, and once an endless herd of humpbacks came by, and she painted the light snow that clung to their backs.

* * *

Traders came by once or twice a moon, hoping to add to their wealth as they went from band to band. The traders' eyes would widen as they ran their fingers over Sky Bird's mixed paintings, and they offered much in trade for her skilled work.

When traders came, Dances In Storms offered the paintings, knowing what Sky Bird, who dared not show herself to outsiders, would ask for. The Holy Woman would sit with traders and point to huge bags of sorted porcupine quills, ready-made paints that took much time to make from gathered plants, medicines she and Sky Bird could maybe learn about together.

Some traders offered humpback robes, and thick hides for footwear that would not wear through so fast when the snow came.

Whenever traders brought out drink in bottles to trade, she would shake her head, and roll up the painted hides and leave.

One trader, who came this day, clearly panicked after she refused the drink he offered. "My travels have been long, and I offer you much more than drink, if you will tell me where to find the golden-red haired girl. I see your band has half-bloods. You must know of her, and must know I will give you met-al knives and the magic that makes them sharp, a special stone."

Dances In Storms laughed and told him only a fool would think such a girl exists. "If I knew of her, would I not speak up for such knives?"

"Then, I would ask to speak to the Holy Man." He untangled his legs and stood.

Dances In Storms raised her chin and crossed her arms. "You speak to her now."

"A woman?" He sputtered as he twisted to face her.

Her eyes bore deep into his, and he backed away. To see a strong woman with eyes that could see into a Soul must have caused him enough pain to look away.

He rubbed his eyes and raised his voice. "I only wish to find the girl with the golden-red hair!"

"I, Dances In Storms, tell you to leave. Leave now or be stripped of all you have, even your footwear. You are no longer welcome here. Do not tell us this girl is here and speak louder when we say she is not. Even if a golden-red-haired girl did exist, do you think we are fools enough to give her to you? She must be worth much, and it is we who would trade her, not you."

Dances In Storms turned away, as did the rest of the band, and left him and his helpers standing alone.

The trader cussed and packed up to leave. When he tried to scratch on hide flaps to gain attention on the way out of camp, he found Dances In Storms and White Elk waiting behind him, lances pointed his way.

White Elk snarled. "Two days ride, you will find another camp. Perhaps, if you do not ask for the golden-red haired one, they will allow you to stay the cold season. Your greed and mistrust of our Holy Woman has made you not welcome. Already, riders have left to warn other nearby bands of a greedy trader with poison in bot-tles that kills Souls. Best if you pour them out now, or we will do so for you.

The trader protested, smiled, and offered met-al knives for free.

Dances In Storms half grinned, but her voice carried a harsh tone. "This black stallion who follows me bites, and bites hard, drawing blood. The Peoples out here tire of being asked for your girl who does not exist, and to be bribed with your drink. She is in the minds of the whites."

She lowered her eyes and nodded toward his chin. "I see some bits of hair on your chin, and grey eyes — you share their blood. Now I understand your greed. Give us the bot-tles before you kill our sister bands. Then go. If you do not, we will take them, and I will allow my mustang to bite you in a place all will know of."

With shaky hands, he offered most of his bottles. He held back five. "They are *my* medicine. I will not share, as I now have so little left." He eyed the snorting mustang.

White Elk poured out the bottles and watched the trader leave with his helpers. "I am going to stay back and see what he does. If he goes toward our sister bands, I will ride ahead and warn them to speak nothing of Golden Fox. This trader and his three helpers might have to make their own camp. It is strange they have no dogs. All traders have dogs and extra mustangs, but he has neither — traded them for words about Golden Fox maybe, or drink."

***

White Elk stood beside Dances In Storms, whose brows tightened.

She shook her head. "Where is Golden Fox? I know she has been upset with me because I told her I had to make you two wait to join, but that was two moons ago. I have much to teach her, and now she must know I made the trader leave, even though traders expect us to invite them to stay for the cold season. I did this for her. He would have seen her."

He straightened and firmed his stance. "She is fine, Dances Is Storms, and knows the trader came. As soon as he left the front of her lodge, she ran up high on the ridge with Frost, Blue Spirit Dog, and the grown pups. I will go get her now that the trader is gone, if you wish to speak to her. It is not anger she feels, but confusion, unsure of what choices to make. She spends much time with Blazing Fire."

Dances In Storms lowered her chin. "I told her she must learn faster than Long Sun. Her Power must be at its fullest for her to be strong. Her moon times take away from this —"

"Must she be old as you and wait until she has no more moon times?" White Elk ground his jaw.

She faced him, clearly hurt by his remark. "I cannot control the Spirits and their wishes. Perhaps it will be but a short time." Her voice broke up. "I am not so old, White Elk. You know I, too, wish for love. I would be a good mate. And... I still have moon times."

She turned and left to be alone. When a woman has her moon time, Power becomes stronger, and can harm a man's Power, make him weaker and unable to go into battle.

My mood changes, as does my concentration.

Sadness crept into her at the thought of not holding a baby, or a man. She knew her own moon time approached — better to be alone than go to the woman's hut. Chatting women would make her sadder. She needed to pray the whole time to keep her power strong.

Spirits, guide me please. My heart is torn.

27

Sister Wind left bare trees with only squirrel nests as reminders of warmer days. Snow lay heavy on the shrubs where once berries had teased birds. Small paths of animals lay imprinted in the more shallow places. Ice lightly crusted the stream near camp, where humpback-robed women hurried to get bladders of water. Children raced through the wind and laughed when branches of snow fell on a playmate.

Along the wide part of the ridge above the camp, Golden Fox and White Elk chased after the pups of both Blue Spirit Dog and Frost. "It is not so cold, White Elk! Even children come out of the lodges." She pushed him into a wind-swept drift and ran away laughing.

He yelled back as he stood and brushed off the humpback coat Golden Fox had made him. The hide's hair, worn on the inside, made for nice cold season wear, and protected him not only from the cold, but from Sister Wind's unpredictable blasts. "I had no idea a *girl* could sew such a fine coat!"

He started to chase her, but a growl from behind froze him in place. Slow as a porcupine, he turned, and bright white teeth greeted him. He raised his arms and growled back.

The white wolf lunged.

They wrestled on the ground until White Elk could not take in air from spilling so much laughter. "Sun Snow, stop! Who would have thought you would outgrow your brothers, Night Wolf and Silent Shadow?"

"One day she might think you taste so good, she will not stop at licking." Golden Fox plopped down, and Night Wolf and Silent Shadow fell beside her. "A *girl* would be the one to beat you up. And one only seven moons old!"

"Sun Snow has many sharp teeth!" He pulled her clamped jaw from his wrists. "She could bite me and take off my arm, if she wished to do so."

The white wolf ran after the pack of nearly grown pups.

Blue Spirit Dog and Frost play-bit each other as they ran with the dog's two grown pups. The smallest female dog, an exact image of her mother, ran past them and jumped into Golden Fox's arms, knocking them both down.

The other female, a darker brown with speckled feet, slid past her with Sun Snow close behind, and leapt into White Elk's arms for protection.

He grabbed Sun Snow on either side of her muzzle and shook her, and she lowered herself and licked his face. The shaking reminded her to be gentle, as the dogs could not compete with the stronger wolves.

White Elk wore a sad smile. "I know they all get along, but one day very soon, the wolves will choose who is who. I worry Blue Spirit Dog's pups will get hurt."

Golden Fox nodded at Frost. "I do not think he will allow this to happen. He knows they are not his daughters, yet still he watches over them."

She stared into smallest one's deep brown eyes. A light hint of blue surrounded the brown. "It was hard to call you any name. I saw the promise of blue in your eyes, and then I saw a branch of orange leaves reflecting back in them. I think Father Sun helped name you. We sat next to Mother as she and I painted on one of the hides those very leaves." She hugged her. "Bright Leaves, I love you."

The other pup came over and pushed her sister away, so she could sit on Golden Fox's lap. "Yes, I love you too. Mother called you Dusty Brown as she shook out the hide you lay on. People laughed and called you that. You know many dogs never have names, never know the deep emotions we have for one another."

She stroked the dog's dense fur. "You are called Dusty, nothing else." She leaned over to stare into the dog's eyes. "Same light blue ring. I do wonder why this is so."

"What do you speak of?" White Elk leaned over. "I see gold-brown eyes only."

She put the dog down and took his face between her hands. "White Elk, why have you not gone through a Vision Quest?"

"How... how do you know such a thing?"

She shrugged.

He hugged Sun Snow and looked away. "I... tried among my own people when I turned thirteen winters, and again when I reached fourteen winters. My father called me aside and told me to stop trying. He told me because I am albino, maybe I only have a half-Spirit, and no one hears a half-Spirit." He crossed his legs, bent forward, and rubbed his face deep in Sun Snow's fur. "I failed."

"A half-Spirit!" She scooted sideways to face him. "No one fails as long as we *believe* in *ourselves*. Creator gives us a choice to believe, as do the Spirits. Grandfather spoke these words to me, and Mother says we are never alone. I believe both of them. Where are your beliefs?"

She let out a slow sigh. "Do you believe in yourself? Or do you believe what others say about you? Can you not see the Great Mystery in the beauty of the land, the Spirits in your dreams, And the sparkle in the white fur of Sun Snow? There is another life, where it does not matter what you look like."

She stared up at the cloudy sky. "I have seen Shining Light! I believe he is why the mustangs and wolves accept each other. No mustang with a baby will be still as wolves walk through their herd, but these mustangs are!"

She dug into the heavy humpback fur on White Elk's collar. "Shining Light came to me in a dream, and I watched him walk among the mustangs with the wolves, only two sunrises after we came here. He must have communicated with them. I did not." She pulled him close. "I will send Dances In Storms to come speak with you when I go down in camp. Listen to her words—become them. I do not know what she will say, but I believe in her... even when she said we must wait to be joined. No matter. Even if it is in the middle of the cold season, or the hottest season when you have your Vision Quest, I will be there for you... and Dances In Storms."

***

Frost followed her as she wandered along the canyon until Father Sun dropped behind the high wall. She turned toward Dances In Storms' lodge at the edge of the camp. The Holy Woman counseled many, and sought to be alone, so others with big ears would not hear the words spoken to her.

A cooking fire burned in front of the lodge. Dances In Storms stirred something in her pot, facing in the other direction. Without turning, she said, "Please, sit at my fire, Golden Fox, and eat with me."

Unable to refuse the request, Golden Fox shuffled over and sat across from the older woman. Frost lay next to her, his chin on his forepaws as he gazed into the flickering flames. She accepted the bowl of meat and tubers and began to eat, while Frost gnawed on the bone White Elk had given him.

After they set their bowls aside, the Holy Woman poured them hot drinks. Over the rim of the bowl, she watched Golden Fox. "Yes, it is important for White Elk to Vision Quest, even though it is the cold season."

She jerked up her head and sputtered, "How... how did... you know?"

With eyebrows raised nearly to her hair, Dances In Storms gave her a gentle look. "I am not unaware of the looks you give White Elk. This is a hard choice that the Spirits have put on all of us. You love him and wish to be his only woman, which is a good thing. A woman's first man should only have one woman in his lodge. It is for older women and sisters to share a man. A young woman has too much fire inside for her to do this. There is a time for women to share a man, and it is good, but...."

She glanced away and shook her head. "I have continued to pray about this, Golden Fox, but the Spirits have been silent. All of us must be sure this is the right choice, or it will become a broken path that we three walk."

"Why now, Holy Woman? Much danger hides in the cold season for one alone."

"White Elk is a young man with heat in his loins. He becomes impatient waiting."

"What about you, Holy Woman? Perhaps, this is as much about your impatience as his."

With a nod, Dances In Storms acknowledged her words. "I, too, would like to know if White Elk is to be the father of my only child. My seasons for bearing children are not many, so I cannot wait long if I am to follow the Spirits' guidance and be blessed in this way."

Golden Fox's head drooped to her chest. "You must think me a selfish child. I have many cycles of seasons to be blessed by children, yet it seems as if I would deny you even one child." She lifted her head. "I do not wish to be selfish, Holy Woman, but I... I love White Elk, and it hurts my heart to think of you and him lying together."

She bolted to her feet and ran into the darkness.

28

Golden Fox shuffled back and forth below in the camp. The wolves and dogs had stayed above the rim of the canyon with White Elk. The snow had begun to fall once more, and every time she tried to stare up at White Elk, the snow hit her in the eyes and forced her to look away.

Dances In Storms gave her a sideways glance as she took the path to the top of the rim, carrying two humpback robes with her. Two women followed her and carried much wood.

When the women came down, they only shook their heads and hurried back into their lodges.

Golden Fox stomped her feet to get warmth back into them.

I am too cold to stay out here much longer. With Father Sun sleeping longer, the cold is harsh. Do I sit out here and make a fire?

"Daughter, you cannot do this any longer." Sky Bird reached for her and tried to turn her around. When she refused to turn, her mother walked around to face her. "Little one, you could freeze as hard as a stone! Deer Woman made us all a good meal, and we wait on you. Stands His Ground even waits. A man should never have to wait on the food he hunted."

Her mother sighed. "You hair is stiff and your lips are blue. Must I ask Stands His Ground to carry you?"

"No, I will." Eagle Thunder scooped up his granddaughter and carried her to his lodge. "I will keep her this night, as I am alone."

Once inside, he offered her a bowl of food.

She shook her head and scowled. "I am not so hungry."

"It is the food Deer Woman made." He shook his head. "Women! Stubborn as rattlesnakes. They shake their tail and move their heads sideways, and Wolf grabs them from behind." He moved the bowl and scooted closer to her. "You must remember that too much worry makes the belly hurt. Your teeth grind and crack when there is no reason. White Elk is not wounded, in pain, or going to the campfires in the sky."

She put her head on his shoulder. "He has no belief in himself. His father told him he only had a half-Soul because he is albino — told him to forget trying to go on a Vision Quest, that he never would be able to talk to the Spirits." She pounded her fists on her legs. "He dreams, Grandfather! He told me that is how he found me, through his dreams."

He pushed the bowl of food at her. "Do you think he would still be up there with Dances In Storms if he did not have some kind of beliefs? Would he not walk away? He would have no respect for the Holy Woman and he would leave. *He listens.* She speaks to him and he responds.

"A person's Spirit would turn black, crumble, and blow away if they did not have some kind of belief. A person could not breathe in and out without belief that they could. They would have no emotions. They would be as empty as last season's bird's nest. White Elk would not love you as much as he does if his heart had no beliefs."

"You are right, Grandfather. I am being silly. You are an elder, and I know what you say to be true."

29

Golden Fox kept gazing up at the rim of the canyon, unable to see the sweat lodge for the snow that fell in large, dry flakes.

Sky Bird walked out of their lodge and laid an arm around her shoulders. "It is his time to find what the Spirits want to tell him. You will only get cold and cough, if you stay out here any longer. Come, Daughter, I have something I wish to share with you."

Settled comfortably near her mother's fire pit, Golden Fox crossed her legs and waited.

Her mother picked up a tunic she was beading and threaded a needle. "You are a woman and a warrior now, and no longer need a mother in the same way. It is time to speak to you of where my heart takes me."

"You want Stands His Ground to move into your lodge." Heat climbed Golden Fox's neck after she blurted her thoughts.

Sky Bird threw her head back and a warm laugh rolled from her. After her laughter trickled into chuckles, she shook her head. "Why did you think this, Golden Fox?"

"Stands His Ground has been your friend since you were a child and... and I have seen how you bend your heads together and whisper. I have heard how you laugh together."

Sky Bird lay the tunic to one side, reached forward, and tossed another small piece of branch into her fire. Red embers flew up toward the night-dark reaches of the lodge, where a smoke flap lay open. "Yes, Stands His Ground and I have been friends since we were barely out of our cradleboards. And you are right: I

212

love him." She caught Golden Fox's gaze. "But, I love him as a brother, not as a lover."

"But he gave you sky beads, and you wear them always. And... and you thought he might become your man."

"I wanted so much to be like other girls in our camp. I wanted to dress like them and learn to cook like them and...." She waved a dismissive hand. "I was not like them, Golden Fox. I knew that in my heart. The boys of the Sun People would not look at me as they did the other girls. This is why I let your hairy-face father take me to his wooden lodge. I wanted to be like other women, but I was not, and so I thought if only I had a child of my own, this would make me like them."

Brows crinkled in bewilderment, Golden Fox stared. "I do not understand, Mother."

A sigh eased from the older woman. "My mother told me that I should be glad for my differentness, but it was too hard. I became the woman of a white man, thinking that perhaps the color of my hair and my eyes was what kept me from being like the other girls and women among the People. Perhaps, among the whites, I would be happy. When that did not happen, I thought a baby would make me like other women. Though I have loved you from the first time you drew breath, you could not make me what I was not. When I returned to my father's lodge, my mother held me and I cried. She told me that someday I would find what I searched for, but only if I learned to accept myself first."

Softness touched the lines beside Sky Bird's eyes and the ones that bracketed her mouth. "Stands His Ground has looked at me with the eyes a man has for a woman, and for a short span, I thought I could try once more to be like other women. But he saw where my heart looked, and he helped me to accept myself. Someday, he will find a wonderful woman and they will have many children. That woman will never be me, for my heart belongs to another."

Golden Fox leaned forward, her elbows biting into the flesh of her thighs. "Who is this man who has claimed my mother's heart? Do I know him?"

Chin lifted, Sky Bird caught and held her daughter's gaze. "You know the one who has claimed my heart, but she is no man."

Mouth gaped, Golden Fox leaned back and stared at her mother. "Not a man?"

"Long I have had eyes for Deer Woman, and she for me."

"Deer Woman?"

"Will you echo the words I speak, Daughter? Or will you ask the questions I see in your eyes?"

"I... I do not know what to say, Mother. You are... Two-Spirit? How did I not know this about my own mother? My eyes must be blind to the looks you gave each other, and my heart must be deaf to your feelings."

"You did not see what Deer Woman and I hid, even from ourselves. Only Stands His Ground saw the love that we had for one another. It was he who echoed the words of my mother, and told me to speak my heart to his sister."

Golden Fox glanced around the lodge. "I will pack my things and move in with Blazing Fire. When will you and Deer Woman have a joining?"

"There is no need to pack your belongings, Daughter. After we are joined, I will move to Deer Woman's lodge."

***

Sky Bird had gone to be with Deer Woman after her talk with Golden Fox. Now, Sister Moon rode high above the canyon rim. Soon the lodge behind Golden Fox would be empty, except for her and Blue Spirit Dog's and Frost's family. Only a moon ago, her grandfather had moved into Sun Rising's lodge after his woman had journeyed to the campfires in the sky.

Golden Fox stared up at the night sky.

So many changes. What changes will happen when White Elk returns from his Vision Quest?

She stomped her feet to push warmth into them.

"Granddaughter, do you wish to become one with the snow and the ice that hangs from the bare branches of trees?" Eagle Thunder stepped from around the lodge. "Where is your mother, that you stand here with snow making your hair white?"

She grinned. "She has gone to be with Deer Woman. How long have you known about her becoming Two-Spirit, Grandfather?"

He bent his neck and stared up. The clouds filled with snow hid the campfires in the sky. "A person does not *become* a Two-Spirit, Granddaughter. Like the color of our hair and our eyes, it is a gift given by the Great Mystery." He brought his dark eyes down to meet hers. "Your grandmother and I always knew Sky Bird was Two-Spirit. We just had to wait for her to know it, too."

30

Inside the sweat lodge, White Elk had prayed and sweated for four days. Dances In Storms and Long Sun had remained with him, fasting and staying awake. Never before had anyone been with him in the sweat lodge. No one had smoked the Pipe of Truth with him; no one had tossed the Sacred Plants on the hot embers; and no one had prayed and sung with him until their voices became like the croaks of the green ones who lived near water.

For the first time in his life, White Elk felt clean — truly clean. Now, Dances In Storms and Long Sun lay curled by the hot embers as he gathered his belongings and snuck out of the sweat lodge.

Father Sun reached shy fingers above the edge of the land. Dances In Storms had already prepared what he would need on his Vision Quest, and left it beside the sweat lodge. He tied the supplies on his mare's back and leapt up. Those who Vision Quested usually walked to find their place. Their bare feet connected them with the Mother and opened their Spirits. In the cold season, however, it was permitted to ride and to shelter in a cave.

Keeping the animal to a walk, he left the lodge behind. Only once did he glance over the rim to the lodges below. Golden Fox slept, as did most of the band. When he returned, they would talk.

White Elk shoved thoughts of Golden Fox to the side, and emptied his mind as he tightened his robe against the cold. At the sound of paws crunching on the hard crust of the snow, he looked back and discovered that Sun Snow loped behind.

Silly wolf!

Still, her presence brought joy to his heart, and the feeling of loneliness that had been growing in his chest lessened.

Once he was far enough away, he tapped his mare's sides, and the mustang broke into a lope.

Sun Snow, tongue lolling from the side of her mouth, ran beside the larger animal.

Mustang breath blew in a cloud past White Elk, where his cloud breath mingled with it. Grey clouds hung low on the horizon. Snow would fall before Father Sun crossed the sky. A cold white blanket already clung to canyon walls and bowed the pine branches of the forest. How well he and his animals blended with the land—albino man, white mustang, and wolf whose fur looked like snow.

As he rode, a grin tugged the corners of his mouth. "Ha! Now I know why Dances In Storms told Eagle Thunder to pack much meat." He glanced down at the wolf. "She did not want you to hunger, Sun Snow."

For a moment, his mind dwelled on Dances In Storms. She was good to look at, with a firm body and a good heart. A man could find a worse mate. Yet his heart refused to yearn for the Holy Woman, and no fire in his loins heated when she was near.

He rubbed a hand down his cold face. He would beg the Spirits to give him guidance; yet, he wondered.... If they told him to take Dances In Storms to mate, even if he lost Golden Fox, would he be able to do this?

Three sunrises passed before he saw the blood-red sandstone boulders in the distance, pushing up through the snow. Dances In Storms had said that a cave entrance lay behind the boulders. The image of a small fire and shelter urged him to hurry.

A white fox appeared before him and kept pace. Overhead, the sky darkened and a deep rumbling shook the air. His mare, never one to fear noise, reared. White Elk clung to his mustang. Wild-eyed, his animal bucked, nearly unseating White Elk. "Easy girl! I should have given you a name long ago. Perhaps then, we would have the connection warriors have to their animals. I must—"

The animal settled suddenly, and he peered around. Alone. "Sun Snow!"

The wolf did not appear.

"I smell rain, though it is the season for snow. What kind of weather is upon me?"

He rode up to the boulders and slid off. The snow slipped under his feet and he fell. On hands and knees, he pushed himself up. "How is this so? For days, the snow has barely touched my ankles. Now it is to my waist!"

He pushed through the deepening snow toward the black hole of the cave entrance, but the harder he pushed, the higher the snow rose. When it reached his neck, he panicked and yelled.

White Fox ran over, sniffed him, then vanished.

White Elk floundered as darkness overcame his mind.

* * *

"You finally wake up, eh? You sounded as if you swallowed gravel all night. I could not understand much of what you spoke. Your mind left you. Oh... and the mare.... Name her Cloud. She will like that."

"How...? Who...?"

"Do not speak in broken tongue, boy." A young man stirred food in a large wooden bowl, which lay on a flat stone next to a small fire. He ladled some into a smaller bowl and began eating. "I know you must fast, at least for a little longer. I made extra to take to my woman. She is a bit crazy, keeping an owl, but I love her." A long, black braid hung over his shoulder. He flipped his head and tossed it to his back

A mouse crawled up the stranger's arm and pawed at the edge of the bowl.

He poured some in another bowl for the tiny creature. "You must share, little one."

White Elk leaned on his elbow. "Who *are* you? A mouse? How did I get out of the snow? Where is my wolf? My mustang?"

"Snow, you say? You must have been dreaming. Flowers bloom." He waved a hand toward the cave entrance. "Birds nest. The forest is awake with baby animals."

White Elk shot up and banged his head on the top of the cave. "Forest?" He rubbed the back of his head.

"My, you really are an albino. I thought the fire in here cast a strange light on your skin. Yes, boy, a great forest that stretches as far as a person can see from a high hill. Where did you think you were?"

"I live in the canyons! There is forest, but it does not stretch for long distances." He tried to rise, but fell backward.

217

"Boy, you are weak. Dances In Storms —"

"Where is she? Have you spoken with her?" White Elk demanded.

"Hmm? Oh yes, she is where she belongs."

White Elk scooted back, leaned on the cave wall, and grabbed his head. "You make my mind crazy! Who are you, and why... are you with me?"

"Well... because I am meant to be, just as you are meant to be here with me, White Elk. The Spirits asked me to show you the forest. You will understand why, when you need to."

"Am I in the Spirit Land? Is the forest there?"

"It is wherever you wish it to be, boy. There are no wrong places in the mind."

"Why is it foggy in here? Are you fading? Do not leave me!"

"I am called Wanderer. Do not worry, for you will see me again."

"Wanderer, are you a Holy Man? Wanderer?"

The cave vanished. He stood in a dense forest, on an animal path covered in damp layers of leaves many cycles of seasons old. Father Sun filtered through the huge branches of the tall trees and puddled around his feet.

Sun Snow rubbed against him.

He dropped to his knees and hugged her. "Girl, I am so happy to see you!"

He stood again and gazed around. A narrow, dirt path led through trees that grew so thickly, he could only see a short ways. Eyes closed, he inhaled until his body could hold no more air. When the damp smell of moss and a sweet aroma floated into his nostrils, he opened his eyes. Flowers sprinkled the forest between trees so huge, it would take several men holding hands to circle their trunks.

He shuffled along the path. Up ahead, beyond where the path bent around trees, the laughter of children rang out. As he followed the sound, a light grey fog swirled between him and what appeared to be a camp. Many lodges rose among the trees, with people moving between them, busy with the life of any camp.

When he reached the edge of the camp, he raised his hand in greeting. No one responded, though he could see that several looked in his direction.

He blinked, and all of a sudden, a white bear and her cub ambled up the path toward him. As she approached, he stepped backward and fell over a log that he would have sworn was not there a breath ago.

Cold. I feel so cold!

He wrapped his arms around himself and rubbed harder as snow touched his skin. "Skin? I stand naked in deep snow! Where is the forest?" Ahead of him rose large, yellow sandstone boulders, partly covered in snow.

Cloud snorted when she saw White Elk, and he rushed toward his mustang. Ankle deep snow lay in front of the cave's entrance.

He twirled around, mouth agape. "Ankle deep? It was over my head!"

Turning in a circle, he stared at the snow barely dusting the ground. He whirled and ran for the cave.

Inside, his robe, tunic, leggings, and footwear lay near a warm fire. Quickly, he jerked his clothes on, wrapped the robe around his shoulders, and scooted closer to the red embers.

On the other side of the fire circle sat a figure he did not recognize.

"Who are you? Did you make this fire?"

"You have been here a long time, boy, longer than most."

"I only... I stood naked in the freezing snow! I have only just arrived! Who... *what* are you?"

"Never say 'what'! I am a being, not a thing. A thing is something Creator did not breathe life into. Creator breathed life into all that is and will ever be. I am Elk. I am man. I am woman. I am Shining Light. You have gone long with no water — maybe five sunrises." He handed him a water bladder. *"Drink. Your body must crave water after so long."*

White Elk reached through the fire as if the flames were not there. He took the water bladder and drank deep. "It does not taste as water, but I no longer thirst. What did I drink?"

"Life. The forest, the canyons, all the animals, Humans, Sky, and the Mother we walk upon. You have taken nourishment from everything there is and everything that will be, Human Who Is Albino. No one can live without taking in all there is. Without such nourishment, you would only be an empty shell. None can live without being every living being at least once."

White Elk grasped his head between his hands. "You make my head feel crazy, as did the one called Wanderer. What is this you say?"

"We are born Human, or maybe Elk, or perhaps Hawk first, so we may experience their existence. Without this, your mind would only fill with useless thoughts. Heh, in the future some Humans will say animals have no ability to think beyond what they call in-stinct. Animals are smarter than Humans. They live in total harmony and balance with the Spirit.

"If you believe in yourself, the rest will begin to grow within you. I wish to speak of your feet. Hush and only listen. I have taught many what I am to teach you. When you feel disconnected from yourself and others, go off alone and take off your footwear. Stand and face in any direction, and sing of how you feel. Ask the Mother to take hold of you. Allow your feet to take hold of her. Close your eyes and allow roots to grow from your feet. These roots are not as tree roots, but from our minds. Think of your feet growing roots. Feel the roots go deep into our Mother. Your feet might itch, but stand firm. If your voice becomes silent, put all of your thoughts, your very being, into growing your roots. Call me Shining Light, little brother."

Shining Light stood, and motioned for him to stand also.

"Sing a song that tells of your need to connect. Sing low, or as loud as you need. Close your eyes."

Barefoot, White Elk sang until his voice could sing no more. He stood in silence and smiled. His feet grew roots, roots that burrowed into the heart of the Mother. Power thrummed through him.

His eyes popped wide. "Shining Light, I...."

He stood in the middle of the small fire, but did not feel the heat. "You... are gone. Thank you. I will never forget." Hunger overtook him, and he stepped out of the fire.

Sun Snow glanced up.

"How long have you been here? You must be very hungry. Come here, girl. Sit with me and enjoy our food." He unwrapped the food and fed Sun Snow a hunk of dried meat.

Water dripped outside the cave. The drip-drip-drip called to him.

He jumped up and peered outside. "No, this is not possible!"

Wet and muddy ground stretched flat to the horizon. Grass grew tall with red, white, and blue flowers sprinkled through it. A new foal whinnied and pushed against Cloud, demanding to be fed. Mustangs grazed with new foals sleeping in the sun, or kicking up their heels and acting foolish.

The warm breeze that ran fingers through his hair made him shiver. "How is this so? Only two, maybe three sunrises have passed since I entered this cave and spoke to Shining Light! It is the cold season!"

Eagle swooped and dove.

White Elk raised his gaze. "Blue sky. No grey snow clouds. How is this so?"

A woman's voice spoke. *"When next you see this season, you must prepare to go with Golden Fox on her journey. Others will come, but Golden Fox must lead. You will be her helper in all things."*

Black clouds raced through the sky, and cold took the land. Plants withered, and shrubs dropped their leaves and became bare. The mustangs vanished.

White Elk rushed back inside the cave and breathed life into the sleeping fire. "I saw no one, but heard a woman's voice!" He snuggled with Sun Snow in the robe. "Have you seen the water, girl? How long have I been here? Ah! The water bladder!" He grabbed for it the same time another hand did.

A woman with bloody wrists tossed it behind her. *"You need to listen, not drink. Tell your wolf to stop growling at me."*

"She can see you?"

"Do you think animals are blind, boy? Of course, she can see me. It is only Humans who are blind to the Spirit Land."

"Why... why are you here?"

The woman tossed her head back and laughed. *"Have you not heard of me, of my shame? I am Yellow Moon."* Her wrist dripped with blood.

"I... I have."

"You must help rescue the people."

"What people? How can I help rescue them? I have no Power."

"All will be known as the sunrises follow the sunsets. The Power to help others, boy, lies within each of us. It is the greatest of all Powers."

"Where are these people? When am I to help rescue them?"

"When the land turns green, you will know what to do. Do not fail, boy. I tire of being trapped in this tightness."

"What tightness do you speak of, Yellow Moon? I do not understand."

Though he strained to see her, she had gone.

He leaned against the rough stone of the cave. Sun Snow pressed against his leg, and he dug his hand into the thick fur around her neck. With his other hand, he rubbed burning eyes. More smoke filled the cave, and he coughed until his chest hurt. Clawing up the cave wall, he sucked in air and stamped out the fire. Finally, the smoke blew from the cave, yet he could not seem to draw a deep breath.

He climbed out of the cave and stared back at it. "Why has the cave shrunk?"

"To force you out of it, White Elk Who Runs With Wolf. Sit, there is much room."

White Elk peered around, but saw no one. Still, he answered the voice. "This is only a small ledge!"

"*Sit, boy.*" An animal with the head and neck of a white elk, but with the body of a wolf, sat next to White Elk.

Intense blue light surrounded the Elk-Wolf, so bright that even as White Elk squeezed his watering eyes against it, he leaned toward it.

The body of the wolf pressed close against his leg, and a growly low voice said, "*Beautiful, is it not?*"

White Elk turned his head in the direction of the Elk's gaze, and sucked in a breath. They sat high on a mountain ledge, and below them, the land rolled out as far as he could see. The beauty gripped his heart so hard that he cried.

"*So much, the eye cannot see it all. Yet, one day, this will not be so. Humans will take and take and give nothing back to our Mother. They will rip into her flesh and dig out her bones. They will care nothing when the wild ones cry, and when the great forests weep.*"

The Elk-Wolf morphed into a woman. Her white hair floated around her, glistening with brilliant blue sparks. Indigo blue swirled around and sometimes filled her black eyes, which held all the sorrow of all the Peoples.

"*We are one. The Mother is where our children will suckle. The animals are our friends and our relatives, and when their voices fall silent, our own hearts will shatter as ice against rock.*"

The blue swirled around her. She became Elk-Wolf again, and her paw reached out to touch his arm.

He stretched out his hand, which sank into the blue around her, and gripped the warmth of her paw.

"*Look below, boy.*"

He leaned over and gazed at the land far below. The air grew thick with black dust. Noises such as he had never heard clamored so loud that his ears ached. Great gashes ripped open the Mother's body, and a black stinking substance oozed out like blood from a deadly wound. Tears of sorrow filled his eyes.

"*Already the Mother cries out in faraway places across the salty waters. Already the air is so black that the Birds breathe it and die. Humans fight to carve up the Mother like a piece of meat. They fight over her body and kill their brothers and sisters. Blood soaks into the dirt, turning it rancid as spoiled meat. Even now, the Humans of every bloodline ride met-al monsters that breathe black smoke.*"

"The blood of the Peoples will soak the Mother. Their bodies will lie beneath Father Sun, with no one to sing them to the campfires in the sky, or to lay them in the trees. Many of the Peoples will turn from the ways of their mothers and fathers. They will go to the wooden lodges to live, and to die.

"Children will cry out beneath the hands of their parents. Elders will die because no one will bring them food. Hope will become as lost as water soaked in the driest dirt."

"No!" White Elk screamed. "No! Please, no." Sobs shook his body, and he hid his face in his hands.

"For many cycles of seasons, our Peoples will despair. Many will drink the poisoned water, so they can hide from their fear and their pain. You, White Elk, must help Golden Fox rescue our Peoples. You must help keep the stories of our Peoples alive, and passed from one generation to the next. Only the stories will save the Peoples. All the Peoples, of many colors, will suffer the same fate."

She nodded her head, and the Mother shook. Pebbles and stones rained down on the land below, and a great cloud of dust billowed up. At the far edge of the land, great walls of water rose higher and higher, then crashed into the sandy shore. People screamed, and bodies of people and animals floated on the churning waters. Fires flashed through forests, until only charred tree bodies stood where once green branches had provided shelter and food for both humans and animals.

"I will take you through what is called 'the true giving,' the Sundance."

He blinked his eyes and found himself standing next to a tree that had been taken from the forest. Its branches had been stripped, and the body of the tree had been planted deep into the Mother. From the top of the tree, rawhide strips hung.

A man came and pierced White Elk's chest with the Eagle claws, then tied the claws to a rawhide strip that reached to the top of the tree.

White Elk gritted his teeth and let no sound come from his lips.

The man placed an Eagle bone between White Elk's lips, and when he blew, it sounded as Eagle calling out.

"The warm season has come, the time of when chokecherries are ripe. The special tree has called to us, and has been taken from among its people so that it might become the center around which you dance. Dance and pray, and blow the Eagle Bone. For four sunrises, give to Great Mystery your body, your mind, and your Spirit. Pull, White Elk. Pull until you become free."

As White Elk danced, he blew hard on the bone whistle and pulled against the claws buried in his chest. A stream of blood ran beneath the claws where they pulled his skin forward. When the pain grew until it nearly broke his mind, he blew harder on the whistle and pulled harder against the claws. All the while, he danced and prayed.

"'Pray for the good of the people, for the sick, the unborn, for yourself, for the Mother. You have nothing that is truly yours, except your body. Give all that you have for all that has been given to you."

The voice floated around his head as he danced.

"Dance until Eagle's claws rip through your skin and you fall to the dirt. When the pain is so great that your mind buries itself inside, and your Spirit becomes open, then a vision will come to you. A vision will show you the path you must follow. Listen to the Spirits!"

The Eagle claws pulled at his skin, and his chest pulled with them. He leaned back, hands at his side, and blew the bone whistle. He danced forward and backward, pulling hard, repeating this many times.

He ripped the claws loose, and fell.

* * *

Many Peoples cowered inside an open space, surrounded by tree bodies that made high walls, but with nothing to shelter them from Father Sun and Sister Rain. A hairy-face stood in the middle, cracking a long rope. Each time the rope touched someone's back, the skin split and blood ran.

White Elk scrambled to his feet and ran toward a woman who bled beneath the hairy-face's rope. "Stop! No more! My people! I come to take them home!"

"Are you willing to die to protect your people, White Elk?"

"Yes!"

An ax swung toward his head. Just before it cleaved his skull, it vanished.

"Will you die to protect Wolf, White Elk?"

"Yes! Wolf is my Soul, my being."

A fire stick roared and something hot burned through his chest. Blood poured from the wound as White Elk fell to the ground. Blackness swirled until he could see no more, and then only silence surrounded him.

When his eyes opened, he stood next to the cave. Sun Snow lay against his leg as Father Sun sparkled on the field of sun that stretched beyond the cave entrance.

A figure wavered into sight beside him. He jerked back, clutching Sun Snow, and the wolf pup licked his cheeks.

"Why do you fear, White Elk?"

"Who... who are you?"

"I am Blue Night Sky. As I once taught Shining Light, I come now to teach you."

Sister Wind blew his hair over his face, but did not touch the long, dark strands of the elder's hair.

"Is this real?"

With a finger, she pointed toward his chest.

He gazed down at the blood trickling from Eagle claw wounds. Tears flooded his eyes. "I am blessed."

"Yes, Brother, you are blessed. More than you know."

"Sun Snow, you speak?"

She raised her muzzle to stare at him. *"I speak, and you must learn to listen. I may not use my voice, but watch me, see how I move. I watch you always. Pay heed to everyone's movement. You will learn much. Watch all life. Pay heed to Birds. Maybe they sing, maybe they do not. Learn why.*

"Keep your inside eyes as open as you do your outside eyes. Always listen to whispers in your mind, in the wind, in the trees, in the squeak of Mouse. Plants make their own words to speak to their kind. Reach out, touch them, and feel what they say. If a stone attracts you, find out why. Stones are the oldest beings on the Mother and have much wisdom. Spirits may not always speak words, but they might whisper signs. Will the sign be written by our Mother, or will the sign be found amid the many noises of Humans? None can say.

"Some humans smile and offer you their hand, while their knife seeks your back. Watch their eyes, movements of their body, as you would Mountain Lion. Feel... always feel. As you need to do now. Listen. What do you hear? Smell? Taste, feel, see?"

White Elk cocked his head and slowed his breathing. "I hear birds, mustangs... smell mustangs... taste... taste dust... feel.... I feel danger." He jumped up.

"Sit, boy. What danger do you feel? Humans? Or animals?"

He eased down next to Sun Snow. "I smell snow. It comes fast. Cloud! I must—"

"Your mustang already knows. She has already found shelter. If you had watched her, you would have known sooner." Sun Snow yawned and stretched, then headed for the cave. *"Come, we will eat, drink, and I will teach you how to be Wolf. And you will see with all of your eyes."*

31

A moon had passed since White Elk had gone on his Vision Quest. When Golden Fox saw him ride back into the Sister Wolf Band's camp, although she was on patrol with Blazing Fire, she pressed her leg into Splash's side and swung the mustang around to race into camp.

Blazing Fire got ahead of her and slowly forced Splash to a halt. "A warrior does not leave her band unprotected. Only a foolish little girl would do this."

Splash pranced sideways. "White Elk has returned!"

A shrug of indifference fell from Blazing Fire's shoulders. "Of course, he has returned. This is his home. We knew he would return."

"But... I have to go see him." Golden Fox attempted to nudge Splash around Blazing Fire's fight-trained mustang, but the larger animal easily kept her from moving forward.

Stern lines bracketed the warrior's mouth. "You have much to do here."

"I will not be gone long. I promise!"

A sigh slipped past the warrior's lips. "It does not matter how long you would be gone. You must never leave your people unprotected. If you wish to be a warrior, you can never forget this responsibility, not even if your heart should break. It is your peoples' hearts that must first be tended. Do you understand what I say, Golden Fox?"

Drawing a shaky breath, she nodded. "I... I am sorry. Again, I have acted as a child."

"No, you have acted as a young woman whose heart is confused."

227

She stared down at the camp as White Elk rubbed his mustang with grass. He picked up his carry-all and his sleeping robe, and walked toward Dances In Storms' lodge. As he ducked under the flap entrance, Golden Fox had to bite her lip to keep it from quivering. He did not even look toward her family's lodge, now hers alone.

A gentle hand squeezed her shoulder. "White Elk has returned from a Vision Quest, Golden Fox. He cannot speak to anyone until he goes to sweat with the Holy Woman. You know this."

"But, maybe, even if Dances In Storms was not a Holy Woman, he would still go to her lodge first." She hated the way her throat clogged.

"No one can know the heart of another. It does not matter. We must patrol to keep our people safe."

As Blazing Fire returned to the path they patrolled, Golden Fox gave one last lingering look, then whirled Splash around and followed the warrior.

* * *

Golden Fox did not return to her lodge until Father Sun had dipped behind the edge of the land. A fire glowed in the lodge's pit, and the smell of roasted meat filled her nostrils. Tired from a long day of sparring with Blazing Fire, and then patrolling the rim of the canyon, she folded her legs and gratefully sank to the ground.

Deer Woman handed her a steaming bowl of tubers and a slab of elk meat. "Stands His Ground brought us fresh meat. It has been cold, so I told Sky Bird I would come and start your fire and fix you a meal."

Golden Fox smiled her thanks as she chewed and swallowed the hot food. "Why did Mother not come to join us for this meal?"

"It would be best to speak of this after our stomachs are filled."

When Golden Fox set aside her food bowl, Deer Woman handed her a hot drink made from plants. The soothing aroma was one of Sky Bird's special mixes.

Sipping it, she waited for Deer Woman to broach the reason for her presence.

"White Elk returned, and has gone to the sweat lodge with Dances In Storms and Long Sun." When Golden Fox did not respond, Deer Woman continued. "There is a story I wish to share with you, Golden Fox."

"I would be honored to listen." She respectfully bowed her head toward the Elder.

Deer Woman cradled the bowl of warm drink in her hands, and spoke. "As a very young girl, I knew in what way I was different. My mother hoped that once I had my womanhood ceremony, my body would make my heart more open to the relationships between women and men. The ceremony only made me sure that I was a Two-Spirit."

She sipped her drink as she gathered her thoughts "My parents were not as Sky Bird's mother and father. I was beaten. Stands His Ground was gone on his travels during this time. When he returned, he put a stop to our parents' cruelty by taking me to our sister band to live.

"As you know, my parents died in a raid long cycles of seasons ago. I did not weep for them, though I helped Stands His Ground sing them to the campfires in the sky. It was then we came back to this band, the one we grew up in."

With one hand, she tugged at the fringe along the sides of her leggings. "I had learned to feel shame about the way I was, and hid it, even from your mother, who was my best friend. Stands His Ground never told my secret."

She set aside her drink and crossed her legs, eyes locked on Golden Fox's. "I also hid that my heart belonged to your mother. For many cycles of seasons, I watched how Stands His Ground's face would light up like Father Sun when your mother was near. My brother did not know how I died inside, each time he spoke to me of how he hoped to win Sky Bird as his mate. When she accepted strands of sky beads from him, I was sure that they would join. My heart shattered like ice on a pond."

"I am sorry you endured so much." Golden Fox felt the other woman's pain and clutched her chest.

Deer Woman's eyes held kindness. "I know that you feel the pain of others, and I do not tell you this to cause you pain. I am happy now. Sky Bird chose me. I tell this story so you might understand that my words do not come from a woman who has never known the hurt of loving someone she may never have."

"How did you live with such pain for so long, Deer Woman?" Voice hoarse, Golden Fox leaned toward the older woman.

"I learned who I was. I used the love I had for Sky Bird to become a stronger person, a person who lived a life to heal others. If Sky Bird had come to my lodge when I was young, I would have become someone very different. Wrapped up in her like I wrap up in a sleeping robe during the cold season, I would not have become whole. I would not have searched out my gifts and studied how to make them better and stronger."

She rose and walked around the fire. Kneeling next to Golden Fox, she took the younger woman's hand between hers. "To make our People stronger, maybe strong enough to survive when the whites come into our land, we must each become all that the Great Mystery has given us to become. We cannot be so wrapped up in another person that we push aside our own gifts, so that we may serve only them. Do you understand what I am saying, Golden Fox?"

"I... I think so." She slapped at a tear fighting its way down her cheek.

"I have watched you grow, and wished that Sky Bird and I could have raised you in our own lodge. Each cycle of seasons, I have watched your Power grow and reveal itself. In my heart—" She tapped her chest with one hand. "—I know the Great Mystery has given you Power to help our people. If White Elk is to walk beside you, it must be beside you, not in front and not behind. It must be because the gifts you have, and the Power you have, can grow stronger with him in your lodge. But, for this to happen, you must find who you are and become that woman, and he must find who he is and become that man."

"I do not think I can share him with another, Deer Woman. I... I know it is selfish of me to want to deny Dances In Storms a chance to have a child of her own, but it would break me into many small pieces if he took her to his sleeping robes. It... it would be better for me to stand aside, for he would make her a fine mate."

Deer Woman embraced her and then stood. The firelight played across her strong cheekbones and firm chin. "That may be the path you must walk, Golden Fox. Go into the canyons and pray to Great Mystery to give you clear eyes, so you might see how you can best serve your people. Remember, our lives are not given to us to use only so we may be happy, but to protect and to nurture and to teach our people."

***

Father Sun still hid below the horizon when Golden Fox rode Splash through the dark space between the canyon walls, which led into the camp. Not knowing where she should go, she let Splash choose the direction, until they had left the camp behind.

Snow glistened on the ground, the crunch of Splash's feet loud in the cold, quiet season. A shallow indentation in the wall of the canyon caught her eye. With bow in hand, she carefully approached. The spot was deeper than it first appeared, deep enough to be a good shelter even if snow fell hard. Nearby, a small stream ran beneath a thin crust of ice. Though the grass that rose above the snow was brittle and tan, Splash would not go hungry.

As Father Sun grew closer to the land's edge, Golden Fox tied Splash's two front feet loosely together with a soft rope, so she would not wander away. With that done, she hurried to gather wood and set up camp. After a quick meal of pemmican and water next to a small fire, she laid her sleeping robe at the entrance to her camp.

Darkness fell over the canyon, and the campfires in the sky burned brightly. A soft whicker jerked her eyes toward the mustang, her ears flicking forward, though Splash stood with one rear foot cocked, resting. From the shadows slinked a darker shadow, and she reached for her bow just as the wavering flames of her fire caught on the silvery tips of his hair.

"Frost! I am glad to see you."

The black wolf ambled over to her and threw himself on the ground next to her leg. She buried her fingers in the thick fur around his neck. "Did you follow me, or did you track me, Brother Wolf?"

He rolled over onto his back, his feet dangling in the air.

With a joyful laugh, she scratched his belly.

The campfires in the sky blinked out one by one as clouds gathered. Soon, tiny flakes of snow drifted down. Golden Fox scooted farther into the shallow cave as Splash came and stood in the opening. The mustang's body blocked the light wind that gusted down the canyon.

Seated cross-legged near the fire, she stared into the blue and red flames.

Frost would tell her if anyone came close to their camp. He rested his chin on his forepaws and gazed outside, even though his back pressed against her leg.

Running her hand back and forth through his fur, she felt the tightness in her shoulders unknot. "This feels nice, Frost. Calm, peaceful." She leaned close, buried her nose in the back of his neck, and sniffed. "You smell clean. How do you keep yourself this way when I have to bathe in the river?"

"Child, too many words spill from your mouth. Over all that noise, how will you hear what the Spirits have to say?"

Golden Fox jumped to her feet, eyes probing the dark.

Frost rolled over and took the spot she left.

She cocked her head and slowed her breathing. *Frost is not worried.* Although this thought was true, her heart pounded against her ribs.

Tiredness made her back sag, and she sat back down. Frost groaned and moved over, so she could have more of the sleeping robe she had laid out. Yawning, she lay next to the big wolf, curled against his back, and fell asleep.

***

Father Sun's fingers pried open her eyes. The campfire had become cold embers. Golden Fox gazed around her. "Frost, where are you?"

Still searching, she walked out of the cave. Birds swooped in an azure sky. Flowers blossomed next to the small stream while a fawn nibbled grass next to a doe.

Mouth agape, she peered around. "This cannot be. It snowed as I fell asleep. It is the cold season, not the season of young animals."

Frost barked sharply. The sound echoed in the canyon and drew her eyes upward. He stood on the rim above her. With another bark, he demanded she climb.

A narrow, rocky path crossed and re-crossed the steep flank. With her breath rasping and lungs burning, she finally reached the top. A water bladder hung over her shoulder. She shook it. Half-full. She took five swallows, then tied the skin cover with the thin strap that assured no water would leak out.

Sweat trickled down the center of her back and along her cheeks. With the back of her hand, she wiped it from her face.

Frost barked again, and trotted toward the place where Father Sun went to sleep when it was time for Sister Moon to shine.

How long she followed the black wolf, she did not know.

At last, he stopped and lay down in tall grass. A blue fog swirled around him.

Her eyes popped wide as she gazed around. "I must be in the Spirit Land!" Laughter spilled from her lips as she lightly slapped a hand on her forehead. "Why did I not realize this?"

Sister Wind blew gently past her, ruffling her long hair. The coolness chilled her heated body. She reached for the thin deerskin robe rolled and tied and hung behind her shoulders. Her fingers touched emptiness. "Ah! I must have left it in the cave."

She turned back in that direction, but nothing except flat grasslands flowed toward the distant purple mountains. "Wha... where is the cave? I climbed straight up."

"Silly one, here, put on your robe."

Golden Fox whirled at the strange voice.

An elder woman dressed in uneven furs sat beside her. White hair fell below her waist and spread out in a circle.

"Are... are you one of the ancient ones I have heard stories about all my life? But, you speak! In all the stories, it is said none of your people speak, that you only show yourselves and chant in words long ago forgotten."

Sister Wind's breath blew colder. She reached out and accepted the robe, and pulled it around her shoulders.

Delight creased the elder's face as her eyes sparked with mischief. *"Ah, the stories. I have heard many over the cycles of seasons. Some say we have no tongue and can only make sounds in our throats."* She stuck her tongue out at Golden Fox. *"Do you see a tongue, Child?'"*

When Golden Fox nodded, the elder's smile faded.

"We speak, child. It is only that others do not listen. Shining Light listened and saved his people."

"Are you here because I must save my people?"

The elder's laughter vibrated. *"You and others who will one day take your place. But first, girl, you must save yourself. You have many questions you have never asked. As a little one, your mind wandered so much, you did not truly hear many of the stories. Sometimes, it is good to stop thinking, to let your mind float, so that it is not so full that thoughts clog your ears."*

"I dream!" Golden Fox touched the elder, felt her furs, her skin. "Yet, you are real."

"Oh, little one, a smile you have put on my face. I am as real as you. We — both you and I — are Energy. The Energy of all living creates the Web of Life. Listen to Spider. Spider spins her web in silence. Many times she has reached out to you, but your mind was too noisy to hear her."

"I am confused. How is my mind too noisy?" She pulled the robe tighter. Above her, where no ground existed, Ancients chanted and danced.

"Relax your mind. The more you think, the more it becomes cluttered with thoughts that have no meaning."

The elder shifted and took Golden Fox's hand. The air wavered. They rose above the land and floated into a blue mist.

"Here, there is less distraction. We see the color of our Spirits, nothing else. Listen well, young one. One day, you will tell others."

"Like my children? Will White Elk be their father, and will I share—"

"Shhh. Your mind is not free. Let go of others. They will be who they are to be. It may not always be what you wish for yourself or for them, but it is not your place to use your mind to trap them. They must be free—just as you must be free—to choose their own destiny. Free White Elk, so you may find yourself, and so he may find himself." A rainbow danced in the elder's eyes.

Golden Fox lifted her chin. "I am to be a warrior then, and live alone."

"Young One, you push for answers before the answers are born. The future moves as it must. Do not push the days to find what must yet grow, or you will find only bare ground where flowers could be. Keep your heart open to beauty, and let go of fear that will cause your Spirit to thirst and never be satisfied."

The ancient one ran her hand through Golden Fox's hair, then took a golden fox pelt from around her shoulders and placed it in Golden Fox's lap.

"Every sunrise, go out alone, except for your wolves. They will guard you and guide you. Walk for a span, for you cannot feel our Mother if you ride. Your feet, even covered with footwear, will feel the beat of life. Become the ground, the air, the clouds, and every animal you see. Do not allow your mind to interfere. Dance, if you wish, but become the dance. Do not force it to become you. Free yourself, if you wish to free your people."

Golden Fox opened her eyes and tried to move, but Frost lay sprawled across her. Her breath puffed in front of her. She rubbed the wolf's fur until his eyes opened. The gold in his eyes sparkled with flecks of blue.

"The Ancient One said you will guard and guide me." She scooted out from under him and hugged him. Tears slid down her face. "I have great need of you. You give me courage when my own fails."

As she released her hold on Frost, she glanced down. Beside her lay the golden fox hide.

* * *

For three sunrises, Golden Fox walked toward Father Sun. Around her neck rested the golden fox fur. Many times, she ran her hand over the fur, and Energy vibrated through her.

Splash sometimes raced ahead, then circled and returned to her. Other times, she lagged behind before snorting loudly and running to catch up.

Frost left her side only to catch his meals.

Ice-crusted waters gurgled in the streams she walked along. Winter birds chattered and flitted among bare tree branches. A skiff of snow covered the land between the walls of the canyons she wandered.

Father Sun rose the fourth time before she stumbled onto a red, half-circle of sandstone that arched way above her. Mud nests attached to the arch. Four Eagles swooped across the turquoise sky as she stared upward, thoughts flowing through her mind.

What is this? Why is it only half of a circle? Is the rest of the circle under our Mother?

With a vigorous shake, she threw the noisy thoughts from her mind. Instead, she allowed the calm rush of water beneath ice fill her head. Whenever she was sure her mind had stilled, White Elk crept into her heart and threw her into confusion. Questions and hopes and thoughts argued in her head, until she wanted to run away from herself.

Perhaps this will be my last sleep out here, before I return to the Sister Wolf Band. I need Dances In Storms to teach me what I cannot learn on my own.

As Father Sun changed the color of the clouds to bright pink and peach, Golden Fox whistled for Splash, and the mustang trotted to her. Since the first night, she had not had to hobble the animal to keep her near. Now, she unpacked her robe and supplies to set up camp. As she dug out stones to create a fire circle, her stick uncovered a yellowed humpback skull.

"Sweet Mother!" Though the bone was brittle, the horns had remained intact

The wet ground made digging easier. She pulled her tuber stick — with its flat oval slant at one end to make it simpler to pop out the tubers — and worked the ground to see what else made the lumps just beneath the dirt.

By the time she uncovered the seventh skull, horns intact, excitement thrummed in her chest. "Long ago, someone used these in a circle. I will flatten the ground and place them as they were."

When she had finished, all the skulls made a perfect circle, horns facing inward. Not one skull was charred, so she spread dry grass inside them, added her robe folded in half, and stepped inside the circle. Her body tingled as she sat on the ground.

Frost lay inside the circle in front of her.

She waited, head bent back and staring up at the sky, as Father Sun dipped below the horizon. Tiredness overtook her, and she lay down next to the wolf.

Sunrise warmed her. She rubbed her eyes as she sat up.

Frost must have gone hunting.

She squinted at the skulls surrounding her. "Nothing happened." She huffed loudly. "Did I expect the Spirits to come simply because I thought they would?"

"Spirits do not come just because you wish them to."

Golden Fox jerked to her feet.

Eagle Thunder grinned from where he sat on the ground outside the circle, running his hand over a humpback skull. "Old, so old. I wonder if the Ancients left them here." With a grunt, he got to his feet. "Come, Granddaughter, it is time to eat. I have brought food."

"Grandfather, how did you get so close to me?" She carefully stepped outside the circle.

"I have seen many cycles of seasons, Granddaughter. Do you think my ears remained deaf and my mind remained empty during those cycles of seasons? That I did not learn how to walk without sounding as a herd of humpbacks?" He chuckled and handed her jerked meat. "Are you ready to return?"

"No. Waking in the middle of the skulls and expecting something to happen have shown me that I have much to learn."

"Golden Fox, I still learn. Only life's experiences can teach you. Yes, wandering alone is good. Many of us do this to clear our minds and our hearts. But some new people have come into camp, and it would be good for you to meet them, to hear their words."

"When you speak of these new people, a chill crawls up my spine. I fear these people mean I am to begin the work I am to do for our people. I am not ready. I do not know enough. I am not strong enough."

She threw her hands in the air and let them slap down against her thighs. "Grandfather, I am not even strong enough to welcome another woman, a good woman, to share a man with me."

Eagle Thunder uncrossed his legs and, with a hand flat on the ground, pushed to his feet. "I would rather face a pack of hungry wolves than to try to untangle the feelings of the heart. Yet it is the heart that gives us strength when we think our strength is gone. It is the heart that teaches us to feel what another feels. To love someone special is to deepen the space inside, so it may hold even more love—love that overflows to all living beings."

He looped his arm around her shoulders and hugged her against his side. "I believe in you, Golden Fox. I believe that you will open your heart and listen to what it whispers. I do not know if you are to become warrior, or healer, or if you are to fill your lodge with little ones. I do not know if you will share White Elk, or if you will find another to share this journey on our Mother. I only know that you will do what is best not only for yourself, but for others, as well." He chuckled. "I *do* know we must hurry. Our guests wait, and it is not polite to make them wait so long."

She began gathering her belongings. "It gives me strength, Grandfather, that you believe in me. I will do my best to always bring honor to you."

32

Golden Fox slipped off Splash.

Her grandfather took the lead rope from her hand. "I will take care of the mustangs. The elder who wishes to speak to you waits inside your lodge. Do not make him wait longer."

She grabbed her carry-all, sleeping robe, and bow, then hurried to her lodge. After dusting snow from her feet, she ducked beneath the flap.

The center fire burned brightly, and a young man of about twelve winters knelt and handed a bowl of food to an elder.

As the elder accepted the food, his face turned toward Golden Fox. "Welcome, Granddaughter. I find your lodge is well-kept, and there is dry wood and hump-back droppings to warm these old bones." The white of blindness filmed over deep-set eyes that had once been dark. His wrinkled skin was creased with the many paths he had followed in his life, some of them cut off by scars.

"I am honored, Elder, that you find rest and warmth in my lodge." She dropped her belongings on her sleeping robe off to the side, and made her way to the fire. Seated across from the elder, she warmed her hands. "Was your journey a long one, Elder?"

His toothless mouth open and sucked in tubers. He chewed and swallowed before answering. "No journey is long, Child, when you know where you are going, and you find beauty as you walk."

She dipped food into a bowl, hoping nervousness did not sound in her voice. "Wise advice, Elder. I am called Golden Fox. I would be honored if you and your boy would share my lodge for however many sunrises you choose."

A wide smile crinkled the skin around his eyes. "I am Has No Mustang, and this boy is my grandson, Boy Who Walks. My grandson will stay with Sun Rising and your grandfather, Eagle Thunder. You, Golden Fox, and I have much work to do. I have come to meet minds with you."

Food slid down the wrong way, and she choked and coughed. Finally, a drink of water washed it into her stomach. "Has No Mustang, what does this mean, to meet minds?"

"Eat, young one. There will be time to speak after our bellies are full."

When she had scrubbed and put away the eating bowls, Golden Fox prepared a medicinal drink for the elder. "This is a hot drink that my mother taught me to make. It eases the aches of an Elder's bones. If you find it soothing, I will send some of the dried plants with you."

Has No Mustang sipped the drink. "It tastes very good. Perhaps, your mother would share with Boy Who Walks how to prepare this."

"Sky Bird, my mother, is always happy to share knowledge of medicine plants."

Though white covered his eyes, Golden Fox had the uneasy feeling that the elder could see right into her heart.

He set aside his drink and folded his hands on crossed legs. "To meet minds is a Sacred Happening between one who is very old and has much knowledge, and one who the Spirits have called to follow a special path. In this way, I share with your mind the knowledge I have gained from many cycles of seasons, so you might be given what you need to follow the path the Spirits have laid out for you. Six moonrises ago, Blue Night Sky came to me in my dreams, and told me the time had come for me to pass on my gifts to you.

"Prepare two sleeping robes side-by-side. Go out and find clean snow. With the snow, wash your hands, your face, and your feet. When you return, bring a woman who has more cycles of seasons than you. She will sing while my grandson pats the drum. We will prepare, and then you and I will join hands and journey to the Spirit Land."

When she entered the lodge with Deer Woman, the Elder held a shiny shell. The inside of the shell glistened with many different blues and purples, as Sacred Sage and Sweet Grass smoldered inside. In his hand, he held an Eagle wing fan made of seven feathers. Leather strips wove in and out of each feather to keep it in place.

Golden Fox stopped in front of the Elder.

First, he fanned the Sacred Smoke over his own body, and even the bottoms of his feet, and then he fanned it over her. After handing the bowl and feather fan to Boy Who Walks, he motioned for Golden Fox to lie down. Once she settled on one of the robes, he stretched out beside her, and linked his fingers with hers.

In a low voice, Deer Woman sang in rhythm to the drum.

* * *

As Father Sun rose above the canyon rim, the rough stone wall burst into a bloody radiance. A gold-red fox peeked out from behind large stones.

Golden Fox held very still, wondering if the fox would come closer or dart back inside.

Barely audible, she whispered her morning song.

Little by little, the fox edged closer, until she sat in front of Golden Fox.

Arms resting on her crossed leg, with her palms held upward, her song drifted to its end.

The fox leaned forward, stretching her neck as long as possible, and sniffed her hands. Then, the fox slowly drew back and cocked her head. "*Sister-Fox, I welcome you to my hunting grounds.*"

Golden Fox blinked and had to clear her throat of surprise before she could speak. "Fox, you speak to me!"

A grin lifted the corners of Fox's gaped mouth. The tip of her tongue curled just behind her white teeth. "*You must learn to hide in plain sight, Sister. The cold season will soon end, and the season of baby animals will come. When the grasses begin to grow green between the cold season stalks of tan, you must save your people. To be able to hide, to sneak like Fox and count your enemies — this is the gift I give to you.*"

"I am honored, Fox...."

Fox gave a sharp bark and Golden Fox fell silent. "*This gift will do you no good, if your mind is still full of chatter like squirrels that argue over last season's nuts. You must sacrifice that which you want most, so your mind will be quiet. Now is not the season for your happiness, but the season for the lives of your people.*"

"What do you mean, Fox? What is this sacrifice I must give?"

"*What brings confusion to your heart? What makes your Spirit too restless to sleep? This cannot be if you will learn the ways of Fox and the ways of fighting. Our hearts cannot be torn, if we are to be fierce. Our minds cannot stumble, if we are to sneak among our enemies."* Fox stood up and stretched, mouth yawning widely. *"Listen, Sister-Fox, and listen well. We are blessed only when we bless others."*

Black clouds boiled across the clear turquoise sky, and darkness descended. Sister Wind whipped through the canyon, tossing ice pellets from her hands.

Golden Fox stood. Sister Wind slapped her, and she stumbled. Panicked, she whipped her head back and forth. "Where am I?"

No one answered.

"Frost?"

Far away, a wolf howled, the sorrow ripping through Golden Fox's chest—pain so great that she fell to her knees. With a hand clutched to her breast, she moaned.

***

Cruel laughter echoed through the air, and she tentatively opened her eyes.

A woman of the People's lay curled in a muddy pool of water, next to boards that the whites walked upon. The hollow thunk of the hairy-faces footwear made the woman groan, and she gripped the sides of her head. A white man walked up to the woman and kicked her side. "Get out of the way, savage!"

The vision changed.

A small girl-child cringed in the corner of a dark space inside a wooden lodge. A white man slung the child, and she slammed into a wall. Blood gushed from her face as she slid to the wooden floor. Not one tear filled the child's eyes, though her heart pounded inside her thin chest.

The white man snatched up the child, kicked open the wooden door, and threw her to the ground outside his lodge. The door slammed closed, and the child crawled to the still body of her mother, curled against her chest, and slept. Neither woke to greet Father Sun.

Tears flooded Golden Fox's eyes and streamed down her face as her hands shook in anger.

And the vision changed.

A boy of the Peoples sat on a wooden bench in a wood lodge, with other children who had brown skin. He leaned over and whispered to the boy next to him. A hairy-face man stormed to the boy's bench and slammed the back of his big hand across the boy's mouth. "I tolja, don' go speakin' Injun 'round here!"

And again, the vision changed.

241

*A white man held a newborn child and smiled down at his brown-skinned woman.
Two more children came running in the wooden lodge and begged to hold the new baby.
The father laughed and showed the oldest child how to hold the newborn. He leaned over
his woman and brushed the raven hair from her face. "Today, I make food for us all.
Today, you enjoy all of our children. My sweet Indian woman."*

***

Golden Fox's eyes opened, only to quickly squint nearly shut as Father Sun
poked bright fingers into them. She rolled to her side and groaned. Her ribs hurt
and her lips felt swollen. Her tongue flicked out and she tasted dried blood.

"Shhh. Lie down, Golden Fox. Be at peace." Deer Woman's soft voice comforted her as strong hands helped her back onto the sleeping robe. "Sky Bird,
close the flap so Father Sun is not so hard on her eyes."

She cracked open her eyes as soon as she heard the entrance flap close. "Thir...
thirsty." She licked her cracked lips.

Deer Woman put an arm around her back and helped her sit.

Sky Bird hurried over with a water bladder and held it up to her mouth. After
a few swallows, Sky Bird took the water away. "Not too much, or it will not stay
in your stomach." Her mother piled sleeping robes behind her. "There. Lean
against them and rest, while I fix broth for you."

"I feel so weak. My side hurts and my lips feel swollen."

Deer Woman dabbed at her mouth with a soft scrap of deer hide. "You mouth
is swollen. It looks as if someone hit you hard and split your lip. On your side,
there are blue and green marks as if you fought."

She barked an abrupt laugh. "No fight. Just... got beat up." Peering around,
she asked, "Where is... Has No Mustang?"

A bowl of broth in hand, Sky Bird squatted beside her. "After two sunrises,
he left to go on his final walk alone. His grandson carried the plants for the
medicine drink for the Elders."

"Two sunrises? I have slept for two sunrises?"

Deer Woman reached out and gently brushed the young woman's hair out of
her face. "Not two sunrises, Golden Fox. You have fought in your sleep for four
sunrises. Dances In Storms has been here, singing for you to return, for three
sunrises. It is only a short span ago that she went to her lodge to eat and to rest.
We worried for you."

"I need to speak with Dances In Storms when she is awake. There is much we need to talk about." She gingerly touched the rim of the bowl to her lower lip, and sipped. The lip split open, and she tasted her own blood with the broth.

* * *

Father Sun rose twice more before Dances In Storms entered Golden Fox's lodge. It was the first day that her mother and Deer Woman had gone to their own lodge.

The Holy Woman eased into a cross-legged, sitting position next to the fire pit. "I am told you wish to speak."

Something in the somber way the Holy Woman sat pricked at Golden Fox's heart. "I have been inside this lodge for too many sunrises. Would you walk in the canyon with me?"

They walked behind the camp and along an old streambed, to where a cleft in the wall led to an open meadow—the back way out of the canyon where Sister Wolf Band lived. No outsider was shown this way, and the brush concealed it, much like brush often concealed Fox's den.

Spears of red rock shoved up from the ground here and there. The canyon that surrounded the meadow twisted and turned, branching off into other canyons.

Golden Fox kicked a loose stone with the toe of her footwear. Not looking at the Holy Woman, she cleared her throat twice before she could get any words out. "Have you always lived here?" As soon as she said it, she wanted to slap a hand across her mouth for such silly words.

Dances In Storms showed no laughter at her question, though. "Yes, my father's father found this place. Come, let me show you something."

For a long span, Golden Fox followed as the other woman led her into a narrow canyon with caves dotting the walls. Scrambling on hands and feet, they arrived in what appeared to be a shallow cave.

As soon as Golden Fox entered behind her, Dances In Storms motioned her to stay close. Stooped over, they followed a bend in the cave. In the dim light, the Holy Woman pointed to a place high up on the cave wall.

At first, Golden Fox was not certain what she looked at. "It is a humpback with two tails," she finally exclaimed.

"Look closer. Only one is a tail, and the other hangs between two very long, curved teeth. A strange animal. In stories of Shining Light, it is said that when he was a boy, he found caves with paintings of strange animals." She pointed again. This time it was an animal with very long, shaggy hair all over its body, and its two tails were much smaller. "I can only think this one must have been a young one."

Golden Fox eased around the cave walls, staring, stopping to examine the paintings of antelopes and bears bigger than any she had ever heard about. Mountain Lion, who did not look exactly like Mountain Lion, snarled from one cave wall. "Did the people not paint the animals as they are? The teeth of Mountain Lion are too large. Perhaps, a child did this painting."

"I asked my mother, who knows many of the old, old stories. She said that long, long ago, even before Shining Light walked on our Mother, such animals as these existed. No one knows why they are gone now."

"Are these the caves Shining Light found?"

"Yes, I am sure from the stories this is so." Dances In Storms pulled flint from her pouch. Small pieces of dry wood lay stacked against a far wall. She gathered it and lit a fire, and firelight reached soft gold fingers through the dimness of the cave.

Golden Fox glanced up and gasped. She pointed. "What is that long bowl with the large hides stretched across the top? I see what looks like people along the edges."

"Stories call it a boat. It is much like our Peoples' canoes, only much larger. It carried the men from across the salty waters. Have you not heard these stories?"

Golden Fox shook her head, then grinned. "Just because I have not heard them, does not mean our people did not tell them."

A loud laugh burst from Dances In Storms. "Ahh, I see."

Human figures chased various animals across the cave walls, spears and bows raised. Some paintings showed great herds of humpbacks and antelopes. Many flowers she had never seen bloomed across the walls. Mixed in with it all were handprints—small ones, not-so-small ones, and very large ones.

Dances In Storms walked over and pointed to one red handprint. "I made that one when I first found these caves. I had only seen eleven winters."

"Who came with you into the canyons?"

She shook her head, her eyes alight with amusement. "Children were allowed to walk where they pleased, after they had seen a certain number of cycles of seasons. When I was a child, the hairy-faces—what we now call the whites—no longer cared about these canyons. Not like when Shining Light's People lived here, and the hairy-faces believed the yellow stone—what they call gold—grew in the canyon walls. They were wrong."

After walking in front of the walls several times, Golden Fox sat across from the Holy Woman. "There is much I must speak to you, Dances In Storms."

"Speak what is on your heart." The Holy Woman sat on the ground and prepared to listen.

"I do not know if we are to share a man or not. It no longer matters." Dances In Storms opened her mouth as if to speak, but Golden Fox held up a hand. "The cold season will soon end, and when the season of new grass comes, I must be ready to *help* save our People. I cannot let the noise of my feelings scramble my mind. Before that time comes, I must be clear to learn all I need to know. My love for our People must be first in my heart, before my love for any one man. These past sunrises have taught me that no one person can do this. We all will do this, together."

She drew in a deep breath, and her heart broke as she blew it out. "You have given much of your life to our Peoples, and you came to find us when our band became broken. If White Elk will join with you, you have my blessing, Holy Woman. If the Spirits say this is the season for you to bear a child, I am happy for you."

She swallowed the lump in her throat. "This season, for me, is one during which I must learn the ways of Fox, and I must learn the ways of fighting. How can I ask others to follow me, perhaps to their death, if I am untaught? And, until our Peoples are brought away from the wooden fort and the poisoned water, I must set aside the desires and confusion of my heart. After this is done, I feel in here—" She clapped a hand on her chest. "—I feel in here that I will know if you and I are to share a man, or if it is my path to follow the ways of a warrior woman."

33

The season of young animals blew in on Sister Wind's gusty breath. All night, the wind howled through the canyons as pink, white, and blue lightning sizzled across the black sky. The growl and booms of thunder bounced off the canyon walls.

Golden Fox sat next to her fire pit with Frost and Blue Spirit Dog sprawled close-by. Their grown pups wrestled along the back wall of the lodge. The arrows she had been making lay in a pile to one side, as she worked on yet another one.

Someone scratched at the flap and she glanced up. "Come."

With hair tossed into tangled strands by the wind, and stuck to her forehead by the rain, Dances In Storms possessed a wild look, which the sparkle in her eyes enhanced. "Come out in the rain and dance with me, Golden Fox, my sister-friend!" She twirled and the fringes on the bottom of her skirt whirled in a wide circle around her.

Dances In Storms grabbed her hand, and they ducked out of the cave.

The crack-sizzle of the thunder and lightning stirred her blood, and she let Dances In Storms lead her into a joyful dance. Rain pounded from the sky as their feet pounded the ground beneath them. Water splashed high on their naked legs, and droplets hung from the fringes on the bottom of their deerskin dresses.

Around and around they danced, their arms flung high and their heads thrown back. They shook their hair and their bodies as they laughed out loud. Water poured from the tips of their fingers as they brought their arms down and looped them around each other's shoulders.

Together, their feet stamped in harmony as they danced a circle in the storm. When, at last, the thunder dropped to a murmured growl, and the flashes of jagged lightning no longer split the blackness, they stumbled into Golden Fox's lodge.

Giddy from the storm, they shed their clothes and dried off. Wrapped in sleeping robes, they huddled shoulder-to-shoulder by the fire.

"Dances In Storms...."

"Hmmm?"

"I am to go with the hunters and Blazing Fire when Father Sun rises. We need fresh meat, and will not return for at least five sunrises."

Dances In Storms reached back and tugged Golden Fox's arm over her side, and linked her fingers with the younger woman's. "Your father, or those he sends, may be closer than we know. Be like Wolf—ever wary—and come home safe. I would miss you, sister-friend, if you did not." She placed a gentle kiss against Golden Fox's knuckles.

"I will be careful, but that is not what I want to speak of."

"Speak, sister-friend, for soon my eyes will close."

"I... I...." She swallowed hard and sucked in a deep breath. It eased from her mouth. "While I am gone, it would be a good time for you to lay with White Elk and make a baby."

Dances In Storms jerked up, and the robe puddled in her lap. "Lay with White Elk? No! We will speak no more of this until after... after we go to the fort and get our Peoples."

Golden Fox tugged Dances In Storms' arm until she lay on her back and stared up at Golden Fox's face hovering over her. With her arms crossed over the Holy Woman's full breasts, Golden Fox rested her chin on her arms, and fixed her gaze on her friend. "While dancing with you in the storm, I... I felt in my heart a deep love for you. I do not know if I am grown enough to lie in the lodge while White Elk takes you to his sleeping robes, but...."

She heaved another breath before she continued. "But, as we danced, I knew that my heart would not be broken if I shared this man with you, so that you might have a child. I would be your child's second mother. I am young and wish for children, but the seasons for you to have a child are quickly passing. I want you to have this happiness."

Dances In Storms' hands framed Golden Fox's face as she searched the younger woman's eyes. "I would let the seasons of having a child pass me by before I would do that which would bring you pain. In you, I find a sister and a friend. I would not give that up. I care for White Elk, but do not love him as a woman loves a man of her heart. I do not know why the Spirits have made this so painful for you, and for White Elk, and for me, but.... Know this: I will not lie with him to get with child unless you are truly at ease in your heart. You do not have to say now. We can wait until the warm season, when everything will be different, before you decide."

Golden Fox shook her head, pushed forward, and placed a light kiss on Dances In Storms' cheek. Dropping back onto her side of the sleeping robe, she said, "In my heart, I feel that your body is ready for a child. As we danced, I could feel the thrumming inside of you. You will make a good mother, and I will make a very good second mother to this child." Turning onto her side, she met Dances In Storms' eyes and squeezed her hand. "This is my gift to you, my sister-friend. When the time comes, you will be the one who joins White Elk and me. But now is the time for you."

***

White Elk walked over to where Golden Fox tied supplies to Splash and readied a second mustang to carry meat back to camp. "I have talked to the Holy Woman. We do not have to make this decision now. When the warm season comes, we can perhaps walk and cry for a vision."

With a firm shake of her head, she leapt onto Splash. "No, White Elk, her body cries out that now is the time for her to be with child. The Spirits have shown all three of us that you are to be the father of her child. It is best that this happens while I am hunting."

When she started to tap her mustang into a walk, he gripped her lower leg. "Golden Fox, I will not do this. I will ignore what the Spirits say, before I will lose you. I have searched too long to let you go so easily."

She leaned over and touched her lips to his forehead. "You will not lose me, silly one. Dances In Storms will have a child with you and, when I am ready, my sister-friend will do the ceremony to join you and me. We will be mates, and when I am ready, we will have a child. But now I have something I must do, and a joining with you must wait."

"You have changed, Golden Fox—grown in ways I only now see."

"Take care of my sister-friend." She tapped Splash's sides, and the mustang trotted toward Blazing Fire's animals.

The hunt went well, and in six sunrises, they had enough meat for the camp.

Stands His Ground and Hawk Watches disappeared as Sister Moon rose in the sky. They would stand first watch.

Blazing Fire finished rolling out her sleeping robe as Golden Fox slipped beneath the warm cover of her own sleeping robe.

"Is it true, Golden Fox, that you sent Dances In Storms to White Elk's lodge while we hunt?"

With hands linked behind her head, she stared up at the campfires in the sky and felt a smile turn the corners of her lips upward. "I am hoping that he will get her with child by the time we return."

"Hmph! I thought you refused to share a man?"

"I do refuse to *share* a man. Dances In Storms cares for White Elk, but they do not have the feelings that a man and a woman who wish to share a lodge all of their lives should have. Their relationship will take nothing from what grows between White Elk and me. It will bring good to all three of us."

"You no longer sound like the child who first begged me to teach her the ways of a warrior woman."

"You have helped me to grow, Blazing Fire. I honor you for that."

Before Blazing Fire could answer, the sound of mustangs coming had them both flipping the sleeping robes aside and grabbing their bows.

Stands His Ground rode in with the lead rope of a second mustang, upon which sat a white man, firmly in his hand.

Hawk Watches rode a little behind and to one side of the stranger's animal. When they drew up to the fire, the warriors slid to the ground and motioned for the white man to get down.

As his feet touched the ground, one leg folded and he fell.

Blazing Fire moved close and stared at the stranger. "He bleeds." She glanced from one warrior to the other.

Stands His Ground gave a slow shake of his head. "We found him riding like a man who sleeps. He was coming to our camp."

Blazing Fire hunkered next to the man. "Why do you follow the People?"

Using his arms, he shoved himself into a sitting position. "I seek my... my daughter, Golden Fox."

Before he could dodge her, Blazing Fire grasped a handful of his hair, bent his head, and laid her knife across his throat. "Why do you seek this daughter, white man?"

He shifted his eyes until he could see her. "Why would a man not look for his daughter?"

Stands His Ground moved forward. "A man does not send other whites with poisoned water to steal his daughter from her mother and her people!" He nocked an arrow in his bow. "I will kill him now."

"Wait!" Hairy-Face No More, one of the two hairy-faces who had joined Eagle Thunder's band during their journey, stepped forward. "This man is not the one who sent poisoned water from the fort. He is not the one who hunted the gold fox. That was the captain."

Golden Fox frowned. "If this man is my father, then he is Captain. This is what my mother names him, if she speaks of him at all."

"I was... was captain at the fort." He squinted at Golden Fox as if he could not clearly see. "You must be... be my daughter, Golden Fox. I never... never sent men after you. Would never send... fire water to your people. I swear." Sweat popped out on his forehead, and he slumped to the ground in the sleep that was not a sleep.

Golden Fox locked her eyes on Hairy-Face No More, and pursed her lips. "There is more to hear." She laid a hand on Stands His Ground's tense arm. "Blazing Fire and I will take care of his leg. We have finished hunting, and are journeying to camp when Father Sun rises. We will take him with us. If he lives, we will hear what he has to say."

* * *

Sister Moon rode the cloudless sky as the man who claimed he was Golden Fox's father swayed on the back of his mustang. Only the ropes, which tied him to the leather thing he sat on, kept him from falling to the ground.

It had taken two sunrises to reach camp, though the hunting party had ridden hard.

As Stands His Ground and Hairy-Face No More pulled the man off of the mustang, Golden Fox wondered if he would see Father Sun rise.

Sky Bird stepped out of the lodge she shared with Deer Woman. She swept open the entrance flap and held it. "Who is this dying white you bring to our lodge?"

Golden Fox touched her mother's arm. "He says he is my father."

Anger flared across Sky Bird's face and her lips tightened into a thin line. "I should let him die. If I heal him, it will only be to kill him. I will not let that man harm you, Daughter."

"Hairy-Face No More says there is more to hear, and that we should perhaps listen to this white man who was once your man. While he heals, Hairy-Face No More and Pale Hunter will tell us what they know. When he—" She nodded toward the man laid out on a sleeping robe. "—when he wakes, we will hear his words, too, before we decide if he is to live or to die. I have many questions for this man who claims to be my father, yet has never been a father to me."

After a long, quiet span, they stepped outside of the lodge and wiped sweat from their faces.

Deer Woman walked out and looped an arm around her mate's shoulders. "We have done all that we can." She looked past Sky Bird to Golden Fox. "I am sorry that you are to meet your father only to sing him to the campfires in the sky. I know you had many questions for this man, but the bad Spirits have eaten into the bone of his knee, and it dies. Soon the bad Spirits will race higher on his body, until they take all of him."

Long Sun's drum sounded softly from behind them, and Dances In Storms' voice raised in song. They sang for a hairy-face that Golden Fox did not know, yet she already felt a sense of loss.

Pale Hunter stepped around the outside cooking fire. "Sky Bird, you are a healer of the People and I honor you. Once, I was known as a healer of hairy-faces. Will you let me and Hairy-Face No More help this hairy-face who claims Golden Fox as his daughter?"

Bewilderment crunched her brows over her eyes. "What can you do? The man will not see Father Sun wake."

"I have seen the bad Spirits get into a wound after battle. There is only one way to save life when this happens. We must cut away the place where the bad Spirits now live. It is better for a man to lose one leg than to lose his life."

Sky Bird's mouth flew open. "Take his leg off? How can you do this?"

"Not his whole leg, but part of it. Will you allow us to try?"

Golden Fox caught her mother's eye. "He will not live if the bad Spirits are allowed to remain in his body, Mother. Perhaps, among the hairy-faces, this is not so bad to lose a leg."

She pointed inside the lodge. "Go inside the lodge, Pale Hunter and Hairy-Face No More. Perhaps, your hairy-face medicine can save this man." Mumbling, she added, "Though I wonder why we save him. If he is the one who sent hairy-faces with poisoned water after Golden Fox, he will not leave this camp."

Pale Hunter squatted by the sleeping robe where Golden Fox's father tossed and mumbled with sick dreams.

Hairy-Face No More took his long knife over to the fire pit, and placed the blade in the embers. As he worked, he talked about what he did. "The fire will kill anything unclean on my blade. If we do not do this, more bad Spirits will crawl into his leg." Letting the blade sit in the embers, he opened his carry-all—the thing he called saddlebags—and took out a strong, short stick wrapped in leather.

He handed it to Golden Fox. "You must put this in his mouth and keep it there, or he will break his teeth." Staring down at her with pale eyes, he said, "We can have Stands His Ground do this, if you want. Your fa... this hairy-face will feel much pain."

She lifted her chin and accepted the leather-wrapped stick. "I am a warrior. A warrior does what is needed."

He gave a brusque nod of respect. "Stand close to his head, then. You may have to hold his head tight."

Pale Hunter gazed around. "Stands His Ground, do not let go of his good leg. Be sure to keep it away from the bad leg. White Elk, hold tight to his arm. Blazing Fire, hold tight to his other arm. It will be you two who must not let his chest rise up."

He glanced over his shoulder at Sky Bird and Deer Woman. "Take the deer-skin pieces that are in the hot water and cool them. Soon they will be needed to press against the piece of leg that I leave."

Pale Hunter held his sword a finger-width from the hairy-face's leg, sucked in a deep breath, held it, and placed the blade on the skin. The smell of burning hair and flesh rose in acrid clouds.

Golden Fox gagged, but swallowed down the bitter spit that came up in her mouth.

With a solid slam of a rock on the blade, the blade sliced through flesh. Blood spattered. Each time that Pale Hunter slammed the rock into the blade, more blood splashed on his arms and hands. The hairy-face fought against the hands that held him, though his eyes only opened once. They looked about wildly and the leather in his mouth muffled his scream.

It took five times of slamming the rock against the blade before the blade passed through the bone. As the leg parted, Deer Woman darted in and removed it from the sleeping robe. Hairy-Face No More pulled the rope Pale Hunter had placed above the wound tight, which slowed the flow of blood.

Pale Hunter rushed over to the fire and shoved his long knife deep into the red embers. When it glowed, he hurried back and placed the blade against the wound. He did this twice before the rope could be loosened, and the blood did not flow fast from the wound.

Pale Hunter wiped his forearm across his face and caught the sweat dripping into his eyes. "Sky Bird, I do not have the medicines of the hairy-faces for wounds. Will you dress this wound and care for it now?"

"Deer Woman and I will care for him. Please, open the bottom of the lodge, and then take the leg far from camp. We must be careful that the bad Spirits do not harm others."

Golden Fox stayed in the lodge, cleaning the blood from her father's body with soft deerskin scraps and warm water. After that, she found a clean, soft deerskin.

Deer Woman took it from her hand. "I know you are a woman grown, but you have not rested since returning from the hunt. Your mother and I will care for this hairy-face. We will come and get you if anything changes. Go to the river and bathe away any bad Spirits that might cling to you, then go to your lodge, eat, and rest."

* * *

When Golden Fox returned to her lodge from the river, White Elk waited. He handed her a bowl of hot meat and tubers and new greens.

She sank to the ground and accepted the bowl.

After eating in silence, she stumbled to her sleeping robes. The last thing she remembered was White Elk brushing the hair from around her face and pulling the sleeping robe up over her shoulders.

34

Three sunrises passed before Golden Fox's father could lean up and drink broth. Two more sunrises passed before he could sit for a short span and talk. Every day, Golden Fox tended to her father's needs.

When, at last, he could speak for more than the time it took to eat, he asked that Pale Hunter sit beside his sleeping robe, that he had words he needed to say to his daughter, Golden Fox. "Pale Hunter has spent much time to learn your language. This is why I ask him to change my words to the words of the People. I know some words, but want what I say to be said with the right words."

He briefly rubbed his leg above where it had been cut off. "My full name is Francisco Riley, but I ran the fort for a long time and people called me Captain. When I met them, I told your mother and grandfather to call me Captain. It had become my name. In a way, it was like your People—the name says something about the person. That was who I was, the captain of Fort Murdock." He reached for a water bladder, but it was too far.

Golden Fox handed it to him. "Perhaps, my mother should be here to hear your words."

"No. I... I will talk to your mother, but now I want to talk to my daughter who is a grown woman. Will you listen?"

She settled cross-legged in front of him. "I am listening."

"When I met your mother, I thought her the most beautiful woman I'd ever seen. That's why I asked her to come live with me at Fort Murdock. I could hardly believe it when she said she would, and when her father agreed to let her go."

Francisco waited for Pale Hunter to finish translating his words before he spoke again. "I don't know why I began drinking too much whisk—er, fire water—but I did. Sometimes, this happens among my people. My own father was like this. When I drank, I became a different man, a man I didn't like, yet I didn't know how to stop drinking, and I didn't know how to keep that bad man inside."

After Sky Bird had cut the hair on his face off, his skin had been very pale. It grew paler as he spoke. "I... I did bad things, Golden Fox. I... I hit your mother and said many harsh things to her. I called you and her ugly. I lay with other women." He clutched his hands together in his lap. "I never blamed Sky Bird for leaving, and I never looked for you because... well, Sky Bird and you deserved a better man than me."

When he fell silent for a long time, Golden Fox asked, "Why did you send whites with poisoned water to hunt us?"

At her father's puzzled frown, Pale Hunter spoke up. "I never met Captain, here. Had no more idea who he was than Stands His Ground did. The captain who sent the whites out with poisoned water to trade for information about where you were... that man is Captain George Henry. A lot of men call him Captain. Maybe it has to do with him being captain of the fort, like your father was."

"Why would he want a woman of the Peoples that he never met?" Golden Fox drew her lips into a tight knot of disgust.

"Because of the story goin' 'round."

"What story?"

"I do not know how it started." Pale Hunter raised troubled pale eyes. "There is a story hairy-faces tell that, among the Peoples, there is a band who has found a rich gold mine." When she gave him a bewildered expression, he explained. "The yellow stone that whites dig holes in the Mother to find is called gold. The holes they dig are called gold mines. This is a very important stone to them. It will make them very rich and very important among others of their kind. Do you understand?"

"Yes. Dances In Storms told me that Shining Light's people had to leave these canyons long, long ago because the whites thought there was a lot of the yellow stone here. She said a white would kill his brother for this yellow stone."

Lips pressed together, Pale Hunter nodded. "Yes, many would. The story goes that the way you know which band of people has this gold mine, is because they have a girl with gold-red hair. She belongs to the headman, and he named her Gold Fox after a statue of a gold fox." Seeing her frown, he hurried to explain, "A statue is... is like a carving, only this one is a gold fox the size of a real fox, and it is made of gold. It is said that if someone captures the girl with the gold-red hair, the headman will trade his gold mine for his daughter.

"It is said that the band who owns this gold mine is a very large band with ferocious warriors, so men seek this girl for the big reward that Captain Henry will give them."

Golden Fox stormed across the lodge. "Why did you not tell us this story, Pale Hunter?" Anger blazed through her body and she rested her hand on the hilt of her knife.

Pale Hunter carefully lifted his hands, palms out. "I... I did not realize that it was important. I am sorry, Golden Fox. I am very sorry I did not tell this to you."

* * *

When Golden Fox had told this story to her grandfather, Eagle Thunder placed a hand on her arm. "Be at peace. Pale Hunter did not understand. A council must be called."

The council decided that a scouting party needed to be sent out to see how many of the enemy searched for this gold mine that did not exist, and for the gold-red-haired woman who did.

Blazing Fire and Stands His Ground led the party, which included White Elk, Golden Fox, Pale Hunter, and Dances In Storms. They left as soon as they had sung Father Sun into the sky.

When they drew closer to the wooden fort, Pale Hunter offered to go inside and count how many whites lived there.

Stands His Ground went with him, acting as if he followed for the promise of fire water.

Together, Stands His Ground and Pale Hunter entered the wooden gates guarding the fort.

* * *

That was two sunrises ago.

Blazing Fire and Golden Fox had gone to scout closer to the fort, while White Elk and Dances In Storms searched for places their people could hide as they gathered to attack the fort.

Upon their return, Golden Fox slid off Splash and rubbed her down with dried grasses.

As Blazing Fire cleaned the sweat off Fast Girl, she tipped her chin toward the cold fire circle. "White Elk and Dances In Storms have not returned yet."

With a mischievous grin, Golden Fox waggled her brows. "Maybe they did not have time to make a baby while we hunted."

Blazing Fire tossed the grasses to the ground, patted Fast Girl on the rump, and headed for the fire circle. "If they take too long, they will have little to eat. I am hungry enough to eat all of the rabbits we hunted."

Splash had learned quickly, so Golden Fox no longer hobbled her. When she released the mustang, she picked up her carry-all and took it to the fire the warrior woman had started. "Good thing I dug these tubers." She added them to the pot nestled on the side of the flames.

The two women ate and cleaned up, then rested.

When Father Sun dropped and ducked behind the trees, Blazing Fire pushed up from where she sat. "White Elk and Dances In Storms should have returned. We need to look for them before Father Sun goes to rest."

The blue of the sky had darkened to that time between Father Sun and Sister Moon, by the time they found White Elk.

He lay sprawled on his face, his faithful Cloud standing next to him.

Golden Fox leapt off Splash and raced over to White Elk's still body.

Blazing Fire nocked an arrow and carefully scanned the surrounding land. Once convinced no one was nearby, she slid off Fast Girl and hurried over to where the young man lay. "Does he live?" She laid her bow on the ground and knelt next to Golden Fox.

"He lives. I must turn him over to see if there are other wounds besides the gash in the back of his head." She carefully rolled him to his back. "Nothing. I will clean the wound, and then see if I can wake him."

Blazing Fire walked around the spot where White Elk lay. "He was not attacked here. He must have gotten away from whoever he fought, and started toward our camp, and then fell from his mustang."

A groan worked out of White Elk's mouth as Golden Fox scrubbed the dirt from the wound. By the time the wound was clean and packed with the moss and plants she always carried, he had awakened from the sleep that a hit in the head can give.

257

"We have to go!" He struggled to his feet the moment Golden Fox turned to pack away her medicines.

She caught him as he swayed, and helped him back to the ground. "Sit, White Elk. You cannot ride a mustang."

Blazing Fire hunkered down in front of him. "Where is Dances In Storms? Tell us what you can, White Elk."

"Three enemies came out of a gully that we passed." Eyes squinted, he sucked air between his teeth and continued. "I hit one with an arrow. He did not get back up from the ground. Two went after Dances In Storms. I saw her push her knife into one. His mustang ran off with him clinging to that leather thing they ride. I did not see the one who came behind me and hit me. I only remember the pain in my head and then darkness. I do not know how long I lay in darkness on the ground. It was Father Sun's fingers on my eyes that brought me to my senses. I jumped on Cloud and she headed to camp. That is all I know."

"We must find my sister-friend." With hands fisted at her sides, Golden Fox marched toward Splash.

Blazing Fire swung up on Fast Girl and motioned toward Cloud. "White Elk, as difficult as it is, you must ride to camp."

He crawled up on his mustang, a stubborn set to his chin, and shook his head. "No. I will go with you. I know the direction we rode and where the gully lies." With no more words, he tapped Cloud and set off at a gallop, clinging to his mustang's mane.

As Father Sun dropped behind the land's edge, clouds gathered.

Blazing Fire glanced around. "We need to find shelter. It is still early in the season of young animals, and the cold may not be done with us yet."

Frost suddenly appeared and trotted up to Golden Fox, and then moved away. He gave short looks over his shoulder.

Golden Fox crinkled her brows, but understood, and she nudged Splash to follow the wolf. She could hear her two companions behind her.

The dip between two short hills became deeper as Frost led her farther into the ravine. Finally, he stopped, circled three times, and lay down.

Blazing Fire looked around. "Father Wolf has found a good place for us. There—" She pointed toward a deeper darkness. "—see how those dead trees have fallen. If there is space, it could be a dry place to sleep."

258

They had barely gotten their sleeping robes and carry-alls into the tight space beneath the fallen trees, when rain pounded down from the black sky.

Frost flipped his bushy tail over his nose and closed his eyes.

Golden Fox gazed out past the tiny fire they made in the entrance to their shelter, and watched the rain turn into tiny ice balls. As the ice hit with a loud *thunk* on the bark of the dead trees, she could not help wondering if Dances In Storms had a place to sleep that was dry and safe.

35

Dances In Storms saw White Elk fall.

As she fought to get free of the enemy, a rope slid over her and snugged her tight, holding her arms to her sides. With a yank on the rope, the white man jerked her off Moon. When she fell, another rope whipped through the air. Just as it would have fallen over the mustang's head, Moon ducked and skittered away.

"Run, Moon!" Dances In Storms yelled at the mustang.

He tossed his head and snorted, as the white man who had tried to capture the mustang eased his own animal toward Moon.

She yelled again. "Run, Moon!"

The mustang tossed his head, whirled, and kicked his hind feet toward the man.

His own mustang darted sideways, and the fast move caused the man to toss the rope too soon—Moon was long gone before the rope landed on the ground.

The man, who had tied the end of the rope that wrapped around her to his strange leather seat, pulled hard, and she fell to the ground. He hopped off his animal and stalked toward her. Before she could roll away from him, the toe of his dirty boot slammed into her side.

"Tha's just a taste, squaw. Give me trouble 'n you'll feel more o' that." Knife in hand, he grasped her long hair and yanked her to her feet. "Move 'n I'll slit yer throat."

He tied her hands in front of her. The rest of the rope was long enough that he could ride while forcing her to walk a few steps behind his mustang.

With the words she had learned from Pale Hunter, she shouted at her captor. "Why you do this?"

He leered down at her. "Know a bit o' civilized language, huh? Maybe you'll make a good squaw to keep 'round. I'll have'ta think 'bout that." He jerked the rope just enough to cause her to stumble. "Now, shut up, woman."

With a tap of his heels, the mustang stretched his legs longer, forcing Dances In Storms to trot to keep up.

When Father Sun finally went to his lodge, clouds had gathered in the sky. The cold season was not yet done, and the rain came hard and fast, and just as quickly turned into balls of ice. The ice stung as it hit her face and bare arms.

By the time she stumbled into the white men's hidden camp, her wrists bled from the roughness of the rope. When the man stopped, she stood with her head down, breath rasping in her throat, and her legs trembling as a newborn mustang's.

The man dove off his mustang and tossed the rope to one of the other men. Not glancing her way, he tugged the rope and led her through a hide entrance and into a wooden lodge. The stale air stank of rancid meat, sweat, and poisoned water.

Dances In Storms nearly gagged.

He shoved her over into a dark corner and tied the rope high on a piece of dead tree above her head. He left only enough slack in the rope for her to slide down to the dirt floor and sit against the greasy wood wall.

Her head sank back against the wall, and she closed her eyes. She did not even know if White Elk still lived.

Great Mystery, Spirits, give me a vision. Help me see a way to free myself.

* * *

A boot prodded her in the side. "Wake up, lazy squaw!" The second time, the boot thumped against her thigh.

Dances In Storms' eyes popped open, and she gazed upon a younger, crazy-eyed man. Kerosene lamps — something she had seen once when she visited her grandmother's sister's family — sat on the rough wood table and cast a dim light through the wooden lodge. A fire blazed in a stone pit that did not look like the fire pits of her people.

The older man that had roped her slept with his mouth open, head sideways on the table.

The crazy-eyed one kicked her again. He grabbed a fistful of hair and yanked her up. With quick motions, he untied her hands and shoved her toward the fire. "Clean them rabbits and make a stew, squaw."

She did not understand his words but, seeing the dead rabbits by the fire, she knew what he wanted. She stared around, not knowing where to get water, or how he expected her to skin the rabbits without a knife.

A third man, younger than the other two, walked over to her and picked up the rabbits. "I will skin them." He spoke in a mix of the whites' language and the language of the Peoples. "There are things to put in the stew over there." He motioned toward a bucket on the floor to one side of the fire. "I filled the pot with water, so chop everything up. I will be back soon."

Between the two of them, the food was cooked and dished out.

The older man had awakened long enough to eat and to drink more fire water. This time, he staggered to a raised hide with pieces of dead trees at each corner, which held it off the ground. He flopped onto it and, within two breaths, fell into a deep sleep.

The crazy one burped food while he held an empty flask of fire water. He staggered toward a pile of smelly robes in a corner, and collapsed with the flask in his hand.

Soon, snores came from them both.

Dances In Storms had not left her place on the floor by the fire since she had fed the men. She finished the stew in her bowl, and glanced over at the third man. "Are you to keep watch during the time of Sister Moon?"

His eyes touched hers briefly before darting away. "Yes."

"You speak my language. Where did you learn?"

"My mother is of the People. I lived with her until I was ten winters old." Hurt peeked out from behind his words.

"Why did you leave the People?"

"My... my mother died... started coughing and... died. The band did not want a half-blood. One of the elders brought me close to here, and told me to go live with my white father." He shrugged. "I have been living here since then."

"You like being here?"

Bitterness twisted his mouth. "I have no other place to go."

"There are half-bloods who live with my People. We see a man's way of living, and the way of his heart, not the color of his skin."

For a moment, hope flashed across his face, but then it died. "Yeah, well, he would never let me go. He will not let you go, either. He will use you, and then he will sell you to men at the fort."

"I am not an animal to be sold or traded to others." Defiantly, she straightened her back. "And I will die before I allow him to touch me as a man touches a woman."

His shaggy, brown hair hung loose about his elbows. He licked his lips and glanced at the men snoring on the other side of the wooden lodge, then bent close to her and whispered, "I... I want to help you. I want to live with your band where half-bloods are not judged by their skin color. Once, I was called Strong Wind. It is the name my mother gave me."

* * *

Frost nudged Golden Fox awake as Father Sun peeked above the horizon. Puddles of water reminded her of the rain and the cold in the darkness. She crept out of the shelter, silently following her Wolf Brother.

Blazing Fire was roasting ground birds over a smokeless fire when Golden Fox rode back into camp.

White Elk half-smiled up at her, then returned to cleaning another ground bird, with Sun Snow sitting at his side.

Golden Fox wondered for a moment how Sun Snow had come to be here, but then thought, 'Of course.'

When she walked over, Blazing Fire handed her a stick with a cooked bird. "Eat, and tell us what Father Wolf showed you."

"How did you know?" She took a big bite of the meat and chewed.

"You were gone, Splash was gone, Father Wolf was gone.... You would not have left to hunt without telling me. I have taught you that it is not the way of a warrior. I knew you left because Father Wolf wanted to show something to you."

"I found her."

White Elk bolted to his feet. "You found her? Come, show us where!"

Before he could get many steps away, Blazing Fire cleared her throat. When he swung around to look, she motioned for him to return to the fire. "Golden Fox, tell us more of what you saw."

After she finished describing the box canyon and the wooden lodge, the warrior woman stared at her for a long moment. "Did you feel danger around Dances In Storms?"

Golden Fox opened her mouth to speak, then closed it and considered her words. "The fat white man.... I felt a... a hole where his Spirit should be. The one with hair the color of dead grass... there is something wrong in his mind, and there is darkness in his Spirit. The other one, the one with the brown hair... I felt no darkness in him."

"Did it feel like they would do her harm while Father Sun is in the sky?"

Lips pursed, she slowly shook her head. "No."

"Good. We will wait until Father Sun goes to his place of rest."

* * *

Dances In Storms watched as Strong Wind kept passing the fire water to the other two men.

Finally, they slumped over.

As soon as the men began to snore, Strong Wind motioned for her to follow. They ducked through the hide flap. Only part of Sister Moon's face shone, but she offered enough light to walk the unfamiliar ground.

Strong Wind whispered close to her ear, "I will take my mustang and lead him out. You take the red one. He has power in his legs. The other mustang will follow." He handed her a nose rope, and pulled the dead trees away so an opening was clear.

She slipped into the small enclosure made of dead trees, and held out her hand to the red mustang. She eased toward him, crooning in a low voice.

When she threw the nose rope over the animal's neck, the mustang panicked and pulled away. The red one snorted loudly and raced out through the opening, feet loud on the ground as she ran past the wooden lodge.

One of the men slapped the hide flap open. The older man's gruff voice yelled, "Hey, stop!"

Strong Wind leapt on his mustang and held a hand down to her. She flew on the already moving animal behind Strong Wind, And with a thump of his heels, he urged the mustang into a flat-out run.

The roar of a fire stick split the darkness. Strong Wind leaned lower on the mustang as the animal raced down the narrow valley that led to the box canyon.

BROKEN PATH

Dances In Storms' hair flew behind as the animal's powerful muscles bunched and released beneath her.

As they burst from the valley and out onto grasslands, Strong Wind pulled back on the nose rope, and the mustang slowed to a trot.

"Strong Wind, he breathes too hard. He cannot carry both of us. We need to find a place to hide."

He glanced around, and then urged the mustang toward the back of a small hill. "We need to get down. This hill is too short, and we might be seen. Besides, I worry that my mustang will call if my father rides past. This way, I can put my hand over his nose and maybe stop his sounds. I left my bow at the cabin—I mean the wooden lodge—so all I have is my knife."

"I have a knife in my footwear on both legs. Your father did not find them in their sheaths strapped under my leggings." Determination flooded her body as her feet touched the ground. "I will not return to be your father's captive. Keep your mustang's nose against you. It will help keep him quiet."

* * *

A mustang trotted out the narrow valley, with the fat man weaving and bouncing on the animal's back. "Where my *trusted* son go with woman not his?"

Strong Wind's animal tried to whinny to his companion, but he pulled the mustang's muzzle close to his body. Body tense, he listened as the animal rode past the small hill and then burst into a run.

Within a few breaths, his father had disappeared into the darkness.

"He will run that poor mustang till she drops. She is a good animal." As Strong Wind began to get back on his mustang, a cold voice called from the darkness.

"Squaw, step on out here where I kin see ya. You too, brother. Make it quick or y'all gonna have some extra holes in ya."

He led Dances In Storms, and they walked out into the weak moonlight.

His brother waved with his gun. "I ain' as stupid as dear ol' daddy. The two of ya kin just walk along real nice 'n slow like. Jus' go on ahead o' me, 'n on back to the cabin with ya."

Dances In Storms edged closer to Strong Wind and whispered, "Move away from me. In five breaths, you must jump on your mustang and run. It will give me time to stop this brother of yours." Not waiting for his reply, she eased away from him.

His brother grunted. "Hey, squaw, don' be gettin' no idears. Jus' get on back over there with my baby brother." He gave a nasty laugh. "I got me some words to say to 'im when we get to the cabin."

All of a sudden, Dances In Storms whirled. Her hand dipped to the top of her footwear covered by her leggings. She scrambled with frantic fingers and snatched a knife from its sheath. As the knife came free, she hauled her arm back and threw it. Before it struck its target, she had hit the ground and rolled.

Strong Wind was impressed with her speed and skill, as the roar of his brother's blasted against his ears.

Dirt sprayed up around Dances In Storms' head, but she kept rolling for a short ways, then sprang to her feet, her second knife in hand.

His older brother lay on his back on the hard ground. The hilt of the woman's knife stuck up from his chest.

Strong Wind walked over and stared down at his brother, whose open eyes saw nothing — the blank stare of death.

He nodded and turned to Dances In Storms. "The other mustang got away. Guess we will both have to ride Daisy."

36

Blazing Fire had tracked the marks of mustang feet shod in met-al from the small wooden lodge. Now, she stopped and wiped the sweat from her face. "Since the mustang went into the river, I had not found the new trail the animal takes. A human must be guiding the mustang. No animal does that on their own."

Golden Fox shook her head. "I fear for Dances In Storms. We only found two bodies, and White Elk said there were three." She stood up straight and stretched. Father Sun's fingers on her back felt good on the tight muscles. She opened her mouth to speak more, but White Elk called out.

"Blazing Fire, a mustang comes."

The warrior woman snapped her head up from staring at the ground, and studied the dust trail in the distance. "The mustang does not run as one who carries a human. Yet I see no reason for the animal to run. Ready your bows."

As the animal drew closer, Golden Fox recognized the sleek black body. "Moon!"

The mustang slowed to a fast trot and hurried to them. Sweat marked his shoulders and neck.

Golden Fox chewed her lower lip as she ran her hands over the animal, check-ing for injuries. After, she turned toward Blazing Fire. "Warrior Woman, what does this mean?"

"We have known that Dances In Storms walked beside the white men's mustangs to the small wooden lodge. The man must have had her riding with him when they left the wooden lodge, because there were foot tracks in only one small space, as if humans waited there."

She cast her eye along Moon's body. "Perhaps, Moon followed Dances In Storms."

"Why is he here then?" White Elk shifted on Cloud and gently touched the back of his head.

Golden Fox winced in sympathy, as White Elk's pain became hers. The hard jarring of his mustang made his head hurt more, and the wound had started to bleed.

Blazing Fire shrugged, but kept her movement too guarded for Golden Fox to feel Blazing Fire's thought. "Perhaps, Moon recognized our mustangs' scents and only wanted to be with us. Mustangs wish to be with others of their kind."

After a nuzzled greeting to the other mustangs, Moon pranced ahead of Blazing Fire. "We should put a lead rope on Moon. We may need him when we find Dances In Storms."

Golden Fox threw herself up on Splash. "I will put a lead rope around his neck."

Each time she drew close to Moon, the mustang danced away. Finally, she halted Splash and propped her hands on her hips. "Moon, what is it that you try to tell me?"

He snorted and bobbed his head, then pranced a bit farther.

Blazing Fire gave a thoughtful look at Frost. "Father Wolf, can you understand what this mustang tries to tell us?"

Frost lifted his muzzle and sniffed deeply, then sneezed. With a shake of his head, he headed toward Moon. Halfway between Golden Fox and Moon, he stopped and peered back over his shoulder. When she nudged Splash in his direction, both Moon and Frost set off at a slow trot.

***

Father Sun went to his rest, and Sister Moon only showed a sliver of her face. Blazing Fire called the three to a halt, and they made camp without a fire. Here on the open grasslands, the smoke and the redness of embers were too easily noticed.

Moon fidgeted tied to Blazing Fire's war mustang, but the lead rope Golden Fox had placed around his neck kept him from wandering away in the dark.

The pemmican tasted dry in her mouth. Golden Fox hoped they found the river again, soon. Only one full water bladder remained in her carry-all. She washed the meat mixture down with a long swallow from the nearly empty bladder in her hand.

The mustang's restlessness must have infected the wolf, because Frost rose and padded away.

Golden Fox stretched out her sleeping robe. *Great Mystery, please keep my sister-friend safe. We have to find her!* She could not bear to lose another sister-friend; the loss of Running Girl still made her cry during the darkness.

Though exhaustion made her muscles ache, her eyelids would not remain closed. She flipped the robe off and went to where Blazing Fire stood. "I will keep watch. You should rest."

Blazing Fire shot her a sideways look. "Dances In Storms is a strong woman. She will be all right until we find her."

"I... I care for her. She will maybe have White Elk's child, and I am to be the child's second mother."

Without a word, Blazing Fire gathered Golden Fox against her in a tight embrace.

When Golden Fox stepped back, she wiped her eyes. "I... I can see Dances In Storms' child in my lodge. She will be older, and will have much to teach my little one, just as Dances In Storms has much to teach me. She... she is the elder sister I have never had."

The warrior woman drew in a breath to speak, but did not let it back out. Her body tensed as her eyes roamed the darkness. The air exploded from her when Frost trotted up to Golden Fox. "Father Wolf, I am glad I did not have an arrow nocked, or perhaps your beautiful fur would have a hole in it."

A mustang's feet thudded against the ground. Blazing Fire swung her bow from her shoulder and motioned Golden Fox to silence.

A blackness deeper than the darkness of the surrounding night showed against the night sky. It halted only a short distance from where White Elk slept.

Golden Fox's heart slammed against her ribs. *Please, please, White Elk, remain asleep. Do not move, Man-Who-Will-Be-Mine!*

The muscles in her back clenched as she too held a bow steady, arrow nocked, string drawn taut.

"That wolf was Frost, or I would not have followed him," a soft voice whispered. "They must be around here close."

"Dances In Storms?" Golden Fox's cry shattered the stillness. She laid aside her bow and ran to her sister-friend.

The Holy Woman slipped off the rump of the mustang and embraced Golden Fox.

Blazing Fire stepped around them, her arrow still nocked, and leered at the man still on the mustang. "Who are you?"

"Yes, answer quickly before you die." White Elk's deep voice rang from the other side of the stranger.

As White Elk moved toward the stranger, Dances In Storms jerked away from Golden Fox. She stepped between White Elk and the man, who continued to sit on his mustang. "Put aside your bows. Strong Wind is my friend, and a new member of Sister Wolf Band. I, the Holy Woman of the Sister Wolf Band, say this is so."

* * *

Golden Fox's stomach growled so loudly that White Elk heard it, and when he laughed, heat rushed to her cheeks.

They rode into the small camp to the smell of rabbits roasting over a fire, and Pale Hunter cooked with tubers and greens in a pot of water.

After eating pemmican for two sunrises, Golden Fox's mouth watered at the delicious scents drifting on Sister Wind.

Stands His Ground studied the stranger, who rode a red mustang beside Dances In Storms and Moon.

Upon arriving, Golden Fox hopped down and rubbed a small scrap of deer hide over the sweaty places on Splash, then walked over to the fire and Stands His Ground. "My sister-friend went hunting." A grin teased the corners of her mouth.

"Hmph! She caught a man of mixed-blood who wears the clothes of a white. I am not so sure that such a catch is better than bringing back a deer." He chuckled. "We maybe could skin him and use his hide. Do you think it would keep out cold as good as humpback hides?"

Dances In Storms stiffened. "Do not speak so disrespectfully of my soon-to-be-mate, Stands His Ground." Though her words said one thing, her gentle laugh said another.

Laughter faded from his face as he cocked his head and stared at Strong Wind. "I hope he can ride and that his mustang is fast."

Strong Wind's eyes snapped toward the warrior. "Why would I need to ride fast?" Worry darkened his green-brown eyes.

"Calls Elk may not think a Holy Woman should give up Power to be with a mixed blood."

Dances In Storms' nostrils flared and she drew herself up tall. "I can be both Holy Woman and have a mate. The Spirits have said this."

A shrug said Stands His Ground would not argue. "Your father believes that he gave up his Power when he took Small Feet as his mate. I have heard the warriors speak of this."

Golden Fox dove for the rabbit. "Can we maybe not worry so much about this until Dances In Storms sees her father? I wish to know what news you and Pale Hunter have about the wooden fort." A bit of juice ran down her arm as she chewed and waited.

Stands His Ground took a deep breath, held it, and let it out slowly. "It will not be easy to rescue our Peoples, Golden Fox. The whites walk on top of a wall made of dead trees. They watch for any who approach. Inside are white warriors and traders. There are white women and children, too, but many of our own people cling to flasks of poisoned water. They will not want to leave." he hunkered down and cut a piece off the roasting rabbits.

Pale Hunter squatted close to him. "And they have fire sticks, Golden Fox."

A grim determination caused her to look at each of her companions one-by-one. "I will not abandon our Peoples. We must find a way to bring them out of the wooden fort, and to destroy the place that has brought so much destruction to our Peoples."

37

As they entered the Sister Wolf Band's camp, Golden Fox rode next to Dances In Storms.

Will Calls Elk be angry that his daughter wants to join with a man? Surely, he will not ignore what the Spirits have said?

Strong Wind shifted on his mustang. "I wonder if your father will be very angry, as Stands His Ground thinks. Maybe this is not such a good thing to do."

She reached over and squeezed his hand. "The Spirits have shown me in a lodge with a child of my own. I was still a Holy Woman. The Spirits sometimes give us great gifts. You, Strong Wind, are a great gift from the Spirits."

As they rode through the center of the camp to Calls Elk's lodge, the people spilled from their lodges and gathered to listen to what the scouts would say.

Golden Fox slid off Splash, and Girl Who Does Not Speak reached out to take the lead rope. "She has ridden long and is tired. I am glad you will take care of her. Splash has a special like for you."

The young woman smiled and hurried away.

Golden Fox walked behind Dances In Storms and Strong Wind into the lodge of Calls Elk.

Calls Elk stood by the fire pit in the center of his lodge. "Who is this stranger, Daughter?"

With her fingers threaded through Strong Wind's hand, Dances In Storms lifted her chin and pulled her shoulders back. "As I have told you, Father, the Spirits have given me a great gift. They have said I am to have a child of my own."

He folded his arms across his burly chest and glared. "This one does not look like a child."

Red crawled up Dances In Storms' neck.

Golden Fox laid a hand on her sister-friend's trembling shoulder. "Calls Elk, the Spirits have spoken to me as well. They wish for Dances In Storms to be with child."

"Is she not with child from your man, Golden Fox? What need does she have of this... this half-blood? The Spirits gave her the gift of a child, not a mate! A mate will steal her Power—Power that her people need to survive the hard times that approach."

"Father!" Dances In Storms' voice lashed out and jerked Calls Elk's attention to her. "I am a Holy Woman. Spirits have given me visions to know that a mate can be a help to one such as me. Strong Wind will be there when I cannot be there for my child. I will not give up such a great gift from the Spirits!" She whirled and stormed out of the lodge, dragging Strong Wind with her.

Golden Fox tilted her head to one side. "Why do you believe a mate will steal Dances In Storms' Power?"

Weariness lay heavy on his features. He rubbed a hand across his face as if he could wipe some of it away. With a wave of his hand, he motioned toward the fire. "Sit, and we will speak, sister-friend of my daughter."

He looked at her and swallowed. "When a Holy Person takes a mate, Power is lost. It has always been this way, even from my grandfather's father." He poked a twig against an ember, then tossed the small branch into the fire. "When the father of Small Feet gave her to me, I was a Holy Man. If I had not accepted Small Feet, it would have shamed her father. I prayed all during Sister Moon's time in the sky. All I heard was Sister Wind telling me I had to accept Small Feet as my mate."

He folder his hands in his lap and met her gaze across the fire. "I rode away with Small Feet, her sister, my mustang, and three dogs her father gifted to me, along with their belongings. I never again heard the whisper of Sister Wind. I do not say this to say how pitiful I am. The Power I lost has come to live in Dances In Storms. Out of four children, she is the only one with Power. Sometimes, I think that her woman's need for a child has perhaps clogged her ears to the Spirits."

Golden Fox nodded. "You still grieve the loss of Power. I feel your pain, here." She tapped her chest. "Dances In Storms' ears have not been clogged by her own desires, Calls Elk. You must believe in your daughter, know that she listens well to the Spirits." She pushed to her feet.

When he got up, she walked toward the flap. As she brushed past him, she froze. Mouth agape, she stared up into his dark eyes. "I... I feel...."

With a step back, he stared down at her. "I have heard that you have a special Power to feel what is deep inside another human. What is it that you feel, Golden Fox?"

Awe filled her voice. "Your Power, Calls Elk. I feel your Power."

"My Power is gone! Do not tease me." His face twisted in anger.

Golden Fox closed the distance between them and laid a hand upon his chest. Her hand landed upon the wolf beaded on the front of his tunic. "I feel your Power, Calls Elk. I feel how your fear has tied it in strong ropes of braided mustang hair. It wishes to be free. Stories from those who did not know — or perhaps from those who felt jealous — have filled your mind, and made your ears deaf to the call of Sister Wind and of Wolf. Wolf howls to be free, Calls Elk, but your own stubbornness has kept them from finding you. Go to a quiet place. Let the smoke of the Sacred Plants open your ears."

Without waiting to see what Calls Elk would say, Golden Fox left his lodge.

As she made her way across the crowded camp, many hands stopped her and asked questions. To each one, she said to wait for Calls Elk and Dances In Storms to speak.

***

Golden Fox sat outside her lodge as Father Sun sneaked above the rim of the canyon. This would be the fourth sunrise since Calls Elk went out into the canyons to pray.

Frost nudged her hand and whined.

"I worry, too, Frost, but what can I do? Even Grandfather will not go to find Calls Elk. There is a place inside me that feels Calls Elk needs me to talk to him." As soon as the words crossed her lips, she hopped to her feet. "We will go find him, Frost."

***

Golden Fox glanced down at the wolf. "Which way did Calls Elk go, Frost?" Nose to the ground, Frost trotted back and forth, seeking a scent, then headed into a winding canyon, in the direction from which the cold season winds blew.

The red-orange-streaked walls of the canyon rapidly edged closer and closer, until the pathway between them forced Golden Fox to lay on Splash's back with her feet on top of the mustang's rump. In some places, water trickled down the sides and pooled at the bottom of the sandstone walls. Even though Eagle Thunder had removed the met-al from Splash's feet, the sound of her walking thudded through the narrow confines.

The walls gradually moved back away from each other, and changed from red-orange to tan-yellow. As she rode, she gawked at the walls. Herds of humpbacks, and deer with long horns bent back over their bodies, raced across the ancient stone. What looked like mostly human creatures had small heads that became pointed. They carried long lances. Handprints painted in reds and browns decorated the walls, some smaller and lower than others.

As she rounded a bend in the canyon, a voice spoke from a shallow cave. "Golden Fox, you have found me."

She halted Splash and tried to decide if Calls Elk was angry or not. "I worried that you may need something. I do not mean to disturb you, Elder."

Beside him sat Frost's male pups.

"Come, child." He tossed another twisted, grey branch on the small fire. "Come, sit and eat with me. It is time to break my fast. I have much to share with you."

As they ate, Calls Elk picked through his words. "It is not often that an Elder shares a vision he has had with someone so young, and who is not a Holy Person."

Golden Fox tipped her chin downward to acknowledge what he said, but held her silence.

The pair of wolves moved closer.

"I am an old man, Golden Fox, and old men become used to things a certain way. Ha! Then a young one comes along and stirs up the nest of the ones who buzz and sting." He sipped broth from his eating bowl. His eyes took on the gaze of one who peered at a place a long distance away.

"I am of Shining Light's people, a sister band of the first Wolf Band people. When I was young, before I took my journey alone, Wolf howled in my dreams. Visions came as easily to me as sunrises. I studied and became a

Holy Man. Our Holy Man was not so old, so I had time to visit other bands, and to learn more." Tears glistened on his cheeks. He did not try to brush them aside.

Night Hunter whined and licked the side of his face.

Calls Elk dug into the wolf's thick black fur. "By the time I returned to my people, I had mated. My father was furious. He had given much to the Holy Man to train me, and now it was all wasted." The slurp of broth passing his lips broke the tension. "These wolves followed me and have stayed by my side." He offered his bowl to the wolves.

"Our people had no Holy Person until Dances In Storms was born. No one could deny that Power sat on her shoulders. When she passed her sixth winter, I rode many days to take her to a Holy Woman to be trained. For long cycles of seasons, we only saw our daughter at gatherings. When she became a Holy Woman, she returned to our People."

When it seemed as if he might not continue, Golden Fox cleared her throat. "You feared that your people would once again have no Holy Person."

He sighed. "I wish that was my only fear, child. I am a selfish man. I pushed Dances In Storms to become a Holy Woman, took her away from her mother and her people when she was only a small child. I thank Great Mystery that the Holy Woman who trained her was not mean, like some are. Yes, I wanted a Holy Person for my people, but even more, I wanted to be the father of the Holy Person."

He would not lift his head and look at Golden Fox. "I took away any chance she had to find a mate, have a child, to be happy. I forced her to live a life that always gave and never received. And when she found someone and had hopes of having a child, I lashed out at her."

Finally, his gaze settled on her face. "She has given much. She deserves to be happy."

"You have changed much, Calls Elk. I would be honored to ride next to you back to camp." Golden Fox stood and gazed down at the older man. Her heart felt heavy as she wondered if he would return to the Band, fearing he would walk alone in the way many Elders did who no longer wished to live.

With a noisy exhale, he pushed to his feet, took a quick scan of the cave, and turned back to face her. "Would you walk with me, Golden Fox, as I did not ask my mustang to come?"

Splash trotted ahead of them through the narrow place, as did the wolves.

Walking allowed Golden Fox to look more closely at the painted walls. A drawing of a man whose head came to a sharp point caught her eyes. She stopped and studied the painting. Some places had become faded, or had chipped off the stone. He rode a mustang, and roped together behind him, six people of dark-skin walked, feet hobbled.

"Slaves." Calls Elk pointed at the dark-skinned people. "My father told a story of dark-skinned people, stolen from their homes across the salty waters, and brought here by the white men. They were worked until they died." He pointed to a painting a bit higher up. "Those are the big canoes that brought the people across the salty waters. I have never seen these canoes, nor have I ever seen the salty waters, even when I traveled. But it was on my travels that I heard of these things. When I returned home, I came here and looked again at these paintings."

Father Sun had lowered behind the canyon rim when they came to a place abandoned by the Wolf People long ago. "On these walls, you will see the story of the Wolf People. Our band believes this is a Sacred Place. We will not speak as we walk through it."

Plants had grown over a pile of rotted lodge poles. Squirrels scolded from nearby trees. High above them on the canyon rim, a new tree grew from the jagged stump of a tree that long ago snapped off. As the canyon curved, a copse of trees grew on the side where Father Sun rose. Bundles that held ancestors of the people lay undisturbed among the high branches.

Sometimes, all she could see was a glimpse of a tattered sleeping robe hanging below the thickness of a branch.

A tree nearer to the path they followed had been lightning struck. The lightning had split the trunk, and the bundle that had rested high in the tree's arms lay on the ground, broken open.

Not wanting to upset the Spirit of the one whose body lay exposed, Golden Fox turned her eyes away as they passed.

The weight of the dead lifted from her shoulders as they stepped out into a meadow.

Frost lay on the ground, tongue lolling from the side of his mouth, waiting for them. Beside him lay Night Wolf, and his children.

Golden Fox's heart lifted as Night Wolf ambled over and sat next to Calls Elk.

When the older man simply stood and stared, Night Wolf gently took his hand between gleaming teeth.

Calls Elk fell to his knees, tears streaming unashamedly down his face.

The wolf leaned forward and licked them off, then leaned the top of his head against Calls Elk's chest.

38

The wet season of baby animals gave way to the hot season. Golden Fox and Francisco Riley, daughter and father, spent much time together, though he seldom walked, as his leg had never quite healed right.

Frost would lie across Golden Fox as Francisco told her many stories. She learned a lot about the land across the salty water, but had no interest in seeing it. She belonged to this land.

He had cried many tears, and even Sky Bird and Deer Woman had often sat until Father Sun woke to hear his words.

As the time to leave approached, Golden Fox looked around. These people would follow her, just as the Wolf People has once followed Shining Light. Her shoulders bowed beneath the weight of that responsibility. Some of them would probably go to the campfires in the sky after she led them to attack the fort. People of Sister Wolf Band would weep, and hearts would be broken, maybe never to heal.

She scrubbed her fingertips across her forehead. Her last vision demanded that she delay no longer.

If only I could go alone.

A glance at the faces standing in front of her told her how foolish it would be to try to sneak away. Blazing Fire, Stands His Ground, White Elk, Pale Hunter, and many other warriors from Eagle Thunder's band and from Sister Wolf Band waited in patient silence.

She grabbed a handful of Splash's neck hairs and swung up on the mustang. Frost padded beside her as the warriors made their slow way through the camp, and passed through the narrow space the led from the camp to the beginning of the grasslands beyond.

Dances In Storms caught up and rode next to her.

"You should not be here," Golden Fox argued for the sixth time. "A child may be growing in your belly."

Moon pranced, neck arched. "I told you. Since Strong Wind has shared my lodge, I have been eating the plants that keep a woman from having a baby in her belly."

"Dances In Storms, may I ask you a question?" Her teeth worried at her bottom lip, a sure sign that butterflies filled her stomach.

"You are my sister-friend. There are no questions you cannot ask." Dances In Storms reached out and squeezed her forearm.

"Why did you not lay with White Elk when I went hunting and gave you my blessing?"

The Holy Woman closed her eyes for a brief span. Kindness shone in their dark depths when she looked at Golden Fox. "Your willingness to sacrifice for my happiness brought to me the need to go to my special place in the canyons. I feared that if I did not lay with White Elk, the Spirits would give me no child with any man.

"When I cried out for a vision, Blue Night Sky came to me. She asked me what was most important to me. I realized that your friendship was more important than my desire to have a child. When I decided I would not lie with White Elk, and would instead become second mother to the children you and he had, I went to White Elk."

A small smile played around the edges of her lips. "He had a fire already built in his lodge, and welcomed me with a warm drink from plants he had picked. He said he expected me, that he had had a vision. In that vision, you and I, our children, and White Elk had gathered in your lodge. However, when he looked into the eyes of the children, he knew he was father only to the ones who called you first mother."

She sighed, a satisfied sound. "When I found Strong Wind, I knew why Blue Night Sky had come to me. It was a test from the Spirits, Golden Fox, to see if you and I valued our friendship more than we valued our own desires."

* * *

BROKEN PATH

Father Sun hung behind the trees as Golden Fox and White Elk drew near to the fort.

Golden Fox wore her fox fur around her shoulders, hidden beneath the dirty tunic she wore, as White Elk pulled on the rope that bound her hands in front of her. She stumbled on the dusty ground, her worn footwear kicking up puffs of dirt.

The fort's big wooden gates stood open, though hairy-faces paced along the top of the wall.

Runner pranced beneath White Elk, and bobbed his head as they entered the noisy space between the wooden walls. White Elk laid the nose rope over the "raling' — a word they learned from Pale Hunter.

A piece of wood hung above a door. The scratchings on the wood looked the same as the ones Pale Hunter had taught them, which meant this was the captain's place.

White Elk pushed through the door, still pulling Golden Fox on the rope. The stink of sweat and body odor from those who never visited the river, along with rancid meat and something nasty burning, slapped her in the face as she crept behind White Elk.

A tall man with a roll of fat around his middle turned from looking out through a dirty space in the wooden lodge's wall. He wore his greasy hair, the color of pale dirt, tied back. He swung around, his mouth stretching in a cruel smile that showed yellowed teeth. "Well, well, look what we have here." He lumbered across the small space.

When he stopped in front of Golden Fox, stink rolled off him, and she turned her head away.

"Shy, too." He reached out toward her face.

Beneath his fingernails and along the lines of his palms, dirt had packed. The fumes of whiskey wafted off his clothes and blew from his mouth on rotted breath. In spite of her obvious discomfort, he grasped her chin tightly, and then dug through her hair as if he looked for bugs.

Offended, she jerked her face, but his fingers tightened painfully.

Why does this filthy man dig in my hair for bugs? I go to sweat and to the river even when the cold season grips the land. And I always use the plants my mother taught me to use to clean myself.

"Good, you have not used plants to color her hair." He let go and stomped over to a wood box, which he stood behind — Pale Hunter had drawn one, and called it a 'desk.' The squeaky thing in which he sat must be the thing named a 'chair.' "Where did you find this gold-red-haired girl, boy?"

"Want gifts promised for gold-red-haired girl. Then I talk."

"You will get your gifts." He squinted and leaned forward, elbows against the edge of the desk. "What kinda savage *are* you, boy?"

The muscles in White Elk's jaw bunched and released. He drew a deep breath through his nostrils. Only as he released it did the tension leave his shoulders. "Albino. My people call me an albino. Where gifts of much fire water?"

The captain leaned back in his chair and belted out a harsh laugh. "Fire water. That is all you savages can think of—fire water. Okay, boy."

He pushed to his feet and walked around to a place covered by a hide flap. He flipped it up and pulled out bot-tles, then walked over and handed one to White Elk.

As he wandered back to his desk and flopped into the chair, he opened the bot-tle in his hand. "Drink up, boy, but do not get so drunk that you forget to tell me where the girl came from."

White Elk had watched as the captain opened his bot-tle, and now did the same. He held the round circle to his lips, tilted the bot-tle up, and swallowed. Afterwards, he wiped his mouth on his tunic.

"You like, boy?"

White Elk nodded and smiled.

"Grab a chair, boy." He waved at a thing that looked much like what he sat on. "Pull it up to the desk. We will drink, and you can tell me about this girl."

Golden Fox stood quietly behind White Elk as he began a long story of how he had found her. The longer he spoke, the louder he became. Soon his words slurred.

The captain's eyes became heavy-lidded, and he leaned hard on his arms propped on the desk. "So, wha' elsh ya shee, boy?"

Father Sun had gone to rest, and this night, Sister Moon shed much light. It would make it difficult to get away, but the children would need to see, so it was good that Sister Moon shone. From outside the captain's wooden lodge, the sound of people yelling and crying, stumbling on the wood path, and cursing, seeped into the darkening room.

Golden Fox slowly and quietly slipped her hands from the rope that bound her. She bent low when the captain wasn't looking, and pulled her knife from the leg sheath. As she straightened back up, she threw the knife.

It thudded into the captain's chest. He raised startled eyes and opened his mouth, but no sound came out before he slumped on the desk.

White Elk sprang to his feet. He grabbed the captain's bot-tle of firewater and poured it on the dirty clothes the man wore. The strong smell made Golden Fox crinkled her nose. "Here. Tie this around your hair so no one sees. Pale Hunter said women sometimes do this."

He darted over to the place where the captain kept many bot-tles, grabbed two more, and carefully opened the door and stuck his head out.

At the motion of his hand, Golden Fox followed him outside.

"I heard some children that way." He pointed.

Keeping to the deeper shadows near the wooden lodges, she crept away, leaving White Elk to his task. Behind the lodges, a couple of hide lodges had been set up. Inside one of these, she found a huddle of children. She put a finger to her lips to signal for silence.

Wide-eyed, they nodded.

With a wave of her hand, she motioned for them to follow. Together, they crept around the edge of the wooden fort.

Golden Fox kept the children behind her, then squatted against the rough wood and waited for White Elk.

Before long, he staggered into sight. He must have been watching for her and the children.

At the base of the fort wall, he held two bot-tles high. "Drink with me!" he shouted, then stumbled over his own feet, nearly falling.

After a whispered argument, the three men who had been pacing the top of the wall eased down wooden steps.

"Give me a drink of that, you strange looking savage." The biggest man reached out a large hand and grabbed a bot-tle from White Elk.

White Elk gave a drunken laugh and held up a second bot-tle, and one of the other men grabbed it.

When the men tossed the empty bottles aside and started to leave, White Elk grinned wide. "Have more fire water. Share with my brothersh." He shifted closer to the shadows beneath the steps that led to the top of the wall.

With a finger to her lips, Golden Fox motioned for the children to stay hidden and quiet. She then eased along the wall. A piece of wood stabbed her finger, but she barely felt it. When she neared the men, she stepped out of the shadows. "Want fire water."

One of the men, the biggest one, turned slowly at her voice. "Well, ain'cha a purty thang?" He staggered her way. "I share with squaw." He used his chest to push her back into the shadows.

The other men gave knowing laughs.

Beneath the steps, she grasped the back of his hair and yanked hard. Before he could yell, she slit his throat. She cut so deep that he made no sound. She then quietly rolled his body against the wall.

White Elk coaxed the other two men into the shadows. "Come, we share woman, too."

Golden Fox grabbed the shorter man while White Elk slit the throat of the taller one. They piled the bodies on top of the first one.

She hurried back to the children and led them to the smaller door in the wooden wall of the fort. The door squeaked, but no one seemed to take notice, so she rushed the children through it.

Outside of the wall, Dances In Storms, Hairy-Face No More, and several other warriors picked up all except the largest of the children, and ran through the dark, away from the fort.

Golden Fox slipped back inside. This time, Pale Hunter, Strong Wind, Stands His Ground, and Blazing Fire slipped in with her. The six crept toward the stables.

The mustangs locked inside the small wood places shifted restlessly when the six entered.

A white man, scratching his chest, wandered from the back of the stables. "Y'all cain't be here. Get—"

An arrow thumped into his chest.

Golden Fox nocked another arrow, in case more hid in the shadows.

When none showed themselves, everyone began gathering armloads of dry grass that Pale Hunter called 'hay.' They spread the hay thick around the back of the wooden lodges.

Flesh hit flesh somewhere near, and a woman cried out.

Golden Fox flinched but continued spreading the hay.

Back in the stables, everyone gathered around Stands His Ground and Blazing Fire.

At a nod from Blazing Fire, Stands His Ground spoke. "There are more children, and many women of the Peoples. Once the fires are set, we will have to gather them quickly, and get them out of the gates before the enemy grabs their fire sticks."

Pale Hunter leaned in close. "I have put much hay around the place where the captain kept extra fire sticks. When it gets to burning good, the stuff that makes the noise and death from the fire sticks will burn fast and hot. I will go inside and start the fire near the entrance, so no one can get more fire sticks."

Stands His Ground settled his gaze on Golden Fox. "White Elk and you will need to work together and work fast. Once the hay burns, the mustangs will fight and run away. Pale Hunter tells me the captain had what is called 'oil lamps.' The greasy water inside burns fast. I will pour this greasy water all over the captain's body and wooden lodge. When you see the fire there, everyone must hurry."

He nodded at Strong Wind and Blazing Fire. "You two will set your fires, then get to the gates and open them quickly. Our warriors will be waiting outside."

Golden Fox frowned. "Who walks on top of the fort wall? Will the whites not see that no one is there?"

Pale Hunter grinned. "Hairy-Face No More, and Luke, the hairy-face you beat up because he harmed his mustang, sneaked in the unbarred small door. They took the blue coats, and now stomp back and forth on the top of the fort's wall." He chuckled. "Long ago, they did this for many nights. Have them tell you the stories."

The others slipped out as Golden Fox walked among the mustangs, soothing and patting them as she slipped the nose ropes on them. White Elk opened the wood gates that held them in the small places, and she led them toward the front of the stables.

She gripped the ropes in one hand, and jumped up on the back of the mustang that stood quietly watching her. The palms of her hands sweated, and she gripped the animal's mane to slow her own heart. The coarse feel of the mustang calmed Golden Fox.

A flash of light appeared in the captain's wooden lodge.

"Now, White Elk!" She twisted her head around and watched as he shoved the torch into piles of hay.

The mustangs fidgeted at the smell of smoke, but before they could get too nervous, White Elk hopped on one and took several of the nose ropes in hand.

Several more fires sprang up, and men began to yell.

The mustang shivered beneath Golden Fox. With her eyes locked on the great gates, her heart raced so hard she could feel it against her tunic.

The gates swung wide as more men and women poured into the center of the fort. Most seemed lost. Only a few grabbed buckets, or dipped water from large wooden bowls that stood near some of the lodges. Women ran toward the big gate.

Golden Fox thumped her heels into the mustang's sides, And the animal lunged forward. People lurched out of her way as White Elk and she led the thundering mustangs through the fort.

Warriors poured into the fort, and nudged their mustangs aside as the other animals stormed out of the gates.

The mustangs raced up the hill a small distance away. Golden Fox leapt off her animal, tossed the ropes to a waiting warrior, and flung herself onto Splash.

Splash spun around on her rear legs and bolted back toward the fort.

Back inside the wooden walls, people fought as firelight danced against the black of night. People ran, screaming. Bows twanged. Fire sticks roared, and some fell with blood gushing from a hole in their chest.

A little boy of no more than five winters stood in the middle of the open space

Golden Fox tapped Splash's sides and she shoved through knots of struggling people. As they drew closer, she leaned over and snatched the child up. With the child seated in front of her, she sent Splash pushing back toward the gates.

After a while, Golden Fox could not remember how many children and women she had plucked from the ground. Her arms ached, and Splash's sides heaved from the work. She whirled her mustang in a tight circle.

Off in the direction of Father Sun's rising, a one-legged hairy-face, without face hair, plunged his long knife into an enemy's chest.

Just as she headed for her father, she spotted White Elk cornered by two hairy-faces on mustangs. In the light of the fires, blood gleamed along Cloud's neck.

White Elk had grabbed a long, skinny piece of wood somewhere. When one fat white man swung a long knife at him, he blocked it with the wood.

The other enemy edged around the battle, trying to sneak up on White Elk's other side.

A snow-white wolf darted at the man's mustang, and the animal jerked back, but the harsh hand of the hairy-face forced the mustang ahead in spite of the wolf's snapping teeth.

A scream became trapped in Golden Fox's throat. She would never make it to White Elk in time.

All of a sudden, a red mustang shouldered its way through the clumps of fighters. Unafraid of the snarling wolf, the animal slammed into the white man's mustang, throwing the aim of his long knife to the side, missing White Elk.

The clang of long knives clashing reached her ears before she got to the knot of fighters.

Freed from having two whites to fight, White Elk slammed the long piece of wood into the side of the closest white man's head.

Another long knife slit open the front of White Elk's tunic, and red blossomed like some terrible flower.

The white man fell from his animal and staggered to his feet, and Sun Snow lunged. Her teeth ripped into his throat, and blood gushed.

The terrified man's mustang squealed, spun, and raced away.

Golden Fox's father plunged his long knife into another hairy-face's chest, and the man slumped over his mustang. When the animal bolted, the body dropped to the ground.

"Father, you are not to be here!"

"I have spent too much time away from my only daughter. I wish to spend all that I have left with her, now."

The heat of the fires pushed them toward the center of the fort. The fighting had died away. The few hairy-faces that remained fought desperately, but arrows and knives soon ended their lives.

The flames roared with a great hunger, and hot embers floated on the heated air.

Warriors led the captured mustangs to the fort, and put the small children and the injured onto them. They then took the lead ropes and headed away from the blood, the fires, and death.

Some children cried, but most sat with wide, scared eyes.

A few of the Peoples refused to leave, even though the fort burned. They huddled together and passed flasks and bot-tles of poisoned water back and forth.

Tears filled Golden Fox's eyes as she sat on Splash and looked at the lost ones.

Her father rode up and stopped next to her. "You cannot save everyone, Golden Fox. They have to want to be saved."

Drawing in a long, slow breath, she wiped her eyes. "Yes, Father, that is what Blue Night Sky told me, too. Still, it hurts, and I wonder if we had come sooner—"

He gripped her hand with his own. "Everything has a time to happen, Daughter. Even things that break our hearts can help us become stronger. Perhaps, their broken path will someday lead them back home. The broken path I walked led me home to you. I was given a great gift." He turned his mustang. "The others are waiting for us. Let us go home."

She turned away from the lost Peoples and nudged her mustang into a walk. Her father's animal kept pace.

Frost trotted out of the darkness and walked on her other side.

"Ha! Where were you, Wolf? The fight is already over."

Dances In Storms heard the question as they neared. "Father Wolf was protecting the young." She pointed toward two hairy-faces with their throats ripped out. "They came after the little ones. He stopped them."

***

They were still a sunrise from the Sister Wolf Band camp when Golden Fox's father slipped off his mustang.

She leapt down, raced toward him, and carefully turned him over. Blood soaked the soft deer skin around the stump of his leg.

When she began untying it, he gripped her arm. "Golden Fox, stop."

She pulled loose and grasped the slick leather tie.

"Golden Fox, please, listen to me."

Something in his breathy voice made her heart stumble. "I am listening, Father."

"Before you left... to get the People... Pale Hunter told me...." His fingers flicked toward his missing leg. "The bad Spirits... they never left. I... I had no time left. I wanted to spend it by your side... doing something... something good, for once in my life."

She gripped his hand as the scent of death wafted to her nose. "Yes, Father, you did something very good. You helped save many children."

Someone began to pat a drum, and Dances In Storms knelt on the other side of Francisco. She said, "You have become a good man. You are no longer Francisco, but Man of the Peoples."

"I am honor... honored, Dances In Storms. Will you sing me to the campfires in the sky? Do you think Golden Fox's grandmother might welcome me? I remember she was kind to me when... when I visited before... before...."

She cradled his hand between her own. "I will be honored to sing you to the campfires in the sky, Man of the Peoples. I know any one of our relatives would welcome you to sit by their fire. Golden Fox's grandmother will welcome you, Golden Fox's father." She began to sing.

Blazing Fire, Stands His Ground, Pale Hunter, Strong Wind, and White Elk came to kneel beside Man of the Peoples.

White Elk reached out and gripped the shoulder of Man of the Peoples. "Brother, you saved my life. I sing for you."

Man of the Peoples smiled, then turned his head to watch the face of his daughter. "You... you are a good leader... Golden Fox. I am... honored to have... been your father." His eyes glistened as they stared up at the campfires in the sky.

As his last breath left his body, Golden Fox looked up toward the campfires in the sky.

Eagle Woman dove from the blackness. Her wings flapped so hard that the air stirred Golden Fox's hair. She swooped down, talons reaching. As her talons touched Man of the Peoples' chest, the talons became hands. As she climbed toward the sky, a blue swirl—the Spirit of Man of the Peoples—rested in Eagle Woman's hands.

Golden Fox bent her head back, watching until she could no longer see the Blue of Spirit.

EPILOGUE

Golden Fox sat cross-legged in front of her lodge, on the prickly grass of late warm season. She tipped her head back, closed her eyes, and let Father Sun bathe her face. Her second child, a daughter with grey eyes and hair black as a raven's wing, lay asleep in her lap. Her four-winters-old son screamed, and her eyes popped open. She spotted him leading several other children as they darted around lodges and ran through the middle of camp.

Dances In Storms' daughter, at six winters old, sat in front of a small group of children, telling the stories her mother and second mother had told her.

The strong scent of pine needles and old leaves traveled on Sister Wind's light breeze. Not too far from where Golden Fox sat, Sun Snow wrestled with White Elk.

"Even though this is not the Land of Tall Trees, this is a magic place my mother's dreams led us to. I only wish Deer Woman and she would have built their lodge here, as well."

Dances In Storms nodded. "They feel they have much healing work to do among the bands that live close to the whites. Perhaps, someday, they will return to meet their grandchildren and decide to stay." She stared at her daughter with much love in her eyes.

Golden Fox chuckled. "Blue Spirit Dog is a healer, too. Without her, I am not sure how I would have healed after my father traveled to the campfires in the sky. It seemed that I had him for such a small time."

"She is truly a healer, like your two mothers, Sky Bird and Deer Woman. I am certain this is why your dog chose to go with them. She is very good with children who have been hurt inside — where we cannot see their wounds."

Golden Fox watched the children play. "Sister Wolf Band has become a very colorful band. The color of skin matters not, only the Spirit within." She smiled toward the children — some with skin so black that it shone in Father Sun's light, playing with others whose brown skin glowed with warmth. They all played with children of pale skin, though none as pale as White Elk's. They possessed grey eyes, or green eyes, or dark, dark brown eyes, but the children saw no differences between themselves.

Wolf pups tumbled around with dog pups, and they all chased after the children.

Dances Is Storms pointed with her chin. "Man Of Night will join with Woman Who Does Not Speak before Sister Moon hides her face again."

"Woman Who Does Not Speak has helped our mustangs when their babies try to come out backward. Ever since White Elk chose her to care for his mustang that day long ago, her gifts with the animals have grown. We are blessed to have Girl Who Does Not Speak become Woman Who Does Not Speak."

"She is a true healer of the four-legged." Dances In Storms chuckled. "And the winged ones. The hawk she healed circles above her even now. I have never seen a hawk who loved a human so much."

Dances In Storms reached over and hugged Golden Fox. Her eyes filled with tears. "Who would know that the Great Mystery would give me not only a child and a man of my own, but also a sister-friend to walk with me on our Mother?"

"We are both blessed. Not only do we have each other, but not one child in our band has tasted the poisoned water. The minds of their parents and grandparents are healed. The only way we know that our people suffered so much from it, is in the stories we tell around the fire circle during the cold season."

"Between you and me, Golden Fox, we will teach these stories to the young so they will pass them to their children. Perhaps, in this way, if some of our peoples should find themselves on that broken path, they will know how to find their way back home."

"Ha!" Golden Fox dispelled the sadness that lingered whenever she remembered how the poisoned water had broken the Sun People's Band, and blackened the Spirit of Yellow Moon.

When Sky Bird had led them here, she said Yellow Moon showed her the trail. Maybe Yellow Moon's Spirit had finally found a way to sit at the campfires in the sky. Perhaps, Grandmother had finally welcomed her.

"Look at Grandfather and Many Walks. See how they laugh and stare at one another, as if they love for the first time." She shot a sideways look at Dances In Storms. "Do you think we will ever find the Land of Tall Trees? I love these mountains. They are full of beauty, even if they are not blue and purple! How could I have not known that distance changes the colors we see?"

Dances In Storms shook her head with a smile. "We do not often think about how things change with the passing of moons and the distance we walk."

Golden Fox stretched her neck, and then rose. "Ho! A stranger comes."

Dances In Storms stood beside her sister-friend.

The Elder stopped a short ways from them, his face split in a big smile. "You are Golden Fox." He turned toward Dances In Storms. "And you are the Holy Woman, Dances In Storms, a relative of Shining Light."

"This is true, Elder." Dances In Storms greeted him politely. "And what do we call you?"

Her question appeared to delight him, and his smile grew even wider. "I am One Who Wanders, and I have come to lead your people away."

Golden Fox and Dances In Storms exchanged bewildered glances, and returned their gazes to One Who Wanders.

He glanced behind him as if he expected someone to appear. "Sky Bird and Deer Woman should be here within two sunrises. That will give me time to tell you the story of your new home—the Land of Tall Trees."

THE END

ABOUT THE AUTHOR

Ruby has been a wanderer, and has seen most of the USA. She's the mother of an amazing son, and the wife of a patient husband who indulges her need for animals. She was also the first woman journeyman newspaper pressman in Colorado at the Rocky Mountain News, A newspaper the survived for over one-hundred twenty-five years.

She spent years rescuing animals and learning from them. They taught her that life does not have to be so hard, if you go with the flow and not against it. Forgive today, because tomorrow may not come.

Her life revolves around writing and her family, which includes, of course, her animals. Two car accidents in the mid-nineties changed her life. She resented it at first, until she understood she had simply been put on another path. It was not an easy one, but she accepted it, and while it continues to be a challenge, she now learns with each step she takes.

She writes because she is compelled to pass on knowledge.

Find out more about Ruby:

www.rubystandingdeer.com

www.twitter.com/R_StandingDeer

www.facebook.com/rstanding.deer

WHAT'S NEXT?

Ruby is currently mulling over and fleshing out a couple of different stories, one of which will be the next offering. One thing is certain: it will represent the culture she has shared so well to date, with another cast of characters sure to capture your heart.

More from
EVOLVED PUBLISHING

We offer great books across multiple genres, featuring hiqh-quality editing (which we believe is second-to-none) and fantastic covers.

As a hybrid small press, your support as loyal readers is so important to us, and we have strived, with tireless dedication and sheer determination, to deliver on the promise of our motto: **QUALITY IS PRIORITY #1!**

Please check out all of our great books,
which you can find at this link:
www.EvolvedPub.com/Catalog

Thank you!